D0916100

UPSY DAISY

HIGHER LEARNING SERIES BOOK #1

CHELSIE EDWARDS

WWW.SMARTYPANTSROMANCE.COM

COPYRIGHT

DEDICATION

For Chris and her King.

CHAPTER ONE

Fisk University
Friday, August 15, 1975

Daisy

"Our father said the Washington Monument really does look like a hooded Klansmen up close. It even has beady red devil eyes."

Dolly's voice came into focus along with the edges of a stately building. I'd mostly spent the last three hours trying to tune her out with varying degrees of success. She was a history buff and had spent the better part of the ride peppering me with facts about Fisk University.

Did I know it was one of the first historically Black universities to be established? Did I know it was founded in 1866? Did I know Jubilee Hall was trying to get added to the National Registry of Historic Places? (I did … it's almost as though I'd applied to go to school there or something.)

Sensing my lack of enthusiasm over knowledge I already possessed, she'd moved on to my father's Washington, DC trip and was giving me—at least I *thought* she was giving me—his assessment of the tour of the National Mall he'd taken yesterday.

My father was sore about missing move-in day for my first year of college, but he was away at the National Association of Black Lawyers Conference in DC, and they were doing good work. Besides, his being away was really a blessing. My sister Dolly was a nut but my father would've been just a little weepy the whole ride.

I turned more fully toward the big building I'd seen and heard Dolly put the car in park and cut the engine. From the corner of my eye I watched Dolly's head turn my way. "Oh, that's Jubilee Hall," she said staring past me out the windshield toward the three-story red-brick castle staring back at me. It had a black turreted bell tower and white framed windows.

It was gothic; it was gorgeous.

Jubilee Hall. *My dorm.*

I get to stay in this fantastic old building. I get to be free!

I imagined the high vaulted ceilings of the place, the wide-open airy rooms it must have. I imagine myself walking across the quad, books in hand, headed back to my comfy room at the end of the day. Of course I'd have an amazing roommate who'd be my best friend and—

THUMP. THUMP. THUMP.

I jumped a mile.

Outside my passenger window a guy had appeared seemingly out of thin air. He was tall—so tall that I could only see his legs and mid torso until he stooped down. He was lean, with an athletic build. He wore charcoal gray slacks and a pale gold shirt, the sleeves rolled up to his forearms. He wore a black and gold striped tie. Unlike most guys my age, he wasn't rocking an afro; he was clean-cut with a neatly trimmed facial hair and his close-cropped hair had a slight wave. Amber brown eyes were framed by thick, long coal lashes. The contrast between those eyes and the deeper umber of his skin was striking. He was handsome. Really handsome. Really, really handsome.

He smirked a little, just as I noticed I was staring. Dolly looked at me, annoyed. "Roll. Down. The. Window." Over-enunciating each word the way she did when she thought someone was a bona fide dolt.

He reached over to tap the window again as I reached for the hand crank to roll it down.

"Freshman?" he said, his voice smooth and untinged with the southern accent I was accustomed to.

"I—uh—yes?" I said unsure of why my answer sounded like a question.

He smiled and the ambient wattage went up.

I mean, honestly. He was a bit much.

"Okay, well that's Jubilee Hall dead ahead. You'll want to stop by there first," he said, leaning back so both Dolly and I could see him. "There'll be a table set up out front for you to check in and get your dorm room assignment. Orientation's at four thirty with your . . . parent? Or sister?" He winked and smiled.

I gaped. He was shamelessly flirting with Dolly.

I turned toward her, expecting her to be indignant and waiting for the dressing down— she ran a crew full of men and never took any mess from anyone—so I nearly fell out of my chair when I saw grinning, her fluttering fingers shooing him away *playfully*.

Since when did Dolly do anything playfully?

"Get out of here, you big flirt, and you best stay away from these poor freshmen girls."

He laughed. "Well I can't stay away today. I'm here to help them all get situated. But I promise to skip the orientation."

"Trevor!" A disembodied voice called out and Mr. Handsome

turned around. He nodded his head and called back, "One sec," to the voice before returning all his attention to me . . . I mean, to *us*.

"Well, duty calls, but if you need any help don't be afraid to ask. I'm here to serve, ladies." His voice dropped at the end as he chuckled and backed away. Dolly was already wagging her fingers at him but she was hiding a grin.

"Well he certainly was helpful," I replied mildly.

Dolly shot me a look. "Yeah, helpful like a viper. You mind me and keep away from that boy. He's handsome as the devil and knows it. Young men like that prey on freshman girls all the time."

I nodded noncommittally as Dolly watched me from the corner of her eye.

She needn't worry. I hadn't come to college to get entangled with young men. I had come for myself and had no intention of getting mixed up with the wrong sort.

Who's to say he's the wrong sort?

I dismissed the thought immediately. Guys that looked like him were always the wrong sort.

Trevor

The girl in the yellow dress with the sunglasses on didn't look familiar but there was something about her profile and her long, beautiful braids that *felt* known. Like the edges of a memory I couldn't quite bring into focus.

My mind was probably tricking me into thinking I knew her *because* she was beautiful. Some primal urge to make her known to me so I could make myself known to her, but I definitely hadn't met her before; I would've remembered that face.

I frowned as my thoughts took a turn I was unprepared for: I wanted to know the shape and color of her eyes. Eyes were unequivo-cally the most alluring part of a woman. Don't get me wrong, I defi-nitely appreciated their faces, and their bodies . . . a lot. But there was something to the saying that eyes are the windows to the soul. Staring into someone's eyes you could tell a lot about what they were—and what they weren't.

Her eyes had been hidden away behind those sunshades that should've and would've looked ridiculous on anyone else. They reminded me of a butterfly—as if one was perched on the bridge of her nose—but instead of looking silly she'd looked like some type of princess or fairy come to mingle with the common folk, completely unaware that we didn't have the power to charm butterflies.

Otherworldly.

Yeah, that was a good word for her. Everything about her screamed out of this world, and I was almost positive that behind those wacky sunglasses hid an uncommonly pretty face.

I shook my head, clearing away the unsettling vestiges of what-ever this girl triggered inside of me. I dislodged the thoughts of the neckline of her lovely yellow dress. I peeled off thoughts of how pretty it looked against her pecan brown skin. I wiped away any trace of how that dress dipped into a little V in the front that stopped just above the good part. I ignored the way it teased and hinted at what lay underneath.

I would give this girl no purchase in my mind. She was too beauti-ful. Greater men than myself had been made fools for pretty faces.

And *yet* . . . I still couldn't turn away. My eyes lingered in the direction of the sisters still sitting and chatting in the car, and they *were* sisters; the resemblance was more than uncanny. The older one looked the way beautifully aged wine tasted: well put-together, balanced, mature, confident, and full of flavor. It was like looking at what the pretty, younger one would be in ten years' time.

I sighed, and instead of following the wild, sudden urge I had to run back to their car, to run back to her, to ask her name, to take those sunglasses off so I could see what would be undoubtedly pretty eyes. Instead . . .

I sighed again, and I turned to face the voice that had been summoning me.

Julian P. Marshall, or Jules as we called him, was cutting across the parking lot toward me, sans his usual swagger.

When he was a few paces away I noticed his expression morph into panic and his steps stuttered to a stop. Ah, he'd finally spotted our student government advisor, Dr. Daniels, in the distance.

Our advisor was a stickler for being on time and for community service. It was a quarter past ten, move-in started at eight a.m., and us volunteers? We were supposed to have arrived at seven fifteen.

"Was Dr. Daniels looking for me?" Jules groaned.

I smiled and scratched my chin, pretending to think.

"Was the advisor to the Student Government looking for the Student Body President this morning? Might've been. Something about it being so important for *student leaders* to show up and *set an example* for all the young, impressionable minds coming in."

"God dammit!" Jules muttered, scrunching his eyes in defeat. A look so bleak and troubled consumed his face, I *almost* felt bad about pulling his leg.

Almost.

Freshman move in was chaos, as usual; Dr. Daniels most definitely had not been looking for Jules.

"Luckily for you, the Student Body Vice President was here to represent the administration and to make us look good." I motioned to myself.

His eyebrows perked up. "So you covered for me?" His tone was so hopeful and grateful it saddened me . . . *a little.* Jules was my very best friend in the world. The fact that he *still,* after all these years, doubted my loyalty even a little bit made me want to take the joke even further.

I'm awful, I know.

"You know I did," I replied keeping my face perfectly straight.

He relaxed a bit.

"I told him you couldn't make it because you'd gone over to TSU last night to help with *their* freshman girls' orientation and all the moving in and out you did . . ." I swiveled my hips just a bit suggestively and his jaw dropped open. "Wore you out! So I left you at home sleeping like a baby."

"You son of a—" He lunged at me playfully, as the realization that I was joking set in.

"Hey, leave my momma out of this before I have to bring yours into it," I warned as I danced out of his reach.

He snorted and relaxed into a smile.

I shook my head. Julian was so easy to rile up.

"In all seriousness, no, Dr. Daniels wasn't looking for you. He didn't even know you were back till I mentioned it. I explained to him that you'd be by later today to help set up the office, and that you were tired since you'd driven the entire way up from Charlotte."

The trip from Charlotte to Nashville had no small number of backroads. Jules was lighter than me by more than a few shades so it made sense for him to drive. No need to increase the chances of getting pulled over for being dark-skinned *and* driving a nice car. It was his car, anyway.

Julian wasn't technically due to come back to school until next Friday with all the other upperclassmen, but he'd pretended he was so eager to get an early start on setting up our office that he needed to come back an entire week early. That answer was, of course, bullshit. He'd never admit it, but *I knew* he'd really done it because *he knew* I'd needed a ride back to school and didn't want to spend, or even have, the extra money to catch the bus or the train.

"I skipped breakfast and I'm famished. You wanna head to Swetts to grab a bite before we get to work on the office?" he asked.

I patted my pockets flat and looked at him, exasperated.

"Oh!" Jules said. "You know I got you if—"

I shot him a look that silenced him immediately.

He held his palms up in concession. "Of course. Let's just go help the freshmen instead, and then we can head to the caf when it opens in a few."

We turned in silence and began walking toward Crosthwaite Hall.

Julian, like most folks, was a walking contradiction: kindhearted, clueless, loyal, scholarly, and mischievous as the devil himself. The type of person who would drive seven or eight hours to get you where you needed to go and never ask for money for petrol or anything. But he was also the type to forget that you couldn't do the same things that he took for granted all the time like randomly eating out at Swetts because you didn't have the money.

It wasn't his fault really.

Honestly. Compared to most of the folks we grew up around, Julian was basically normal.

Jules was my third cousin, twice removed or my second cousin, thrice removed—something like that. Our great-grandparents were siblings. Whatever.

Growing up I knew *of* the Marshalls. Folks in my family occasionally spoke of kin in North Carolina that were well off. But they hadn't been to any family reunions or functions that I recalled, so I'd thought of them in the same way one thinks of rumors that your family was royalty back in Africa. Mighta been true but probably wasn't, and definitely wasn't relevant to your day-to-day either way.

Needless to say, crash landing on their doorstep in the dead of night when I was eleven had been difficult. *Crashing.* Yeah that about summed it up.

Because although we were allegedly related, our families were nothing alike. Our *worlds* were nothing alike. And in the beginning, *we* had been nothing alike.

For starters, there were a lot of rules and most of them weren't said out loud. You see, the Marshalls were not just well off after all.

The Marshalls were *rich*, rich.

Sent us to a fancy-ass boarding school from eleven to eighteen years old, *rich*.

Jules had private tennis lessons and I had an art instructor when they'd discovered I could draw, *rich*.

Spent half the summer at his nana's house in Oak Bluffs, *rich*.

Spent the other half of the summer at the best sleepaway camp in the entire world, *rich*.

But putting all those privileges aside, that wasn't how I knew the Marshalls were loaded.

After all, they could've been leveraged up to their eyeballs in debt the same way my parents had been.

No, forgetting the house in Martha's Vineyard and the fancy school—the way I knew the Marshalls were rich, was that they never, ever, discussed money.

Ever.

And we weren't allowed to discuss it either, hence Jules and I having a terse exchange wherein he wanted me to accept his charity and I would not. Julian was generous to a fault sometimes, but he was the exception, not the rule.

The thing about rich people was that they knew how to hold on to money. That's how they *got* rich.

Well . . . a lot of them got rich through human pain and suffering, but they *stayed* rich because they knew how to hold on to that money, by hook or by crook.

So while I was well cared for, at least, materially while I was growing up—and was given opportunities most folks could only ever dream of—the Marshalls' money was not and would not ever be my money. And I never forgot that.

They never let me forget it.

Case in point: they were very graciously footing the bill for my college education, with the caveat that I begin paying them back as soon as I graduated, with eight percent interest.

"Eight for the number of years we've done your parents' job for them," was how May so graciously phrased it.

It wasn't the repayment or the interest that upset me; it was the spite.

And the helplessness. I would never have qualified for student aid; the Marshalls had too much money and they were, for better or mostly worse, my guardians. Just to add insult they'd encouraged me to turn down scholarship money over and over again telling me to "consider people who really needed the money," and "that they'd make sure my education was paid for."

And they'd made good on that promise. They just hadn't mentioned it came with stipulations until after I'd already turned the scholarships down.

So yes, I had . . . complicated feelings about the Marshalls. On the one hand they took care of me, on the other hand they never let me forget my place. And my place was firmly beneath them in their convoluted minds.

But I'd learned to get by all right.

I lived a decidedly frugal life. Eating out, dinners, movies, *dates* were luxuries I could not afford. I sometimes ventured out with Elodie, but that didn't really count. Besides, she was kind enough to make sure whatever we did was free. I supposed I was lucky, in a way, that real dating hadn't been in the cards for me. The very thought of spending money unnecessarily made my heart race and my palms sweat. I had a plan for paying back Julian's parents and every spare cent I had went toward that.

You're already in debt just like your parents, Trev. Soon you'll be giving your own kids away in order to get by.

I rejected the thought immediately. If I were blessed enough to have children, I'd never let them out of my sight.

I squinted at the bright sun as we walked. Jules had started going on endlessly about this fine girl he'd seen and how she must've been a supermodel. I was listening but I wasn't really paying attention.

Julian's suggestion that we go out to eat still weighed on me.

It was the kind of thing that niggled and burrowed deep under your skin because it was so simple. It wasn't always easy to grow up with personal lack surrounded by folks whose excess had excess.

But I didn't mind paying my dues. One day, maybe in the next six or seven years, I'd be able to go out to eat without care. One day, I'd be able to treat Julian to pay him back for always looking out for me. Maybe I'd even be able to take a date to a nice restaurant and have a steak.

"God, I'm tired," Julian said, as he lifted his frames from his face and rubbed his eyes. "Who the hell called the house so early this morning? It took me forever to drop back off to sleep."

It took everything in me not to groan. "My father."

"What?" Julian slowed, his head whipping up. A little of my disgruntled tone must've seeped into my voice despite myself, because Julian stopped walking altogether and his eyebrows were near touching as he stared at me with concern.

My parents were a touchy topic.

"Yeah. Caught my ass at six thirty in the a.m."

Jules whistled low, shaking his head.

At the Marshalls' house the switchboard operator knew how to rig the lines; both his parents and mine were perpetual recipients of the busy tone. Julian's parents were gone a lot so when we were in Charlotte we were mostly left in peace.

At Fisk, there was no one to bribe into doing our bidding so the call had come through, and I'd been dumb enough to pick up.

"What did he want?" Jules prompted at my silence.

I sighed. "He wants me to come 'home' for the Christmas break."

Green Valley was not home.

Not anymore.

I hadn't lived there in years and could hardly remember what life was like when I had. I *did* remember my parents being stressed about money, all the time, especially after my little brother was born.

I remembered the distressed look my mother gave me every time she measured me fearing I'd grown another inch and would need new pants. I remembered willing my feet not to grow because I didn't want to ask for new shoes. That—the feeling of actively trying to be invisible so as not to burden my family—was how I remembered my time in Green Valley more than anything else. I knew they were pouring everything into trying to keep their business afloat, so I'd tried in my own way to stay out of the way.

It hadn't worked. You were a burden and they sent you away anyway.

Julian looked at me, his expression carefully neutral. Too careful. "What did you say?"

I caught myself before I sighed again, frustrated that I couldn't get a read on Julian's thoughts. "I told him I'd think about it."

Julian gave a small smile and a nod. "For what it's worth, I think you should go, Trev. They've been trying, I think—"

I shot him a thunderous glare that had him pivoting. "I *know* I'm not in any position to give advice on parents." He really, really wasn't. Julian's relationship with his parents was as fraught as my relationship with my own. "But can you honestly say you've never wanted to go back?"

No.

That wasn't the whole truth. I didn't think about going back *anymore*. When I'd first been deposited with Julian's family, going home was all I could think of. The desire for the familiar terrain of Green Valley, for the way the air smelled up in the mountains, for the faces of townsfolk that knew you and your kin—going back generations—was piercing. I'd missed my friends, but above all else I'd missed my *family*.

The yearning for home had been so strong, so acute, that I'd ached with it. I didn't sleep, I couldn't concentrate on anything else.

It wasn't just that I'd lost my family; it felt like I'd lost my world. Everything and everyone that I'd ever known. Maybe my family didn't have money in Green Valley but I'd had a sense of belonging. But as weeks trickled to months and years, without my parents coming to retrieve me the dream of returning home withered slowly and then died. All that longing turned to bitterness. And now?

And now I wasn't sure how I felt about the idea. While Green Valley wasn't home, Charlotte wasn't home either. I had no particular desire to spend my break at Marshall House. The place that felt closest to how I remembered a home feeling was Palmer Memorial, our boarding school, and even that was gone now.

I didn't feel as though I had a home to go to.

Julian took my hesitance as a sign to keep pushing. "Trevor, your parents have been trying to reconnect with you for more than three years now."

I flinched. Julian was right; they'd started really hounding me my senior year of high school and had been persistently reaching out with cards, calls, and letters throughout my entire time at college.

I mostly ignored them. As the saying went, too little, too late. It seemed cheap to me, to give me away as a child only to try to establish a parental relationship once I was almost grown.

I knew Julian didn't see it that way, as the child of people whose interest in his life was inconsistent at best, he took their persistence as something greater than what I saw. He'd come up with all types of conjecture to explain their spurt of interest in me in recent years. "Maybe they regret their actions, perhaps they've changed, or maybe they had a good reason for their actions. You should give them a chance—at least hear them out," he'd lectured over and over again.

I didn't want to have this conversation with him again today, as part of me—a very, very small part—was curious about my "family."

"I needed to check with you first," I replied and before Julian could get too high on his soapbox or the conversation got too deep, I ribbed him again. "After all, if I'm going to the backwoods of Tennessee for almost month, I'm sure as hell dragging your pretty, city-boy, siddity behind with me."

He bristled at the word pretty but cracked a smile in spite of himself. "I'll check my schedule."

Daisy

An hour later we were still standing in line and I'd made at least one good life decision. I'd decided my senior thesis would be titled *Freshman Move in Day: A Study in Controlled Chaos.*

A big brown-skinned lady with hair bumped up like Diana Ross and wearing a red dress with white capped sleeves sat at the check-in desk in front of Jubilee, Hall just as Trevor promised.

With her at the table? A definite fire hazard.

Extension cords ran a mile through the grass, across doorjambs and under people's feet, all to connect to a dusty old fan that sat atop her desk.

Considering the building was up for historic recognition, it was a little alarming.

I couldn't really blame her; it was ninety-four degrees in the *shade,* and we weren't in the shade.

I managed not to pass out while listening to the big lady methodically call, "Next!" over that hour. Following each "next" a girl and her family would shuffle to the front and the big lady and her two aides would pick through banker's boxes filled with letter-sized brown envelopes. After a moment, the envelope would be located and handed to the big lady and she'd hand the envelope to the girl.

Repeat for one hour . . . and counting.

There must've been one hundred and thirty girls trying to sign in all at one time. And not just girls; there were fathers overheating and mothers fretting while little brothers and sisters ran around making up games to entertain themselves. Boosters walked the line selling cups of water for a quarter, and I was told there were plates of yams, greens, and smothered chops on their way up from who knows where that would be sold for a dollar and a quarter to anyone that got too hungry.

My mind began to wander while I waited. I was determined not to let Trevor or whatever his name was hijack my thoughts. I finally managed to get a daydream going about being at a Temptations concert with a tall stranger who maybe looked a tiny bit like him, but not really.

What did his face even look like? I'd already forgotten.

Finally, *finally* it was nearly my turn, and I began paying attention again. It was the last part that made this whole thing real and exciting. I noticed that the big lady handed the envelope to the *girls*; not the parents. When two adults interacted the documents were never handed to the child.

We're the adults now!

I'm an adult! Jesus! I can't wait for Dolly to leave.

I'm an adult. JESUS! I don't ever want Dolly to leave.

Those two thoughts battled it out in my head and I realized I was being ridiculous. I would be fine. Plenty of people have gone off to college, and they all turned out fine.

They mostly turned out fine.

I would be one of the fine ones.

Dolly eyed me like she knew exactly what I was thinking as I vacillated between biting my lip and grinning like a fool. Her look conveyed that I'd better not get any overly bright ideas about my newfound freedom. I dropped my head to hide my smile, but my grin didn't fade.

When it was my turn the girls working with the big lady became and more and more flustered as they searched for my envelope before the big lady finally turned to me said, "Are you sure you're in this dorm?"

I looked to Dolly who was already squinting at the lady. "Yes, she is. She is a freshman girl. Is this not the freshman girls' dormitory?"

The lady eyed her levelly before looking at me and asking, "What was the last name again?" I'd originally given it to one of the assistants who was now looking very nervous.

Dolly interjected before I could respond. "Payton, P-A-Y-T-O-N," she said in the same voice she used when speaking to a Mill foreman who was dangerously close to feeling her wrath.

I wanted to die. Why, oh why couldn't Dolly just once let it go when someone gave her a hard time.

Oh Lord. The folks behind us were starting to whisper.

The big lady dug back through the boxes and after a moment she pulled free an envelope whose flap had nestled snugly behind another. She scanned the front once, twice, and then lingered on it for a third reading.

The lady's eyes cut to me. "You're Daisy Payton from Green Valley," she said, staring, incredulous.

Oh God. Did anything good ever come from anyone staring you dead in the face and asking you to confirm your identity? What did they think, that you were a liar? Were they disappointed that you were you?

I stared back at this lady trying to decide if I wanted to be a disappointer or a liar . . . She was portly and pretty; her eyes were surprised but not unkind.

Better to be honest.

I nodded.

Her cherry red lips broke into the biggest smile. It transformed her face. Where she'd been methodical and all business before, she was warm and open now. I realized she was much younger than I'd thought.

"My momma always says the world gets smaller every day! I went to school here years ago with your brother Adolpho! He talked about you all the time. Back then he was the biggest flirt, but that didn't stop me from having a crush on him." She laughed self-deprecatingly. "Is he here today?" she asked, eyes darting past me hopefully.

Dolly opened her mouth and closed it twice so fast that she looked like a fish. Before she could say anything, I cut in. "Nope. Couldn't make it today, but I'll send your regards."

"Please do. Tell him Bessie Mitchell said hi," she said a voice that was a bit dreamy and breathy before she blinked and hastily shoved my envelope into my hands.

"Now, you're top floor—penthouse level, we call it. Corner room diagonal to the stairs. Curfew is at eleven, room inspections are on-demand, any of the—" She waved about to guys wearing fraternity insignias and ROTC uniforms. "—can help you get your stuff upstairs. Complete dorm rules, welcome letter, freshman directory, and maps are in the back of the packet. See your advisor first thing Monday morning to pick your classes. Orientation today at four thirty, parents invited. Freshman mixer starts at six p.m." She looked at Dolly. "Students only."

I nodded, clutched the packet a little tighter and tugged Dolly away. I managed to quickly flag down one of the guys dressed in an ROTC uniform to help us get my steamer trunk from Dolly's car. I could feel my sister boring holes in the back of my head but I continued to smile and didn't face her.

Yeah . . . so about those wide-open airy spaces in this giant building? Not so much. Maybe folks in the olden days were smaller or maybe they just had less stuff.

My room was small with pale yellow walls, one window on the far wall, two closets, two raised beds, and a single dresser. I'd beaten my roommate there and claimed the bed closest to the window. We'd made quick work of the cleaning and had gotten a good way through the decorating and hanging my clothes before Dolly flopped on the bed and called me to sit next to her.

I knew what was coming next. It was one of my favorite Dolly speeches. It was the "Today You Become a Woman" speech. My conservative guess was I'd become a woman twenty-three times in the last few years. It'd happened when I'd gotten my driver's license, when I'd gotten asked to the junior prom, when I'd gone to the senior prom, graduation day . . . you get the drift. Dolly was good with marking milestones with big speeches.

She'd begin gently but I knew it wouldn't stay gentle for very long; she would poke and pry and try to get me to cry and suddenly I was tired and ready for her to go.

"Do you like your room?" she asked innocuously.

I nodded, because I knew she hated when I nodded. Instead of reacting she simply stared and stared until I said, "Yes, it's nice. A bit small for two people, but I'm sure my roommate will be nice and we will make do." I said it more hoping than knowing.

Dolly smiled, and then after a moment said, "Don't be angry with your father . . ."

I stared at her confused, waiting for her to go on. She seemed to be struggling for words and so I patted her leg reassuringly. "Don't worry, I'll write him a letter. Or better yet, I think I saw a pay phone at the end of the hall, I'll call him and tell him I'm not angry he couldn't make the trip."

She sighed. "No, Daisy, I know you're not angry over that."

There was another pause and she took a deep breath. "Daddy wanted to surprise you. He thought you might be more comfortable in your own room here since you have your own room at home."

I continued to stare at her. "He called in a favor with one of his friends at the Alumni Association and they made special accommodations for you. Someone will be by to collect the extra bed—"

"No," I said more forcefully than I intended. I wasn't angry with Dolly.

Although she had kept this from me until now, so maybe I should've been. In fact, I definitely should've been.

"Dolly, why didn't you tell me?"

"I knew it would make you upset. There is no use trying to change what's done."

"No use? Would make me upset? I am way past upset. I don't want special accommodations. I don't want my own room. I don't want to be treated *differently*," I hollered.

"Daisy, calm down. This isn't the end of the world."

How could I explain that it wasn't the end of the world, it was a continuation of the same world.

And that was the problem.

I wanted to be Daisy Payton here, not *Daisy Payton*.

Because Daisy Payton played a mean game of spades, and knew how to cornrow in every direction. She had a natural head for figures, and could even do three-digit multiplication in her head. She loved the Temptations and could cut a rug on the dance floor with the best of them. She could bake better than your eighty-five-year-old granny. She studied geography for fun. She got a four-point-oh during the worst year of her life. She was good with potted plants but terrible in the garden; weeds were foes she could not defeat. She'd been kissed twice. Once was awful and once was amazing, so amazing that she did it again, and then again—so really four times, but three of the kisses happened in one session. And she wanted opportunities to roll that fifty-fifty dice again to find out how the next kiss would be.

But *Daisy Payton*?

Daisy Payton had a powerful father. (That poor man.)

Daisy Payton was a rich girl. (She's not, but it doesn't matter if people think you are.)

She had a dead brother, who got murdered in Vietnam. (What a useless war.)

Daisy Payton had a mother who was there and then—*poof!*— was gone from breast cancer. (Poor *Daisy*.)

Daisy Payton went from rich girl to poor girl. Poor little rich girl that everyone looked at with pity.

And she hated it.

She hated that everyone, *everyone* thought they knew her.

She hated the assumption that if they hurt with her, or worse, for her, then it made the pain better, as if that made it the entire community's pain; but it absolutely didn't.

She hated that she still read and reread the letters from her brother. Some of the pages had wrinkles from being crumpled in fits of anger because oh, she was so angry when he left. And then she felt guilty and stupid and horrified that she'd almost destroyed his letters when they were all that was left. Some were starting to show signs of age, yellow in some spots and the ink fading in others, and she hated that too because how could so much time have passed without him?

And she hated that her mother had been helping her shop for homecoming dresses and was buried before Thanksgiving. It had spread so fast.

No junior prom dress shopping. No junior prom.

She barely remembered her senior year.

She hated that her friends and family and perfect strangers spoke to her in hushed tones and assumed she was broken.

She hated that they were right.

Because the ache inside her was relentless. It constantly missed her brother. It constantly missed her mother. It would not abate. It could not be moved. She was thoroughly, horribly broken and all that brokenness was put up for examination by an entire town. That just couldn't happen here.

For the whole of her life, the whole of Green Valley had treated her differently, and she absolutely hated it.

But she wasn't in Green Valley now.

And Daisy Payton had a plan.

She would have a roommate, her father's meddling be damned. No one would ever know she was the daughter of the owner of largest lumber mill in eastern Tennessee because she was going to do what everyone else did with their influential connections: hide them.

And she was going to do what everyone else did with their hurts and disappointments: tuck them away and ignore them till they didn't hurt anymore.

She was going to be just like everyone else.

But first she was going to get rid of Dolly.

CHAPTER TWO

Daisy

Dolly had to go but I knew I wouldn't be able to get rid of her without a fight. Just as I was about to spout a wildly ridiculous lie like, "I think I'm having an asthma attack!" Or worse, fake a fainting spell during which Dolly would rush to find someone to help and I would hastily write a note explaining that I'd left to explore the campus alone and that Dolly should not wait for me, I was saved from having to resort to subterfuge.

There was a soft *rap-rap-rap* at the door and I bounded from the bed.

I opened the door to see two girls. One was tall, wearing a picked-out afro that was perfectly spherical, a blue and white infinity scarf over her bosom that left her midsection on full display, and a pair of hip-hugging dark denim bell-bottoms. She was rail thin with an oval face, strikingly high cheekbones, deep set brown eyes, and satiny skin that seemed to shimmer like it was freshly oiled even under the dim hall light. She was drop dead gorgeous. The other was shorter and more buxom. She was softly pretty with a perfect face of makeup—

perfect half-moon, coal-black eyebrows and blue eyeshadow expertly applied—and wearing a bright orange shift dress with yellow trim that stopped just above her knees.

"Hey! We're all about to head to Spence to grab something to eat before orientation," the tall one said. "I'm James Jones, by the way. Before you ask—yes, my parents wanted a boy. Yes! I *am* named after my papa. And, yes! I know the alliteration is amazing!"

James rattled this all off at a sonic clip and paused ever so briefly to throw me a knowing grin. I liked this girl instantly. She didn't just talk, she acted as she spoke, her hands fluttering, her face animated; it was fascinating to watch. There was something about her presence that just drew your eye to her. "This here is Odessa Mae Boyd!" she said, hands fluttering in the other girl's direction.

"Daisy Pay—erm, just Daisy," I said, not wanting to potentially relive the mess of being recognized from earlier.

She raised her eyebrows at me and exchanged a quick sideways glance with her friend. "Okay. Daisy, just Daisy. Odessa is from Charleston and I'm from Murfreesboro."

Oh great. Now they thought I was a nut. I would need to get my story straight about who I was and was not sooner rather than later.

"I'm from Green Valley," I volunteered, wanting to avoid embarrassing myself any more than I'd just done with the Daisy, just Daisy nonsense.

The shorter one, Odessa, spoke up. "My friends call me Odie. You should too," she said with a smile. Odie had the most distinctive voice; it was very soft, slightly smoky, and lingered the way barbecue smoke lingers even after you'd walked away from it.

"Bye, Dolly!" I shouted.

I threw my hand over my shoulder waving goodbye, then I hazarded a glance behind me. My sister looked not at all like herself; she looked . . . flummoxed.

But it was not enough to deter me. I headed out with my two saviors, leaving her behind on my bed.

On the way to the cafeteria we seemed to pick up another two or three girls every ten paces as word spread around the dorm. We made our way down the drive in front of Jubilee and by the time we reached the cafeteria there were probably thirty-five of us total; we'd even picked up some guys along the way.

We were stopped short outside the doors to the building. A petite, elderly woman wearing a starched blue collared shirt with "Dining Services" written in yellow on it barred our entry.

Her shirt was layered with a royal blue apron that read "Mrs. Dot" in script over her heart.

Her mouth was snapped shut into a firm line, gray whiskers jutted from her chin, and the hairnet atop her head let no curls or strands escape.

When she spoke it was *not* what I was expecting from a lady that frail looking—her voice thundered.

"Nah lissen here! Make this the first and last time you show up to Spence Dining Hall without your dinin' coupons. I know you ain't got your coupon books because none of y'all showed up to sign them out."

I was bewildered. The faces of my new classmates looked equally puzzled, but it was Charlie from South Carolina, a boy who'd joined us on the walk from the dorms, that voiced our thoughts. "Excuse me, ma'am. No one told me to come here to pick up a book."

She stared at him like he was a bug in her soup before she responded slowly, speaking so it was perfectly clear she thought Charlie was a simpleton.

"But you've got to eat, son, haven't you?"

"Yes, ma'am," he replied.

"And how you think you were supposed to do that?"

He opened his mouth again, but she shut it.

"Let me tell you something."

She pointed her finger at him and then waved it toward the larger crowd. "Let me tell *all* of youse something. Your mamas, daddies, memaws, nanas, and aunties ain't here no more to think for y'all. You need to open your mouths. You need to ask questions, and if the good Lord ain't gave you enough sense to ask how youse supposed to eat, well . . ." It hung in the air for a second before she delivered her final barb. "Maybe you ain't Fisk material."

Her words pressed on us for just a second longer before a voice sniggered behind us.

I turned and I saw *him*: tall, lithe, and a face full of mirth.

His smooth black waves glistened in the sun as he easily maneuvered through the crowd.

He was accompanied by another guy who was just as handsome; black horn-rimmed glasses, reddish-brown, wavy hair that was cut lower on the sides and transitioned into loose curls at the top. The cut made him look a bit like a boyish Malcolm Little. He was laughing even harder than the Trevor boy.

I could feel the girls on all sides of me eyeing them, and I was quite suddenly enveloped in a cocoon of swooning.

Life's not fair.

"Have mercy, he's handsome," James whispered beside me, reaching over and squeezing my hand. She averted her eyes from both guys, and when she looked up again she looked dead calm, totally unaffected.

"Yes, he certainly is," I said benignly.

They moved like a pair of homonyms—the same kind of fine, sounding two different ways, and it was patently unfair to every female in observation distance.

Trevor sauntered right up to the cafeteria lady, scooped her up in an embrace, and kissed her cheek.

"Mrs. Dot! Mrs. Dot! I been thinking about your candied yams all summer long!"

She broke into a big grin. "Trevor! I ain't know you was coming

26

back so soon or I'd have them ready for you." Releasing Trevor, she reached over to give the other boy a light pat on the cheek and then a hug.

"That's all right, I can wait till next Thursday." He glanced around as if he was just noticing the cadre of freshman standing in line trying to get in.

Of course he'd just noticed us. He hadn't just cut the line, he'd charmed it. Even the boys with us had parted like the Red Sea for the two of them.

Our eyes briefly met, he winked at me and I looked away quickly, feeling unsettling flutters low in my tummy.

I could hear the smile in his voice. "You getting the newbies straight?"

She nodded her head and looked back at us with dagger eyes.

The boy with the glasses picked that moment to speak up. "Let me guess. None of y'all have your coupon books?" he said mockingly as he reached into his breast pocket and theatrically extracted his and handed it over.

"Why thank you, Jules," Mrs. Dot said equally dramatic.

"Jules," James whispered at my side. "His name is Jules."

I gave her a sideways glance.

Interesting. Her Mr. Handsome was not Trevor.

I felt oddly relieved by that.

"You two may enter," Mrs. Dot said giving them another of her genuine smiles before adding, "Tell Jimmy to pull the pecan pie out the freezer. I popped one in this mornin' and was gonna save it for the uppers next week but seein' as how I know you both love it, y'all can eat it today."

"Mrs. Dot, you're the sweetest," Trevor crooned, giving her another kiss on the cheek and stepping toward the dining hall. As he passed, she stared at us—lips pressed together, arms crossed, and chin jutted.

Sweet was not the adjective I would have used.

Before he slipped through the doors, Trevor glanced over his shoulder and met my eyes again for a second before he called back to Mrs. Dot, smile still in his voice, "Be easy on them—they know not what they do."

We were treated to the grace, wit, and charm of Mrs. Dot for another *fifteen* minutes while she detailed the dos and don'ts of the dining hall.

And when I say detailed, I mean *detailed.*

"Y'all are welcome to get more juice but for Pete's sake, don't use the same cup to stick under the juice fountain! No one wants your spit rim touching on the lever or the juice spout. Same goes for water and soda."

The entire lecture could've been summed up in about thirty seconds with a succinct, "Use common sense, don't be gross, don't be rude, don't steal."

I finally signed my coupon book out from a table in front of the cafeteria and by that time I was well and truly starving.

As I entered the cafeteria doors, I noted Trevor was holding court on the far side of the cafeteria near the windows with Jules at his side.

They really were an unfair vision.

We moved through the line selecting from the dishes then descended on the tables all at once. The saying "there's safety in numbers" had never felt truer and I was grateful for each of my freshman classmates in that moment.

I end up seated between Odie and James with three guys sitting directly across from us: Maurice, Rufus, and Charlie.

Someone had crammed the tables together and soon we became a rowdy, boisterous bunch.

It felt more like a family reunion than the first meeting of a bunch of strangers. That instant acceptance was a big welcome contrast to the cafeteria of Green Valley High, where I'd mostly eaten quietly by myself.

My high school had been integrated but that didn't mean that the Black kids and white kids sat together at lunch.

Oh, no.

Quite the contrary; while we were content to sit together and learn together, we did not socialize together. With the exception of a handful of brave souls, the smattering of Black kids congregated at three tables and the white kids ate everywhere else.

Neither of those groups ate with me.

Don't get me wrong—I wasn't picked on, and I wasn't an outcast.

No one was dumb or daring enough to do that directly. I just wasn't *included.*

I was to be *examined,* not included.

I didn't blame them. I didn't.

As far as my classmates were concerned, they may as well have been eating with their teacher.

As it was, most of them would've been eating with their parent's boss's daughter. I eventually got why they'd wanted to avoid me.

After all, would *you* have wanted to take the chance that you'd let it slip that when your dad called out sick last Thursday, he'd actually taken you on a surprise fishing trip to the very best water hole in the Great Smokey Mountains for your birthday? Or that your mother came home complaining about her job every day?

No. You wouldn't have risked it. No one wanted to take those kinds of chances.

Besides, the few times I was invited to join of my peers, I'd had to decline anyway. My mother and father had fielded the requests as delicately as possible, declining sleepovers, birthday party invitations, and picnics on my behalf when I was younger.

I'd been angry and confused. It felt like I was being punished for something I had little to do with.

Dolly had been the one to add perspective and per usual, Dolly was right. She'd succinctly summed up my parents' actions. *"Daisy,*

29

trust me, it's better if you don't. You never can tell folk's motivations for these kinds of things."

It wasn't until I'd been a tad older that I realized what she'd meant. The thing about being the child of everyone's boss is that everyone thought they could get something from you.

Ev-vor-ree-bod-ay.

Like that time I was discussing my grade with my English teacher and she causally mentioned that her husband was hoping to pick up extra hours at the Mill to be able to afford a new medicine their infant daughter needed for her asthma. Medicine that was "unfortunately, not covered by the insurance offered at Payton Mills."

Or who could forget the time in fifth grade when my class presented their annual "All I Want for Christmas" essays and every single person had included a line hinting that their Christmas morning joy was contingent upon their momma or daddy's Christmas bonus being issued.

Yeah, that one had been particularly painful.

I took a sip of my juice, aware of the chatter around me but suddenly a little melancholy at the memories.

At home—my siblings, my momma and daddy, and I—we were as regular as any other family.

But in public?

Well, there were a lot of spoken and unspoken rules to being a Payton in public.

Never let them see you cry. *Never* let them see you sweat. *Never* let them see you unkempt.

I realized even at that age that some of my actions weren't about me at all. They were always tied to the larger mythical Payton family narrative.

Therefore, instead of crying as each classmate implied that my family was personally responsible for the success of failure of their *Christmas,* I'd sat there placidly doodling in my notebook, and after each one finished, I'd briefly looked up at the speaker and clapped.

Because if I had cried, there's a good chance that one or more persons would've assumed this meant that their parent was *not* getting their Christmas bonus. When in fact, ten-year-old me was simply overwhelmed by being implicitly tasked with a request I had no power to grant.

I knew sitting in that classroom that when I got home to a safe space, I *would* cry. But by that age I'd already gotten really good with deferring my feelings for an indefinite length of time. It was a useful life skill.

The great Christmas debacle ended up teaching me another useful life skill—handle it on your own.

Because my parents? They were wonderful yet terrifying. Dolly words, not mine. Coincidentally enough those were the same words I now used to describe Dolly.

It was best not to involve them in whatever was happening unless you were prepared for things to escalate. Quickly.

I had gone home and I had wept mightily, asking my father— pleading with him really—to give people extra money to buy their children gifts at Christmas. I'd offered to forgo my own gifts if it meant it would help. It wasn't that I was so good and charitable. I just didn't want to have to face the disappointment of my classmates and the knowledge that it had been my fault if their parents didn't get that money.

My father had looked bewildered but had hugged me and kissed me on my forehead and rocked me until I calmed down and then he'd sat me in a seat and asked me what in the world was going on.

So I'd told him.

And then my father calmly replied that Payton Mills had never in all our years of existence failed to give employees a bonus at Christmas. It was built into the budget.

That moment of relief and elation was pierced by my mother's voice saying in a tone I hardly recognized, "I'm having Gloria

LaCroix fired tomorrow and don't you"—she'd pointed at my father —"'kindness, Kendra' me."

I'd turned more fully toward my mother, shocked. I was blown further back by the rage I saw on her pretty face. My mother was actually shaking.

I didn't know what was more surprising: her words, her anger, or the fact that Mother and Mrs. LaCroix were—I thought—friends.

She couldn't be serious.

My father nodded but then said, "That might make things worse for Daisy."

"Make things worse? My baby just came home crying because her classmates were allowed to bully her all day. Glo should have put a stop to that mess after the first or second student!"

She was serious.

"I don't want her to be fired," I offered trying to diffuse her anger. "I like Mrs. LaCroix."

More than that, everyone liked our teacher. If she was fired it would just be one more thing I was responsible for.

"Besides, that's not right," I continued. "She's your friend. She shouldn't be fired just because I had a bad day at school."

My mother looked down at me, gentleness returning to her eyes. She smoothed my hair, and said softly, "You've always been the sweetest of my children."

I didn't know if it was true but my father said the same thing often —that I was sweet and that it came from my mother. He said Dolly was steel and that she got that from him and Ado had been strong and he said that he got that from both of them.

"Daisy," my mother said gently. "I don't expect you to understand this but what Mrs. LaCroix did today—"

"She didn't do anything!" I protested.

"That's right. She didn't do *anything*. Sometimes doing nothing *is* what's wrong, Daisy. If something wrong is happening to someone, and you do nothing to help or to stop it when it's within your power to do so, then what you are doing is wrong."

Her eyes had cut to my father's. "Adolpho, fifteen children didn't just decide to do this out of the clear blue."

"I was thinking the same thing," he'd said with a look of consternation on his face.

Then he turned to me and said, "Sweetheart, I have some calls to make. Your sister was waiting for you earlier. She wanted to wait for you to get home so you could make Christmas cookies together."

Right on time, and in retrospect, *too* on time, Dolly walked into my father's study and declared she'd been looking all over for me.

Eavesdropping was more like it.

She'd ushered me out of the room but before I'd gotten out of range it sounded like I'd heard one of my parents say something like *". . . find out which one of the employees decided it would be a smart idea to send a message to us by taking a hit out on my baby."*

Things got . . . uncomfortable in school after that. Mrs. LaCroix disappeared for a while and we had a substitute, Mr. Jackson, leading into the Christmas break. He was not loved.

And when I'd returned to school the week after the incident, I'd received a handwritten apology note from every single classmate.

The whole thing had been disconcerting and had only served to widen the gulf between myself and them. As any child who'd ever been forced to spitefully mutter the words "I'm sorry" can attest, the only thing worse than the original offense was having an adult force you to give or receive said apology.

I'd suspected Dolly was behind those overtures right away. My parents would've spoken to their parents but most likely wouldn't have made any requests of the children.

Dolly though?

I don't think there was anything my sister *wouldn't* do for me, including threatening my classmates.

And Dolly was in the perfect position to do it, she went to high school with half of the class's older siblings.

Furthering my suspicions? For several days after the incident, my class picture from that school year had been missing from its place on my desk in my room and it'd magically appeared back in the same spot just after the apology notes began appearing.

"Odie Mae, is that all you're eatin'?"

Charlie's voice broke through and pulled me back from my ruminations.

I looked at Odie's plate and saw a limp-looking salad and an apple on the side.

She ignored him.

Instead she flashed her brilliant smile at a boy named Maurice and said, "So tell me where you're from?"

Maurice looked from her to a crestfallen Charlie and shrugged his shoulders as if to say, "What you want me to do, man?" He wiped his mouth, gave Odie a timid smile, and answered, "Atlanta, Georgia."

"You don't say! Jewel of the South, they call it. We went there on family vacation one year. I've got a pen pal that lives on Peachtree."

"Uh, which Peachtree—" He paused suddenly, as he realized Odie was grinning quietly down at her salad like she was the cat that caught the canary.

He chuckled. "Peachtree, eh? I'm sure I know your friend. Is her name Lucy? Or maybe Mary?" He caught her subtle humor, matching common names to the common street name.

She looked up delighted and shook her head. "Close. It's Linda."

James smiled catching the joke and added, "If that ain't the truth! I had a Linda Gilliam, Linda Gillian, Linda Gillum, and Linda Gaines in my class." She huffed and made an exasperated crossed-eyed expression.

We all began laughing, well, all of us except Charlie who cut in over the din.

"Odie, I think I saw some sweet potato pie out with the desserts. I know how you like it. I can go grab you a slice, if you'd like."

Odie took a bite of her apple, the hard crunch resonating even over the hum of the chatter all around us. She chewed it slowly as if she was savoring the tiny bite and we all remained silent until it became uncomfortable.

I saw James open her mouth because it was evident Odie's intent was to ignore Charlie again, but Odie surprised me.

"Why are you here, Charlie?" she said in that breathy, smoky voice of hers. Her tone was not soft or gentle; it was cutting. I wouldn't have even thought her capable of such sharpness, given the sweetness she'd greeted everyone else with.

James looked up at me, startled.

"Actually, scratch that question. It doesn't matter why you're here. The real question is, do you remember what I said to you in the gymnasium after graduation?"

Charlie flinched and stared at her for a second, searching her face for some sign.

So they did know each other from home.

My suspicions had been raised by the way Charlie gravitated toward Odie like an eager puppy from the moment we'd stepped out of our dorm doors.

Like he'd been waiting for her.

He nodded almost imperceptibly.

"Good," she said simply. "I meant every single word, Charles Love."

Charlie stood abruptly, mumbled something about having lost his appetite, made his apologies, and left.

Odie took another bite of her apple and chewed it like it was the most delicious thing she'd ever tasted. Her accompanying grin was absolutely vicious.

"So sweet Odie Mae has a sour side . . . Um, what the hell was that?" James quizzed.

Odie shrugged and then said softly, sweetly, "That was nothing. Nothing at all."

Before we could press her further, another girl, ironically enough named Linda, plopped in Charlie's seat and started chatting with James right away. I noted how James was instantly absorbed, giving her undivided attention to whatever occupied her mind at the moment, her hands waving in animation.

My awareness of what was happening at my table was pulled away. My stare detector had been going off at random intervals since I entered the cafeteria, but it must have been malfunctioning because each time I'd looked up I'd found nothing but folks minding their own blessed business.

I glanced to the far side of the room where the upperclassmen were still crowded together, laughing, joking, and utterly disinterested in what we were doing.

Trevor was gesturing widely; I couldn't even imagine what they could have been talking about.

His strong arms flexed as he moved his hands.

Why must he be so . . . eye-catching?

I sighed and gave up searching for where the disconcerting feeling of being watched was coming from. I turned my attention back to my new friends just in time to hear Maurice ask, "So Daisy, where about are you from?"

"Greenville," I answered automatically, having sorted my origin story on our walk to the cafeteria.

I braced for Odie or James to look at me oddly or to otherwise indicate they'd noticed the change but neither of them reacted; they just continued eating and chatting and I chalked it up to having met so many folks that day.

"North Carolina?" Maurice continued.

"Tennessee, eastern part of the state."

He shrugged as if it was unfamiliar to him and I smiled, thanking the geography gods.

This was going to be was absolutely perfect. Greenville, Tennessee was a tiny town, four hours away near the North Carolina line. Notably, it was also almost one hundred percent white, meaning the chances that someone from Greenville would be attending Fisk were slim. On the off chance someone did, it was even slimmer possibility that I'd ever even meet them.

The rain started just as we reached the front door to our dormitory. James was lamenting that the freshman social planned for tonight would be cancelled due to the bad weather when I spotted Dolly the dogged waiting for me in the lobby of Jubilee. I motioned for James and Odie to head on back upstairs and I decided to greet Dolly head-on.

I'd found my bravery.

I would tell my sister that I'd be fine and she could head back to her hotel for the night. Dolly and I were just prolonging the inevitable. She had originally planned to return to Green Valley early Sunday morning but honestly, there was no reason for her to stay. In fact, I'd be fine if she decided to head back to Green Valley tomorrow instead, a full day ahead of schedule. I was just about to vocalize my thoughts when she surprised me and beat me to it.

She pulled me into a brief, tight hug and whispered in my ear, "I'm proud of you. Never forget that. You're smart and you're strong, and you deserve every good thing that you've worked for, Daisy. Never forget that either."

Then she stepped back, still holding my hands. She spoke down at them softly adding, "Funny enough, I ran into one of my classmates from Howard here with her youngest sister and their parents when I went . . . when I looked around after you left."

It was almost imperceptible the way her voice wavered around the word "parents," but I heard it and my throat closed inexplicably.

Probably choking on that apology you owe Dolly.

"I'm going to go to orientation with her. I know you'll probably head over with your new friends. Afterward, she and I will probably grab dinner and catch up. And I'm going back to Green Valley at first light tomorrow. You know how the Mill falls apart when I'm gone for longer than a day. Besides, I want to make sure I'm back with enough time to rest for Sunday service—you know how I hate to miss it. And so I guess this is goodbye."

She squeezed both my hands again and then pulled me in for an even tighter hug. I held her for a long time.

Guilt, of course, was a boulder. I'd hurt her feelings; that much was apparent. I saw through her excuses. Usually Dolly didn't bow out for anyone.

Anyone but you, apparently.

And while I wanted to apologize, I also still wanted to be *done* with these feelings. The sadness that had settled over us like a fog. The expectation of greatness. The expectation of strength bordering on perfection.

My emotions bubbled up and collided all at once. *Ah, there's the tiredness I knew was coming.*

Dolly was my only sister, and this semester would be the longest we'd been apart in a good while. My desire to clear the air before she left welled up to an unbearable degree.

"I'm sorry," I blurted. "I don't want you to be mad, or sad, I just . . ."

"Oh, Daisy, love." She forced a laugh. "I'm not upset." She shook her head for emphasis.

"Ignore me," she continued emphatically. "I'm just remembering you toddling after Ado when we moved him in here. And I remember you and Mommy helping me decorate my dorm room at Howard. I can't help but wonder what today might be like if they were here."

Nope.

That fathomless, bottomless well of what ifs? I couldn't. I *wouldn't* think about that.

She took a deep breath, and stole the words from my mouth. "But today is for celebrations, not sadness. So I'll be happy, because I *am* happy." She took another deep breath. "And because if Mommy and Ado were here, they'd be overjoyed."

"I had hoped . . ." She paused again then regrouped smiling a bit too brightly. "It doesn't matter what I'd hoped. Today isn't about me. I heard what you said earlier, Daisy—"

I opened my mouth to defend myself, and she quickly raised her voice.

"And I don't blame you."

That brought me up short.

"This place is your own. Make it your own. Our brother was so happy here. College was the best time of his life. You deserve to be happy here, and you deserve to be in the sun and not the shadow of his life . . . or his death." She gave me one last sad smile, gave my unoccupied hand a quick squeeze, and then she was out of the door.

Sidestepping Dolly's planned trip down memory lane had been difficult and if I was being honest, I had been a little hard on her by disappearing into the ether.

Dolly tried—I know she did—her best to relate to me, to understand me, to advise me, to *mother* me.

And I knew she was trying to fill impossibly large shoes that she never, ever wanted to wear.

And there I was being ungrateful and making her feel bad. However, today was case in point on why it was time for me to be on my own, far away from Green Valley.

Don't get me wrong; we loved one another fiercely and we weren't moping around the house all the time. But we were constantly managing one another's feelings, and it was exhausting and suffocating. It seemed there was never going to be a time when all three of us were doing okay at the same time, and that was before all the well-meaning town folk dragged us down with constant reminders.

In a town so small it should have been impossible to continuously run into folks for over a year that "hadn't seen you since you'd lost your mother." And that they'd "really been meaning to get by the house." That line was a cue for when you had to reassure them that no, they were not bad people for abandoning you in your time of grief.

After comforting words had been shared by me or Dolly or my father, it often led to them sharing some arbitrary memory of our loved one that was supposed to bring comfort but usually only served as a reminder of what was missing. Worse was when their stories rang suspiciously out of character for my brother or mother, making me wonder if this person was inventing something for my benefit or if they were just mixing my loved one up with someone else. Sometimes after this revelatory story the person would cry.

At any rate the net result was that you ended up comforting *them*, late for wherever you were headed, exhausted, depressed, and still alone to work through your own grief.

Back inside my room, I bypassed the bed that should've contained my overly shy or maybe super chatty roommate and, spurred to action by Dolly's words, I moved to the closet and pulled out the small, nondescript box that I'd smuggled in.

You deserve to be happy here.

I thought of my family and of how much I loved them.

You deserve to be happy here.

I thought on my family's name and how much it burdened and suffocated me.

You deserve to be happy here.

I thought on happiness and freedom and what that might look like for me.

And then I committed to my plan.

I had no idea if it was a good idea or the dumbest thing I'd ever done, but I was going through with it.

I began picking up the mementos around my room—ones Dolly had just painstakingly placed.

A stationary set that read *From the Desk of Daisy Payton* in fancy script, an early graduation gift from my mother who must've known she might not make it until my senior year. She'd said I could use it to write home when I went away to college.

A framed picture of my brother and sister and me standing in the Mill lumber yard . . . *You deserve to be happy here.*

I smiled remembering how me and Dolly had gotten in trouble for playing in the Mill shortly after the photo was taken; it was one of the few times my father'd lost his temper growing up. He was endlessly patient except where it came to safety and the Mill. He had no tolerance for slack there.

I placed the picture in the box and picked up a picture of my father and mother and me at my debutante ball just before she got sick.

A tiny Eiffel Tower from a family vacation in Paris, a cartouche containing my name we'd gotten in Egypt, and knickknacks from Milan and the Bahamas.

A framed picture of my brother in his dress blues.

I gathered the pieces of Daisy Payton's life reverently.

You deserve to be happy here.

And I contemplated what it meant to be both Daisy and *Daisy.*

I placed them gently in the box.

I closed the lid.

CHAPTER THREE

Trevor

On Sunday morning I arrived at church about twenty-five minutes before service was scheduled to begin. The sidewalk in front of the Fisk Memorial Chapel, or the Chapel as we called it, was a sea of black and white. The girls dressed in white dresses and the boys, like me, were dressed in dark suits with dark ties and crisp white shirts. Everyone was hurriedly congealing into a mass headed toward the front doors. I funneled myself into the stream steadily filing in.

I wanted to say I hadn't taken extra care with my appearance this morning, that I didn't make sure my shirt was pressed extra crisply, and that my real gold tie clip—one of the few gifts from my parents I'd kept—gleamed extra brightly against my solid black tie, but that would've all been a lie.

"*Freshman?*"

"*I—uh—yes.*"

She'd sounded so demure and unsure I'd wanted to reach into that car window, tug one of those plaits, give her a wink, and reassure her that all would be well.

It was baffling. I didn't even know this girl, but I hadn't been able to get her off my mind or to shake the lingering desire to protect her.

We hadn't even really spoken. I didn't know her name, and yet . . . and yet, I'd been replaying that insignificant five second exchange in my mind for the last twenty-four hours.

What was it about this girl?

The first ecumenical service of the year was traditionally just for freshman and their families, so I was pretty sure she'd be present, maybe even with that sister of hers.

I'd wondered where her parents were. I'd never ask of course; I'd gotten enough of *that* when I was moved into college myself.

People were so nosey sometimes.

Most folks didn't know Jules and I were distant relatives, they certainly didn't know I'd been raised by his parents, and that was exactly how we liked it. As the saying went in our household, "Marshall business is Marshall business."

I told myself that after my long hiatus it was past time for me to attend a church service. I told myself that I had a duty to participate as a role model, as Student Body Vice President. Then I came clean and told myself I was a liar.

The simple truth was, I went to church because I'd wanted to see her again.

From the moment I'd watched her depart the cafeteria yesterday I'd been both anticipating and bracing myself for the impact of seeing her again.

And it felt just like that: impact. My body reacted viscerally to her; she'd already hijacked my mind.

And that couldn't stand, because there were plenty of reasons I shouldn't want to see her again. Not the least of which was that I didn't have time for her, no matter how pretty or intriguing she was.

I'd also made a promise—a vow—to Elodie and I never broke my promises. I gathered my resolve as I filed through the church doors and determined that I didn't want to see her. My mind corrected me immediately, *No, Trevor, you don't want to* want *to see her.*

I sighed too loudly and it earned me a hard, censorious look from a lady dressed in a St. John suit and a white pillbox hat who walked in beside me.

Ashamed, I dropped my head as the usher escorted us to our seat. I glanced over my shoulder, searching for any other upperclassmen that may have been in attendance. This was my way of preventing myself from searching for the one person I really wanted to see.

I recognized a few faces and offered either quick smiles or nods by way of greeting. When I turned back around, I realized I'd made a miscalculation.

One pew up, seated *directly* in front of me was the girl. I didn't need to see her face to know it was her; my body reacted the same way it reacted each time I'd seen her. My heart hammered, my hands twitched as if wanting to reach for her, and it became harder to breathe.

It was too late—church was too crowded to try to move.

I resigned myself to two hours of torture, because while I'd wanted to see her, I didn't want to be this close to her. I couldn't afford to be this close to her, with the way she made me feel out of sorts.

After our initial meeting, I'd taken to calling her Sunshine in my head, because of the pretty yellow dress she'd worn and because of the way she'd lit me up inside.

But perhaps I should've named her Angel because she was a vision in white. Her dress dipped slightly in the back, teasing the skin between her shoulder blades. She wore a strand of pearls around her neck—and her *hair.*

That hair.

She'd undone the French braids and her hair just grazed her shoulders, cascading in dark, kinky, coily waves.

Shoulders that appeared to be freshly oiled, that looked soft and *biteable*. Shoulders I most definitely should not have been noticing, but noticed just the same.

I felt a rush of blood to my nether regions and on cue my groin began to tighten.

Oh no, oh no. My palms began to sweat.

This was *not* happening! Not here in the house of God.

I diverted my eyes to the floor, while strategically placing the program over my lap. While doing so I noticed the opening hymn, which the congregation sang *standing*, was happening next.

Wonderful.

I breathed deep. *I wouldn't let this happen, I was a grown man in control of my body, not a fourteen-year-old boy, for Pete's sake.*

I spotted a Bible sitting in the back of a pew and focused my mind on scripture, *For God so loved the world . . .*

In my periphery, I saw motion. I looked up just in time to see her glance over her shoulder.

I immediately wished I'd never looked up.

Imbecilic, bad move, Trevor.

She wasn't wearing sunglasses today and her eyes were revealed to me.

That revelation felt like a gift and a punishment. All at once I was swamped with forlornness, because I'd been right. She was a manic kind of beauty.

The kind of beautiful that stole a man's breath and sanity all at once. The kind of beauty that made men warriors, that made them fools. This girl was dangerous.

Her eyes captured mine. Our gazes clashed and held. The feeling of forlornness gave way to something more . . . something I couldn't or wouldn't put a name on. I allowed myself to give in to the feeling of sinking—of drowning, and cataloged as much of her face as I could.

Her eyes.

Chestnut brown, hypnotic, wide, and indescribably deep—those eyes held multitudes, they held secrets, they held *promises.*

They called me. I couldn't look away. I didn't want to. I felt my palms twitch; my breath was already gone as my heart had already begun doing calisthenics in my chest.

She stared back at me, unblinking, seemingly frozen and then in a burst, her long dark lashes fluttered in rapid succession.

Mercy, she was literally batting her eyelashes at me, and for one morose second I thought, she was *trying* to kill me with her beauty.

Her breathing hitched—or mine did—and I could hear it, the din of folks settling in around us fading into the background.

It felt apropos to see her face close and clearly for the first time in this hallowed space because something about the experience felt holy.

My body's *reaction* to that sight was anything but holy, and react it did, in a painful way despite my efforts to stay in control.

I was already suffering, painfully hard, close to mortification, and still unable to stop from looking my fill.

Those *lips.* They were pillowy, perfect, and coated in eye-catching pink. She parted them ever so slightly and if any of my earlier progress with controlling my body had remained it would have been erased with that simple motion.

The blare of the organ startled us. She blinked as if dazed then slowly turned to face the front.

The sudden intrusion of the opening chords of the Call to Worship had been a sobering dose of medicine allowing a modicum of self-control to break through quickly followed by a flush of shame.

You are in church, Trevor! The house of God!

And while I still felt warm under the collar, I realized it was prob-ably God letting me know first-hand that I was going straight to hell.

Forgive me, Lord.

I worked to concentrate my attention on the service, to ignore the girl in front of me, to focus on *anything* except the way my blood seemed to race through my veins in her presence. In the end, my tenuous grasp on self-control was moot.

She did not turn around for the remainder of the service.

Daisy

Thank God for the opening chords of "The Lord's Prayer" or I might have developed a permanent crick in my neck with how hard I was staring.

Shame. Shame. Shame on you, Daisy Marie Payton.

I buried my face in the hymnal Odie and I shared, and endeavored to block out the prickle of awareness from the hairs on the back of my neck that radiated throughout my whole body.

I squirmed, trying to get comfortable, fighting to ignore the fluttering low in my belly.

After the third time I shifted in the pew Odie raised her eyebrows and mouthed, "Are you okay?"

I smiled weakly, apologetically, and nodded.

James, that devil, looked at me, inclined her head slightly in Trevor's direction, and cut her eyes back and forth between us.

Oh Lord, am I that obvious in liking this boy? And why did James have to be so obvious in looking between us? Had he seen her do that? I wouldn't turn and look at him again.

I wouldn't. One glance and I might've gone up in flames. Trevor all dressed up in his Sunday finery was just too much.

As if my thoughts were written all over my face, James smirked and then she reached forward to dramatically hand me a church fan.

I wanted to kill her.

Smiling her devil smile, she raised her own fan, and began rapidly flickering it in a motion that covered her mouth. She spoke lowly, "My, it sho' is warm in here, Miss Daisy. You look *overheated*. I thought you could use some air."

But because I *was* warm. I flicked my wrists rapidly, taking in the cool air of the fan as I covered my mouth and responded quietly, "James, as of today we are no longer friends."

She hid her grin—but not her snicker—as she continued fanning and pretended to skim through the second chapter of John.

When we stood a moment later, I could feel the heat radiating off Trevor's body like a touch. I battled the urge to sway toward him, certain his arms and chest would feel divine.

Divine.

It was going to be a long service.

―――――――――

"Well if they gave out medals for church service length, this would be a contender for the gold," James quipped as she stood, demurely yawned, and then walked toward the end of the pew.

She was right; church had felt unendurably long, and not just in the traditional Southern Baptist way. The true torture was being saturated in Trevor's nearness. I could hear the deep tenor of his rich, melodic voice when we sang the hymn. I felt him looming behind me both in and out of my space when we stood for prayer.

I was too aware of him.

When service ended, I pretended to be extremely fascinated with my hymnal, leafing through Responsive Readings and studying the musical notations on my favorite hymns. Odie, still seated to my right, gave me a sympathetic smile and then rifled through her purse to hand me a mint.

I took the mint and unwrapped it *slowly*. I was stalling after all, trying to stay still, and more importantly staying facing forward until the gentleman behind me left.

Unfortunately, everyone wanted to speak with him. There must've been nine or ten people who swooped on him immediately after service ended.

Trevor, when will the packets for the freshman officers be up?

"Two weeks and some change. Gotta get Jules to sign off on the qualifications. I'm assuming you're running? Good for you—we need everyone to be interested in being a student leader."

Iceman, when's the first party?

"Gotta wait for the rest of the bruhs to return, but best believe it'll be the coldest party."

Trevor, I'm taking Dr. Long for Intro to Differential Equations and he says you've got the best study notes of any student he's ever taught.

"Ha! He told me he was changing all his tests this year because he was tired of my notes being the blueprint for everyone else. I knew he wouldn't go through with it. He's a curmudgeon for sure, but he wants everyone to succeed. Come by the office next week and I'll give you a copy. Better yet, check with Francine—she has a copy from last year. Also, don't forget Long works for you the same as all the professors. Don't be afraid to use office hours—how do you think my notes got so good? I spent half that semester in his face making sure I had things down."

He was kind to everyone. He was *helpful* to everyone. And that *voice*. It was smooth and deep and had a quality that made you feel like he knew you or wanted to know you.

Also, differential equations? Of course. *Of course* he was good at math because close to perfection wasn't enough. Someone made a joke behind me, and when he laughed in response, my heart thudded hard, then raced.

After what felt like an eternity, his fan club began to dwindle. *Finally.* However, my gratitude at the fact that Trevor was about to make his leave, and that *we* in turn could finally leave, was short-lived. From the corner of my eye, I saw James turn from where she'd been standing at the end of our pew. She took two short steps toward Trevor, threw him a friendly smile, and extended her hand saying, "I don't believe we've formerly met. I'm James Jones."

Trevor's response was simple, wonderful. "Pleasure to meet you, James."

I was impressed.

There were no follow-up questions or jokes about her name. In the three days since we'd met, I must've heard every variation of James joke, from King or Queen James, James Brown, James Bond, to St. James. It was exhausting for me and it's wasn't even my name. Apparently, James must've felt the same way because she didn't wrap the conversation up—her usual response when someone said something idiotic about her name. Instead I heard my friend formerly known as James, now known as Brutus say, "This is my friend Odessa."

Odie looked up from where she'd been doodling on her program beside me, gave him a slight head nod and breathed, "Hello," in that Marilyn Monroe voice of hers.

"And this saint—that seems content to live in church instead of leave—is Daisy."

I was going to *murder* James.

He smiled at me, warm, gorgeous, affable. I felt a twinge of annoyance at the friendliness and instantly chastised myself.

What did you want, Daisy? For him to look at you like he wanted . . . to . . . like he wanted?

No.

I definitely, positively did not want that.

"Daisy," he repeated slowly. He said my name as if he were tasting the way it sounded. I angled myself toward him, still seated and definitely not meeting his eyes—I'd learned my lesson with *that*, as I offered him my hand.

51

He nodded his head in greeting and added, "Did you get all settled in at Jubilee?"

He captured my hand.

The second we touched, I felt a tingle in my toes that zipped up through my spine. My stomach burst with butterflies and my thighs clenched.

Trevor's hand was firm and warm, even through the white lace of my gloves.

His thumb slid back and forth over my knuckles, causing my breath to catch and those butterflies took flight full speed.

My eyes—of their own volition—snapped to his.

Trevor looked down at my hand, something like confusion on his face. But then his expression morphed, he looked at me, smiled, released my hand, and slid his own into his pocket.

My own hand felt his departure acutely. It felt colder, abandoned.

No that's not right, Daisy, you're being silly.

A hand couldn't feel abandoned, could it?

I realized I hadn't answered him and rushed to add, "Yes, thanks for your help. You were very . . . helpful."

I sounded like an idiot. A bona fide dolt.

James's widening eyes confirmed it.

"It's funny that your name is Daisy. That pretty yellow dress you had on the other day was fitting for a Daisy, but to me it made you look like a ray of sunshine," Trevor said in a tone that may have been teasing, but I was suddenly too distracted to tell.

My muscles seized, locking involuntarily at the innocuous little word. I dully heard him say on what seemed like a rush, "Are you sure your name isn't Sunshine?"

I wanted to respond. But all I heard was Ado's voice clear as a bell in a memory I'd buried.

"You can do it, Sunshine! That's it! Keep it balanced! Just like I showed you." My brother's heavy footfalls as he ran, keeping pace beside me. The click of the wheels of my sister's ten-speed as she rode

just in front of me to make sure no cars were coming up the drive. My
mother shouting for us to be careful as she watched from the veranda.

"Steady . . . Steady! Go, Sunshiny! Go! Go! Go!"

My brother had taken the training wheels off my bike and stayed
with me as I'd mastered riding on two wheels. I'd been so proud.
He'd been so proud. And the first time I'd worked up the courage to
follow him and Dolly as they rode downhill . . . there almost hadn't
been words for the joy. I'd felt like I had gone to heaven and was an
angel flying.

I heard someone cough. I blinked and the memory dissolved as I
became aware of my surroundings again, but a heaviness still clawed
at the center of my chest.

Trevor's expression had turned concerned. He stared at me with
his brow furrowed and James and Odie and were looking equally
puzzled.

I slipped into my best *Daisy Payton* smile. It was my default
response to any tense public situation.

"Kill 'em with kindness," my mother always said. What were we
talking about? He'd asked me if I was sure about something . . .

I looked up at those amber eyes of his, looking so troubled and
confused, and in that moment I would've said almost anything to
reassure him.

"I'm sure!" I blurted a little too loudly.

James eyes grew even wider.

Trevor rubbed the back of his neck with his free hand, nodded to
James, then turned to Odie and said, "It was nice meeting you, ladies.
I've got to attend to some business but I'm sure I'll see you around
campus."

He avoided looking at me directly but gave a polite nod in my
direction then turned and headed out of the church doors.

I sighed. *Bona fide dolt.* Dolly's voice reverberated through my
ears as I fought the urge to smack my palm against my forehead.

"Coulda been worse," James said eyes still wide.

I shot her a look. "How?"

She opened her mouth to speak and then paused, no words coming out.

"Well, even if I have made a fool of myself . . . at least I have the distinction of saying I'm the first person in maybe the entire world that has rendered James Jones speechless."

We held each other's gaze for a second before our laughter broke.

CHAPTER FOUR

Trevor

Stupid. *Stupid. Stupid.*

That was the refrain in my head as I walked the two blocks from campus to the small apartment Jules and I shared. I should not have flirted with Daisy.

In church, Trevor. In church!

I definitely hadn't *meant* to flirt with her in the house of God.

I hadn't even meant to say that I called her Sunshine, it'd slipped out. Daisy was the perfect name for her; she was bright and sunny.

Perhaps, I should've said that to her, instead.

No, Trevor. Get a grip. You most certainly should not have told her that.

Maybe I should have said, "Pleasure to meet you." I groaned biting my lip as I walked. *No, don't use pleasure in a sentence related to Daisy. You won't be able to control your thoughts.*

Unbidden, a thought of how I could please Daisy hijacked my mind and I shuddered despite the ninety degrees heat.

I sighed. *Nice to meet you. I should've said nice to meet you.*

It was clear that my comment about how pretty her dress was had made her ten shades of embarrassed and uncomfortable.

She'd actually lost a little of her coloring.

I felt like a right ass.

You should apologize. No, you should stay away from her. No, you should apologize and then *stay away from her.*

I was a jumbled-up mess. I'd known this girl less than twenty-four hours, spoken not more than a handful of sentences to her, and was completely tied up in knots over her.

So much for not giving her any purchase in your mind.

I chuckled ruefully at my hubris from only a few days ago.

My apartment was dark and quiet when I entered. Jules had left late yesterday.

I began to strip and methodically put away my church clothes.

I hung my tie and then my shirt. After unbuckling my pants, I paused to pat my pockets making sure no loose change or sundry items would fall when I folded them over the hanger. I felt the folded church program in my pocket, removed it and tossed it on my dresser in one swift motion. I walked to the closet, hangar in hand, but stopped short as something on the program caught my eye: a small line of Fisk blue text in a sea of black ink. I wasn't sure how I'd missed before.

Today: We are Fisk! Family Fish Fry and Barbecue 3 P.M. 1000 17th N Ave

Hallelujah! I know I don't deserve it, Lord, but thank you for this day and for this opportunity for free food!

If there was one thing you learned quickly in college, it was that you never *ever* turn down the opportunity to get free food.

Still smiling, I checked the clock.

It was already two. I'd have to skedaddle if I wanted to actually get any of said free food; it was bound to go fast.

And, if Mr. Jimmy from the Dining Hall was frying the fish, he'd be nice enough to give me an extra piece or two so I could make a sandwich in the morning.

I put a little pep in my step as I changed into my casual clothes. And who knew, maybe Daisy would be there.

This could be your only time to talk to her. Once Elodie returns on Sunday you'll have to slip back into the role you play . . .

I tried to dismiss the thought. I didn't want to ponder why the thought of pretending to be involved with Elodie made me anxious, when that had never been the case before.

I quickly changed and headed back toward campus, formulating a plan in my head as I walked. First, I would get Daisy away from her friends somehow, although that in and of itself would be a small miracle. Freshman girls in particular traveled in packs. Then I would apologize for being a jackass to her earlier. I would let her know that she didn't have to worry about me ever saying anything like that to her again. Then I'd ask for her forgiveness.

And then I'll spend the rest of my collegiate career avoiding the five-eight beauty and hope she has a fantastic life.

Admittedly the plan had some flaws. Alas, it was all I had. *Besides, no plan was perfect*, I reassured myself.

I did not feel reassured.

Nevertheless, I resolved to stick to it, because the alternative . . . My reality came into sharp focus and with it the sharp weight of responsibility. I reminded myself for the hundredth time that there was no alternative. Daisy and I could never be anything other than acquaintances.

Daisy

The delicious smell of fish hot out the fryer filled my nose as I made my way toward the barbecue. For the first time in my collegiate career, I was alone.

The fish fry was for both students and their families, a last little hurrah before parents got on the road and left us newly minted young adults behind.

Odie met up with her parents, who'd insisted we call them Mom and Pop when they stopped by the dorm.

James said no one from her family was here, so I thought we'd go together until she announced that she had to get going and had mysteriously disappeared without giving an explanation.

I got the feeling that James had a lot of secrets—or maybe carried a lot of burdens—that we didn't have a clue about. At any rate, she hadn't seemed like she was in the mood to talk about it and I wasn't going to pry. I understood—oh, how I understood. Family stuff could be complicated and private.

I took in the scene before me as I arrived: blankets had been spread out for us on the grassy lawn behind the administration building. Under a tent set up with long tables and pans covered in aluminum foil, folks were steadily streaming through to collect their food.

Mrs. Dot, our most friendly and esteemed ambassador, was playing hostess at the top of the line. I heard her saying, "Welcome to Fisk," over and over again—with surprising cheer—as families made their way through the line. Blue and gold balloons had been tethered to one of the tentpoles. They bobbed and swayed high in the air as if they danced to the music that was playing softly in the background.

Instead of heading toward the food, I popped a squat on an open blanket, fished my sunshades from my purse, put them on, and lay back. I closed my eyes, enjoying the solitude.

Inevitably my mind drifted toward Trevor as it had these last few days whenever I had time to dream, be it day or night.

I wished he was here. Maybe he would've sat beside me. Maybe we would've talked and he'd tell me all about himself, and maybe this time I would be witty; nothing like the unintelligible mess I was around him in reality.

"Is this seat taken?" his voice says.

"Of course not," dream me replied.

"In that case, may I take it?"

"Of course, but only if you lay beside me," I said, a little breathy.

There was a slight pause and his laugh sounded so rich and real as it filled my ears. And then I felt something warm and soft brush against my leg.

I felt that.

My eyes popped open, I snatched my glasses off, and sat up all in one motion. He was there in the flesh.

He sat next to me, leaning back, amber eyes glittering with amusement, long lean body stretched out, feet splayed and propped on his elbows.

He raised one eyebrow at me, and the motion was . . . well, there's really no other word for it. He looked sexy.

"Hi," he said.

My heart raced. "Um . . . hi," I squeaked.

"Now don't go clamming up on me now that I've sat down. You did invite me to sit—or rather, to *lay*."

"NO—I'm not. I'm—"

I'm a moron.

I'm going to die of embarrassment.

I am going to leave.

As if he could sense my rising panic, he touched my arm reassuringly and I instantly relaxed.

"Hey, it's okay. I was just messing with you. You want me to leave?" he asked concerned.

"No, stay! I mean, if you want to stay you should stay."

He nodded his assent and squinted up at the sun. I took the moment to suck in a deep breath to calm my hammering heart.

"I didn't mean to disturb your rest, honestly. If you want to lay back down on the blanket you can—of course. Pretend I'm not even here."

Ha! As if it were possible to ignore him. As if half my waking minutes hadn't been spent daydreaming about him.

I didn't want to rest but I *was* going to lay back down. I would close my eyes and pretend like he was dream Trevor, and I was dream Daisy. The Daisy that was able to talk to him like he was any other person.

I lay back and let my hair fan out over the blanket.

I sensed him shift on the blanket.

He swallowed loudly before saying, "So why aren't you eating?" His voice sounded a little hoarse suddenly.

"Oh, I'll grab something a bit later."

That laugh I loved rolled over me and set my heart to dancing again, so much so that I almost didn't hear him say, "No, you won't. That's a rookie mistake. Free food does not last around college students. *At all.*"

"What on earth are you talking about?"

His laughter continued. "You'll see, dear Daisy."

I shuddered a little at the word *dear*. *He didn't mean anything by it*, I reminded myself. He was just being polite.

"You'll see. It's about, oh three fifteen—I reckon you got another half hour before the upperclassmen that are back on campus start showing up to the dining hall only to see a sign posted on the door telling them to come here to pick up their meal. And then . . ."

I turned my head toward him and opened my eyes. His gorgeous light brown eyes were full of mirth. "It'll be like locusts descending on Egypt, you mark my words."

I burst out laughing and his smile grew.

"I'll keep your spot warm if you want to grab a plate, even if you don't eat it till later. The real tall guy down at the end wearing the hairnet over his bald head is Mr. Jimmy. If you bat those pretty eyes at him and tell him you need some foil, he'll wrap your whole plate for you."

He thinks my eyes are pretty? HE THINKS MY EYES ARE PRETTY.

"Is that how you got your foil? By batting your pretty eyes?" I blurted unthinkingly.

He barked a laugh. "No, indeed. He don't give a damn about my eyes. I had to beg for it."

"But you . . . you should never have to beg for anything . . ."

He looked a little uncomfortable and then sucked in a deep breath and added on a rush, "So listen, earlier at church when I called you Sunshine." I winced at the word and he winced in return.

"And complimented your dress . . . I think you maybe thought I was flirting with you when I said it was pretty. But it's empirical—as much as fashion can be empirical—*empirically* speaking, it was a lovely dress. Anyway, I'm really sorry if I offended you or made you uncomfortable."

He thought my dress was pretty?

He . . . wait, what? He thought he was flirting with me?

WHAT?

No that's not right.

He thought *I thought* he was flirting with me?

"No," I said quickly. "That's not it. I knew you weren't flirting with me." I gave a little laugh and added, "As if that would *ever* happen. It's just . . . I hadn't . . ."

Dammit. Why was this still so hard.

I took a deep breath.

"I haven't been called that name in a long, long time." I looked him in his eyes so he could see that I was sincere. "I took no offense and there's no need for an apology. It just caught me off guard, is all. And thank you. I love the dress too—it's my favorite color."

He smiled and then frowned. "I take it you kicked this someone, who gave you the name I shall never again repeat, to the curb?"

Trevor was fishing. But instead of being offended I smiled, not minding the nosiness of the question at all. Maybe it was because I'd been meeting new people for days and had been giving up tidbits about myself. Or maybe I wanted to get to know more about him, for him to know more about me. I answered his question unthinkingly, honestly.

"No . . . it wasn't—it wasn't like that."

I closed my eyes again. "It was my brother. My brother gave me that name, and I . . . haven't seen him in a very, very long time."

He exhaled on a *woosh*, and I expected him to say I'm sorry or why not or something akin to what folks normally say when they become aware that the Payton girls weren't always just the Payton girls.

He didn't.

"I know exactly what that's like."

My eyes flew to his.

"You do?"

"I do."

In his eyes I saw everything—*everything*—I felt. Pain that was old and somehow still new. I saw heaviness and I saw strength. I saw a kindred spirit.

"I really, really do. I also haven't seen my brother in a very long time."

I nodded because what else was there to say. I knew very well how little any of my words would mean to him.

"You wanna talk about it?"

I shook my head vehemently.

He smiled ruefully. "Yeah, me neither."

He nudged my shoulder. "Come on. Let's go get you a plate before you starve."

As we walked to the line, he joked that we should make a list of things we didn't want to talk about.

"I agree!" I said a bit too enthusiastically, glad of an opportunity to avoid future awkwardness.

He smiled slightly then rubbed his hand across the back of his neck and said, "All right, dear Daisy. While we're avoiding brothers, can we add families to that list?"

"By all means, yes." I laughed. "Let's just avoid talking about family altogether."

"Also, hometowns. Can we add that to the list?" I volunteered.

"Absolutely! We can file that one under 'it's complicated,' too."

"What else?" I asked getting into it.

"Exes," he said quietly.

I had none to speak of but didn't mind avoiding discussing other women with Trevor. I didn't mind *at all*.

I nodded in agreement. "Sounds reasonable. Should we shake on it?"

He looked down at me, grinning like I was funny. Then he stuck out his hand. I extended mine and I held my breath, wondering if I would experience the same jolt I felt when he'd shook my hand in church.

He slid his palm against mine and I was glad I was already holding my breath because if I hadn't been, he would've stolen it.

This time was better.

Warm and soft, he slid his palm back and forth against mine. Skin to skin I could feel all the details my gloves had denied, like the grooves of his fingertips.

The delicious mixture of rough, soft, and warm sent tingles through my palm, and then quite suddenly, he splayed his fingers and slid them between mine. Our fingers flexed at the same time, and just like that he was holding my hand.

"I shake hands with everyone the other way. Maybe this can be the way only you and I shake hands?" he asked softly, cautiously, almost shyly.

"Yes!" I said a little too emphatically.

He responded with a smile that was brighter than Edison—both the genius and the bulb.

God. Between that smile and those eyes that were like jumper cables to my heart, I was done in.

"Good. Then it's settled, friend."

Friend struck a discordant note and I reminded myself that Trevor was just being friendly. Hadn't Dolly told me he was a natural flirt? A special handshake didn't mean anything!

Still . . . he shook my hand as we walked through the line and I collected my plate. After some playful ribbing from Mr. Jimmy, Trevor collected another plate too as he advised, "Hey, you never can have too much food when you're in school."

Both our plates were loaded to the gills with potato salad, string beans with ham hocks, baked mac and cheese, two pieces of fish, and a controversial barbecue sandwich.

"What on earth do you mean Tennessee barbecue has nothing on Carolina barbecue! What blasphemy is this?" I said as we found our way back to our blanket, balancing our plates in one hand while we shook hands with the other. We let go only once when it was time to sit, and as if by some miraculous silent agreement, his hand found my own the moment my bottom hit the blanket. Just like that we were shaking hands again, now while eating.

"First, dear Daisy, can you even blaspheme against a sandwich? Isn't that reserved for God Almighty? And second—"

"You can blaspheme against anything you darn well please, as evidenced by the folly you're spouting right now."

He looked at me serenely. "Well one day we'll just have to have a taste test, won't we? But it'll have to be blind, because I wouldn't want you to cheat."

"Cheat?" I screeched, indignant with faux outrage. For emphasis I set my sandwich down and pointed a finger at him. "Let me tell you something—you Yankees are a trip! You come down here and insult all the barbecue in the great state of Tennessee and then when I defend it you call me a cheat!"

His eyes crinkled with how hard he was laughing. He took a deep breath and then another bite of the alleged inferior sandwich, leaving a dab of barbecue sauce at the corner of his mouth.

I had the sudden, powerful urge to lick that corner, followed by an uncharacteristic rush of heat.

Get a grip, Daisy.

As if on cue, the tip of his tongue darted out, cleaned the sauce from his mouth, and then he patted the corner with a napkin. Trevor continued on as if he hadn't just sent a heatwave straight through me.

"First of all, I'm not a Yankee. I'm originally from Tennessee."

"How?"

The word was out of my mouth before I even registered I was speaking. That was one of the dangers of Trevor; he made me speak before thinking.

He smiled at how miffed I sounded as he replied, "I'm guessing you're surprised I don't have an accent?"

I managed a nod.

"Without getting too far into our taboo topics, I went to a school that had *mandatory* elocution classes. Our headmistress felt that we'd do better in the world if we didn't sound like we were from 'the back-woods of the boondocks.'"

"Well that certainly is . . . I mean, I . . . that's not very . . ."

"I believe you're looking for the word snobbish?"

"Yes! And . . ."

It was snobbish but . . . was it wrong? There were plenty of people that looked down their noses at the way folks from the south talked.

But I hadn't thought Trevor would be one of them. Though clearly, if he'd worked to lose his accent, then he must see something wrong with accents like that. With accents like mine.

Embarrassment—swift and strong and sure—hit me and I released his hand.

"Daisy?"

"It's nothing."

He leveled those eyes on me and repeated my name in censure as if I should've known better than to try to fool him. He said it like he knew me, like we knew *each other* and that made me want to open up.

"You think my accent is—"

"No. *Never* think that. Please. Don't think that." He retook my hand and stared down at our joined fingers, frowning. "I think your voice sounds like . . . home."

He cleared his throat and continued before I could wrap my head around what *that* could possibly mean.

"My headmistress was somewhat correct, colorful language aside. There's a bias against southern accents, especially in the sector that I want to work in, but I love hearing them and . . . sometimes I regret losing mine." He looked bashful for a moment but then smiled. "My friend Julian has a great ear. He can turn his off and on, but for me it was just easier to learn to say the words the way they wanted them said."

I picked at my plate with my free hand, releasing the embarrassment I felt into the air as I willed my heart rate to return to normal.

"What sector is that—the one you want to work in?" I said, returning us to a safe topic.

"Finance."

"Finance?"

He looked at me from under those long lashes as if amused by the distaste in my voice.

"*Yes*, finance."

"Why?" I said, trying to reconcile the image of a slimy hedge fund manager or a corrupt banker with *Trevor*—who seemed so sweet and caring about folks.

"Because of that face you're making right there. Daisy, good people get hurt when they can't buy houses because they can't get loans. They get hurt when they're taken advantage of by an investor that sells them a junk bond, promising some ridiculous rate of return without explaining the probability of that return or how likely it is that they'll lose their shirts instead of getting money for their kids' education. They're hurt when they try to start a business and have to mortgage their house and their kids' futures and . . ." He trailed off. I'd never heard someone speak so forcefully and so passionately about bonds and loans.

"Someone gets to be in those positions. Someone gets to be the decider. They get to say who gets a loan to buy their first home or to open start their own business. Someone gets to decide if you're worthy of your *dreams* and if you are, how much it's going to cost you. And since someone has to decide either way, shouldn't that person be a good person? Someone who wants to be in finance not just because of what it can do for them, but for what it can allow them do for other people? The assholes are going into finance in droves—the good guys need to do it too."

My father and mother had often said that it was important for the people who controlled capital to be compassionate.

I took stock of how Trevor breathed just a tad harder than usual, how a different light shined in his eyes. *This. This was what he looked like when he loved something,* my mind catalogued dully.

"It seems like you've found your life's calling."

He nodded slightly, still staring down at his hand that was holding mine, or maybe my hand holding his. In a motion that was both familiar and new, I ran my thumb across his knuckles reassuringly, the same way he'd done to me at church. The feeling was still just as strong as before, and he looked up at me, surprise written all over that face.

Surprised was a good look on Trevor; he looked more boyish.

Every look was a good look on Trevor.

He bit his lip and then said, "So what about you?"

"Me?"

"Yes, you. What's your calling?"

"Ha! Isn't figuring that out why people come to college?"

"True, it's why most people come to college. Well, that and the fact that their parents tell them they have to 'get out of their house!'" We both laughed and he continued, "But you don't strike me as most people."

"Oh yeah? What do I strike you as then?"

"You strike me as the type who knows exactly what you want."

The way he said it, deep and low while he absently bit his lip, had my insides clenching and I had to shake my head to clear it before I responded.

He was wrong though; I didn't know what I wanted. All I knew was what I didn't want.

That's a lie, Daisy. You know it's a lie.

Because the truth was I *did* know what I wanted. I just didn't know if I was brave enough to admit it. But since Trevor had been so open with me about his dream, I decided to open up about mine for once.

"You ever wanted something so badly you were afraid to admit it, even to yourself?"

His eyes bounced between mine, probing, deep, and a little tender.

"Might do, being a Black man that wants to work in finance and all." And it struck me in that moment that Trevor still spoke with a southerner's cadence, that they'd taken his accent but not his dialect and I found that both wonderful and sad. Trevor had already sacrificed a piece of himself for his dream and here I was too afraid to even admit mine.

"I want to be an entrepreneur. I want to have my *own* business. *Businesses.*"

He smiled as broad as I'd ever seen him smile.

"Well now, seems you and I may be a match made in heaven. After all, you'll need a good banker to help jump-start those businesses, right?"

I laughed at his freshness instead of replying.

"What kind of businesses will you be starting?"

I loved that. Loved that he spoke as though it would be, just because I wanted it to be. That belief alone made it possible.

I groaned. "You're going to laugh."

He shrugged. "I may, if it's funny."

It's funny.

"Daisy's Doughnut House."

He laughed, surprised and splendid.

"That's a mouthful. I take it you make doughnuts?"

"I do," I said through a smile.

"How does one even make a doughnut?" He scratched his chin thoughtfully, playfully, "Are they baked in the oven or . . .?"

I rolled my eyes. "There you go blaspheming again. Doughnuts are deep-fried. Everybody knows that." I nudged him with my shoulder and he laughed.

"I can't wait to have my first deep-fried Daisy's Doughnut."

"It'll melt in your mouth," I assured him. Because my doughnuts were really, really good.

He stiffened and looked at me wide-eyed. With that deep voice of his he replied, "Oh I have no doubt about that at all."

And just like that he had me all hot and flushed again.

Trevor and I talked for a long time.

We discussed his favorite book, *Shakespeare in Harlem*, and mine, *Sula*.

He nodded at my pick, replying, "I think Morrison is going to be one of the preeminent writers of our generation."

And I fell in love. With those words, not him; with his words about Toni Morrison.

He revealed his favorite color was brown and challenged my

assertion that, "No one's favorite color was *brown*," by gesturing around him at all the families—representing different hues of brown skinned people—and said simply, "Did anyone tell God that?"

I snapped my mouth shut with a grin, one that only broadened when he said, "Your favorite color is yellow, and it fits you because you light up a room." I was surprised and delighted that he remembered. Before I could get too moony, he'd moved the conversation forward.

"Home fries. That's my favorite food. I love that they're simple. And versatile—they go with almost any meal. But mostly they just taste really good and they're hard to mess up, so I know how to make them."

That got me laughing again and I told him I couldn't name my favorite food for the life of me; there were just too many.

And we argued.

First about the sandwiches and then *again* when he stated that the Delfonics were better than the Temptations.

I'd actually placed my hand on his forehead to see if he was running a fever, after he'd said it. That move had earned me another of Trevor's deep laughs, a sound I was coming to cherish more and more. Laughter came so easy with him. Everything came easy, even arguing.

I'd been debating with my siblings all my life—it was something of a tradition in my house—but it had never been as fun as arguing with Trevor.

We talked until the sun started to get low and families started to leave. Until it was no longer comfortable to sit, so we laid side by side, Trevor's long legs trailing off the blanket. And still . . . talking.

We discussed whether Blaxploitation films were helping or hurting our people. He argued helping because at least those films were employing Black actors and actresses, and giving us a presence on film. I argued hurting, because they just reinforced too many stereotypes.

We talked about anything—everything.

When someone from the dining services started collecting the blankets around us, I sat up, surprised that we were alone.

I knew that people had been leaving but I hadn't realized we were the very last ones there.

Trevor looked around equal parts amused and surprised and said, "I guess we've overstayed our welcome. I should be walking you home now."

He released my hand for the first time in hours, and stood agilely. He extended his hand to help me up, keeping hold even after I stood.

We quickly relinked our fingers, in the handshake that had been our near constant since we first shook hands in line. He grabbed his to-go plate in his other hand, and we set off on the short distance to Jubilee.

We were both quiet, walking slower than normal, but finally the building loomed and he stopped at the bottom of the stairs.

"I'll watch you get in from here," he said quietly.

I nodded because I wasn't sure where my voice had gone. Instead of moving, I turned to stare up at him; the moment felt tense, charged in a way I couldn't quite understand.

He frowned before looking down at my fingers still entwined with his. His expression seemed pained as he raised my hand to his and placed the softest kiss on my knuckles. The warmth of his breath and the feel of his lips made my breath hitch.

"Thank you for spending the afternoon with me. It was . . ." He struggled to choose the right word but finally settled on, "Unexpected."

"Anytime," I said. I paused for a beat, waiting for him to ask about the next time we'd see each other. For him to ask if I had a phone in my room, and if I did, what my phone number was.

Instead he shifted on his feet uncomfortably and then he looked in my eyes and said, "You should go inside now, Daisy, before it gets too late."

I nodded. Disappointment flooded through me. Of course. Hadn't he called me his friend all afternoon? Didn't I remind myself not to get too caught up in his flirtations? That was just how he was built.

I found my voice. "See you around, pal," I said as I released his hand. For a second his eyes flashed with something I couldn't place. It looked like anger or maybe sadness. I erased the thought; I was probably just reading too much into things again.

Like you did this entire afternoon, Daisy.

I turned and walked up the stairs. I felt his eyes at my back the entire time, until the moment I slipped inside and closed the doors.

I walked into my room and took a step back in surprise. The lights were on, there was music playing on my radio and Odie and James were sitting on the bed across from mine. Both their heads popped up at the sound of the door opening.

James jumped up from the bed and ran to me. "You didn't lock your door, so we made ourselves at home. And I heard you had a *very* eventful afternoon. Tell me *all* about it," she eagerly demanded as rapid fire as ever.

I laughed, but it didn't sound natural. Disappointment from how things had ended with Trevor lingered.

I shook my head, looking at Odie with accusation.

James's head bounced back and forth between us. "Don't blame Odie! She didn't tell me about your rendezvous—she didn't *have* to tell me! It's *the news* around here. Roxie Jones, no relation, who lives on the second floor? She told me—she said she saw us eating together in the caf and figured we were stick girls. She said everyone was going on and on about how some handsome, and I do mean FIIINNNNEEE—her words—guy and Daisy were all over each other."

I groaned. "We were not all over each other."

72

"She's right, they weren't. They were only holding hands," Odie supplied a bit too innocently.

I opened my mouth to deny it. To explain to Odie that we'd only been shaking hands, then snapped my mouth shut. She was right. We had been holding hands.

"Ha!" James said seeing my face.

"It's not like that," I said weakly.

"Not like what?" James pressed bouncing on her toes.

"I don't think . . . it's just not like . . . we're just friends," I said remembering the crushing disappointment I'd felt moments earlier.

James reared back and cocked her head at me skeptically. "Friends?"

I took a deep breath, but before I could explain, Odie swept in, throwing me a sympathetic look as she spoke. "Give her a break, James. It's clear she's had a long day. Let Daisy tell us when she's ready."

I smiled my gratitude at my endlessly patient friend.

James grumped, "When she's ready? We're her *friends,* the ones that—you know, *figuratively hold her hand* through life," she finished with a dramatic flourish of her fingers.

Then she threw herself back on the bed.

"James, you actually do hold my hand sometimes."

It was true. She did.

She threw her hands up. "In a uniform showing of sisterhood! Not as a potential romantic overture! Why would you keep stuff from us? We're the Daisy pep squad. *And* I need to be armed when I go forth into the world."

"Armed?" I asked wary.

"Daisy, people talk to me. Okay? I don't know why. They tell me things. I try to set them right when they share misinformation. So now I will go back to Roxie and let her know that *nothing* is going on?"

Her eyes glimmered, curious as ever, and her smile was teasing.

I shook my head, she was impossible. "I will tell y'all what happened, but I do not need you to defend me."

"I do that for free," James quipped bouncing the balls of her feet against the floor as she propped her head up on a pillow.

I shook my head and tossed myself onto my bed, having been able to finally make it away from the door where James had accosted me.

"And I do not need y'all to repeat it to anyone else." I sat up on the bed and stared at Odie, who nodded in silent agreement, and at James, whose eyes were still all lit up. But she made a zipping motion across her lips.

I recounted the story quickly, leaving out the more personal details. That felt like too much to share, even with my friends.

He makes you feel like being just Daisy is enough.

When I got to what had happened by the stairs, Odie and James were as confused as I was.

James said that he was probably just afraid and Odie said he was probably a true southern gentleman that wanted to take things slow.

I weighed both of their conclusion and decided that neither sat right. I felt like there was a very obvious explanation to Trevor's behavior that we were missing.

But it was Odie who finally helped me let the whole thing go. "Daisy, boys are dumb."

"Amen," I affirmed.

"Amen!" said James.

Odie lifted her hand in praise. "Amen," she said.

CHAPTER FIVE

Trevor

W hen my eyes opened at four a.m. Monday morning, it was to a sticky, rapidly cooling pool of embarrassment between my legs. I sighed at my predicament. I'd been sighing a lot since meeting Daisy.

Inappropriate hard-ons, wet dreams, and daydreams. It was official. She'd turned me back into a preteen boy, and I resented the hell out of her for it.

No, you absolutely do not. You adore her.

I didn't think it was possible to resent someone as sweet as Daisy. Someone as funny and kind. I'd never had a problem striking up conversation with strangers, but I'd never experienced anything quite like the connection I'd felt with her.

Partly because it didn't feel like I was conversing with a stranger when we spoke. It felt like—*she* felt like—coming home. I didn't really know how else to describe it, as crazy as it sounded. It felt like I was speaking with someone that had known me my whole life and I was just catching them up on what they had missed.

Daisy was so much more than just her physical beauty; her dry wit made me laugh so hard my belly ached. She loved math just the same as me. She had big dreams, and I could see that her spark matched my own. Maybe even surpassed it.

Being with her yesterday had been beautiful and it had been torture. I sighed again and hauled myself up. Dread coursed through me as I fumbled around for clean clothes. I was going to have to find time to wash my sheets today since I only had the one set. Extra sheets were a luxury, and now was not a time for me to spend lavishly.

If I didn't have to live so frugally, if my life were my own, I knew exactly what I'd spend my money on. I'd ask Daisy on a date, I'd borrow Julian's car, and I'd take her to eat someplace with real good food. Maybe Swetts, or someplace even fancier.

I would love that—the opportunity to enjoy another meal with Daisy. To observe the dainty way she'd patted the corners of her mouth when she ate. To watch the way she threw her head back when she thought something was particularly funny. To fight the grin she pulled from me whenever I said something she thought was suspect and she cocked her head and stared at me like I was a lunatic.

Having stripped the bed and changed into clean boxers, I flopped back on the bed, mildly frustrated.

I mulled over my fantasy in my head, turning it around to see if I could find a way to make it happen. But I couldn't see my way to a right path; I couldn't see a right way to Daisy.

I closed my eyes, suddenly very frustrated and a tad angry. Those emotions were easier to deal with than the alternative: sadness. Because what I wanted—to be able to ask a girl I liked on a date— should've been a simple thing.

I heard a familiar soft voice in my head say, "Wouldn't it be nice if we could all just date whoever we wanted without a care?" Elodie's words chastened me.

Elodie.

The words of my childhood friend were too poignant to ignore. Elodie *wasn't* free to date the person of her choosing, at least not publicly. Instead, bad luck and bad people had forced her into deceiving our closest friends by denying who Elodie truly was. Elodie had been through enough at the hands of inconsiderate people who claimed to love her and want what was best for her. I couldn't—I wouldn't—allow myself to be another person that let her down.

I knew how the charade we kept up wore on her. I'd been privy to some of the battles she fought, both mentally and the fights she had with Gracie. Behind her good looks and popularity she struggled mightily, and I'd promised I'd help to lessen those burdens. I didn't get to abdicate my promise to a friend just because I'd met a wonderful girl.

The sadness I'd tried to keep at bay swamped me. I should have been able to ask Daisy on a date. And I absolutely would've.

If I didn't have so many financial constraints.

So many *emotional* ones.

And just like that, the truth of my situation calcified, hard and unbreakable.

I felt a sharp stab of pain in my side.

It didn't matter what I wanted.

It never had.

It hadn't mattered that I'd wanted to stay with my parents—they'd sent me away. It hadn't mattered when I gotten straight A's year after year—May and Marcus had never even acknowledged my grades.

That's not precisely true.

They had acknowledged them, but only to shame Julian.

"If Trevor—*Trevor*—" the implication behind my name being obvious, "can get straight A's then why did you get a B? Get out of my sight. Both of you disgust me. You for failing, and you for showing off." And just like that, we'd both be dismissed.

I could never win. If I got straight As, I was a show-off. If I got a

B, they were wasting their money on an education that I obviously wasn't equipped to handle.

And the way May had treated Elodie? I felt queasy just thinking of all the things she'd said to her over the years about how she was defective—how she'd implied she was disgusting.

I could never win. Not then, and not now.

Daisy—sweet, beautiful, perfect Daisy—wasn't for me. Even if I were unyoked from all my burdens, I knew she'd never be mine. I never got what I wanted. And if I didn't push her from my mind and concentrate on starting and finishing the school year strong so I'd have my choice of jobs or grad schools come spring, then I never would.

CHAPTER SIX

Daisy

On Monday morning I rose early and headed to the Registrar's Office, Operation Deliver Daisy in full effect. I'd work-shopped the name a lot in my head and had decided this one was most worthy.

I arrived just as it opened, and to my surprise, there was already a crowd of twenty or more students assembled.

Thankfully, I didn't see anyone I recognized.

A lady stood at the door and handed each student a slip of paper with a number on it as we crossed the threshold. We filtered silently into the room and slouched in chairs or sat on the floor and leaned against the wall. By some miraculous unspoken agreement, it seemed we'd all agreed it was too early for speech unless it was absolutely necessary, so aside from the typing at the front and the dull hum of a machine in the distance, the room was graced with library-level quiet.

Despite the sleepy calmness of the room, I felt anything but. My leg bounced nervously, and I bit my nails in rapid succession as I waited for my turn. A row of teller-style windows lined the front of the room and the whole area had a sort of chemical smell that I couldn't quite place.

I was particularly afraid of running into the Bessie lady who'd helped me check in. Spotting her would mean I'd have to abort the whole mission. I wasn't sure if I'd ever work up the nerve to try again.

Be cool, Daisy. Be cool. It's no big deal. It's only one letter.

I wished . . . I wished James and Odie were with me. If James were here and she knew—really knew—what was going on, she'd tell me to be fearless, wouldn't she?

And Odie would be understanding and encouraging the way Odie was.

I wondered if they'd wonder where I was this morning when they eventually stopped past my room to retrieve me for breakfast.

Yet another lie you're going to have to tell. If this was a spy movie, Daisy the Deceiver would be your code name. No, Daisy, your code name wouldn't have your real name in it. Unless Daisy the Deceiver is so deceptive that she factors people's inherent disbelief into the equation!

I fought the urge to slap my forehead and told my internal monologue to downshift from hyperdrive and shut up.

I heard a lady say, "Twenty-four." I rose and headed to her teller station, finally placing the weird smell and the mechanical noise as I approached. Xerox machines, about fifteen of them, were going full speed, spitting out reams and reams of paper.

In the background monitoring one of the machines was a lady who looked suspiciously like Ms. Bessie from the side.

I kept my head low and prayed she didn't turn in my direction.

I willed my heart to slow down as it galloped in my chest, and tried to calm my nerves by focusing on the person at the window. She was young, perhaps a student, and entirely disinterested in waiting on me. She picked at her nails as I stepped close enough to speak quietly.

I had no intention of raising my voice above the bare minimum with the Bessie doppelgänger hovering so nearby.

"Name?" she said without looking up.

"Good morning," I paused biting back the ma'am I'd been programmed to add. This girl wasn't much older than me, she would definitely have been offended by it. I refocused. "That's why I'm here," I said getting right to the point. "My last name is Paxton," I said with a lot more confidence than I felt. "But somehow it got misspelled on my file. They had it as Payton when I checked in."

She rolled her eyes and never looked up at me as she shouted behind her, "Carmen, who did the P's? Was it Sheila?"

A disembodied voice called from somewhere in the back, "I think so."

"ID?" she said still not looking at me.

"I'm getting migh-tee tired of fixing her mess," she called back to the voice as she rolled her eyes again. "This is the third student that's had something wrong with their file."

Relief swelled in me. This was going to be a piece of cake!

Thank you, God, for no-typing Sheila and her two left hands.

My nerves caused my hands to shake before I was finally able to retrieve the fake ID I'd procured before leaving Green Valley.

I slipped the ID from my purse and finally handed it over to the girl.

All my nervousness was for nothing.

She barely even glanced at the ID, instead she slid me a duplicate form and instructed me to check the box that read Name Correction. Then she motioned for me to stand to the side while I completed the form.

Inside I was a mess of emotions. Fear because I couldn't believe I was about to go through with it. Excitement because I couldn't believe I was about to *get away* with it. But most of all, I felt free. Free to be just Daisy. I reassured myself that the plan was good. I'd thought about it a lot. *A lot.*

I wouldn't leave my last name different forever, I'd have it "corrected" second semester . . . or maybe at the start of following year. I'd pretend I didn't notice first semester and I'd show them my real ID.

I realized there was a small kink in my plan as I completed the triplicate, there would be a record of this original change. But, given my experience today, I doubted whoever processed the next name change would even check my file and see this paper.

And . . .

Don't think it, Daisy.

But I couldn't stop the thought from coming.

If they give you a hard time . . . you can always call your father.

I hated myself for thinking it, but the thought occurred all the same. I recommitted myself to total independence and vowed that I would not, no matter what came, call my father.

When I handed the form back to the girl, she ripped off the top copy, placed it in a wire basket to the left of her elbow. The pink carbon copy, she slid under the window to me as she intoned, "We'll process this change as soon as possible but in the event that an updated class roster doesn't get to your professors in time"—she gestured to the Xerox machines—"you can show them your copy and they will manually update your name on the roll."

"Thank you," I said.

"Twenty-nine!" she replied.

And just like that, Daisy Payton was dead.

And Daisy Paxton had been born.

I was so caught up in my relief at having finished what I believed to be my most daunting task of the day that I didn't notice James until I almost slammed into her in the hallway just outside the Registrar's Office.

She spoke in her normal clip, "If you're on your way to financial aid it's already too late. It's a zoo down there!"

"Thanks for the warning. I'm headed out, but did you get you get what you needed?" I asked eager to pivot the conversation.

"No," James replied glumly. "My financial aid still hasn't posted."

She bit her lip and stared past me. "I don't know what I'll do if it doesn't come soon."

I linked arms with her. "I'm sure it'll come this week. There are probably just a lot of people who need to have their funds dispersed. Maybe they just haven't gotten down to the J's yet." I tried to strike a cheerful, hopeful tone.

She smiled at me, but it wasn't her usual James smile and worry for my friend began to creep in.

James and I bumped into Odie in the cafeteria almost as soon as we arrived. She promptly declared with more than a little dismay that she'd "been looking all over for us."

We downed a quick breakfast and were greeted with a surprise as moved toward the exit to leave. Charlie Love, donned in the beautiful royal blue and gold dining services shirt, was bussing tables and by the look of it, was hating every second.

"Heya Charlie!" James called, because it was clear Charlie hoped that we, or most likely that Odie, hadn't spotted him clearing the table closest to the door.

Charlie stopped—his back still to us—holding a cup in mid-air for a second before he finally turned. His eyes zeroed in on Odie immediately. I wasn't even sure if he knew he was doing it. It was honestly kind of sad to watch.

"Hey, uh everybody," he mumbled and shifted from foot to foot.

Odie didn't respond, but I saw a small grin slip at his clear discomfort.

Talk about bringing out the worst in a person. Odie was a kitten, but with this boy she was all claws.

"New gig?" I said asking the obvious, taking pity on the boy.

"I—yes. Work study."

Charlie was still looking at Odie, his mouth was doing this weird thing where it kept forming words but nothing was coming out. He looked to be truly at his wits' end as he stuttered and stammered silently.

And Odie?

She just looked . . . bored. She's wasn't even looking at him; she was busy waving to Karen Smith who sat five tables over.

"Okay, well I guess we'd better—" I started before I was cut off.

"Boy! It's your first day and you're already slacking! Don't let them pretty faces get you in trouble. I see I'mma have to watch you real close. You ain't no worker, are you? No. No. No. You ain't one, but I'mma make you one." We all turned to see Mr. Jimmy making his way over to Charlie.

I thought poor Charlie couldn't look any more uncomfortable, but I was wrong. Now, true misery was upon on his face. He wasn't even looking at Odie anymore. His eyes were fixed on the six-foot, old, bald man lumbering toward him. Charlie looked like he would've been completely fine with vanishing through the floor or even dropping dead on the spot if it meant he'd get to avoid being chastised by Mr. Jimmy while we watched.

"I guess we'll be going now. Have a good shift at work," I said as I pushed James toward the door. Odie didn't need any prompting, she moved as soon as we did.

As we crossed the threshold I heard Mr. Jimmy's voice reverberate behind us, "Listen, son, help me help you! If you can't handle something as simple as tables, I'm going have to put you on latrine duty."

I parted from my friends outside of Spence and headed to meet my academic advisor. I arrived at nine a.m. sharp, ready to put the final part of my plan in place.

Before I could knock on the closed office door a clear, a prim voice commanded, "Come in."

I walked in and she motioned for me to take a seat.

"Daisy Payton, I assume."

I started to nod, but something about the lady reminded me of Dolly so I decided against shaking my head and answered.

"Yes, ma'am. But actually, it's Paxton." I reached into my bag to pull out my correction form.

She saw the pink duplicate copy in my hand and waved it away as she spoke. "I see you've already been to the Registrar's Office to have it fixed. Well done."

She scribbled a note in my file, and I gulped.

"All right, Ms. Paxton. Let's get started."

Her office was neat, medium sized, with an unstained mahogany desk with ornately carved footings. There was a matching bureau to her left and she was seated in a cream-colored tufted and mahogany chair. The contrasts around the room were striking.

Also striking? The woman sitting across from me. Her hair was pulled into a bun high on her head, and bright white diamond earrings shone from her ear.

From her immaculate French-manicured nails to her soft pastel pink suit with pearl buttons to the matching mauve lipstick and ivory peep-toed sling back pumps that peeked from under the desk, everything about her screamed class.

Dolly would've loved her outfit. Dolly would've *worn* her outfit, and that really was the highest praise. My sister had the most exquisitely discriminating taste I'd ever seen. As it was, I was feeling a little wardrobe envy myself. One thing my sister and I had in common was that we loved fashion, and dressing to the nines was our signature.

We hadn't really had a choice; not that we minded. It was expected that we never leave the house unless we were neatly turned out. I smiled a little thinking of my mother whose motto was, "Never face the day without your face on."

I peered at her desk, noticing a large stack of manila folders bearing student names. There were several other rows of file folders neatly organized behind her. They appeared to be color coded using some obscure system.

"I am your advisor, Dr. Gwinn. Now, first things first. You were late to your meeting with me this morning. Do not repeat that behavior in the future. I do not tolerate tardiness, and neither will your professors."

I glanced down at my watch, the time read nine precisely.

I looked up and she chuckled at my furrowed brow.

She took a deep breath and said, "Oh, Daisy. To be early is to be on time. To be on time is to be late, and to be late is *unacceptable*." She smiled brightly and continued with a dismissive wave. "That is the law around here. Now tell me about your goals for your time here at Fisk."

I was eager to change the subject, as I'd never liked that old adage anyway.

My father said it all the time, and once Ado went to school he'd squawked it too. I was wise enough *now* to know that trying to convince its followers that being early was being *early*, late was *late,* and on time was, well, *on time,* was absolutely fruitless.

"My long-term goal is to graduate in four years, summa cum laude, preferably number one in my class."

She smiled back at me. "Your ambition is admirable. A woman after my own heart. And what of your interpersonal development?"

I sat up a little straighter.

Interpersonal development? Did she mean she wanted me to get in touch with my masculine side or some other such nonsense?

"Ma'am?"

Her smile turned patient. "You—Daisy—how do you want to develop your person while you're here? Any clubs or service organizations you want to join?"

"I'd like to earn a spot in the Phi Beta Kappa Society."

"Of course. Anyone with your academic ambitions would, but what of your social ambitions?"

Again, she'd lost me.

"Daisy," she said with a *tsk* and a chuckle. "College is not only a time for you to tend to your mind. We are not just growing brains here. We're growing whole beings that will need to go forth into the world and contribute. You are not here to just take knowledge for yourself and go, you're here to give of yourself and of your time and of your talents.

"You are here to learn about yourself—and how you fit into the world. And that means interacting with more than just books. It means interacting with people, trying new things, joining clubs. Sometimes it even means quitting them and moving on to things that fit better."

She slid me a book with the words *Student Life* stamped across the top. "Here are some of our clubs and organizations. I'd strongly suggest you look through it and select a few that you may be interested in. Your time here at Fisk is but a blink in the grand scheme of your life, but it's my job to guide you on how that time can be best spent. I'm here to put you on the path of life-long success, learning to build connections is a big part of that."

I nodded. She was right; there was nothing wrong with trying new things, and goodness knows the importance of making connections had been stressed to me my whole life. I stopped nodding and began speaking when I caught her frowning at the motion. She was definitely a Dolly-type.

"Of course. I'd overlooked that. I'll take a look and decide on something."

I'll just have to recalibrate my schedule. I think there was a half hour on Thursday between four thirty and five that wasn't—

My musing was cut off as she continued, "No doubt you've already looked through the course catalogue and decided what you'd like to take. Even though"—she looked me in my eyes

—"your academic advisor is supposed to guide your course selection."

I smiled wryly. Busted. I already knew exactly what I wanted to take.

"Well, let's have a look." She opened her palm and I slid my course booklet with its circled selections across her desk.

"I can't wait to see what the valedictorian of 1979 will be embarking upon this—"

She stopped abruptly. Her eyes ran over the courses I'd circled as she flipped the pages in silence.

She looked back up at me, her lips pressed firmly together.

"No," she said in a tone that indicated it was final.

I sat up straighter in the chair. I hadn't expected her to deny me outright without any conversation.

"But—"

"No."

"If you'll let me—"

"No."

"I believe that I am owed the chance—"

"No."

"If you'll just be reasonable—"

"No and no, forever and ever, amen. I am not being unreasonable. I'm the only one of us using reason. *No.* You are not owed the chance to speak on this. No, I will not allow you the opportunity to try this lunacy."

To my horror, she began drawing lines through the courses I'd selected as she spoke.

"I do not allow freshmen to double major. And *I* know that *you* know that the course load you've selected would equate to just that. It is not a good idea. It is, in fact, a terrible idea. It will set you up for failure, both academically and socially. You will end up sitting in my office next year this time, trying to repeat your freshman year because you failed all your classes. Other ambitious freshman before you have tried and failed to carry this course load. It's my job to put you on the path for success, not to rubber stamp half-baked delusions of grandeur."

"Dr. Gwinn, if you'll just let me expl—"

"I'll hear no more on the matter. Report back here at quarter past the hour and I will have your perfectly reasonable, perfectly challenging courses selected for you."

She closed my folder and reached for the next one, glancing at her watch as she did so.

I was shocked. I'd never in my life been so summarily dismissed. She was definitely a Dolly-type.

But if she's the Dolly-type, you know how to persuade her: cold, hard, logic. You can do this, Daisy. You can beat her at her own game.

Me, Dolly, and Ado had been encouraged, prodded . . . okay, forced to discuss and defend our positions on various topics around the dinner table growing up. It hadn't mattered that I'd been in elementary school, while Dolly was in middle school and Ado in high school and then later college. I had not been exempt from the conversations.

While I was not a sore loser—okay, maybe I was just a little, but no one wanted to lose all the time—I could never beat Dolly in a debate. Ado, I now suspected, took it easy on me, but Dolly was ruthless. When she was right—which occurred annoyingly often—everyone was going to know it.

A gracious winner she was not.

I focused so much on how I hated the "spirited discussions," as my parents had called them, that I'd missed the ideas they'd been trying to teach me. That is, until my mother took pity on me. She'd touched my face and gently explained, "The purpose of these discussions isn't to win, Daisy. The point is to ground you in a firm foundation. I always want you to be able to know yourself, and to defend your beliefs against small-minded people."

I thought of my mother's words and realized I *did* know how to convince Professor Gwinn. I'd grown very good at making my case. It was a natural by-product of having to do it so often when I was so outmatched.

I knew if I was going to have a chance to change Professor Gwinn's mind I'd need to speak fast.

"Professor Gwinn, you value time, right? I assume that means both yours and mine. Unless the things you said about utilizing my time here wisely were all hogwash."

She reared back and stared at me for what felt like a full minute.

Be patient, Daisy. Just make sure your logic is airtight.

Then she'd sighed, and it almost unnerved me. She did not seem like a woman given to sighing.

"Yes, I value your time," she said, sounding totally exasperated.

She opened her mouth, undoubtedly about to kick me out again, so I dove in speaking faster than James Jones.

"Well if that's the case, then I'd like my twenty-three minutes." I fought against the urge to call her ma'am. I needed her to see me as someone that was worthy of standing before her and advocating for myself.

"It's nine-oh-five, and I estimate that your next appointment will be on time and arrive at nine twenty-eight." I calculated that she'd want me to incorporate the "early equals on time" lunacy to prove I was listening. "Then that leaves twenty-three minutes for me to make my case to you for why this should be allowed."

She said more gently, "Daisy, I do value your time. It's for that reason that I don't want you to waste it. Even if you were to spend the next twenty-three hours making your point, I wouldn't be swayed. I've just seen this too many times. People come in and they're at the top of their class and they are brilliant and bright, but college is meant to challenge you. And some—most, in fact—are in for a rude awakening with a regular schedule. Forget about double majoring."

She had a point, and she was right.

Here's the thing though: she was also wrong.

Not about those other kids. About me.

I wasn't one of those kids. I'd lived with beyond high expectations all my life. I wouldn't fail. I didn't know how. It wasn't in my constitution. When you're one of a handful of Black kids in a white school and you're the daughter of nearly everyone's employer, you learn very quickly that excellence isn't *an* option; it's the *only* option.

"Dr. Gwinn, I know you're trying to do what's best for me. But you have been very insistent that I should try new things. That I should have an open mind, and that I should be willing to accept that I am ill-equipped for the challenges coming my way.

"All I ask is that for just a few moments you apply those same principles to yourself. I ask that you have an open mind. That you allow yourself to consider that you could be wrong, and that I may be perfectly equipped to handle an extra-rigorous course schedule."

I wasn't just top of my class. What she didn't realize was that I'd grown up under pressure on all sides. My sister was a straight-A student, my brother was straight-A student, my mother had been crowned Miss Negro Tennessee in 1945 and had been salutatorian of her class at Howard, and my father . . . well, my father was in a class by himself, literally. He'd been the first Black person appointed to the judgeship in the state of Tennessee since before the Reconstruction Era.

I came from coal stock. We were diamonds under pressure.

And I knew no words would be enough to prove that to her. What I needed was a chance to show her.

"All I am asking is for fairness. I am asking for the opportunity to show you that I can handle these classes. I am asking to prove to you that I am not those other students. If you think it appropriate that a blanket principle be applied to me and that I be penalized for the failings of others—"

"Now wait a minute—you are not being penalized, Daisy."

"But I am. I'm being held back from fulfilling my academic

potential because some other student, at some other time, wasn't able to live up to theirs."

She sat for a moment with her fingers steepled under her chin, mulling over what I had said.

Know when to hold them, Daisy.

After a moment she gestured to me with her palm open. "All right. What do you propose, Daisy? How do you intend to *prove* that you can handle the course work?"

I was going to have to wing it, because how do you prove something until you've done it? But this was important to me. It was my whole future. She wanted to test me before saying yes.

Tested.

She wanted to test me? Well, she could throw all the tests at me.

"Usually exams are given at the beginning of the semester. I'm here a week earlier than classes are going to start. I can take the tests now, for all of my desired courses. When I pass, you'll know I can handle the work."

"That won't do. That will only prove to me that you're smart. And I already know that. It isn't just the work, it's the time. I don't know if you'll be able to manage all these classes at *once*."

Another brilliant idea came to me.

"Professor Gwinn, the deadline to drop classes isn't until September fifteenth. What if we do this as a trial? By that time, I should have had my first round of tests. We'd be four weeks into the semester! I can show you my grades from my first set of exams and then you'll know I can handle the classes. If I am doing well, then I get to stay in all the classes. And if I can't handle the course load, I'll drop the home economics classes. No arguments."

She steepled her fingers under her chin again and I could see she was seriously considering my proposal. I hastened to add, "And of course I'll still join a club or social group while I maintain my grades." I rolled my eyes and waved my hands like it would be a piece of cake.

She laughed softly. "You sure will. And I think I know just which club you'll be joining."

She held her hands in front of her, palms up in a conciliatory manner. "Okay, Daisy. I'm willing to give this a try."

I broke into a grin. I felt like breaking into a dance.

"A *try*," she repeated. "Under two conditions."

"Yes!" I agreed quickly. "Anything."

She raised her eyebrows. "You might not be so quick to agree once you know what they are."

"I'm sure they'll be fine. I trust your wise and just counsel."

She laughed fully at my joke and I beamed. I had the feeling Professor Gwinn didn't laugh nearly as much as she should, and it was nice to be able to make her smile.

"First"—she held up a finger—"I'm going to monitor your grades closely. Now, ordinarily I'd have you meet with me . . ." She glanced down at the oversized calendar on her desk.

Ordinarily?

I thought she said she'd never done this before.

"*Ordinarily!*" I screeched. "I thought you said you've never allowed anyone to do this?"

She grinned like the cat that caught the canary.

"Did I say that?"

She tapped her chin theatrically as if thinking. "I don't believe I used the word *never*. I don't allow it *now*."

My chin dropped.

She raised her eyebrows defiantly. "Now are you going to let me finish? Or ...?"

I bit my tongue.

Her eyes were definitely brighter and her lips were curved like she was holding back a smile. Professor Gwinn was something else.

She took my silence as encouragement to continue. "Now, as I was saying, ordinarily I'd meet with you on a weekly basis, but unfortunately, Professor Dixon is out this semester so I'm teaching almost double the number of classes. Before you make any very funny jokes about my having a double major this semester—don't." She pointed at me with one eyebrow raised, and I bit my tongue to keep from smiling at her humor.

"I am not nearly as enthused by the extra work as you are. Between my busy schedule and your own schedule, I don't think we will be able to meet as often as I'd prefer, so I am going to set you up with a mentor. One of my student aides is double majoring as well, in business and mathematics. I'll arrange for you two to meet weekly, and you will not miss any meetings."

"But what if she's too busy to meet with me?"

She waved me off. "That won't happen—best time manager I know. You'll learn a lot." She quickly jotted down something on a pad of paper then ripped the sheet off, folded it in half, and handed it to me.

"There. You can meet there later today and then arrange the rest yourselves. Do not miss any meetings," she repeated, emphasizing each word.

"I'll get the weekly report on how you're progressing during my meetings with my aides. I assume you're staying in Jubilee with the rest of the freshman. If I have concerns and need to contact you, I'll leave a note for you there. If you need me, you can check in during office hours."

Then she took the course selection sheet, signed it with a flourish, ripped off the carbon copy, and slid it back to me along with my course booklet.

She slipped the original copy in my file, closed it, checked her watch, and then reached for the next manila folder.

I grabbed my things and walked to the door, still smiling at my good fortune.

I was good. I was so good, I was great. I walked in there and made my case and—

"Daisy," she said, and I turned, startled.

"There's a second condition that you seem to be forgetting."

I hadn't forgotten; I'd hoped she had. She was smiling a bit too broadly and I suddenly had a very bad feeling about this.

"Oh, yes!" I said, trying to sound enthused while looking at her expectantly.

"I've figured out the perfect social activity for you."

"Great!" I said through a smile that felt like a grimace.

"Anyone that can come into their academic advisor's office, who happens to be the acting dean of the school no less—"

I felt my mouth drop open.

"And successfully make the case for why they should be allowed to double major as a freshman, even after being asked to leave, is a natural fit for the debate team."

I wasn't good.

I was an idiot. *She* was good. As the saying went, I was playing checkers and Professor Gwinn—Dean Gwinn—was playing chess.

"Public speaking?" I croaked.

"Oh, yes. And before you come up with all the reasons why you're not doing this, let me save you the time." She glanced at her watch again. "After all, I know how much we both value time." She blinked rapidly at me grinning while turning my argument against me. "So, let us skip whatever argument you're concocting to get out of this and just say you agreed to do *anything*, and this is the *anything* you've agreed to. But, I have fantastic news. The debate team doesn't start until spring, so you have the whole fall semester to vanquish whatever trepidation I heard in your voice just now when you mentioned public speaking. And as an added bonus, your mentor is the captain of the debate team, so you have a whole semester to practice together."

"Thank you, Professor Gwinn," I ground out, feeling less grateful by the second.

She looked at me, eyes brimming with humor and sincerity. "Oh Daisy, it was my pleasure."

CHAPTER SEVEN

Trevor

Dr. Gwinn holding court was a thing of beauty. The President of Fisk University had just announced to a handful of student aides that supported the Department of Business Administration that Dr. Gwinn would become acting dean while Dean Dixon was out on maternity leave.

The whoops and the hollers that erupted with the announcement should not have been unexpected, but our slight, bookish president seemed taken aback. I understood why. Dr. Gwinn had a reputation for being the most exacting professor in the entire department. Having had her as a professor three times in the last three years, I could say with no uncertainty that the reputation that was absolutely deserved.

So much so that Jules, who was an English major but a business minor, had switched his schedule no less than three times to avoid taking one of her courses.

She was also the best teacher in our college, maybe even the best teacher on our campus, and for that reason she was as beloved as she was feared. I was admittedly biased; I'd learned more from her than anyone else in my collegiate career and the depth to which she cared for her students couldn't be faked.

We'd had a rocky start with her initial reluctance to allow me to double major, but now she was one of my favorite people. I was honored to call her my mentor, prouder still that as one of the youngest professors at Fisk she'd come out the front runner for interim dean. Dr. Gwinn was one of the few people that never asked me to tamp down my career ambitions—at least not after I'd proven I could handle the work.

President Young turned to Dr. Gwinn with a hopeful smile. He joined the clapping before dismissing the aides to greet the professor they'd support or chat with classmates. It was the first time most of us had seen one another since last year.

I hadn't checked the assignment roster. I knew I'd be assigned back to Dr.—well, now Dean Gwinn. I'd often tried to get her to admit that I was her favorite student and I was never successful. She'd evenly state, "Trevor, I love my students equally." But then with a bit of mirth in her eyes she'd add, "But I'm keeping you as an aide because you're the only student who has bigger ambitions than me. I have to keep my eye on you to make sure you don't try to take my job!"

The real reason she kept me around was because I knew how to make myself useful. Three years into being her assistant and I pretty much knew how she liked things run. I would head back to her office in a few moments and begin organizing her returning student files for when the upperclassmen returning next week, but for just a minute I was content to soak up another form of education.

I knew many wealthy individuals and many more smart people and in all of that, I'd never seen a person who commanded a room more completely than my mentor. I had no shame in admitting I aspired to be like her. I caught snatches of her conversation as she moved from student to student and spun her magic. She had the uncanny ability to remember details from previous conversations and would never forget ask about your mother's fiftieth birthday celebration or sick relative.

In the classroom, she was all business all the time, but in small settings like this, she was more relaxed and made us students feel more comfortable too.

Dr. Gwinn once told me the most important gift you could give a person was to make them feel valued. She'd mastered doing just that as she worked her way around the small gathering.

When she got to me, I was all prepared to discuss my own summer knowing she wasn't above prodding for details about the gossip she'd heard about me or my close friends.

Therefore, I was surprised when she placed her hand on my shoulder, her bright smile dropped, and she said, "Meet me in my office after this."

But then her public face was back and she drifted away, on to other students.

An hour later, I was nearly done organizing her returning student files, and was about to move on to skimming a 200-level course syllabus for grammar and typos. Although, mercifully, I was not taking any of her classes this semester, she still wouldn't let me see any of the 300- or 400-level materials.

I chuckled and remembered her chiding me when I'd asked about it.

"I know that I'm younger than most of the professors, but it is apparent that you believe I was born yesterday."

When I'd objected she continued, "I know that students, even you honors students who are smart and who are good and who are noble, think it's better to 'cheat than repeat.' You're not getting anywhere near my tests, so get that out of your head now."

I wouldn't have stolen a test or cheated, but there was a reason that Dr. Gwinn's tests never ever got out. She changed them every semester and sometimes between classes. She wasn't playing around. You couldn't fake your way through her class.

She'd been in and out of the office since the gathering ended but hadn't said more than two or three words to me, and I was beginning to feel more uneasy by the minute.

I honestly couldn't imagine what I could've done—over the summer, no less—to earn her censure.

Maybe one of my bosses down in Charlotte called her.

The door opened and she walked in looking a bit more tired than usual. She took a seat in her chair, slid her feet out of her high heels and wiggled her toes around for a second before placing them back on.

I was shocked. I'd never seen her do something so informal.

"Pick your jaw up off my carpet, Trevor."

I immediately snapped my mouth shut.

"Now, how was your summer?" she said, looking down at the notepad on her desk.

"It was—Dr. Gwinn?"

"Yes, Trevor?"

"Are you—upset with me?"

Her eyes flew from the paper she'd been skimming.

"Why on earth would you think that?"

I don't know, maybe because you called me to the side and said ominously that you needed to speak to me and then you've been kind of ignoring me for the last hour.

"You said you wanted to speak to me privately but you've been on the move since I got here. I didn't know . . ."

"Oh no." She flinched, and added softly, "Oh, I am so sorry, Trevor. I wasn't ignoring you. I took for granted that you didn't need anything because you're so self-sufficient."

Relief washed through me.

Huh. So her leaving me to my own devices was actually a compliment.

"I've been so busy with my added duties now that I'm acting dean, I didn't make time for *you* and that is my primary job. Forgive me. I know your internship went well. I got a glowing letter from your supervisor down at First Union," she added.

It was my turn to be surprised. I didn't know Dr. Gwinn had been in touch with my boss.

"Don't look so shocked. Of course I checked up on *one* of my favorite students during the summer." I laughed loudly at her non-concession that I was her favorite student.

"Speaking of favorite students—or should I say, favorite non-students—please pass on a message—" I grinned and ducked my head. I knew who she referred to before she even said his name.

"To that rapscallion friend of yours, Julian P. Marshall. You tell him I said the time is nigh. No more running." She pointed her finger at me imperiously. "He may take my class first semester or he will take it second semester, but all roads to graduation lead through my classroom."

I burst into shocked laughter.

Julian had no idea she *knew* he was avoiding her.

Jules was going to be devastated.

I, admittedly, was not devastated for him. It was about time he took a class that challenged him instead of skating through American Literature: The Past as Prologue or whatever they had him taking for an English major.

English courses were not a challenge for Julian; he could teach most of the courses by now. Hell, he was an English TA this year, so he probably *would* teach a class at some point.

"Where is that layabout anyway?" she continued jokingly. Jules was a hard worker; proof of that was how hard he'd worked to avoid taking Dr. Gwinn's classes. "I don't recall seeing him helping out during freshman move in this weekend."

I feigned a look of confusion. "Jules? Manual labor?" Dr. Gwinn laughed.

"He's at his cousin's wedding in Kentucky." I looked down at my watch. "He oughta be back here in about two hours."

"Well, speaking of freshman, I have a favor to ask of you."

I raised my eyebrows in surprise but continued listening.

"There's a freshman that has somehow convinced me, against my better sense, to allow her to double major."

A shocked laugh escaped before I could stop myself. "How on earth did she get you to agree to that?"

When I'd gotten approved it had been like pulling teeth. I shook my head thinking of the argument that had almost led to me choosing another school.

"She was quite dogged. Sound familiar?"

I smiled despite myself. Whoever this person was, she already had my admiration. I knew just how big a hill she'd had to climb to get that approval.

"And I'm a sucker for a good argument. She made a good case for herself. She told me she shouldn't be held accountable for the failures of other students."

I nodded in appreciation for this very valid argument, as it was an echo of my own.

Dr. Gwinn continued, "I'd usually supervise her myself, but since you're wrapping up a very successful run here as a double major, I thought she might glean a little more insight on balancing the workload from someone that's actually done it. I'd like you to act as her mentor."

Her request surprised me. I knew just how seriously Dr. Gwinn took mentorship. She'd been a lifeline to me. She challenged me when I needed it, listened when I was struggling, and gave valuable advice on how to further my goals.

I must've paused a bit too long because she added, "It would only be for this semester, Trevor. By next semester, Dean Dixon should be back and I'll be able to mentor her myself."

"Of course," I replied as I recovered from my shock. "I was just surprised. I'd love to do it."

"Excellent. You and I can work out the details about when you'll meet and how you'll be reporting back to me, but for now here's what you need to know."

Just as she began to write, one of the economics professors poked his head in and said, "Dean Gwinn, staff meeting in two."

She nodded in acknowledgement, sighed a bit wearily, and hastily handed the paper to me as she stood and walked to the door. She called over her shoulder, "You'll need to get going. I told her you'd meet today." I heard the sound of her heels clicking as she strode down the hall and I unfolded the paper in my hand.

Harris Music Building.

11:30 AM.

The Harris Music Building was the small house that belonged to first African American Trustee of Fisk. These days it held classrooms and practice space used by the Music Department, with beautiful pianos dotting the corners and walls.

The building was one of the few places I'd spent little time, since, ashamedly, I was not musical.

I'd peeked through a few rooms before I heard the notes of a piano floating from the other wing of the building. I drifted toward the familiar soft melody of "Someone to Watch Over Me." As I moved closer, I heard a voice, low, but under the notes it struck me like a bell all the same.

I knew.

Without having seen her, without even having heard the voice clearly, I knew it was Daisy.

Daisy.

I stood near the threshold of the room where she played, not yet ready to enter, not yet ready to see her again. I listened to her voice. I closed my eyes and let it wash over me.

My body reacted in the same odd way it had all the other times I'd seen her. My heart raced, I couldn't catch my breath, and my palm ached as if it was punishing me for keeping it from its mate.

I took a deep breath and braced for the moment she would fill my vision. I stepped into the space.

And there she sat.

Daisy played with her whole body, not just her fingers. Her voice was velvet, melodic, and clear as a bell. She sang the refrain and I wished more than anything that I could be the one to watch over her.

She was in blue today. I could see hints of her shirt peeking from beneath that gorgeous fluffy hair that reached down past her shoulders. Hair that I wanted to twist around my finger so I could feel its deep texture. Hair that I wanted to play in and separate coil by coil, wave by wave, curl by curl. Hair that I want to fist and tug as I . . .

I stopped my brain from going down that lethal track. This was the girl I was supposed to mentor? A girl so goddamn beautiful I could barely think straight?

How the hell was I supposed to do that? For a second I was almost angry with Dr. Gwinn.

I allowed myself another moment to drink her in, her voice, her body, her spirit . . . hoping to draw a bit of strength before facing her.

I would be careful today. I wouldn't shake her hand and I wouldn't tease or flirt.

I'd . . .

I didn't know what I'd do. The danger of Daisy was that all the things I shouldn't want to do felt like the most natural things in the world around her. She was dangerous for another reason too: Daisy made me weak. Or rather, to put the blame on myself where it belonged: Daisy was my weakness. She made my resolve crumble. I hadn't meant to spend the day with her yesterday and I could already feel my mind whirling, trying to think of ways to extend what should only be a brief meeting between a mentor and mentee to set up future dates.

Future dates. Good God, I was going to have to see her all semester long. How on earth was I going to do that?

I reminded myself that I was in a position where I was supposed to guide her for Pete's sake. I reminded myself that Dr. Gwinn would have my head and every other part of me if she got so much of a whiff that I had taken advantage of Daisy.

Besides, there were plenty of other reasons that being anything other than completely platonic with Daisy was a very bad idea.

She was a freshman and I was a senior, for starters. She was too young for me. I needed to concentrate—*she* needed to concentrate—if she was going to double-major successfully. And then there was the commitment I'd made to Elodie; the relationship may have been fake, but that didn't matter. The commitment was real.

Longing, strong and sure, pierced me. The combination of Daisy's beautiful, wistful notes and my own frustration at the futility of wanting anything more with Daisy created palpable pain.

Lost in thought, I shifted my feet and Daisy must have heard because she stopped singing and playing abruptly.

I expected her to turn around, but instead she just froze.

A few uncomfortable seconds ticked by and she didn't move.

"Daisy?" I asked in concern, sounding a bit raspier as I crossed the room, a sixth sense telling me something was wrong. I wanted and needed to provide her comfort if she was upset, caution and keeping my distance be damned.

"Trevor?" she said, but her voice was too watery, as if she'd been crying.

I slid next to her on the piano bench, and threaded my fingers through her hair, gently nudging the riot of hair behind her ears. I needed to see her face. I needed to see if I could help fix whatever had made her cry.

"Hey. What's wrong?" I said by way of greeting.

She released a shuddering breath and I wanted to ball my fist.

Whatever was wrong—I would fix it. And then I would annihilate whoever was responsible for making her feel such melancholy.

When those deep brown eyes met my own, they were clear. She hadn't been crying but she was definitely feeling something sad and strong. She gave me a weak smile, looked down, and her hair spilled over her shoulder and curtained her face from me.

None of that. This girl hiding that face from me felt criminal.

"Daisy, whatever is wrong, you know you can tell me."

She looked up at me again and offered a halfhearted shrug. I suspected it was meant to look casual before she replied, "Oh, nothing. I'm just being overly emotional. I haven't played since . . . I haven't played the piano in over a year." She paused and continued softly, like a confession. "I missed it."

The question *Why did you stop playing?* pressed at my throat, but I got the feeling that Daisy wouldn't tell me. She didn't seem to want me to know how strongly this was impacting her so I reckoned she wouldn't want to talk about why she stopped playing either.

"I hadn't realized just how much until I came in here and I saw all these beautiful . . . and I hadn't missed it until just now."

"That was beautiful," I said because it was.

She smiled up at me ruefully. "You are too kind. *That* was quite rusty. But . . . it's my mother's favorite song," she added the last part so quietly I almost didn't hear it.

I was definitely not going to ask Daisy, who'd arrived parentless, about her parents. If playing her mother's favorite song brought a bout of sadness this palpable then the story couldn't be good.

I wanted to reach over to hug her, give her some comfort and then encourage her to get back to playing full time if she missed it, but before I could she jumped up from the bench.

"Oh!" She looked around like she'd just remembered where she was. "Oh! I was supposed to meet someone. And I saw the pianos and . . . I have to go." She grabbed her bag and was ghosting away from me before I could get a word out. *As if I was going to let that happen.*

"Daisy!" I shouted and she halted with one foot out the door. Something about that image—Daisy with one foot out the door—had me rushing to speak.

"I'm the one you've been looking for." I cringed at the unintentional double meaning. "I mean, I'm your mentor. That's who you were going to meet in the foyer, right? Your mentor?" I clarified.

She walked back toward me slowly. Her big brown eyes blinked rapidly, making connections.

She stood in front of me, almost eye to eye since I still sat on the bench, her eyebrows raised in delight. "You're my mentor?"

I was so caught by those lovely eyes it took me a second to answer. When I finally did, I had to look away. "Yes I am, I—" I stopped short because I'd made the mistake of looking down.

Now that she stood, I could clearly see her outfit, and it became clear Daisy has a sadistic streak.

Her shirt . . . well, it was really a sorry excuse for a shirt. It was cropped off above her belly button and showed off a tantalizing sliver of her taut belly. The sleeves of the shirt were little arm bands, leaving her shoulders completely bare. The way the light blue color of the shirt contrasted with the rich brown of her skin, the way her collarbones dipped and curved, the way those bell-bottom jeans hugged her figure . . . it was all too much.

My eyes snapped shut.

I fought the feeling that this girl—only this girl—made me feel. Something akin to flying and fear and hope and lust, stronger than I'd ever experienced. When I opened them again, her magnetic eyes were right there, inches from my own.

I want to kiss her.

I fought against the thought. Of course I wouldn't kiss Daisy. But I did stare right into those the big oval eyes. I memorized their shape and the vibrant nut-brown color. I noticed for the first time the flecks of black within her irises.

The tension between us felt so thick it was like another presence in the room. Then Daisy—blessed, beautiful, innocent Daisy—broke it. She looked away shyly and that was enough to snap me from my stupor and I stood.

I had to get out of there before I got myself into trouble.

I looked toward the door as I plotted my escape but Daisy's sweet voice pulled my focus back to her. "This will be fantastic! Teach me everything you know."

I looked back down at her with those magnetic eyes staring at up me waiting and—

Lust, white hot and burning, slammed through me once again and I felt my spine crackling as my body began to change. I prayed it wasn't noticeable. I closed my eyes to get a reprieve from all of Daisy's . . . Daisiness. When I opened them again, I sighed in defeat. "I intend to do just that, mentee."

She smiled and scrunched her nose in response and then dug into her purse and produced a pen and small scheduler. "So when do we want to meet?"

Daisy and I decided on Fridays at four in the library.

I was eager to have our session wrapped up. I was overheated and in desperate need of some air. I made it as far as the other side of the threshold before my lips moved without my brain's permission, and I heard myself ask, "Would you like to get out of here? Maybe go on a tour of the campus?"

She was beside me in seconds, her easy smile back on her remarkably pretty face. She laughed. "Well, we can leave but I've already been on a tour of the campus."

I smiled back automatically, because I couldn't seem to help it when she smiled. "Yes, but you haven't been on the Trevor Boone tour of Fisk."

Her pretty eyes meet mine from beneath her lashes. They sparked with curiosity and maybe a bit of humor.

"Well how can I resist that?"

"No need to resist at all," my mouth involuntarily responded.

What are you doing, Trevor? That sounds a lot like flirting. Get a grip. You cannot flirt with this girl.

"Lead the way, dear mentor."

God have mercy on me. She should never be allowed to use the words lead, dear, or mentor.

She was definitely gonna notice if she looked down now.

CHAPTER EIGHT

Trevor

I held the door open for Daisy, squinting as the light hit my face. I tucked my twitchy hands in my pockets so I wouldn't grab hers. I was quiet—my mind working to justify asking Daisy for any extra time. On the one hand, it was selfish, and I knew that. On the other hand, she had been sad. The echo of that misery still haunted me, even if I didn't know the source—maybe even especially since I didn't know. An hour or two of distraction wouldn't hurt her, and it would go a long way in settling my mind.

I was happy to see that her mood improved as we started toward Fisk's most well-known landmark: a statue of W.E.B. DuBois. Daisy had already been on a tour so instead of giving her pure history, I'd just have to improvise.

She reached into the small purse she had slung across her body and pulled out some shades.

She looked up at me with those butterflies perched on her nose and it was the sweetest thing I'd ever seen.

Maybe she was a fairy or a goddess. Yesterday she'd lain on the blanket, hair fanned about her head, and she'd looked the very picture of Isis or Aphrodite. Perhaps I'd been bewitched the way Greek goddesses would sometimes toy with mortal men.

That was, sadly, the most rational explanation for my reaction to her. After all, I hardly knew her and here I was thinking of excuses to extend our time together. *That isn't true*, my mind automatically contradicted. I hadn't known her long but after yesterday I understood her. I knew her favorite color and her favorite books and her favorite songs and her favorite music group.

Maybe today I'd have the chance to find out a few more favorites. *Just to get to know her as her mentor*, I quickly justified to myself.

I glanced at her still cheerily looking up at me, and because I couldn't seem to control my body, my thoughts, *or* my mouth when I was around her I blurted, "You look a like a fairy queen with those glasses on."

She laughed. "My sister said the same thing but I think they're cute."

It's not the glasses that are cute.

I stopped us in front of W.E.B. DuBois and gave her my most somber, scholarly face as I began speaking, "As you know, this is a statue—"

"Of W.E.B.—" she interjected.

I quickly cut her off as I smiled at her knowledge and a little at her know-it-allness.

I didn't fault her for that; in fact, confidence in your intelligence was a major turn-on for me.

Everything about this girl is a turn-on for you.

"Of W.C. Pennington," I countered.

She stopped short and those butterflies stared up at me, perplexed.

"Trevor." There was surprise and laughter in her voice. "I think the name you meant to say—"

I slapped my hand on my forehead. "Yes, you're right. I forgot his *name*! It's *James* W.C. Pennington." I nodded assuredly. "How could I forget his *first,* first name." I rolled my eyes theatrically.

If Jules could see you right now, yours wouldn't be the only eyes rolling.

"Pennington, who, as you may be aware, was famous for being an—"

"Abolitionist—" she said flatly, lips twisted and eyebrows raised.

Of course she knew who James W.C. Pennington was. I wasn't surprised so I didn't miss a beat.

"I believe you meant to say arborist," I corrected graciously. I hoped my plan worked. I hoped Daisy would go along with my joke. I hoped she got my sense of humor, otherwise I was going to look like the biggest fool.

"He was responsible for . . ." I moved my hands in an arc as I gestured to the campus. "Hand planting most of the trees that dot our beloved forty-acre campus."

I kept my face absolutely straight.

A long moment went by, and then . . . her lips broke into a full smile.

And then she *laughed.*

My breath caught a little and I exhaled my own chuckle in response.

I balled my first inside my pocket. I would not reach for her hand. But I did feel like I was flying, soaring really. Daisy and I had laughed together yesterday, but this was different. This was the first time I'd set out to make her laugh. The fact that I could earn that laughter, earn those smiles, made me feel fifty feet tall. It made me want to spend a lifetime earning them.

You can't. I reminded myself.

Why not? my brain said.

Because you're her mentor. You're in a position of power over her.

We are not responsible for her grades, my brain countered.

Okay well maybe not power, but . . . leadership. And school, too! Senior year. Stay focused. And maybe after yesterday she doesn't want to shake your hand. She's been nothing but friendly today. And what about Elodie? my brain nagged.

My smile fell a little at the reminders. Daisy was fatal because she made everything that had been my top priority feel less important. I knew it was wrong, but in that moment I felt like earning more of Daisy's laughter was the most important thing in the world. I couldn't have a lifetime, but I was greedy enough to want these next few hours.

"Well," she said after her laughter died down. "I'm so lucky to have you mentoring me. It would seem I've been deeply misinformed and need someone to help get me up to speed on my Fisk-tory," she said, still grinning.

I bit back my grin, and nodded somberly. "Very common for freshman. How can we expect them to know about the rich and vast history of this great university when they don't even know how to pick up their meal vouchers?"

I winked.

"Oh, that does it!" she exclaimed whipping off her glasses and gently poking me in the shoulder.

"You and that boy were impossible! With your"—she lowered her voice and her chin while adopting a more manly posture—"I love you, Mrs. Dot. You're the best cook in heaven or hell, Mrs. Dot!"

Was she imitating me?

I burst into laughter. *She was definitely imitating me.*

"Firstly, my voice does not—"

I didn't even get to finish the sentence. She slid her sunshades into her hair and pounced on me like a kitten assaulting its prey—claws out, poking, and tickling.

How does she know I'm ticklish? I hadn't told her that.

I danced in front of the statue trying to avoid her probing fingers as she shouted, sounding a little deranged, "How in the world were we supposed to know—"

Poke!

"—to just show up!"

Tickle!

"To sign out the coupon books? And your timing was more—"

Poke!

"—than—"

Tickle!

"Uncanny!"

I managed to dance away but she wasn't finished.

"You planned it!" she shouted, assailing me with her fingers. My heart raced, tears streamed down my face, I was completely breathless, and I had no idea if it was because she'd made laugh so hard or from her touch. Or both.

"Innocent!" I yelled back. I moved, trying not nearly hard enough to get away from her.

"Liar!"

She poked me especially hard between my ribs and it caught me off guard enough that I lost balance.

My hands flew out automatically, seeking stability and finding Daisy.

We both tumbled on the soft grass and she landed on top of me.

Her hair fell around her face and I was struck with the need to touch it, to tuck it away, to see her face. The urge to run my hands over her body to check for bumps and bruises, to make sure she was okay even though I could feel her soft, warm body on my own, was nearly overwhelming. Daisy's body was flush with mine, her lips so near my ear I could hear her soft pants as she tried to catch her breath.

And I knew I needed to get her off me quickly or she was going to feel my not-soft body under hers.

And I would, absolutely. I would roll us both to the side so that we could move apart . . . but not yet. I took a second, just a moment, to indulge. I'd wanted to play in her hair since the first moment I saw those two long wavy braids trailing down her back.

And so I did.

I gently took a piece that had fallen around her face, I slid it between my thumb and index finger. Then I wound it around my index finger, once, twice three times and gently tucked the tendril behind her ear.

Her hair was so soft. Its texture was a silky mixture of coily and wavy; it left a delicious sheen of oil on my fingertips.

And since I was indulging, I allowed myself to stare into those big, pretty eyes. Eyes that were becoming familiar to me. I wondered if I could draw them from memory yet.

It wasn't as if I really even had a choice. Her eyes compelled me to stare, and although our fall was short, looking into her eyes made me feel like the wind had been knocked out of me.

The longer we lay pressed against one another, the more it felt like our entire bodies had become magnets. To break us apart would require a force stronger than my mere human strength. The air around us grew charged, growing even hotter in the Tennessee summer heat. It may have taken me several seconds, but I finally noticed that Daisy wasn't scrambling to get off of me. She wasn't moving at all. In fact, she stared right back at me, lips slightly parted.

Speaking of lips . . . I let my mind wander and wondered what would happen if I slid my hand from the warm, soft, bare skin of her lower back where it'd gone instinctively on some wild attempt to protect her as we fell to her lips, mere inches away. Would they feel as smooth as they looked? Her lips were plump and she wore lipstick that made them the color of ripe berries. I wondered if they'd taste as sweet.

Too far gone in my imaginings, I realized I had leaned closer and closer, but it wasn't until I heard the hitch of her breath and her saw her eyes flutter closed that reality crashed into my fantasy and I paused.

Are you out of your entire John Brown mind? You almost kissed her.

I cleared my throat and looked at the sky, at the grass, at anything but her. It would kill me to look at Daisy and see her so close and so willing and yet so far out of reach. After a long moment, her eyes opened and she retreated off me.

Shame swamped me strong, fierce. An apology burned my tongue. I shut my eyes tightly and when I opened them to look her in the eye—because she deserved to be looked in the eye when I told her that I was terribly sorry and that I would completely understand if she wanted a new mentor. One that could keep his hands to himself.

I expected to see her sitting near me, confused, hurt, maybe even angry. Instead, I found her already standing on the sidewalk, smiling brightly.

She spoke before I could. "So what about Jubilee Hall? Does it actually date back to 1876?"

I stared at her in confusion before realizing she'd gone back to the history game. I cleared my throat, stood, and brushed the blades of grass from my trousers, not sure if I should be relieved or disappointed that she seemed content to ignore the intense last few moments between us.

Be relived, Trevor. She's too young for you. She's too innocent for you. She's too beautiful for you.

But relived isn't what I was . . .

I was crestfallen.

Idiot.

I was screwed.

Daisy

And the Academy Award for the leading actress, in Of Course He

Doesn't want to Kiss You, Dummy, *goes to Daisy Payton. I would like to thank my sister for letting me know I was perfect for this role, and of course, the Academy.*

My smile was screwed on so tight if it got any bigger my whole face would give like a screw tightened one turn too many.

Nevertheless, I was determined to get the day back on track. I couldn't very well run off in a fit of tears when he'd rejected my advances.

You basically threw yourself at him, Daisy. Pressing yourself against him like a pair of cheap press-on nails the first chance you got.

Shame. For shame, Daisy.

I did not feel ashamed. I felt . . .

Hot.

Turned on. Embarrassed. Remorseful.

Poor thing. What must Trevor have been feeling? Here I was, thinking he was working himself up to make a move and instead he'd been politely trying to give me time and space to get the hell off of him.

But the way he looked at you . . .

Is probably the way he looks at everyone, Daisy.

The boy couldn't help that he had eyes. *Gorgeous eyes.* They were light brown with even lighter, almost golden, flecks in the center. I'd never seen anything quite like them.

And his stare? I fought a shudder as I recalled the way Trevor looked into me like he could see my soul.

Both James and Odie had been wrong, and Dolly, per usual, had been right. The boy was a natural flirt; he didn't even realize what he was doing. It wasn't his fault he had charisma oozing out of his pores. It wasn't his fault he was charming and funny and had eyes that could set a room ablaze.

Your face is going to wrinkle from how hard you're smiling, Daisy.

I was not going to make big deal out of this minor thing.

Was it embarrassing? Sure. Yes, Lord, yes! It was the same level of mortification as when you waved at a stranger who you thought waved at you in a moment of human kindness and connection but had actually waved at the person they knew standing behind you.

But it wasn't devastating.

And anyway, I'd just gotten to school. I needed to hold my horses.

Yes, consider the horses held. There was much to do and to learn and I needed a firm foundation under my feet before I rushed headlong into kissing practical strangers.

Yes! Good plan, smart Daisy. Great plan.

Therefore, I was hitting the reset button on my day, and on our non-relationship. I was gathering the butterflies I felt whenever this boy came near and sealing them in a jar.

No, Daisy, they'll die in a jar. Yes! Good riddance. Those flutters can be smothered and die in the vacuum jar of no feelings.

I'd backed up so that Trevor knew he was in no danger of being attacked again and waited for him to open his eyes and see that I wasn't a threat anymore.

When he did look at me, the expression on his face was so strange, I contemplated apologizing. Quickly realizing that the only thing that would make him even more uncomfortable was me pouring out my heartfelt regrets, I jumped in with the first benign thought that popped into my head. "So what about Jubilee Hall? Does it actually date back to 1876?"

He paused for a second—comprehension and I hoped a little forgiveness dawning in his eyes—before responding with a small smile that didn't quite reach his eyes. "Yes, that part is true. Jubilee Hall does indeed date back to 1876. But . . ."

He stood and brushed blades of grass from his pants and when he looked back at me, the mischievous glint had returned to his eyes. "There was a lumber shortage that year."

"A lumber shortage?" I couldn't help but ask because of course Trevor would weave lumber into a story. I wanted to roll my eyes.

"Yes!"

"In Tennessee."

"Yes."

It was the most ironic tall tale in the world but of course he didn't know that. He had no clue that he was talking to one of the few people whose family was very capable of manufacturing a lumber shortage, even though we'd never operate that way.

"Trevor, there was no such thing," I replied, unable to keep a wry smile from my face.

"I think, Miss Daisy, that we've already established that I am the expert in—what did you called it? Fisk-tory?"

He raised his eyebrows at me, smirking.

I pretended to think, "Hmm, is that so? I'm not sure I recall saying those exact words. Well, it sure looks to the untrained eye like the exterior is made of wood," I ribbed back. It didn't. Jubilee Hall was definitely made of brick.

He turned toward the building and we moved toward it at a leisurely pace.

"Well I was getting to that part before I was rudely interrupted."

I cut my eyes to his.

"It's made of wood, but since lumber was so hard to come by they had to source the wood however they could."

Those intense brown eyes caught mine. He took a deep breath and seemed to pause for dramatic effect. Then he gestured to the building. "What you're looking at is ten to the twelfth power's worth of popsicle sticks."

Ten to the . . .

A trillion popsicle sticks. Oh brother.

I couldn't have stopped my incredulous reply even if I'd wanted to. "And from where, pray tell, did they get a trillion popsicle sticks?"

He opened his mouth to respond but I continued, not finished mulling through the lunacy of his claim.

"And how were they cleaned? And did those poor, diabetic founding fathers and mothers have to consume all one trillion popsicles?"

"Course not," he shot back. "They were twin pops, two sticks to a popsicle. They'd have eaten five hundred billion popsicles, max."

That might've been the most incendiary thing he'd said yet.

"You can't honestly be one of those kinds of people." I sniffed. I kept my face impressively straight, showing I could give as good as I get.

"Beg your pardon?" he replied, genuinely confused.

"Twin pops are two popsicles, not one. And if you're the type of person that can't do basic math . . ." Injecting my tone with a hint Mrs. Dot's, I finished him off with, "Maybe you ain't mentor material."

I saw the spark of recognition in those deep brown eyes and realized that his jaw ticked when he was trying hide his grin.

He placed his hand over his heart, leveling me with an earnest gaze that made my heart beat double time.

"I'm sure my beloved Mrs. Dot would agree with me, culinary expert that she is, that it's a twin pop, singular, with a single wrapper." His voice turned solemn and a little rough. "Daisy, I'll be the best mentor. I want to teach you everything. I want this to be good for you."

I felt a shiver down my spine, looked away quickly, and nodded my head.

It was going to be a long semester.

Trevor and I visited a handful more destinations around campus before deciding to call it quits in front of The Wall, Fisk's unofficial gathering place for students, and split for the day. I needed to head back to my dorm to start getting ready for the rescheduled mixer that, to my surprise—and if I was honest—delight, Trevor mentioned he would be attending.

"But only for the beginning. Jules and I will do our introduction as Student Body President and Vice President, talk a little about the position of freshman class president ,and then we're going to get out of there. I mean, it's not like we'd actually party with *freshman*." He pulled an exaggerated face and rolled his eyes. He reached over and playfully swiped his thumb across my nose.

It happened so fast that I was sure I'd imagined it, if not for the heat rushing to my face and the semi-embarrassed look on his.

Before our goodbyes could turn awkward I heard a voice calling my name and turned to see James exiting Spence Hall, followed by Julian just a few paces behind.

Trevor spoke so highly of his cousin and best friend that I was looking forward to meeting the person behind the pretty face.

I gave James a glare as she approached as a warning not to pull any of the funny business she tried at church.

James gave Trevor a quick nod in greeting and he smiled and nodded in return.

By way of introduction, Trevor affected a long-suffering sigh and said, "I'm sure Julian will do a more-than-adequate job of listing his many accomplishments, accolades, and laudable traits during tonight's festivities, but I'll spare you now. His most important accomplishment is being my best friend."

Julian scoffed.

Trevor winked at me, and I bit my bottom lip to keep from smiling.

Julian, on the other hand, looked truly put out as James dipped her head to hide her smile.

"Daisy and James, this is Jules."

"Thank you for that glowing introduction," Jules said dryly, extending his hand to me and then to James.

Jules squinted at James as if he was examining her and then said, "Has anyone ever told you how gorgeous you are for a dark-skinned girl?"

James eyes flashed with anger so quick I almost missed it. She dropped his hand and her face briefly. When she raised her head again, her expression had been wiped clean.

I looked at Trevor agog.

Trevor looked at Jules agog.

Julian looked at James as if he expected her to kneel at his feet and kiss his hand for that backhanded compliment hanging there like a rotting fish.

"Interesting," James replied, not sounding the least bit interested —and pointedly not saying thank you.

She gave Julian her back, turned to me and said, "Daisy, you ready to get out of here?"

"Past ready."

Trevor was still looking at Julian like he'd sprouted horns. Which would've been appropriate.

Julian, not content to make an ass of himself only once in a day, began talking again. "The proper thing to do when given a compliment by a man is to say thank you."

He looked to Trevor for back-up. Trevor's expression was vacillating between frowning and bewilderment so quickly it would've been funny if . . . well if the situation was even a little funny.

I shot him a look that said, *Get your crazy ass best friend before I hurt him.*

James turned back to examine Julian, her head cocked. "When I receive a compliment from a man, I'll respond accordingly."

Julian rocked back on his heels, eyebrows high on that sinister pretty face. I got the feeling that he hadn't been dressed down by many—maybe any—girls.

"Trevor, Daisy. I'll be on my way now. Whatever you name was . . ."

Julian's eyebrows shot up even higher.

"Pleasure was yours, I'm sure."

Julian laughed, harshly. "Whatever my name is? I'm Julian *P.* Marshall."

He was clearly trying to regain control after James's dismissal and it was a bit pathetic. He affected an overly bored tone. "But of course freshman don't know anyone. I'm Student Body President. I'd suggest you ask about me," he said, waving dismissively in *my* general direction.

This guy was an asshole. How could Trevor be friends with him?

James spoke in her usual staccato tempo but mimicked Julian's bored intonation, when she replied, "I'd ask about you, Mr. Marshall, but I'm sure that tale would be short." She looked down at his groin pointedly. "And unsatisfying."

Julian's face turned beet red.

With that final barb finding its mark, James turned to me. "Daisy, if you're staying, then I'm going to head out by myself."

"Oh no, I'll go with you," I said emphatically and looped arms with my friend. We headed out without another word.

Julian couldn't resist a parting shot though. "Goodbye, gorgeous," he called as we walked toward our dorm.

James paused mid-stride, lifted her head higher, and straightened her shoulders before continuing on without acknowledging that he'd even said a word.

CHAPTER NINE

Trevor

I watched as Daisy and James sashayed their fine asses away and took a deep, calming, pointless breath before I rounded on my friend.

"What the hell?" we exploded at the same time.

Okay. Not what I was expecting.

Why the hell was Julian mad? He'd started this.

A boy walking out of Spence looked up startled at our explosion, registered the two of us, turned, and walked in the other direction.

"Not here," Jules said gruffly.

I could see him running the same calculation through his head that was running in mine.

We had a little over an hour before the mixer was supposed to start. We didn't have time to go home, and we couldn't do this in public—our arguments were Hamilton-Madison level of debate. Our office atop the third floor of Spence was not ideal; we could be overheard if we weren't careful, but it was our only real option. Besides, most upperclassmen weren't back yet. Hopefully the other offices would be empty.

We walked circumspectly into the building. We were, after all, student leaders. Once inside our space, Jules closed the door and collapsed into the club chair, legs draped over the arms like the weight of the world was upon him.

He closed his eyes and tilted his head toward the ceiling, not saying a word, which was fine by me.

I gave him a minute to collect his thoughts. In truth, I needed a minute to collect my own.

I am an easygoing person by nature. I'd much rather be debating the nature of twin pops than confronting my friends.

But there was something about a body that you've shared a room with and a home with, Christmases and Easters and everything in between for years and years with, that could drive you to levels of anger you wouldn't have thought possible.

Be a leader. Do not give in to your anger.

To keep myself from doing so, I surveyed the work that Jules had completed since I'd been away at my work-study assisting Dr. Gwinn and then with Daisy.

Our office was small—cramped, really—as it had come stuffed to the gills with furniture. A small conference table was crammed into the far end for cabinet meetings and two smallish writing desks with chairs were right near the doors. There was window seat to my left and the club chair which Julian was currently occupying to my right.

Jules had hung a framed print of one of our campaign posters on the back of the door. On the corner of his desk I saw a small, folded piece of yellow circle that I knew was from Felicity, Julian's ex-girl-friend's six-year-old sister who was in love with Julian.

It was cute and it was terrible.

When the girl had found out he was running she'd sent him a handmade "Jules Marshall for President" button. Jules had worn it everywhere.

And when Julian and Francine had broken up at the end of last semester they'd both been unaffected, but Felicity had wailed that Julian was supposed to be her brother. She'd taken it so hard that even though they weren't a couple, Frannie still routinely phoned us over the summer so that Jules and Felicity could chat.

It was off-putting; it was puzzling. Julian could be an asshole, but he was nearly always respectful. I shook my head again trying to tamp down the rising anger I felt when I thought of what he'd said.

I focused on a previously empty bookshelf and I saw that Julian had already began to unpack our books. *Roberts Rules of Order, The Student Code of Conduct*, and *The President's Book* were in the center of the bookcase. They were flanked by two bookends: a tall letter T on one end and a letter J on the other. I saw Jules' favorite books filed neatly behind the letter J. On the other end there was space behind the T, waiting for me to fill the shelf with my math and finance books.

A placed reserved for me. Always looking out for me.

I didn't even know he'd purchased those.

I sighed. Julian Marshall was indeed a study in contrasts. Big heart, big ego.

I wandered to the window overlooking the sidewalk where we'd just stood and tried to sift through my emotions rationally.

I wasn't trying to fight with Jules on this otherwise lovely day.

Daisy's sweet face popped unbidden into my mind and I allowed myself a moment to recall the way she raised her eyebrows and scrunched her nose when she disbelieved something I said. The way her brown hair had changed in the sun, the surprise I'd felt when I noticed some strands of copper and red, while unlit, her hair looked almost black. I felt protective of this information, of this revelation of the beautiful secret her hair carried. I felt like it was mine.

I wanted to know all her secrets. I wanted to know everything that would make her smile.

"You're smiling like you have a secret," Jules said, cutting through my memories.

I needed to deal with Julian's pigheadedness, but I stalled, trying to find a path that wouldn't lead to us both blowing up.

It was rare that we both went full throttle because the result was unpleasant.

But Jules was gonna apologize to Daisy.

And to the person he'd actually offended.

Right!

He was certainly going to apologize to James.

I turned from the window, looked my best friend in the eye, and what I saw looking back at me took me by surprise.

Underneath Julian's anger was hurt, clear as day.

And then fear gripped me, cold and clammy. Julian had a way of finding out information about anyone and everyone.

Impossible. He doesn't know. He can't know.

"When did you get back?" I asked cautiously.

"A little while ago."

I exhaled a little, but it was short lived.

"Just long enough to hear that my best friend has been cavorting around campus with some *freshman* girl. The Trevor Boone I know is a good guy and would never do that. We're not those guys that prey on new arrivals—we're disgusted by those guys. We blackball them from our social settings, we warn girls off them."

Fuck! He knew.

He took a deep breath and said, "And then there's my cousin—"

Elodie.

El and I had always been close, even before her parents died. Growing up she was the harmonic force that Julian and I needed to keep from killing one another sometimes, but after she'd lost her parents ,she and I acquired an unbreakable bond forged through a shared understanding of loss and abandonment, displacement and discontent.

I loved her like she was my own sister. And I wanted what was best for her. I would do anything to protect her, which was why I'd offered to pretend to be her boyfriend in the first place. I hadn't seen it as a hardship. If anything, it had been beneficial to me. I was too broke to date anyone and having a girlfriend gave me the cover I needed to never have to answer for my finances. And I was a double major, staying attachment free left me free to focus all my energy on my schooling.

Everything had been so uncomplicated.

Until Daisy.

I cut him off. "That's complicated and you know it." Julian had done an admirable job of trying to mind his business considering Elodie wasn't just his maternal cousin, she was his other best friend. With the exception of one tightly held secret, the two them were as close as close could be. They even resembled one another.

He raised his eyebrows at me and said, "You're right. The less I know about you and Elodie's relationship, the better off I am. *Probably*," his tone was exasperated, "because God knows I don't understand it."

It wasn't the first time Jules had expressed bafflement about the peculiar mechanics of my relationship with Elodie. He thought it peculiar that we "broke up" every summer and allowed one another "freedom to explore." Elodie's words. He knew my rebuttal would be that Elodie wasn't back at school, so we weren't technically back together. He and I were smart enough to know that my excuse was bullshit, or at least it *would've* been if Elodie and I were a real couple.

Right on cue he spoke. "I think we can both agree that it's mighty big of me to even be *willing* to put that aside."

I nodded my agreement.

"Right now I'm so fucking angry at you, Trevor, I'm liable to do something rash."

"Dr. Gwinn asked me to be her mentor," I said weakly.

"Is that what I saw on the sidewalk just now? You mentoring her? Because the way you were playing with her face didn't look like something a mentor should be doing."

He was right to be pissed. He was right to hold me accountable; it's what we did for each other. Growing up we'd seen too many of our schoolmates surround themselves with folks that would only tell them what they wanted to hear. And when we got to college it was even worse; too many friendships where guys only encouraged one another to act on their worst instincts, particularly when it came to women. Julian was right to call me out. I'd absorb his anger, but for that same reason I couldn't absolve his behavior, because no matter what I did, Jules' comment had been way out of line.

"Jules, you may want to apply some of that righteous indignation to yourself," I said quietly. "I want you to publicly apologize to James tonight."

He bristled. "I'm not apologizing." His voice was dead calm and flat, and I knew he was well and truly pissed.

Too bad.

"You are too smart to buy into that bullshit your family has spouted our entire lives, Julian." My voice rose with each word.

Worry had me losing it a little because I was devastated by what he'd said but not as surprised as I should've been. Growing up Jules' family had been . . . weird about skin color. They didn't prefer white folks; they just didn't like their Black folks *too* black. I was already too dark by their standards so they didn't bother with me much, but keeping Jules from getting a tan had been a borderline obsession for his mother and grandmother. He hadn't been allowed to swim in their outdoor pool because his mother was afraid the combination of the chlorine and sun would "blacken him up."

Jules was light—light enough that you could see his blush, light enough that the dark brown and white freckles splashed across his face were highly visible. Yet still they'd lose their minds over the slightest change in his coloring. He'd actually had to stand up and be inspected anytime we came from playing outdoors, and if they felt he was getting too dark, we'd be indoors for a few days.

Jules had seemed as dismayed and annoyed by his parent's antics growing up but I'd never heard him repeat their craziness.

Until now.

I squinted at Jules as he squinted back at me.

The faces of the girls Jules had dated over the years from grade school on popped into my mind. Always very thin, always straight hair, *always* as pale or paler than him.

How could I have been so blind? Jules had been dating the same girl.

He looked uncomfortable, shifting from foot to foot, and I realized he'd been expecting me to refute his denial but the moment was much bigger and scarier because if my best friend was truly color struck . . . then where did that leave us?

All I could bring myself to say was, "Why?" It was harsh, torn from me in fear and anger.

"I didn't say anything wrong to her. I just stated a fact. She is dark-skinned." Adding quietly after the fact, "She is gorgeous." Fists balled at his sides like he wanted to fight the notion.

Julian mistook my question when in fact it was about something so much bigger.

He looked so uncomfortable with the notion that James could be both dark-skinned and pretty, as if there was something innately wrong with it, that my frustration boiled over.

"Jules, you can't possibly believe that crock of shit your parents spout about light skin being better!"

"I never said anything about anyone being better than anyone else!" he hollered, defensive.

"You didn't have to say it, Julian, it was implied. Do you even hear yourself right now? You sound like a bigot! Mary Washington, Katherine Hale, Persephone Shaw, Francine Deveroe . . . they all look mighty similar," I countered, naming his past girlfriends.

He rocked back on his heels and shoved his hands into his pockets. He looked back at me, face hard and lips pressed together, defensive as hell.

Guilty as hell.

And hell, while I was thinking on it Romona Wells might as well be added to the mix. Romona was the girl his family had been pushing him to marry since before he'd even known me.

I let that sink in. From what I could tell, Julian's parents had his spouse selected for him practically since he was born.

And since Jules' parents usually did whatever they had to do to ensure they got what they wanted, she very likely would marry Jules. Green eyes, light skin, thin ski-jump nose, softly pointed chin, ramrod straight honey-colored hair.

Pretty in a particular type of way.

"There's nothing wrong with having a type. A preference," he said more softly.

"You're right. Nothing wrong with having a preference."

He exhaled at my words, though his shoulders were still bunched because he knew me well enough to know I wasn't done.

"But that ain't what this is. And if it is, whose preference is it? Yours? Or your parents'?"

Because here's the *other* thing about living with a body and sharing summer vacations, and holidays and bedrooms: you got to know their personal preferences—all of them—very well.

Jules only used Mighty White toothpaste. He could not abide sleeping in a hot or even mildly warm room—it had to be colder than the arctic tundra in there. He was meticulously neat; one might even call him anal. He had a collection of watches that rivaled the Timex Corporation, he collected books and read obsessively, and the Jet Beauties of the Week that he preferred, the girls that turned his head on an unconscious level, didn't look a thing like the girls he dated.

What the hell did they do to you, Jules?

He looked at me, eyes stormy and full of so many emotions I couldn't name them all.

He cleared his throat and then said, "I didn't call you up here to talk about me."

Typical Julian.

"You didn't call me up here at all, *Prince*," I said through gritted teeth.

He'd always been that way, since we were kids. Because his parents treated everyone that wasn't a Marshall like they were their servants and they expected Julian to mimic that disgusting behavior.

You ever seen a twelve-year-old tell a seventy-year-old cook to remake their dinner because they'd changed their mind about what they wanted to eat? You ever seen the parents laugh at his "antics" when he did it?

Yeah. When Jules and I met, we did not get along. At all.

Being a young asshole, he'd called me Eeyore, claiming I was sad and stubborn. He was right at the time, but he didn't need to know that.

And I'd called sarcastically called him Prince, his middle name and the one he hated most of all.

He flinched now at the nickname.

"Fine. I'll apologize tonight." He exhaled in frustration. "And you'll set some damned boundaries with your mentee."

I opened my mouth to try to dance around his request because I didn't want to limit my time with her.

But Julian was right.

I don't care.

Before I could speak Julian leveled me with a look, one that said *I know you. Lie to me. Try it.*

Then he spoke. "Did you think I didn't notice that your eyes and head kept drifting when we were in the cafeteria the other day?"

Busted. Here I thought I was being stealthy.

"I didn't pay it any mind, because they're a couple of stunners. Truth be told, I was looking myself."

The idea of Julian looking at Daisy has my pressure rising and my vision going blurry. I blinked and took a deep breath as he continued, "But just then? The way I saw you looking at her, the way you casually reached over and thumbed her nose, and yesterday—holding her hand? Trevor, none of that was innocent." He shook his head and looked at me with confusion, like he didn't know me.

Then he sighed. "You're supposed to be a good guy, Trevor. You're supposed to be better than me. So why are you leading that girl on?"

I wasn't.

I'm not. Am I?

I thought about my actions over the last few days and suddenly I felt sick, like a piece of lead had crash landed in the pit of my stomach. I wasn't leading her on. I wasn't. It was just Daisy made it easy to forget things I shouldn't have forgotten.

Jules mumbled, "You know what. I don't even want to know what was going on or what was going through your head. The less I know, the better."

He sounded so tired and I remembered all the stuff my best friend had done for other people in the last forty-eight hours. Driving me to school and then turning around and driving to Lexington to be a groomsman in his cousin's wedding, when Jules absolutely loathed weddings. Then he'd driven back here and got to work setting up our office, because he knew I had work-study and wouldn't get to it until the end of the week.

That knowledge made me look at my best friend through a familiar filter. Julian was a lot of things: cunning, giving, a braggadocio, loyal to a fault, and sometimes entitled. But he wasn't cruel.

And that was why what he said to James struck me as discordant. It was out of character, dating history aside. It was cruel and it was stupidly insulting, and Jules wasn't either. He had to have known she'd be offended, that she'd leave.

That *they'd* leave.

Jules was aware that Daisy and James were friends. He'd observed them from the cafeteria.

I paused. And everything clicked into place.

This wasn't about James. This was about me.

"Why did you come outside just now? Where were you going, Julian?"

"I was on my way to nowhere. I came outside to save my best friend from making a fool of himself."

And by saving me, he meant getting me away from Daisy.

"Did you insult James so that she'd leave? So that they'd both leave?"

He looked away and then back at me, all the weariness in the world on his face. And I bit back the need to apologize to my friend.

I've done nothing wrong.

"Is there some reason you wanted to keep both girls around?"

Not a confession, but not a denial either. Dammit, Julian.

"Trevor, people are already talking about the two of you. Even if no one had told me about yesterday, I picked up from *inside* a building, three stories up, and one hundred yards away that you two were more than just friendly. What do you think is gonna happen on Friday when *everyone* gets back? What do you think is happening now to that girl's reputation?"

"Her reputation? I haven't done anything for Pete's sake! We haven't done anything."

"It doesn't matter!" he hollered. "You're gallivanting around with this girl that you've clearly got a thing for. You're holding hands in public! People are gonna fill in the blanks on their own! You think none of the freshmen here have a brother or a *sister* that's a year or two ahead at this school? You think folks aren't talking? You're not dumb enough to believe that. And that girl . . ." He stopped, like he was trying to work something out in his head. "Whoever she is, she has no clue what you're pulling her into.

"So, now I'm telling you, you're going to find her tonight and you're going to tell her that you're not going to see her anymore unless it's for whatever thing Dr. Gwinn has you doing. Because you're one of the good guys, Trevor, and it's my job to remind you of that."

Daisy

We were in my dorm room, which was kind of becoming our dorm room, and I was raging. "Arrogant, imperious, smug bastard! I mean, does he think you're stupid? Like you can't tell the difference between a compliment and a backhanded compliment. He's immature and can't have anything close to common sense to say something so ugly and . . ."

"Amen! Yes, ugly!" Odie seconded from her place in the bed waving her hand like a church lady.

It was the church lady wave that caused me to pause my litany. Odie cracked a smile and said, "Welcome back, Daize."

I smiled at the use of the nickname she's given me, exhaled the rest of my anger, and flopped backwards on my bed. James was sitting on the edge of my bed picking a piece of lint off her black V-neck halter. She'd been silent. She didn't say anything as we made the trek back to my room or as I explained what happened to Odie who was already in my room, picking through my makeup.

"James, are you okay?"

She didn't even look up from the lint.

"Oh. Yeah," she replied mellowly and then added, "Daisy, can I borrow your snakeskin platform sandals for tonight? I'm considering wearing my orange jumpsuit—you know the one with the little diamond cutouts at the side that you thought was so cute? Those shoes would look righteous with them. I love having a friend with the same shoe size. It's like my shoe collection doubled overnight."

"James?"

She looked up, batting her eyelashes playfully. "Daaaaiiisssy."

"How can you be so calm about all this? How can you just sit there talking about shoes?"

"What would you have me do, Daisy? You're worked up enough for three people." She shot an exasperated look at Odie who tried unsuccessfully to cover her laughter. I tossed a pillow at her. She caught it and pressed her face to it shaking with laughter.

"We need to—he needs to—we should make him—ARGGH-HHHHHHH!!"

There were no words for the futility I felt.

"Daisy," James said softly, gently, and it bothered me that she felt like she had to comfort *me* in this. I needed to calm down.

"Do you think Jules is the first person to say something like that to me?"

Yes, I wanted to say. *Yes, I imagine that Jules is the first person to say something as awful to you because why would anyone go out of their way to say something terrible when shutting up was a perfectly viable option?*

But I knew better.

As much as I wished society were different, that *we* were different —the reality was, what Julian said wasn't all that out of bounds for a lot of people. And for many more, it was, unfortunately, completely *within* bounds.

James continued. "Do you think he'll be the last person to talk like that to me?" She sat up and shook her head dismissively. "Even if it's not about my skin, it'll be that I'm too tall for a girl . . . or about my weight."

Odie made a strangled little sound and said, "Amen," again softly.

"If I had a nickel for every time someone called me Olive Oyl." She rolled her eyes. "I'd drop out 'cause I'd already be rich."

"There will always be a Jules there to tell a woman she should be less dark or less large or less loud. Folk who feel like they aren't enough so they spend their time making everyone around them feel like less."

She gave a little shrug. "*Julian* doesn't deserve any more head-space. And so I won't give him any. Instead I choose to focus on better things like, that divine cheetah print bra-top that's hanging in your closet. Are you wearing it tonight? If not, I am! It'll look great against this dark skin."

She winked cheekily and continued her perusal through my closet.

James and Odie had previously declared my closet and makeup "The Shop."

James was a fellow lover of clothes and had nearly fainted when she'd seen my neat-but-well-appointed closet. And Odie had been able to name the maker of all my cosmetics when I didn't know some of the brands myself.

I'd explained it away with a simple, "My sister has a good job and she and I are the same size." Then I'd added, "She orders her clothes in bulk and gives me lots of things."

There was no need for them to know that the ordering happened from the best couturiers in Paris, Milan, London, and sometimes from the seamstress we employed. My clothes didn't have labels on them—since I was young, they'd been removed when they arrived.

I waved to the closet from my spot on the bed, indicating James should take whatever she wished to wear.

As she grabbed the top, she looked at me with that gleam in her eye. The one that I was learning meant trouble and said, "Speaking of things I *do* want to talk about . . . What was little Daisy Paxton doing with big fa-fa-fa-fine Trevor when I walked up?"

"Nothing at all," I said sighing.

"That don't sound like a 'nothing' sigh to me," Odie teased.

I looked back at my two friends staring expectantly at me.

No. Not expectantly, knowingly.

"Trevor . . . is . . ."

How could I describe Trevor?

Trevor was remarkable. He was so much more than just a handsome face. I hadn't expected the funny. Or the sweet. And he was so clever. I thought of the nonsensical facts he'd come up with during my tour and the advice he'd given me on how to talk to professors, how to keep up with my course schedule, how to get ahead of my assigned reading. He'd also shared more about himself, his life . . . It had been lovely. *He* was lovely.

"Nice," I settled on.

"Oh yes!" Odie said. "I bet he is vera vera nice," she purred in her soft soprano.

I burst into giggles. "In all seriousness, he is very smart and generous with his time."

James opened her mouth to make join in teasing me and I raised my voice to say, "And he is my *mentor.*"

"All right now! Your mentor? Exactly what is he supposed to be showing you? Something *big* I hope," James said shimmying her shoulders up and down.

"Jesus, James! Does everything have to be that way with you?"

"Oh, Daisy, it's that way with everybody, I'm just *honest about it.*"

"He's my mentor since I'm double majoring and he's double majoring. My advisor appointed him and neither of us knew the other was the person we'd been paired with. That is all that is going on."

I wasn't sure if I was trying to convince myself or them, and by the look they both gave me, they knew it.

CHAPTER TEN

Daisy

When we arrived at the mixer it was well underway. That was to say, we were late.

And not the fashionable kind of late either. Or maybe we were "fashionably late" in the truest sense of the word . . . because the reason that we were so late could be summed up in two words:

James Jones.

She had first tried on my cheetah bra-top paired with my white chiffon bell-bottoms that billowed beautifully at the bottom. She'd torn those off in a fit and put on a purple minidress with a flaring cape, which she also rejected, saying she looked like "goddamn Lynda Carter and not in a good way." After that, she had tried her orange jumpsuit, stripping it off almost immediately after she put it on, saying she looked fat.

I'd had to bat down Odie's hand as she reached toward the back of James's neck. James had been way too absorbed in rifling through her own clothes to even notice Odie's momentary consternation and attempted strangulation but the look dear Odie gave her back was enough to make me worry that James would end up looking like a clown during the makeup portion of our preparations.

She finally ended up rocking a denim jumpsuit that dipped almost to her navel—hers—and python print platforms—mine. She pulled her hair up into a giant curly puff—she'd slicked her baby hair down—and she topped it all off with a gold chain that dangled low between her bosom.

James was a fly dresser. But tonight she hadn't opted for *fly* at all; tonight it was pure foxy.

Odie worked her usual makeup magic, lining James's eyes with heavy black eyeliner and a coral lip.

So yeah, no other word but foxy would suffice.

I'd opted for the shortest cream shorts I'd ever donned in my life and the rejected cheetah bra-top. I paired it with knee-high patent leather red boots. I let my hair fly free like it'd been doing all day, threw on some pink lipstick, lashes, a bit of blue mascara, and called it a day—or rather, a night.

Odie wore high-waisted, five-button bell-bottom jeans, and a cropped peasant top that showed off just the tiniest bit of her midsection when she moved. Her makeup was flawless as usual, her blue eyeshadow never out of place.

In short, we looked *fine*.

The mixer was in the same location behind the administration building as the cookout the day before. We could hear faint music and chatter, as we'd dressed with the window open, and the disc jockey was still spinning tunes as we approached. The sun was sinking below the horizon, getting to the time of the day where everything looks just a little purple as day wanes to night.

The lamps that dotted the street were starting to blink to life as we headed toward the tables set at the far side of the grass. James's fashion show had caused us to miss dinner in the caf and now I was a little hungry.

A long low whistle from somewhere to my right and as I looked over. I caught Trevor leaning idly watching the scene unfold: the girl who was being whistled at by the nearby guy rolled her eyes and kept on strutting.

My stomach fluttered with the butterflies I'd tried to capture, tried to smother. He'd changed clothes; he now wore a simple black T-shirt with his fraternity insignia in gold and jeans. But the way he wore it made my mouth go dry. The T-shirt stretched over his broad shoulders and was tucked into his jeans to show off his narrow waist. Those jeans confirmed what I felt earlier: his thighs were built of hard muscle and were magnificent.

Our eyes met, his amber to my chocolate brown, and I stopped breathing.

I wasn't sure how long we stared at one another with the world spinning on its axis and everyone else turning right along with it. In that moment there was only him, and I might have stayed stuck there forever if not for the whisper at my side.

"Looks like your tutor wants to teach you something."

I blinked the world back into focus and saw James at my side smiling like she stole a car.

I shot her a look warning her to behave and couldn't help but correct her. "Mentor, not tutor. I don't need him to teach me anything."

"You sure about that?" Odie eyed me skeptically.

"Oh no, Odessa Mae! Et tu, Odie?" I gasped theatrically.

I heard her faint laughter over the sounds of LaBelle singing about some truly scandalous acts.

"Don't look now, but I think your mentor is coming this way. *Vou-vou-whoo-you say avec moi?*" James sang huskily, raising her eyebrows playfully and butchering the French lyrics for . . . well never mind what she was singing.

James laughter died suddenly as I heard a voice say, "You are beautiful."

We both turned and saw Julian, black horned-rimmed glasses

gleaming in the dim light. He was wearing a shirt similar to Trevor's, except where Trevor's was black with gold letters, Jules' was gold with black lettering, the reversal of coloring seeming somewhat indicative of their personalities.

It was a real shame Julian was a waste of a perfectly good pretty face. There really was no other way to describe him. Trevor was handsome, but Julian was pretty. And somehow being out of their dress shirts made them both *more* attractive. They looked younger, more accessible.

I saw the flare in James eyes before she schooled her expression like a pro and I mentally gave her a hip bump.

That's it, stick girl. Don't let him see any emotions.

"You are beautiful, James," Jules repeated, more sure of himself now. "Full stop. No qualifiers. You may be the most gorgeous girl I've ever seen. You look amazing tonight, and you looked amazing earlier. And I'm sorrier than you'll ever know that I said something so ugly and hurtful to you earlier." I reached for her hand the way she'd done the first time we'd seen this beautiful, poisonous boy at in front of Spence.

Jules was all dewy eyes, the kind that looked a bit like the person might cry. Combined with the way he wholly owned what he had said to James melted my anger.

James squeezed my hand so lightly it was barely noticeable.

Trevor's voice cut through the tension of the moment startling me. "Daisy, would you like to get some punch with me?"

"I would love to." My response was automatic.

I went to take a step but James's hand squeezed mine a little tighter.

Dammit! I couldn't leave James.

So cool it seemed the ambient temperature had dropped, I heard James say, "I do not forgive people, Julian P. Marshall, and you are no exception."

Then James let go of my hand, offered her most brilliant smile to

Trevor and said, "Now what's that you said about us all getting punch?"

Trevor

Breathtaking. That's the only word for how Daisy looked. The teeny-tiny short-shorts that she was wearing were short-circuiting my brain and my willpower.

Jules and I had reached an agreement whereby we both agreed to do the right thing.

He would apologize to James, and I . . . I would stay away from Daisy. Except when mentoring her.

His apology had seemed real to me, though the wet eyes were a bit much. If it hadn't been for our conversation I wouldn't have even suspected him of being disingenuous. I leaned toward believing he was actually sorry because he'd looked like he had been slapped when James brushed him off. Either way, it didn't matter. I didn't care if I'd gotten through to him. I didn't care he meant it—I cared that he'd said it.

We were supposed to have been long gone from this shindig but Daisy and James and their other friend whose name I couldn't remember had taken forever to turn up.

It was worth the wait. They looked like three stone-cold brick-houses.

That's beside the point, I reminded myself. The point was there was no way I was letting the sun set with this ugliness between James and Julian still hanging in the air.

It was the right thing to do.

But that's not why you twisted his arm to do it. You did that because Daisy was upset and something inside you balked at her ever being upset or hurt or afraid or anything other than completely blissed out.

I eyed her legs in those boots. I could think of one hundred ways I could bliss her out tonight.

No, you're going to say goodbye to her. You're going to let her know that you're busy and you're going to keep your word, because that is what you do, Trevor.

I'd given Julian my word and it was my bond. It was absolute; I never broke it. Julian knew that more than anyone. He'd seen the consequences of broken promises, same as me.

We reached the station and I doled out three cups of punch, regretting that this was a school sponsored affair. I could've used a real drink, and it would've been nice if the punch had a hit of scotch, or better yet, bourbon.

I handed the ladies their cups of virgin punch.

Julian was making small talk with a group of eager freshman girls but every few moments his eyes flickered in our direction. I knew what he was trying to convey—it was time to go. He'd done his part. Now it was my turn.

"Daisy, may I speak to you for a moment?"

She looked up at me wide-eyed, wild haired, and smiling shyly.

Why does it feel like you're breaking up with her? You've just met her. She's not yours.

I sobered at that thought.

She's not mine.

She never would be mine, not as long as I was at Fisk.

Something in me cracked at the thought. There was something about Daisy. She just drew me in; she drew everyone in. I thought about the way I'd seen her with her friends, how protective and furious she'd been on James's behalf. How her friends seemed to gravitate around her. There was just something about her gentle spirit that made people feel welcome. The idea of being so near her all year without truly being allowed to bask in her warmth felt bleak. It felt like intentionally depriving myself of the sun.

We meandered away from the crowd slowly, my steps leaden with dread. We made our way to the other side of the grass, exited the lawn, and walked a few paces on the sidewalk. The sound of the music and the crowd faded. My fingers trailed along the warm brick wall that separated us from the party a few feet away. I stopped under the shadow of a massive, mossy oak tree.

In a move that surprised me, Daisy stepped behind me and launched herself on the wall with impressive agility. She sat perched there, my fairy, my diminutive goddess, swinging her legs and searching my face with those *eyes*.

It's too soon. I can't say goodbye. I need more time.

The streetlamps set her gorgeous hair ablaze, revealing all its secrets to me.

The space around us—between us—was quiet except for a few lonely notes from the Chi-Lites singing about being in trouble if their girl left them.

I can relate.

My heart was already hammering so that when she touched my shoulder and looked at me smiling shyly, I was undone. We were nearly face-to-face with her sitting high on that wall like a queen come to conquer. I knew what I should do.

I absolutely did.

But I didn't.

I *couldn't*.

"Go out with me," I blurted.

The grin on her face was immediate.

I grabbed the tip of one of the fluffy coils that rioted around her shoulders and wrapped it around my fingers.

It was only fair. She'd already wrapped me around her fingers.

"On a date?" she questioned sweetly.

I nodded, my voice having abandoned me.

Her smile bloomed. "Yes, of course."

Her acquiescence coursed through me like an elixir. Daisy said yes, to *me*.

I felt drunk and sobered all at once.

Those magnets she called eyes seized me for a moment and I sucked in air, trying to do the right thing, trying to make it right even though it was a lost cause.

I couldn't have broken eye contact in that second if my life depended on it.

Logically I knew it was way too soon for me to be so taken with her, but I wasn't running on logic right now.

Logic can get stuffed.

She squeezed my shoulder and slid her hand to my neck still staring into my eyes. And that small, innocent touch was enough to make me suddenly, painfully hard.

My body temperature rose all at once in a way I'd never experienced.

I was on fire.

I couldn't think.

I couldn't see anything that wasn't *her*.

For the second time that day, I heard Daisy's breath hitch in anticipation.

Pulling away wasn't an option.

I leaned in and captured her lips, just a soft, sweet press of her lips against mine.

Then she opened for me and her tongue darted out quickly, teasing mine.

It was enough to send me into overdrive.

I was frantic to feel the friction of her tongue against mine.

I wanted to kiss her neck, to place soft kisses over both her eyelids. I wanted to kiss her forehead in a way that would let her know she was all that was on my mind.

I was desperate to feel her pressed against me. I was desperate for her.

"Trevor, you ready to go?"

I jumped back. And I dropped my head low at the sound of my best friend's voice.

"Yeah, gimme a minute," I said, not turning to see his face.

I knew it would be twisted in disappointment.

I took a deep breath and exhaled. A portion of my sanity returned and with it a slither of dread.

What had I done?

I'd broken my word. *I never broke my word.*

Your word was all a man had.

But maybe there was more than one right thing. Maybe there was a way. I needed time to think, time to make this right. And I couldn't do that and be around Daisy. Spending the whole week around her—and not touching—her felt impossible now that I know she wanted me too.

And so I told her the smallest of lies, and I hated it.

"Listen, I have to go. I may be a little hard to get up with this week with my work-study and all. I will . . . I will meet you at Harris on Friday at six to take you out, okay?"

Daisy smiled and nodded. She still looked a little dazed and a lot hot. I knew I should leave but before I did, I swiped my thumb across her nose and kissed her forehead, eliciting a soft gasp from her. I pulled her into a hug, inhaled her scent, and allowed myself to be drunk for just a moment on Daisy.

Daisy

Burning.

Trevor's kiss—just the slightest press of lips had burned.

Was it possible for lips to feel singed?

I didn't know the answer but I was still on fire as I turned to leave. Trevor watched me from his place in the shadows as I rejoined the party. I knew I should feel ashamed for sneaking off from my first college social with a boy. But I couldn't find my way past the heat and the giddiness coursing through my veins.

As I made my way over across the grass and approached my friends, James eyed me suspiciously.

I held my out my palms in a conciliatory manner and offered her a sheepish smile. She couldn't have seen us kiss. No one had. Well, no one but Julian. But somehow she seemed to know.

"Have a good *talk* with your mentor?" James asked.

Odie stood, resting her head on James's shoulders and batted her eyelashes at me. "You look a little overheated, Daize. All that . . . talking?"

"Shut up." I grinned. "He asked me out," I said softly. Dreamily.

"Of course he did, beautiful," James said laughing. "Anyone with eyes could see you two have *chemistry.*"

Chemistry. I'd never thought about it like that, but that's exactly what it was. We were elements and whatever this was, it was causing a reaction.

"This is cause for a celebration!" Odie declared as I rolled my eyes.

"We're going on a date, not getting hitched," I reminded her.

"Not yet," she teased in a sing-song voice.

She stepped forward, grabbed my hand, and pulled me onto the grass near the speakers.

We bumped and we boogied and we got on down. We laughed—oh, how we laughed—as Odie broke into the Bus Stop halfway through Stevie Wonder's "Don't You Worry 'Bout a Thing."

Up until that point, most of our peers seemed to be content standing in little clusters around the perimeter of the lawn but once we began to dance they started to migrate over, gyrating, snapping, and groovin' to the beat.

Odie's soft smile found mine and she said, "See, everybody wants to dance. All it takes is a few brave souls."

––––––––––––

Later that night Odie and James lay draped across the bed they'd claimed as their own, too tired to go back to their own rooms.

"I'm huuuungry," James whined.

I shot her a look. "You're the reason we missed dinner, James. By the time we got to the mixer all the free food was gone."

I smiled at the thought. Trevor had been right. Free food did not last around college students. I wondered what other tidbits I'd learn from him this semester.

"I knoooow but I'm still hungry."

I took pity on her. "Stop your moaning. I'll feed you." I climbed from my spot on the opposite bed and moved to get my supplies.

"How?" she asked hopefully, lifting just her head from the bed.

"I think I danced my soles off. Not my shoes, my actual feet," Odie whined.

"I have something for that too," I said throwing her a tin of *Dr. Brother's Get on the Good Foot* cream.

I slid a box from underneath my bed containing all the contraband I'd smuggled from home for just such an occasion, ignoring that *other* box.

I unpacked its contents as my friends stared on—a hot plate, a skillet, and a few cooking utensils.

"Daisy Paxton, you're a miracle worker."

I bristled a little at my fake last name. For a moment I wanted to tell them everything.

These are your real friends, Daisy. You don't have to keep this a secret from them.

It's too soon. What if it changes things? You can't tell them now.

For the first time in my life I was Daisy, just Daisy. And things were as wonderful as I'd dreamed they could be. If I had to fib a *little* about my last name and my hometown, then that was a small price to pay for having friends who loved me for me. Besides, my friends would understand.

I'll make them understand. And then we will all have a laugh about that crazy time I changed my last name.

I would tell them before the end of the semester.

"Earth to Daize!" Odie's sweet soprano cut through. "Whatcha thinking about, Daisy? Or should I ask who?" she teased.

I realized I'd been holding my breath and absently staring at my mini-fridge. My hands fluttered to life grabbing the cheese, ham, and bread and, with a smile that didn't feel quite as natural as the one before it, I announced, "Hot ham and cheese for dinner and then . . ." I dug into the small freezer compartment and pulled out a saran wrapped packet. "Homemade cookies!"

"What the hell, Daisy? You got a hat stand and an umbrella that can make you fly in there too?" James asked incredulously. "Where did you get cookie dough?"

"Oh. I bake."

"You bake?"

I pulled foil from the box and snatched off a piece with a satis-fying *zzrrrrpp*!

"Yes, I bake. I love to bake. In fact, I love it so much I'm majoring in home economics."

"Business too, right? You could open a bakery!" James declared, answering her own question.

I wrinkled my nose and she laughed.

"I'm not sure I'd like that at all. People popping in for a second and just grabbing their goods and going? Using me to get what they want and then leaving straight after." I sniffed. "I am not sure I'm that kind of girl."

James and Odie exchange looks of wide-eyed surprise at my scandalous joke.

I smiled widely, proudly.

They burst into laughter.

This. This was what I wanted. I wanted to make food and bring people together. I wanted to laugh with them and tend to them.

I plopped the sandwich I'd assembled and wrapped in foil onto the hot plate. I grabbed the iron from my closet, wrapped the face in foil, and turned in on.

And I don't want to work at that damned Mill.

I pressed the iron down on top of the sandwich cooking on the hot plate.

I knew my family expected me to follow in Dolly's footsteps and join her at Payton Mills, especially since our brother was gone.

It was in the Mill charter that the Mill could not be sold and majority ownership could not be transferred. It had to stay within our family.

My sister could've left Green Valley.

She could've left everything to my father and the trustees but Dolly was big on legacy and, for better or worse, the Mill was ours.

I sighed and then chastised myself.

Stop being ungrateful, Daisy. The Mill has provided a great life for you. It's given you opportunities that most people never, ever get. Most people were figuring out what they wanted to do, whereas I had my life preplanned for me. See! No work. So blessed.

I sighed. I was being ungrateful still.

It wasn't that I hated the Mill. I just didn't love it.

It was loud and busy and serious.

People got hurt if you were not paying attention. It was no place for goofing around, because being playful could be deadly.

And I didn't want to spend all my days being serious.

So no, I did not hate the Mill. I just wanted something different for myself.

"What are you doing to that previously delicious sandwich?" James asked bewildered.

"Oh, we don't have a grill so I'm making a panini press with the iron," I said a little absently.

"A pay-wha-dee?"

"Panini. They're these delicious sandwiches my sister and I had when we went on vacation one year in . . ."

Rome.

I couldn't tell them we holidayed in Rome; that would lead to too many questions.

Too many lies. Better to fix it with one small one.

"Oh, you've caught me. My sister and I made these sandwiches up. But trust me they're really good."

"What on earth," James said skeptically, "would possess you and your sister to put a clothes iron on a sandwich?"

I rolled my eyes and ignored her. "Just try it." I set the iron down and opened the foil to reveal a perfectly golden, pressed hot ham and cheese sandwich.

I dropped Odie's on the hot plate next.

James didn't wait.

She took a bite of the sandwich and moaned in delight.

"Now what was that you were saying about me and my sister?" I raised my eyebrows.

"Apologies! Your weirdo iron sandwiches are *divine*." She moaned again adding, "I'll eat them any day."

She took another big bite and had to *ha-ha-hah* it with her mouth open to avoid burning her tongue in her eagerness.

"That must be some sandwich," Odie laughed.

A few moments later I pulled hers off the hot plate, slid it onto a waiting plate, and handed it to her.

She took a small bite and her face spit into a grin.

"Daisy, you domestic goddess! You're a regular Julia Child!"

I put my own sandwich on and then began to break the cookie dough into rough chunks. Odie and James stared, amazed.

I pulled my sandwich off after a few moments and added a little butter to the skillet before returning it to back to the hot plate for the butter to melt. When it was hot, I dropped in a few pieces of the dough while I munched my sandwich.

Odie and James waited for the cookies to be finished like kids on Christmas, asking every thirty seconds if they could eat the dough yet.

The familiar smell of baked goods wafted through my room and I was reminded of my mother. A sudden bout of melancholy threatened to swamp me, but the laughter of my friends and their chatter grounded me.

BOOM, BOOM, BOOM!

There was a knock, or rather several knocks, at the door.

We all stiffened.

If that was a room check I was dead. We were all dead. I couldn't put the hot plate away; it was too hot. And we couldn't cover it either.

James saw my wide, panicked expression and jumped into action.

"Yes?" she croaked sounding sleepy and giving me a helpless shrug.

"This is Diana and Ruth from down the hall . . ."

James cracked the door open and we saw the two girls standing there in PJs, slippers, and bonnets.

"Are y'all . . .? Is someone baking cookies? The hall smells amazing and I'm hungry," Diana said hopefully.

James laughed and opened the door.

"I hope you've got enough for two more."

I smiled, relived and happy.

I had more than enough.

This was more than enough.

CHAPTER ELEVEN

Trevor

I awoke on Friday ebullient.

My mind hadn't had an idle second since departing from Daisy at the mixer four nights prior. It'd been filled to the brim planning how I could walk the delicate tightrope of supporting Elodie while moving forward with Daisy. Because after our kiss—brief and sweet as it may have been—moving forward without her was out of the question.

It had taken two days, but I'd finally figured it out. There was way for everyone to get what they wanted.

Jules had been distant and stonily silent most of the week, but he'd agreed to let me borrow his car all day. He'd left the keys on the countertop and was already gone when I headed out around eleven a.m.

Deciding it would be a day for indulgences—dinner with Daisy being the finest one—I made my way to the barbershop in town treat myself to a professional haircut. I was man enough to admit that I wanted to look my best for her and if that meant spending a few dollars, then so be it. I also wanted to make Daisy smile. We'd passed a particularly pretty flower bed during our campus tour on Monday and she'd oohed and ahhed at the blooms.

I'd been delighted at her joy and couldn't stop myself from teasing. "I'm sure you're used to having flowers placed at your feet all the time. The guys back home were probably tripping all over themselves to present you with bouquets."

She'd rolled those gorgeous eyes and retorted, "Ha! Does my father count? That's the only man that's ever given me flowers."

The guys from her hometown must've been blind or idiots. I told her that and she'd laughed. Memory of her smile had me grinning as I made my way into the local florist shop.

I'd cajoled her into telling me her favorite flowers were peonies but to my disappointment they were out of season. Maybe, if things went well between us, I could save up a few dollars and return in the spring to buy her some.

I would definitely need to save up.

I made my way back home a short time later with a dozen long-stemmed roses and my pockets *significantly* lighter. I shook my head at my antics. I was breaking all my rules for Daisy.

And it didn't bother me one bit.

I headed into my kitchen to set the flowers in some water. I glanced at the clock on the stove and saw that I had about two hours and forty-five minutes until my date with Daisy. Not that I was counting the seconds or anything. I estimated that I had time to take a brief nap, shower, then dress and head to Harris to meet Daisy.

I headed to my room with sleep on my mind, opened up my door and . . . froze.

My best friend sat atop my bed with *his* best friend.

"Hello, darling," Elodie purred without missing a beat, while leveling me with a look.

I took two steps back in surprise.

Jules said nothing. He just squinted at me, eyes narrowed in warning. He stood, gave his cousin a hug, and left the room. He closed the door behind him, presumably to give Elodie and me privacy.

El dropped her act.

"What's going on?" she demanded quietly. I understood the reason for her hushed tone. Julian had left the room, but who was to say he wasn't right outside the door?

"I—I—you weren't supposed to come back until Sunday," I stammered, still trying to get my bearings. I was going to kill Jules. The last thing I needed was Elodie showing up now.

"Trevor. What is going on?" she repeated.

"Did Julian call you? If so, he shouldn't have. He should've minded—"

"*Julian* shouldn't have? Let's maybe pause on what Jules should and shouldn't do and talk about you—besides it wasn't just Julian. He was just the last straw."

I struggled to find the words I'd rehearsed in my head a hundred times this week.

"I met someone," I blurted.

"So I've heard."

"I was going to tell you."

Elodie's voice held a touch of frustration and sadness when she spoke again. "You don't have to do this you know. You're standing there like a caught philanderer. I feel like we're acting now even when there's no one around but us. Is that what we've become? Nothing but an act?"

"*No,*" I countered immediately. The shock of her sudden appearance wore off upon hearing the hurt her words carried. "How can you say that? You know you're like a sister to me."

She shrugged in response. Then added, "Come sit. Let's talk this out." She gestured to my desk chair across from the bed.

Elodie and Julian shared more than similar looks as cousins. They both acted like they owned every room they walked in to, even if the room was yours. The irony of Elodie giving me permission to sit down at my desk, in my own room, wasn't lost on me as I made my way from the door and sat on the edge of the wooden chair.

"Trevor, Jules called me on Wednesday and told me he needed my help with preventing you from doing something colossally stupid. He explained that I needed to get back to campus as soon as possible. He was—is—legitimately worried about you. You know how he feels about women being taken advantage of. He said you're so far outside your character he feels like he doesn't even know you."

I groaned.

"In addition to Jules calling me, I've been contacted by no less than four sorority sisters asking if everything is okay between us."

My eyes bugged out of my head. *Did people have nothing better to do?*

"Now I am asking you, my oldest and dearest friend, what is going on?"

"I met a girl and I'm crazy about her. I'm taking her on a date tonight. This wasn't how I intended for you to find out that I wouldn't be able to keep up my end of the bargain. But I can't. I need to—if you met her . . . She's special." The words poured out on a rush.

She exhaled slowly. "I was hoping you *wouldn't* say that."

I hurried to make my case. "I've been thinking about it a lot and, El, we were going to end our charade in May anyway. Moving it up a few months won't hurt anything. Besides the girls that started that rumor about you have all graduated and—"

"I agree," she said simply.

"You—you agree?"

"Yes, I agree, Trevor. Even if you hadn't met anyone, I am *not* May. I know what it's like to have a 'relationship' forced on you just to keep up appearances."

Shit, she did.

"I would *never* do that to you. Gracie and I would've just been even more cautious whenever we were together. I never asked you to do this in the first place. You *volunteered.*"

I closed my eyes in relief. I hadn't given Elodie enough credit. It wasn't that I thought she would be against my being with Daisy, per se . . . I just hadn't trusted that she would be okay with prematurely ending our agreement. Before my brief calm could take hold, she pierced my joy.

"There's just one problem."

My eyes flew to hers.

"You didn't tell me about this plan!" Her tone was exasperated and the redness that appeared when she was angry started to show through.

"I was going to tell you on Sunday when you got back."

"Sunday? Trevor, did it never occur to you that Sunday would be too late?"

I didn't know what she meant, precisely. It had occurred to me that Sunday would be too late for Elodie to try to pressure me into continuing our arrangement. By that time my date with Daisy would've already occurred and falling back into the status quo would have been untenable.

Elodie exhaled a deep breath. "Trevor . . . can you even imagine what it feels like to have your love life scrutinized all the time? Of how many girls are jealous of me because of you? Of how many were waiting for the day they could gleefully call me to inform me that my time with you was up?"

I knew Elodie bore the brunt of the speculation about our relationship. She'd told me once that women got questioned about their love lives in a way no one would dare do to a man. But I did know what it was like to have people sticking their nose in your business.

As evidenced by the fact that we are having this conversation now and not on Sunday. "I've been in this thing with you for three years now, haven't I?" I reminded her.

She snorted. "Then you had to have known that this would get back to me. And you had to have known that I would deny it!"

I knew people talked. I just didn't think word would have travelled as fast as it did. I honestly couldn't see why anyone would care enough to call her on . . .

Wait, deny it? My stomach dropped.

"I've spent the last couple of days categorically denying that anything—anything—untoward was going on with you and Daisy." Elodie hissed urgently.

"Why would you do that?" My voice was harsh and laced with panic. I saw where this was going, and it made my heart race and my mouth dry.

"Because I *didn't* think there was anything going on between you and Daisy! Trevor, there are three people in the world I trust. My girl-friend Gracie, my cousin Julian, and you. Why on earth would I believe what anyone said about you, knowing what I know about how destructive rumors are?"

Her words were like a sock to the gut, but she wasn't near finished.

She paused to take a deep breath. When she spoke again her voice was nearly a whisper. "Surely, if my dearest friend had found someone he would've told me."

I winced at the hurt in her voice.

"Unless he didn't trust me." Her eyes met mine and I could see all the hurt and accusation in them.

I hung my head, ashamed, as silence fell between us. She was right. I hadn't trusted her not to put my own interest over her own; in my experience people rarely did that.

"I thought, if nothing else, we had trust between us. Especially since I've given you all my secrets."

I fucked up.

"I messed up." I was only beginning to realize just how badly I'd messed up. Not just with Elodie but with Daisy. "I'm sorry. You're right, I should've told you."

My heart rate had begun to tick up as the size of my miscalcula-tion sank in. My mistrust had backed us into a corner where my original plan—to simply pretend that we'd broken up over the summer and both moved on to other people—wouldn't work.

Oh my God. What if someone tells Daisy Elodie is my girlfriend? I flinched, physically recoiling at the idea.

She exhaled wearily. "So now what are we going do?"

My mind spun trying to figure out a way to save the situation.

Elodie's words reverberated through my entire being.

What was I going to do?

How would I fix this? I either had to make Daisy look like a fool, or Elodie a liar.

Or . . .

There was a third option.

My head snapped up and I looked at Elodie, whose posture was suddenly ramrod straight. Her eyes were narrowed at me as if she was preparing for a battle and I was a target she needed to annihilate.

"Let me tell her the truth, Elodie. The whole truth."

CHAPTER TWELVE

Daisy

On Friday morning I awoke for the first time ever with breathless anticipation.

I don't think I really even knew what the term meant before this week.

Because, Lord, *Lord,* did Trevor ever make me breathless.

The term breathless was invented for Trevor and the word anticipation was created for when one has been waiting a whole week for a date with Trevor.

True to his word, Trevor hadn't been around all week.

I'd seen a few glimpses of figures from afar that could have been him, but I couldn't tell. I hadn't seen him and we hadn't spoken since the night of the kiss.

The kiss.

Just a touch of lips really, but that didn't stop it from being on constant replay in my mind.

And the way he'd kissed my forehead at the end? *Sigh.* Somehow that kiss had been even more intimate than the one on the lips.

That kiss felt like a confession.

Like he wanted me to be his, like he was saying he was mine.

You want him to be yours.

I rolled my eyes at how far I'd travelled mentally in a week. Because Dolly had been wrong; Trevor was definitely the right sort. And there was nothing wrong with getting to know a wonderful gentleman in addition to mastering my schoolwork. In Trevor's case the two things wouldn't even be in competition since he was my mentor. Even with all those positives I reminded myself to take it slowly. There was no rush. We had all semester; all year, really.

And tonight? Well I wasn't going to overthink tonight.

Correction, I wasn't going to overthink tonight *anymore*. I'd spent all week going through every possible scenario for how the evening could play out.

I'd fretted myself out.

Therefore, I'd just go with it.

James and Odie would meet me in my room at 4:45 when they got back from dinner. I would be skipping dinner as I would be eating later. On my date. *With Trevor.*

I couldn't help it. Breathless.

I didn't know who was more excited about this date: me or my friends.

Definitely me. But still, it was great to have friends that were excited with me. James because I trusted her fashion sense even though I had insisted on final veto power over wardrobe choices. Odie was over the moon because I was finally relenting and letting her try her hand at my makeup.

"I prefer *understated*," I'd stressed.

She'd rolled her eyes then retorted, "You prefer beautiful and you'll look that either way."

Distracted by thoughts of tonight, it took me a moment to realize that something was going on outside.

I peeked out my bedroom window and witnessed a miracle. Where freshman move in day had been chaos, this was a waltz.

I heard folks yelling for their friends to "Hurry the hell up," or "Slow down for a second!"

I saw ABC boxes, moving boxes, and bankers' boxes being handed from friend to friend and carried into Crosthwaite Hall. I saw folks unloading duffel bags, dragging over-stuffed clothes hampers that over, carrying lamps, and struggling with steamer trunks all on their own.

Students were balancing boxes on their shoulders or setting them briefly on the ground, pausing to dap their friends up or hug them in greeting.

What I didn't see during this move in?

Confusion.

There were no fretting parents, no children running free, and no students wandering around lost and overwhelmed.

Everyone moved with purpose and surety.

I was wrong on my first day.

We're not the adults; *they're* the adults. There were probably four times as many upperclassmen moving in and half the support staff roaming around.

I turned at the sound of my door opening and saw Odie fly in excitedly.

"Lucy's here! Lucy's here! Come on, you've gotta come meet her."

I smiled at her enthusiasm. "All right. Who is Lucy?"

She stared at me blankly. "I can't believe I haven't mentioned her. She's only my very best friend from back home."

James was conspicuously absent as we headed over to Crosthwaite to meet Lucy.

Odie shrugged when I mentioned it to her. "Checked her room earlier. Her roommate said she wasn't there and she did not know where she'd gone or when she'd return."

"Should we be concerned?"

James's roommate Lolanda was eccentric, and the pair did *not* get along. Her roommate couldn't take a joke.

If you said something funny like "well, I'll be a monkey's uncle," she'd respond with, "While primates and homo sapiens share a common ancestor they are too genetically dissimilar to ever mate. Even if they were able to mate, the likelihood of carrying viable offspring to term is next to none, making it unlikely that you become the uncle of a monkey. Furthermore, and admittedly, I have no empirical evidence, but given our current living situation, I am operating on the belief that your sex is female. That would make the English relational pronoun aunt. So even if you were able to overcome any genetic barriers, you'd still be a monkey's aunt." And then she would inevitably crack a big smile that would fall by degrees as silence filled the room.

Yep. Like I said—eccentric.

Odie threw me a look and shook her head.

"Probably. But in all seriousness, she probably just went to Spence early to grab something to eat. You know James can eat her body weight in food and never gain a pound."

We arrived at Odie's friend's room and the door was wide open, boxes and one duffle bag dotting the floor and an empty bed in the corner.

Lucy noticed me eyeing it and piped up. "Feel free to pop a squat. My roommate isn't coming back till Sunday night, just in time for class on Monday."

She stopped tucking the corners of the bedsheet and turned toward me, hand extended. "Lucille Love." She squinted her eyes and added, "If you make an *I Love Lucy* joke, we're not gonna be friends."

I flashed my broadest smile. She was funny but . . . Love?

Why did that last name sound familiar? When I really looked at her, I realized she had the same oval face, same deep-set brown eyes, and same sienna brown complexion as Charlie Love.

I could see her watching me put the pieces together. "You're Charlie's sister, right?" I blurted.

She rolled her eyes that looked just like his—or rather his eyes that looked like hers, as she had to be older—and sighed. "Guilty."

My head was spinning. Because if there was one thing I'd learned for certain over this past week, it was that Odie Mae hated Charlie Love completely.

Charlie had continued to plead for Odie's attention in great and small ways the entire week. And she had continued to operate as if he were invisible.

The only thing worse than watching Odie ignore Charlie was the few times she'd broken her silence and acknowledged him.

On Tuesday, she had leveled him with a glare and told Charlie, a biology major, that the mitochondrion in her body hated each and every mitochondrion in his body.

On Thursday, she told him she hated his cytoplasm too because there was no space in between her mitochondria that did not hate his guts.

It was awkward as hell but I watched with a kind of morbid curiosity. He seemed perfectly content to self-flagellate on the altar of Odessa and I knew there had to be more to the story than the nothing Odie had told us.

My curiosity exploded and my head bounced between Lucy and Odie in a way that felt cartoonish even to me. "Not to be too forward, but, um . . . how does that work?"

"What do you mean? Odie not speaking to Charlie and all?" Lucy shrugged half-heartedly. "Easy. We both think my brother's an idiot."

Odie cracked a smile but her eyes looked a little sad.

Lucy unpacked an 8-track player and popped in a tape.

Music filled the room the sound of the Shirelles crooning about boys kissing girls floated over us and Odie shot me a grin and wagged her eyebrows. I hid my face in the book I was putting away.

I stayed with Odie and Lucy for the rest of the morning listening to them trade stories about growing up in Charleston. There was something soothing about being in the company of friends that knew one another well. I was content to unpack knick-knacks and listen. They'd lived next door to one another their entire lives. Odie said she'd been more devastated when Lucy moved away to college than when her brother Buck had gone a year later.

"Oh! Remember when you and me and Charlie and Buck went to the fair and we ate so many of those dogs on a stick that I thought we were gonna be sick!"

They doubled over laughing.

"How about the time somebody put the snake in the cigar box stank-breath Mr. Turner kept in his desk drawer? Always smelling like those stinky cigars and getting right in your face."

"Somebody?" Odie asked her, raising her eyebrows dubiously. "We all know it was—"

"They never did catch who did it." Lucy sniffed.

I burst into laughter at Lucy's denial and Odie shook her head.

My stomach growled and I realized that I'd missed breakfast and was ravenous.

Odie looked up from where she sat on the floor organizing shoes under Lucy's bed, smiled, and shooed me with her hands.

"Get outta here, little helper. Me and Lucy have more catching up to do and you should eat."

We exchanged goodbyes and Lucy surprised me by giving me a hug and making me promise I'd visit her with Odie in the coming week.

I headed to the cafeteria, keeping a lookout for James, or if I was being honest, Trevor.

Wouldn't it be nice to run into him early? Maybe we could have lunch together and dinner together. Don't be greedy, Daisy, I reminded myself.

You'll see him for dinner. And you'll have all night.

Well not all *night,* I cringed, flustered. It wasn't going to be that kind of date.

Neither James nor Trevor were around and the cafeteria wasn't as crowded as I'd expected with all the other students returning today.

I found a table near the windows and dove into the roast beef sandwich they'd made from last night's pot roast.

After a while I got that familiar Green Valley lunchroom feeling and looked around to see if I was being watched. I told myself that I was being paranoid but when I looked over to my left, I saw that I was not.

Trevor was nowhere around but Julian—in all his beautiful, horrible glory—was sitting there staring at me.

Really staring. And not in a way that made me feel warm or hot and bothered; he was examining me. Eyes squinted, brows furrowed, head tilted, like I was the missing factor in an equation he was trying to solve. I didn't really know what to make of Julian. His apology seemed sincere but . . . first impressions were hard to overcome.

I stared back for a second widening my eyes meant to convey "stop staring at me." Usually being caught was all it took for a person to look away, but Julian, ever the rebel, just continued to stare.

After a moment I shrugged my shoulders, looked away, and returned to my sandwich. If Julian wanted to look at me there was nothing I could do about it. I'd mention it to Trevor later but I refused to let anything get in the way of me enjoying this day.

When I returned to Jubilee there was a note on my door from our dorm mother, Mrs. Johnson. The message inside was succinct.

"Call Dolly."

I'd elected to not have a phone in my room for this very reason. I didn't want Dolly calling me every day checking in.

I would call Dolly, later. I was sure she just wanted to see how I'd been settling in and I would happily tell her I was doing great. And she'd mentioned on the drive up that I'd need to call her to provide my student account number so she could wire my tuition payment.

So yes, I would call my sister but . . . not now.

Right now, I needed to set myself up for success. Taking a piece of advice Trevor had given me on Monday, I pulled the calendar off my desk, and began setting up blocks of study time, color coding by class to keep them straight.

He also mentioned that I should try to visit my teachers the first week during their office hours, introduce myself, let them know I was double majoring, and ask for tips on how to be successful in their class.

"Isn't that sucking up?" I'd playfully ribbed.

"Absolutely!" he said with a wink.

Then he added, "But seriously, professors usually go out of their way to help you. They don't get any benefit from seeing us fail and if they know you're double majoring they may give you tips on where to focus your attention. That will save you a world of time when it comes time for exams. Now don't get me wrong, some won't—I don't want you to think it's all roses—or should I say, daisies—all the time, but most will be very helpful."

My grin at his help, his concern, and his little joke had been enormous, and I'd thanked him for all his advice.

He'd bitten the left corner of his bottom lip and then he'd smiled and said, "Well thank you for your trust in me. I want you to know that I'm never going to steer you wrong, Daisy."

Those words had made my heart fly and blood rush everywhere.

I felt myself smile at the memories of that day for maybe the millionth time this week. The ridiculous conversation about popsicle sticks, our tumble into the grass, his kindness and intelligence, and the way he'd talked to me about student life had been little gifts that my mind opened at random intervals throughout the day.

I checked my watch again for the sixty-fourth time that day. It was only 2:46 p.m. Waiting another three hours and fourteen minutes to see him felt unbearable.

Therefore, a nap was in order.

Someone was shaking me. "Daize! Get up! It's almost five, you are going to be late!"

I gasped, sitting straight up.

"Well, she's up now," James said drily from somewhere in the room.

She was right, I was suddenly AWAKE.

It was time.

Actually, it was past time, I realized as Odie's words sank in. I tore my scarf from my head and jumped out of bed in one smooth motion.

In a rush, I began grabbing my things to head to the shower. Odie's stomach growled loudly and in the back of my mind her discomfort registered.

"Didn't you go to the cafeteria?"

"No," she said with an odd finality.

I paused one foot in and the other outside the door.

Concern for my friend warred with my need to jump in the shower. I debated if I'd have time to whip up something for her to eat really quickly.

"Long story and we don't have time for it right now. Go get in the shower," James added seeming to read my mind.

I took the quickest shower of my life and was back in my room ten minutes later.

I immediately began plying Odie with snacks; I did not want a hungry beautician doing my makeup.

While I'd been away, James had pulled one potential outfit off its hangers and tossed it haphazardly onto my bed. She was still inspecting another two.

"The ruffles on this one are going to make you look like a rejected member of The Jackson 5."

She tossed it on my bed.

Okay. Well, not that one then.

"I guess it's the red hotpants with the orange bra-top."

She was shaking her head before I'd finished the sentence.

"No. That's not going to work. You said you were going for hot and fun. You're not going to look hot, you're going to look like an actual flame if you wear those red pants with blue stitching and an orange top."

I grumbled. She was right but it was five fifteen and I didn't have time to look for a new outfit.

I was about to launch into defense of the ruffles when I saw that James was looking at me with that glint in her eye and then she smiled like she was up to absolutely no good.

Odie was munching on a breakfast bar and hiding a smile.

"What am I missing?" I said, tugging the ends of my robe a little tighter.

"Now don't be mad," James started, "but you've been excited about this all week. And well . . . you're the first one of us to go out on a real date. A *college date*. And maybe we got a little carried away . . ."

Odie chimed in excitedly, "We don't mean to pry. At all. And Lord knows we understand."

"What in the world are y'all talking about?"

Wearing secretive smiles, Odie and James ran to my closet and rummaged around before emerging, each concealing something behind their backs. With a flourish, Odie revealed a medium size bag and James a smaller one.

"We got you a gift! A new outfit for your date!" Odie said excitedly in her breathy voice.

"And shoes too!" James declared.

My face was frozen. I didn't know what to say or to do. And suddenly my eyes were glassy.

And then inexplicably I was crying, *hard*.

Now I usually preferred not to cry in front of people. I was an expert at delaying my feelings until I was alone or with my family where it was safe to feel vulnerable.

But these girls . . .

You feel safe with them.

"Oh Daisy, don't cry!" Odie said even more softly that usual as she looked at James with alarm.

And then suddenly my two friends were there surrounding me, hugging me.

"I'm sorry. This is just . . . this is the nicest thing anyone has ever done for me."

Anyone outside of my family, that is.

Someone buy me a gift?

The rich girl?

Please.

Never.

It wasn't even about the gift. It was the thoughtfulness that I appreciated.

"It's not charity, Daize, please don't cry," Odie pleaded.

"Charity?" I asked stepping back and taking a deep breath to quell my tears. They took a seat on their bed and I sat on mine, lovingly touching the braided straps of the bag marked Berkmann's.

"James and I . . . we noticed that you don't talk about your folks much, or where you're from or what they do. And we thought . . . Well, we both know what it's like to come from humble beginnings."

Oh no. A prickle of dread shot through me, making my stomach clench.

"You deserved to have something special for tonight. So we pooled our money."

175

Oh no.

Guilt cloyed at my throat making my heart race and my throat clog. I was struggling to breathe and the tears were back for a very different reason.

Tell them. Tell them. Tell them. My brain chanted.

I can't. Not now. Not after what they've done for me.

"Oh Daisy." I saw James exchange a sympathetic look with Odie and the tears I'd been holding back spilled over.

"There is no reason at all to feel ashamed," she said grabbing my hand and squeezing tightly.

Oh there is every reason in the world to feel ashamed. They've pooled their money together to buy something for me.

Oh no.

"This is what friends do for each other," she added trying to be helpful.

Tell them. Tell them!

They'll understand.

My friends looked at me with so much empathy, so much trust, and kindness.

And I realized I'd made a grievous mistake.

They won't understand. How could they?

The second jarring realization was that there was a Lie Meridian, an imaginary line which one crosses after telling a certain number of untruths that, once crossed, means revealing the lie cannot be navigated without hurt feelings and broken trust. The realization that I'd sailed past that line before I even knew it existed was earth-shattering.

I have to tell them, but not now. When I have time to explain and make my case, and definitely not right before this date. I will tell them later.

"Thank you," I managed to croak. "This is the nicest thing anyone has ever given me," I added, feeling like I owed them at least that truth.

Odie gave a relieved little laugh. "But you haven't even opened it yet, go on."

So I did.

What I pulled from the bag in delicate pink paper was the sexiest black jumpsuit I'd ever seen.

I let out an audible gasp at the soft silky material with a herringbone pattern. It had a deep V in the back almost down to the tailbone. But the front was modest with a keyhole cutout at the bosom and sweet bows on the shoulders.

"It's so gorgeous," I said touching it longingly, lovingly. "How much did it cost?" I demanded. Somehow I'd figure out a way to pay them back. Even if they never knew it was me.

"Nah-ah," Odie said in a sing-song voice. "It is remarkably bad form to tell how much a gift cost."

"It's bad form to ask too." James leveled me with a look and then burst into laughter.

"Besides it's not as bad as whatever you're thinking. James told me she charmed the pants off the sales guy, and I've seen the receipt —she ain't lying!"

James gave an unrepentant shrug.

"Now let's get you into this thing!" James said.

"*Don't* you move a muscle!" Odie commanded—well as commanding as Odie's voice got. "James, you just hold your horses. She won't be touching that outfit until I'm done with her. Jamesy, you do something different with her hair, while I do her face," Odie directed, going into full director mode.

I lay my gorgeous jumpsuit on my bed, tissue paper beneath it, and then plopped down on the bed opposite. James began grabbing hair pins from a ceramic dish on my dresser as Odie started laying out my makeup—plus things I'd never seen before that must've belonged to her. Odie's face, usually lit with a soft smile, took on an expression of intense concentration as she got to work on me.

While she worked, Odie told me everything I missed during my nap. After they'd finished unpacking, she and Lucy had headed to The Wall which, according to Lucy, was the place to be on Fridays. It had been crawling with folks, talking and catching up. Music played, fraternities and sororities stepped. There were even a few vendors selling food, drinks, and knick-knacks.

"And this happens every Friday?"

"Yes! Just about, while the weather holds. And Lucy told me there's a block party every Friday night. And lots of after-parties too. She told me about this club we have to try called The Met," she said waving her brush theatrically.

I laughed. "Okay, okay . . . but I wonder if I'll have time to fit in any school at all with this full semester of partying you have planned."

She bopped my forehead with a clean brush.

"Don't sass me, Daisy Paxton, I have your life in my hands right now!" Her eyes squinted menacingly.

I didn't know it was possible to love folks you weren't related to as much as I'd grown to love these girls. But maybe that's what real friendship was: people you found along the way that became your family.

I laughed a little at Odie's antics and James smacked my arm. "Hold still!" she ordered, tugging my hair.

"Ow!"

"It wouldn't hurt if you'd hold still!" she declared unapologetically.

"Odie, how much longer is it gonna take you to beat that face? I need her to put her head down for a few."

With her own tongue stuck out to the side, Odessa was using a brush to paint red lipstick onto my pursed lips.

"Awl . . . mosh . . . done!" she declared waving her hands with a flourish.

James immediately shoved my neck down and began applying pins with fury.

"James, hello! I have a scalp—Ow! That—"

She let go. "There! Good grief. Tender-headed people are so dramatic."

"Lemme see!" I said making grabby hands toward the mirror Odie was holding.

James snatched it. "Hell no! Put that outfit on. Nothing less than the full effect!"

I tried to make a beeline for the floor-length mirror near my closet but James was faster and blocked me.

"Five forty-eight!" Odie sang.

At that my heart slammed into my rib cage, doing a jig of antici-pation. *Da-da-da-dung-da-da-da-DUNG!* I tore off my robe and grabbed the garment from my bed.

Odie and James were on me as soon as I stepped into it, pulling up the front and tying the dainty bows at my shoulders, readjusting the fit at the waist.

They made me close my eyes as they placed me in front of the mirror.

"Oh my." I heard James say as I felt them withdraw.

"Open!" they declared in unison with smiles in their voices.

My eyes fluttered open—and I do mean flutter with the weight of the mascara Odie had applied—and then . . . my breath caught. The butterflies in the jar of no feelings?

Yeah, they'd tipped over the jar and were flying free.

I reached toward the mirror because I didn't want to touch my own face.

Oh my, was right.

Odie had gone for more subtle colors. She'd use a grayish, smoky shadow around my eyes that made the brown of my eyes pop. My lips were the most perfect shade of tempting red. My high cheekbones were highlighted and contrasted with my face, making me look more mature. And my outfit? It looked as if it was poured on me, made for me; it perfectly accentuated all my curves and dips.

For the first time *ever*, I looked sexy.

And I *felt* sexy.

My hair was pinned up in the back—all my coils pushed forward falling haphazardly around my face.

"I can't believe y'all made me look this beautiful."

I felt tears prickle my eyes again, but they were quelled by a warning glare from Odie.

"Daisy, I do *not* have time to fix your mascara if you run it. You wanna meet Trevor looking like a raccoon?"

All three of us laughed.

I sat on the bed and quickly unboxed my shoes—patent leather, black on black oxford brogues. I slid them on, tying them tight.

I took another deep breath, stood and pulled my best friends—*yes,* these girls were now my best friends—into a hug.

"Y'all are the best."

"We are," James agreed. "Now let's go get your man."

I was not used to being sexy.

Walking out of my dorm and down the hall I heard girls shout, "I see you now, Daisy," and, "All right now! Looking foxy."

I could feel my grin stiffen into a grimace because it was nice to be admired, but I also felt slightly embarrassed and a bit out of sorts.

How on earth does James deal with this all the time?

I shot her a glance and I saw her beam back at me knowingly.

While walking down the front drive painted with sorority and fraternity insignia, I was besieged by even more attention thrown my way. Random boys were whistling at me like I was a dog or yelling, "Mm Mmm MMMMmm," or, "What's your name, brickhouse?"

I smiled politely, uncomfortably, until I heard James whisper at my ear, "Don't smile, it'll only encourage them. Don't make eye contact. Don't frown. Keep your face perfectly neutral and don't respond. Do not even turn your head in the direction of the person. Act as if it's just us three here on a wonderful walk through our storied campus."

I nodded my comprehension and she gave me a sympathetic look.

We walked toward the music, where the day party had started to morph into the Friday night block party.

I had to walk through the party to get to the Harris Music Building and my friends decided to escort me that far since it was on their way to the cafeteria.

There were tons of people on the sidewalk and the street had been closed off, so folks spilled into the street too. The mood was festive, everyone enjoying their first weekend back at school after a long summer. The music got louder as we pressed through the crowd until we were right in the thick of it. People stopped to chat with each other or paused to buy food or trinkets from the vendors.

Sorority calls bounced off the walls and just about every frat was represented by boys wearing their colors or doing their calls. Sometimes they'd break out into a stroll, moving in syncopation while the crowd parted to let them through. I wondered if Trevor would be sad that he was missing the fun with his frat brothers.

"Odie Mae!" a voice yelled, and we all turned to see Lucy working her way toward us.

"Lucy!" Odie shouted in return greeting.

She waved in my direction then did a double take as recognition sunk in. "Daisy, Daisy, who you trying to let pick your petals tonight?"

I burst into laughter. "I owe you an *I Love Lucy* joke for that one."

She winked and we all resumed our walk together.

"Seriously did you get all dolled up for this?" She waved around and then gestured to her *Fiskite Forever* T-shirt and jeans. "Much as we appreciate it, it wasn't necessary."

"No, Daisy, has a date, with—" But Odie's words were drowned out as the opening notes of "Betcha By Golly Wow" by the Stylistics filled the air.

Up ahead, a small semicircle had formed in the wake of an evaporating Soul Train Line.

James jerked to a halt at my side. I looked at her stricken expression and followed her line of sight to see what had her frozen in place.

Julian. Dead ahead. Standing on the perimeter of the circle looking directly at James.

Julian saw me and flinched away.

And then I saw . . .

All the air left my lungs.

Up was down, down was up, and nothing made sense.

I was trying to find the words, but my mind was blank and my ears were filled with the *whoosh-whoosh-whoosh*ing of my heart.

James found the words that I lacked. "Who the hell is that!?"

Lucy looked over to the circle—at the *guy* in the circle, at the *girl* in the circle, the two of them so close I couldn't tell where Trevor ended and she began. Her hands ran gently over his deep waves of hair, his hands were at her waist, hips pulled tightly together.

They swiveled, swerved, and gyrated.

Calm down, Daisy. It's just a dance. They're just dancing.

His lips mouthed along to the song, making promises about her being the one that he'd been waiting for.

Then he kissed her neck.

I'm going to be sick. I have to get out of here.

"Oh, them." Lucy's tone was bored. "They're royalty. Literally. I believe they were Mr. and Miss Sophomore a few years back. That's Trevor Boone and Elodie Mayhew. Fisk University's golden couple."

Some part of my mind registered Odie making a surprised, strangled growl at my side but I couldn't turn to look at her.

I couldn't turn away from *them*.

I couldn't turn away from *him*.

The way he looked at her. The thought from the other day popped into my head. This was what Trevor looked like when he loved something. No. Not something. Some*one*.

Why was it so hot all of a sudden?

The heat was suffocating, making it hard for me to breathe.

He caressed her cheek. She smiled and turned her head into his palm, giving his wrist a kiss. The movement was easy, so natural, as if they'd done it a hundred times, a thousand.

I couldn't breathe.

My stomach felt like it had been placed in a vise; it kept clenching painfully.

And I could not look away.

Not when they stopped dancing and walked to the perimeter laughing and holding hands. Not when another couple took center stage.

I stared at the way she leaned her entire body back into his and he wrapped his arms around her automatically, letting his big body be a wall for her.

To comfort her. To protect her. To cherish her.

I stared because they looked perfect. They looked like they made sense. She was tall and light, with an hourglass figure. Her bone straight hair was pulled up into a ponytail high on her head, so long it trailed to her mid back. And her hair color? It was the exact same unusual, stunning color as Julian's.

She was gorgeous and he was gorgeous.

They made sense.

Of course, Daisy.

Of course a guy who was smart and charming and attractive wouldn't also be *single*.

Staring at them felt a bit like having my irises singed by the sun. They were so bright, and so shiny, and so pretty, and *so in love*.

Still leaning on Trevor's shoulder, she glanced our way without recognition until another girl wearing her sorority colors approached and snagged her attention.

In that brief second she looked our way, I saw why her hair was the same color as Julian's: they looked almost exactly alike. Her features were soft where his were sharp, but the resemblance was uncanny.

She was obviously related to Julian.

She had to be . . . and Julian had watched us kiss.

No wonder he stared at me in the cafeteria.

Did he know about tonight?

Of course he did.

Julian and God only knew how many other people had seen Trevor and I walking around that day. Had I been something just to pass the time until Trevor's girlfriend came back? The idea stung way more than it should've. There was no telling who Trevor had told. For all I knew, he'd boasted to his whole dang fraternity about the stupid freshman girl he'd led on.

The giggle that burst forth from my lips sounded manic even to my ears.

I was doubled over in laughter, the kind that makes your chest heave the same way sobs do.

It was either laugh or cry and I would not cry. Not in front of all these people.

"Daisy!" Odie yelled. It was loud enough that I realized it may not have been the first time she'd called me.

She tugged at my hand.

When did she start holding my hand?

"Let's get you out of here."

No!

If I leave then, they win. If little dumb Daisy Payton goes back to her dorm room and cries her goddamned eyes out, then these . . .

"Fucking bastards," James muttered under her breath.

Yes, that about summed it up. The fucking bastards would win.

And while I would most certainly be retiring to my room, later, for a long night of bawling my eyes into puffiness, right now?

Right now, I needed to be a Payton. I needed to put on my bravest face and tuck my emotions away until it was safe for me to cry. I needed to let these men know they would not win.

Why, oh why, does Dolly always have to be right? She'd warned me off this boy.

I took a deep breath, squeezed both my friends' hands—I realized James at some point had also grabbed on to me—and I gave my best *Daisy Payton* smile. My momma called them pageant smiles. *"They're not real but no one expects them to be. They just have to look pretty,"* she'd said.

"Get out of here? But we just got here, ladies." I raised my eyebrows meaningfully. "I was promised a Friday night block party and this right here looks like the place to be. So many interesting things percolating. I think we should stay."

Odessa surprised me by agreeing immediately. James, on the other hand, glanced between us and said, "This is a bad idea."

I gave James my most serene look. "This is the best idea I've had all week."

She looked at me for a long moment and then said helplessly, "Odie."

"If Daisy wants to stay, I think we should stay."

James shook her head and shrugged. "Okay." The music kicked up again and I think I heard her say, "But if we end up in jail, you can't say you weren't warned."

CHAPTER THIRTEEN

Trevor

Daisy was probably near furious with me.

On Monday when I'd asked Daisy out, I'd dreamed of a beautiful start for the two of us. Now I was facing a nightmare.

I had tried, desperately, to get Elodie to come around to my way of thinking. We'd argued for over an hour, but there was no way, none at all, that she would agree to letting me tell Daisy.

"Let me get this straight, you want to tell my deepest secret—a secret that I've kept from my own blood, who I would die for . . . That secret is the one you want to tell to a girl you've known a *week,* Trevor? *A week*?! In what world does that make sense?"

And there was no way I would tell Daisy without Elodie's permission.

And without telling Daisy that my relationship with Elodie wasn't real there was no way for me to explain my actions over the last week.

I'd put the cart before of the horses and now I was paying for it.

Instead of tonight being full of beginnings, it would be the end of Daisy and me.

I glanced down at my watch. It read 6:08. I'd promised her I would meet her at six.

I have to get going before she thinks I'm not coming.

I would meet Daisy at Harris, take her to eat, and then I would take her walking along Cumberland River because I thought she'd enjoy the water. And then . . .

You're going to end it.

I swallowed hard, thinking of the lie I would tell Daisy at the end of the night.

I thought I was over my ex, but I saw her a few days ago and I realized I have some issues I still need to work through with her. I'm so sorry for wasting your time.

If all I ever had of Daisy was just tonight, then tonight would have to be enough. But I wasn't without hope; I was still Daisy's mentor. Maybe in time she would forgive me. Perhaps over the course of some months I could even earn her friendship. And if I could earn her friendship then there *might* be a chance in the future for something more. I could wait. I'd waited most of my life to get what I wanted, and if I could earn Daisy's forgiveness then the moment my foot crossed that graduation stage, I would come for her. They said timing was everything, and maybe now was not our time.

But this night was ours.

I needed to go.

"I have to go," I whispered to El's hair. She was pressed against me, leaning back casually stroking my arm in the same comforting way she would do when we were kids.

I felt her nod against me and let my arm go.

Julian appeared next to me, an intense frown on his face.

"I honestly have to go this time, Julian. No more delaying." I'd been trying to leave for about twenty minutes but each time I tried to go Jules would tell me one of our frat brothers needed me and that person would magically materialize to ask an asinine question or someone would pull me into the circle for a dance or push me to the top of the Soul Train Line. I got the distinct impression that folks were getting in the way of my leaving on purpose. Or maybe I was being paranoid.

"No, you don't." His voice sounded off, strained.

I inhaled and exhaled. I didn't want to arrive in a fit of fury. Jules and I had been at odds all week, our relationship was strained, and I *hated* it.

But I was done being a good friend. Elodie had asked me to show my face at the block party for a few minutes. While I'd wanted to say no, I suspected showing a united front meant a lot to her. She'd been the target of a handful of vicious rumors over the years, and I knew just how important quieting the speculation about our relationship was to her.

I hadn't been expecting to dance, but when she'd grabbed my hand and looked at me with pleading eyes, I knew what she was asking. I still felt awful for not trusting her enough to tell her about Daisy.

I needed to make a mea culpa for my colossal mistakes.

I realized bleakly that although I may have ruined my chances with Daisy I could still try to do right by Elodie. It was a simple truth that Elodie would always feel most protected with the shield of our faux relationship to hide behind and I no longer had a worthy reason to tear that security away from her. With that in mind, I'd responded affirmatively.

We'd fallen back into our roles effortlessly. I'd laughed with joy I did not feel and danced with passion I did not feel, and I was very sure from the outside looking in we looked very much in love.

Mission accomplished.

That would put any rumors of a rift between us to rest and any lingering rumors about Elodie into the grave with it.

Now it was time—past time—for me to leave and face Daisy.

"I'm leaving, *now,*" I said to Jules, as Elodie stepped to the side.

"No, Trevor. What I meant is, she's here."

My head whipped around looking for her. *Daisy was here?*

Why was she here and not at Harris?

It only took me a second to spot her—well, them. James was tall for a girl so her group stood out in a crowd. And there was Daisy, standing not ten feet away from me, almost close enough to touch.

Almost.

It seemed like everything was destined to be *almost* with this girl.

She was talking to someone and just her profile stole my breath.

Daisy was always beautiful, but it was almost unbearable how gorgeous she looked with all the icing on her cake.

And that outfit . . . I took in her curves, the way the material caught the light and accentuated her pert, round bottom. I let my eyes roam up her soft-looking thighs to her flat stomach and that peekaboo cutout between her breasts that was made for driving imaginations into overdrive.

I was on fire. She was close—so, so close—and she was dressed like that for me.

"You're not thinking." Jules voice was a mosquito in my ear.

He was right; I was not thinking. I was feeling—just feeling.

And right now I was feeling like walking over to Daisy, lifting her up around my waist, and carrying her where no other eyes could ever see her body in that jumpsuit ever again.

I was feeling like I wanted to whisk her away to a place where only we existed and kiss her 'til she was excited and breathless.

I was feeling like I needed her to turn so I could see those eyes that made my heart gallop and my stomach swoop and drop.

As soon as I thought about her eyes, she turned, and—*BAM*—those magnetic eyes found mine. Her makeup made her eyes look even larger, browner, deeper, and more hypnotic, and my heart was stuttering and somersaulting in my chest.

I didn't think I'd ever get used to the way my heart reacted when I stared into her eyes. The way my whole body reacted.

But then Daisy's eyes changed, becoming turbulent, undoubtedly hurt, before falling totally flat as if a light inside her had been snuffed. She broke eye contact, and gave me her back as she turned toward a person to her left. It was like someone had socked me in my stomach and a bucket of cold water had been thrown on me all at once.

Oh God.

I never wanted her to look at me like that again.

I never want her to look at *anyone* like that again. What on earth was wrong? I took an instinctive step in her direction.

I admit my brain was working a little slowly because Daisy in that outfit had redirected most of my blood flow away from my brain.

But Jules was there to enlighten me. "What are you going to say to her? She's *been* here, Trevor. She didn't just get here. She saw *everything*."

I turned to him, eyes flaring in panic. The music, the dancing, the laughter around me all contrasted with the cold dread snaking through me. My body flashed hot, then cold, then hot again, and I had the sudden urge to throw up.

I swallowed a few times.

"What—what do you mean, she saw *everything*?"

"She saw you dancing, she maybe even saw you kiss. You can't very well go up to her and say, 'So are you ready for our date? Please, Daisy, ignore the fact that you just saw me kissing my girlfriend. Should we go grab a bite?' And even if you could somehow manage to trick that girl into going out with you, what would be the point? El is back now. You just need to—"

Jules said this all so calmly—so rationally, like it was no big fucking deal—that I walked away mid-sentence.

Oh God.

She wasn't supposed to see any of that show.

Oh God. Oh God. She wasn't supposed to find out like that.

Oh God.

Look at me, Daisy. Look at me so you can see the truth.

Look at me, Daisy.

My feet were moving toward her.

I had to get to Daisy to explain to her.

It was an act. Everything she'd just seen—the dancing, the kissing —was an act. I needed to tell her that. I would shout it from the rooftops if I needed to. And then a thought worse than all the others struck me:

She won't believe you.

Elodie and I had been pulling this act off for a long, long time. We weren't good at it—we were *great* at selling the lie.

Daisy would see though, wouldn't she? She would know the way I looked at Elodie was nothing, *nothing*, like the way I looked at her.

The thought left a wake of desperation in its path. Panic, clammy and hot, gripped me and left an acrid taste in my mouth. She would see. She would know. She had to see.

My brain short-circuited as I pressed my way through the crowd, firing all the things I needed to say to her in random order.

She's like a sister to me.

I didn't lead you on.

It's not what it looks like.

I do like you.

I never meant for you to see that.

I do want to date you.

I had to get to her.

I continued weaving through the crowd, which all of a sudden had seen fit to coalesce in front of me, in between us. It felt like the universe was trying to keep me from her.

The universe be damned.

Nothing mattered except getting to Daisy. Except *explaining* to Daisy. Except pleading with Daisy. Except begging Daisy.

I offered a quick prayer. *God, I don't ask for much, but if all those*

Sundays I banked growing up meant anything at all please give me the words to get Daisy to understand.

God, *please* make her understand.

I glimpsed her through a hole in the crowd. She was partially blocked, but it was clear she was talking to Jermaine Thompson, my frat brother. Correction—my dog of a frat brother. And like a dog, he was looking her up and down, openly assessing her in a way that made me clench my fists. If he touched Daisy I was going to be tempted to violence.

I was almost there.

I saw her smile up at him and ignored the jab of jealousy that speared me.

She was not mine. I did not have the right to be jealous. I was not a jealous person.

I exhaled deeply, and resigned myself to the truth.

Except when it came to Daisy.

Then all your bones are jealousy bones, Trevor.

I sighed in frustration again. Would this girl be the exception to every one of my rules?

Without warning, my path to Daisy was suddenly cut off by Daisy's friend. Her name was something with an O—Ophelia or Octavia or something.

I remembered thinking she reminded me of a teddy bear when I'd first seen her, but now, she looked more like a mama bear.

"Don't be stupid," she said out of the gate. "We're all here to be seen, not to make one. Go back to your friends and leave her alone. You've done enough."

If it were Jules I'd have walked past her without responding. Every second spent talking to someone else was a second not spent not explaining to Daisy. But this was Daisy's friend and I didn't want to piss Daisy off even more by making her friend angry.

Presently, she was looking at me like if she could set me on fire, I'd already be a pile of charred ashes.

"It's not what it looks like."

She cocked her head, examining me with a probing glare.

"It's not what it looks like. Hmmmm. And just what do you think this looks like to me? To Daisy? To all of her friends? To half the freshman class?"

I opened my mouth, but no rejoinder came out.

She continued to stare me down, which was ironic because I towered over her and I literally had to look down at her.

Daisy chose that moment to look up from her conversation and looked at her friend quizzically. She took a step in our direction but was stopped when James touched her arm and shook her head. Daisy turned her back and—she didn't even glance at me.

"It doesn't matter," her friend said, calling my attention back to her. "Whatever is going on with you and Elodie Mayhew—"

My head snapped back as if I'd been slapped.

Julian was right. People talked. I had been a fool to think that Daisy and I had gone unnoticed simply because most students weren't back on campus yet. Daisy maybe would've been fine seeing anyone else, but I was already too well known.

I hadn't been thinking. Daisy made it too easy not to think. She made it easy to block out the rest of the world.

"Whatever is happening with y'all, Daisy is out of it."

"Then let that come from Daisy's mouth," I snapped. I knew that my anger seemed unfounded to her and probably wouldn't help my case, but I was just so frustrated. She stood there giving me commands like a tiny empress as if she was the authority on Daisy and me.

Fatigue began to claw at my edges. This was not how this night was supposed to go.

I exhaled deeply, planning to soften my tone. I was not a man who snapped at women, but it was unnecessary because Ophelia or whatever her name, was not cowed by me at all, in fact she still glared at me.

"I only want to explain what—"

Cutting me off, she opened her arms expansively and I took in all the folks around us dancing, laughing, *watching.* "Even if you have a perfectly reasonable excuse—not reason, an excuse, and it would have to be an excuse from God himself—do you think this is the time and place to have that conversation?"

She had me and by the look on her face, she knew it.

"Leave her alone, Trevor. You've humiliated her enough. Just . . . leave her alone."

Daisy's friend turned her back to me and in desperation I grabbed her shoulder because I needed to get a message to Daisy. She shook me off, rearing back like she was absolutely sure I'd lost my ever-loving mind.

Maybe I had.

"Ask her to meet me later. I need to explain. I owe her an explanation. Just tell her to meet me in the spot where we were supposed to meet up tonight." Daisy's expression had broken me; in that moment I would've told her the entire truth if it meant forgiveness.

"I will not."

I growled.

"*She* doesn't owe *you* anything. *Anything.* You *hurt* her. You *played* her. And now you want her to go out of her way to let you explain your side? Why should she? If I tell her to come meet you, what could you possibly tell her that is gonna make her *not* look like a fool in front of everyone, Trevor?"

I didn't answer because I couldn't.

She snorted in disgust, shook her head, turned, and in a few short strides, was swallowed by the crowd.

And then Jules was there at my side joined by a few of our other friends. I don't know what my face looked like, but Jules looked at me and for once he didn't say a word. He simply placed his hand on my shoulder gave me two quick pats and sipped his drink.

Tumult.

That was the only way to describe how I was feeling. Daisy had come into my world and in the span of seven days she'd flipped the entire thing upside down.

Her friend was right.

I'd hurt her. The way she'd looked at me . . . just recalling it made my stomach plummet.

You were going to end it anyway, Trevor.

Just let her go.

I felt sick again. Hot and cold, palms sweaty, heart racing, sick. I hurt her. I never wanted to hurt her. Her friends' accusation rang in my ear over and over again.

You hurt her. You hurt her. You hurt her. Each one stabbed me in my chest.

I thought I'd known hell, I thought I'd known misery, I thought I'd known jealousy.

But I'd been wrong.

I was just beginning to know those things.

Because hell was watching man after man walk up to the object of your affection, hitting on her, admiring her, wooing her.

Agony was watching as she took interest in one as he handed her a drink. It was hearing the wind carry her voice so full of curiosity as she said, "No, I've never drank before." It was watching him gaze at her as her nose scrunched as she took her first sip.

Jealousy—hot, sick and green—was standing back as Daisy had a first experience, any experience, with another man. It was watching her make *memories* with another man.

And hopelessness was feeling like I'd never get to make memories with her in the future.

The longer the night went on, the more out of reach she felt.

I had not given up hope of explaining to her in the future, but her friend was right. Now was not the time. I didn't try to approach her for the rest of the night.

Instead, I watched her.

I watched her laughing with her friends. I watched the way the light caught her mystery hair. I watched as she went from thinking liquor tasted terrible to thinking it tasted great.

I watched as she drank, drink after drink . . . and I felt guilty because, while I recognized Daisy was an adult and could make her own decisions, I couldn't help but feel like she was drinking in part because of me.

I watched as she pointedly ignored me.

My misery turned to worry as I realized she was past her limit and guys were *still* hitting on her and plying her with drinks. Mercifully, James intervened just as I was about to confront Dexter Hines, who was persistently trying to get a tipsy Daisy to leave with him.

She and her friends finally left the party and headed back in the direction of their dorm.

My friends, having sensed my mood, had left me alone for the rest of the night, which was fine with me. This was a special type of misery where company wouldn't help. Instead of sticking around I headed off to walk home, glad to have this hellish day finally winding down.

Elodie caught up to me a block into the walk and looked up at me in that beautiful haunted way of hers. Her arms went around my torso, giving me a squeeze.

"Thank you, Trevor. Just . . .thank you."

I wrapped my arms around her back, hugging her tight because this embrace was real, not for show, and not for anyone but us.

We walked in silence for a minute before she grabbed my hand and whispered, "You're doing the right thing you know, letting her go."

I swallowed and nodded but I didn't agree—not really. Because it didn't feel like I was letting Daisy go at all. It felt like I was letting her slip away. And it felt as if I'd never be the same.

Daisy

WHY DID I WAIT SO LONG TO DRINK LIQUOR! IT FELT AHHHH-MAZING!

And then it didn't.

And then it really, really, did not.

I knew it was morning because light was coming through my dorm room window. Demonic light. Hellfire light, that burned unholy and bright.

My head was splitting and my mouth tasted like rot. I rolled over and—

Oomph!

The floor greeted me, hard and sturdy as ever. The pain felt fitting.

Lovely. I hadn't fallen out of the bed since I was four.

I groaned from my spot on the floor.

James sat up, took one look at me and deadpanned, "Well, well, well. Look who's back from the dead, like Lazarus."

I groaned, again. "Why on earth does it feel like this?"

"Because you can't go from having a learner's permit to being a goddamn NASCAR driver, Daisy. I told you to stop after three!"

I shuffled through my memories while lying on the floor because the floor felt cool and my head hurt and I may have broken my arm when I landed on my side. It throbbed so badly it had to be broken.

I'd gotten dressed. I'd gone to meet Trevor. And . . .

Trevor . . . It felt like someone had placed their boot on my chest and stepped until they cracked all my ribs. Like there wasn't space for my heart or lungs to fully expand.

Pain. Sharp. Humiliation. Sharper. *Anger.* Sharpest of all.

Those three emotions had held me in their grip until the alcohol had taken over and muted them all.

I willed my mind to clear. I couldn't think about Trevor. Getting drunk had been accidental but not a bad plan, in retrospect.

I sat up and the room spun.

Okay, so not a *good* plan either, but it had kept me from crying my eyes out over someone who clearly wasn't worth the tears.

I sighed. "I think I remember all of last night, but I can't be *sure* I actually remember all of last night. Did I do anything or say anything to Trevor that would lead to me having to transfer schools immediately?"

James rolled her eyes, stretched, and yawned. I noted from my place on the floor how utterly unfair it was that she looked like a magazine cover model even when she had just woken up. I was sure I looked like feral rats had performed a mating ritual in my hair as I'd slept.

James lithely hopped down off her bed and extended her hand to me.

"Get up," she said, pulling me up with more strength than I'd thought possible from someone so thin.

"James," I said meekly, trying to find my balance on legs that felt tired and shaky.

"Daisy."

"I didn't make a fool out of myself last night, did I?"

She looked at me hard for a moment and I felt a little afraid of what she might say.

After a second she sighed. "Daisy." She paused before trying again. "It depends on what you mean by making a fool out of yourself. I don't know what kind of Mayberry-ass-Leave-it-to-Beaver town you grew up in—"

I opened my mouth to defend Green Valley and snapped it shut because I'd have to defend *Greenville,* instead.

"That you haven't drank before the age of eighteen, but Daisy, you can't ever get so drunk that you have to ask someone else what happened the night before. Do you understand me? And you can't accept open drinks from guys either. You never know what they might've put in it. So no, you didn't make a fool of yourself in the way you're talking, but you were reckless and girls that look like us—girls, *period*—can't ever afford to be reckless. At least not in that way."

Another kind of shame flooded me swift and strong. James was absolutely right, and not because I didn't know any better. Even though I'd never drank before I had common sense. I'd been angry and willful, and that combination made my actions idiotic.

Thank God no one drugged me. Thank God my friends didn't leave me.

I looked at her to apologize for my behavior—for making my friends worry—but she held up her hand.

"No need to feel ashamed. Rookie mistake. I'm just trying to speed your education along and make it less painful. Since whoever raised you apparently never let you or the Beaver go and play with the other kids."

I cracked a smile at her joke. She had no idea.

"Do I need to explain the birds and the bees to you too?" she teased gently. I laughed it off, but it sounded shrill even to me and I waved her away. Laughing was a mistake. My head pounded harder at the sound of my own voice.

She eyed me for a long minute before shaking her head and smiling ruefully. "That's a conversation for another day. Right now, I need your first-aid kit and you need to run down the hall and grab a glass of water to take some aspirin. Then you need to get back in bed and sleep off this hangover until Odie and I come back with some pastries from the cafeteria."

Chastened and chastised, I did as she instructed.

James drew the curtains and before she left said, "Oh, and for the record, of course you didn't do anything that you'd regret last night. Trevor never even got near you. Your friends were by your side and we would never allow that."

She flicked off the light and exited.

I slept most of the day and it was dreamless and untroubled. Probably because I felt exhausted. James and Odie woke me with time enough to shower and then head to dinner.

I held my breath as we walked through the cafeteria doors and breathed a sigh of relief when I noticed Trevor and his friends where nowhere to be seen.

In fact, the cafeteria was fairly empty. A glance down at my mother's gold watch on my arm told me it was 6:48.

A nagging suspicion began to claw at me, but I was hungry. Starving, in fact, and I wanted to eat every single thing. However, James and Odie warned me that I should start slow and simple and not eat too much or it would make me sick.

The temporary euphoric feeling of last night was so far in my rearview mirror, I couldn't see why I'd thought drinking was a good idea. The after-effects were awful.

We got through our meal and made it back to the dorms before the other shoe dropped. We entered the lobby of Jubilee and it was like a record skipped. All the girls in the seating area immediately lowered their voices.

I sighed as it clicked as to why we were eating so late; James and Odie and I never went to the cafeteria that late. I'd chalked it up to them generously letting me sleep my hangover off, but I now realized they knew the later we went the emptier it would be and the less likely we'd run into whispers.

Notoriety and Gossip, you bitter hags, how I have not *missed you, my old friends.*

Back in my room I lay down on my bed and closed my eyes. "James, talk."

James, the chatterbox incarnate, floundered as she tried to figure out a place to start, so I knew the rumors were bad.

Finally, I opened my eyes and put her out of her misery. "Whatever the rumors are, James, just spit it out. This waiting is killing me."

I was delivered from my curiosity by Odie. "Well the good news is that most of the upperclassmen aren't paying this any attention. Lucy says she hasn't heard a blip."

I nodded. College was larger than high school so it made sense that rumors would take longer to spread. And also, not all the upperclassmen were even back yet. And most importantly, they probably had lives and just didn't care.

"But amongst the girls in this dorm you've been branded as . . . a hussy," James said the word lowly and shamefully.

But I laughed. Big peals of laughter that had Odie and James looking at each other like I was a nut.

A hussy? Nothing could be further from the truth.

Whew! I'd needed that. I'd thought the rumors would be closer to the mark. That I was an idiot. Or a naive country bumpkin.

My friends continued to look at me strangely, like they thought I'd gone a step further and became a *cracked* nut.

I took a big gulp of air, breathing fully for the first time that day and ignoring the way my heart twinged. I would not think about him. I would not.

"Let me guess. I used my feminine wiles to try to steal Elodie's boyfriend?" I twisted my lips and raised my eyebrows expectantly.

James looked stunned. I took that as confirmation that I was correct.

"Gossip is predictable, James."

I sighed. So very predictable. Of course I'd get blamed for Trevor's bad behavior. Women usually were.

On the bright side, at least there was no way this would get back to my father and Dolly since I was using a fake name. I didn't have to worry about them calling or driving up here like a couple of dueling white knights trying to save the day. Lord, Dolly and my father showing up would be the second worst thing that could happen to me this week.

Besides, if the rumors were just some bored freshman girls gossiping about me in their dorm rooms, then it would probably blow over in a few days.

Or the rumor might grow wings and fly through campus. You never knew with rumors.

I decided I didn't care either way.

I'd thought I'd feel . . . I don't know, upset. Or maybe compelled to set the narrative straight—that was why I'd asked James to begin with. But I didn't feel any of that. Maybe because the narrative they came up with was so unoriginal. Or maybe it was because folks had been talking about me my entire life that another week or two—hell, another month or two—wouldn't kill me. It would make life uncomfortable and irritating, but it wouldn't kill me.

It would make it so that some people who didn't even know me wouldn't want to socialize with me, but it would not kill me.

And eventually something shinier would come along and the wagging tongues would all move on.

This too shall pass, Daisy.

"Daisy, how are you taking this so well? They're saying that you slept with him to try to get—" I held up my hand.

"James, I can't care."

I meant it literally. From the depths of my battered spirit which still felt exhausted, either from the alcohol or from the events of the night before or both. With my whole heart I could not find it in me to care what those girls thought of me.

I would not give it my time. I could not. I had *two* majors to focus on. If I went down the path of trying to refute every dumb thing that was said about me I would never have time for class.

I'd dated—well not dated, but I had been taken with a guy—and I got burned. End of story.

And all those girls that were blaming his behavior on me?

I suddenly felt bad for them. Because if they blamed me for

203

Trevor's bad behavior then they'd blame themselves for the bad behavior of the men in their lives.

"I just can't care," I repeated looking at my friends, letting them see the tired truth of my words.

"I don't want to hear about the rumors unless they'll impact my physical well-being, my enrollment status, or my grades. Otherwise, let them talk, let them have their fun." I repeated James's wise words about Julian, "Those girls don't deserve any more headspace than what's absolutely required. So I won't give them any."

James smirked at me in approval and gave me a curt nod.

Odie picked that moment to inform us both that Lucy was on her way over with ice cream pops.

My stomached grumbled in appreciation and anticipation. Dinner had been too light and unsatisfying.

We ate the ice cream pops and we played spades well into the night. Odie and I kicked James and Lucy's butts until James called reneging. After a good-natured scuffle, James was finally able to wrangle the cards from Odie's hands and we all collapsed in a cloud of cards and laughter.

Eventually, Odie and Lucy headed back to their respective rooms. James climbed in the bed across from mine.

"Not going home tonight, Jamesy?" I asked, not wanting her to feel like she needed to mind me. She'd done enough. After all, she'd stayed with me last night already. In fact, both of my friends had done more than their share to take care of me.

"This is home," she said on a yawn.

I shut off the light, climbed into bed, and let sleep claim me.

Sunday evening after dinner I was finally able to convince my friends that I was well and truly all right. I gently pointed out to them that they had their own first day of classes to prepare for, and that I did not need a minder to sleep in the room with me. I was going to be absolutely fine.

It was only a partial lie.

I did and do love having my friends around but it had begun to feel a bit suffocating. They seemed determined to keep me from falling into a slump, but I needed to think and I needed to brood a little and then think some more.

And I loved them for it . . . but the thing was—

I needed the slump.

I needed to ruminate on how I had gotten here, and more importantly, what I could do to make sure I never ever ended up being so stupid over a boy again.

I needed to work through all the feelings I had around Trevor and there were a *lot* of feelings. And then I would come up with a plan for what to do when I saw him next.

Because I would see him again, every single week. I'd contemplated asking for a new mentor for about two seconds before I realized that I would rather drop out of school altogether than bring Dr. Gwinn into my personal drama.

And if what Trevor told me about his affection for Dr. Gwinn were true, then he felt the same way.

But was it? I found myself questioning just about everything I'd experienced with Trevor.

Was brown really his favorite color? Was he really even my mentor or someone that had just wandered into Harris and decided to take advantage of an opportunity?

No, Daisy. He's really your mentor. Fate is exactly that kind to you.

I decided to work through my emotions in chunks. Trying to do it all at once would likely lead to tears.

I'd already dealt with the humiliation, so that left anger . . . and devastation. *Enough hurt to bring an elephant down without a tranquilizer gun.*

So, anger it was! I thought of Trevor kissing me, holding my hand all the while—

Nope!

Turned out anger wasn't safe either.

None of your emotions are safe.

Happiness wasn't safe because happiness was kissing Trevor. Sadness wasn't either, because sadness was watching Trevor kiss someone else. Trevor had tainted them all. He'd even tainted missing folks. Because the part of me that had believed the Trevor I knew was real still missed that person.

Pathetic.

This is why your friends didn't want you to slump, Daisy.

My emotions had gotten me into this mess, so I decided to use logic to get me out of it. The jar of no feelings was getting upgraded; I was going to make it pitcher sized, maybe even gallon sized. A gallon sized jar of no feelings sounded lovely right about now.

I regrouped. Maybe working through all the feelings wasn't the most important thing right now. I just needed to focus on getting through this week, on *enjoying* this week. After all, it would be my first week of college classes. Enjoyment was—I cut my mind off. *Don't think it, Daisy.*

I figuratively straightened my spine and decided as of that moment to put an embargo on ruminating on Trevor. *Logically* speaking I didn't need to feel anything about him at all—all I needed to do was come up with a plan for seeing him next.

And just like that the solution came to me.

Trevor would get nothing from me. No reaction, no emotion, no conversation. I fleshed my plan out and turned it around in my mind looking for holes. I realized I needed to make an amendment: I'd likely have to speak to him *some,* but one-word answers or the shortest possible variation would do.

I held on to my plan like a life preserver and finally drifted to sleep.

CHAPTER FOURTEEN

Daisy

My first week of class went by mostly in a blur. Dr. Gwinn was right; it was going to be a lot of work. *A lot of work.*

My teachers didn't shirk from giving reading assignments or projects just because it was the first week. Each course syllabus has proven to be a lifeline. I grudgingly acknowledged that Trevor's method of filling out my blocks of study time with chapter numbers was helpful. Additionally, he'd shown me a grid he kept with major milestones for each course, like the first exam or when term papers were due. I replicated it, color coding each class and it turned out to be a very, very effective way to track what I needed to study at any given time.

Another thing I'd learned was that there was no review period. I'd laughed at myself the way I'm sure Dr. Gwinn had scoffed when I'd assumed the first week would be determining what students already knew. Professors were way more focused on teaching new concepts than figuring out what we already knew.

And even though the course work was a lot and I was barely seeing my friends, I loved it.

I loved my Introduction to Textiles class and I loved my Introduction to Culinary Arts Class. I did not love biology and I absolutely loathed statistics.

Here's the thing: I loved math. Math was beautiful, and its beauty was in its simplicity and constancy.

Statistics was *not* math.

Its calculations were deceptively simple, but its applications? Complicated, clumsy, and situational. It was the awkward offspring of math and sociology that did not fit into either world.

Statistics was messy.

Nevertheless, I would need to figure out a way for it to make sense. I couldn't afford to get behind in any class.

Maybe I'd ask Dr. Gwinn . . .

No, she'd wonder why I wasn't asking my mentor. It would be a cold day in you-know-where before I asked Trevor to recommend a statistics tutor.

Trevor.

The other reason having a crammed schedule was great, aside from keeping me challenged, was that I barely had time to think about Trevor.

Except at night. Nights were . . . hard.

Because I thought of Trevor, no matter how hard I tried to push him out of my mind. I didn't want to think of him, but I'd close my eyes, exhausted and ready to sleep, and without fail that dimple in his left cheek that only showed when he smiled would appear.

Or I'd see those striking eyes and their strange, rich shade of brown. The worst was when I saw his whole face—lips curling in laughter or eyebrows raised high as I challenged him on a point. I missed him.

No that wasn't exactly right.

I didn't miss him.

I missed the Trevor I'd spent time with, the one I thought I'd started to know. I couldn't reconcile the guy who'd stomped on my heart last Friday with the Trevor who was so clever and kind all the times before. Mentally I knew they were the same, but my heart was having a lot harder time catching up.

I hope, I hope, I hope, it would beat.

Or *maybe there's a reason, maybe he can explain,* it'd thump. And then my brain would have to explain the facts of life to my heart; the reason would not matter.

Give up hope because it's hopeless, it would lecture.

I wasn't sleeping well. But I hadn't cried and I counted that as a win.

At the end of my first full day of classes I finally called Dolly. The chat was mercifully brief and mostly pleasant. I gave her my student account number so she could wire my tuition payment. Her voice pitched up an octave when I'd given her the total amount owed. Then she'd quipped, "I had no idea Fisk had become so expensive." I immediately came clean and told her that my tuition was high because I was carrying twenty-one credits and that I'd decided to double major.

She was quiet for a very, very long beat and then surprised me by saying, "Well, Daisy, I admire your gumption. That's a lot of work . . . if you feel like you're drowning, make sure you raise a flag to your professors."

I'd been bracing myself for her reaction and her acceptance was a balm. My immediate instinct was to assure her that I'd be fine, that I had a wonderful mentor that would help me out, but the words turned to acid and died on my tongue.

So instead of telling her that lie, I sang the praises of my advisor and told her that she'd gone through great lengths to make sure I was supported. And because hell was freezing over, I was suddenly overcome with a bit of wistfulness, missing my sister, wishing she were here and that I could tell her about Trevor. Wishing I could trust her fully—trust her to not just bulldoze her way through and to *Dolly* Trevor into submission. What would count as Trevor submitting? An apology, maybe?

Yeah, an apology would be real nice.

But I digressed. Dolly didn't second-guess my decision to double major and I was so happy that she trusted me in this at least. And so I said it apropos of nothing, cutting her off mid-sentence as she talked about a new pair of shoes she'd gotten. "Thank you, Dolly."

She paused for a second and then said, "Whatever can you be thanking me for? Is it being the world's best big sister?"

I rolled my eyes. Oh brother—or rather, oh sister.

"Just, thanks . . . I know you do a lot for me. And I know this whole thing hasn't been easy for you, me leaving home and all."

"Oh . . . I know you're an adult now, Daisy, and that you have to do things your own way," she said airily in the voice she used when she knows she should believe something but absolutely doesn't.

We moved on to the news from back home. Dolly filled me in on local gossip and the latest with the Mill. Listening to her tales, not only did I miss my sister, but for the first time since I'd been gone, I missed home.

But Dolly was an emotional ninja. She could blindside you by stealthily sneaking all of your emotional pain points into the most innocuous of conversations. And just like that, my homesickness vanished when she suddenly asked me if I was coming home for the upcoming long weekend and offered to pick me up on Friday. I— artfully, might I add—sidestepped her question by telling her I had a lot of work (true) and that I'd have to think about it (untrue) because the unspoken subtext between us was that it wasn't just the long weekend, it was the weekend of my mother's birthday.

I was absolutely not going home.

My mother hadn't been too far from my thoughts—that's why I'd been playing her favorite song—but it wasn't the pit of despair that it had been last year.

Dealing with it here would be difficult enough. Going home and being in that house with all those memories would undoubtedly be worse.

So on Saturday I would wake up and feel . . . whatever, but I wouldn't stop. I would keep going and I wouldn't fall apart the way I would if I were at home.

My sister sighed resignedly then let the topic die before we ended our otherwise pleasant call. But I didn't buy it for a second; she was going to pester me about this again. Dolly might retreat for a moment, but she never conceded defeat.

I hardly saw James and Odie during that first week. James had two early classes so breakfast was out. Odie had a late lab class on Wednesdays and, much to her dismay, Fridays.

We were finally able to connect for lunch on Thursday, and afterward we decided to head to the bookstore to pick up our books.

We were *not* prepared. We weren't prepared at *all*.

A line longer than the Great Wall of China, twisted, snaked, bunched, and curled almost back to where we entered. It was overflowing with students.

"I guess we should've come before lunch. This is insanity," Odie said, bewildered.

A guy turned around to respond to her, saw James, did a double take, and then rapidly shook his head like a cartoon character.

James smiled wryly and looked away pretending not to notice his reaction to her. I didn't know how she managed; being stunning had to be kinda exhausting. To the guy's credit, he didn't hit on her. Instead, he stammered to Odie, still clearly unsettled by James, "Th-th-this is nothing. Earlier was worse."

"Worse," I said perplexed. "How is that even possible?"

"We're standing inside the building," he responded.

Over the next forty-five minutes we learned that some students were there trying to sell back their books from the previous semester while others, like us, were there to buy them for the current semester.

We had a lot of questions. And maybe it was because they were bored standing in line too, or perhaps it was a little schadenfreude whereby they were intensely amused by our growing distress, but either way, the upperclassmen answered our questions.

"Okay, so you said the best way to get books in the future is to get the book from a person that's already taken the class. But you also said that books change from semester to semester. How will I know before the next semester starts if the book I got is still usable?"

"You won't."

Odie's face bunched in confusion as she mulled this over.

"My professors have given me a lot of reading, due this week, but I didn't have the class until today and I didn't get the syllabus before now, so I'm already behind on my reading. I'd like to avoid repeating this predicament in the future. Is there any way to know which books I need before the semester starts?"

That from James, who'd been assigned volume one of *War and Peace* in addition to her regular textbook reading for her English 202 class. James was majoring in English and had tested out of most of the 100 level English classes. Her reading schedule was already more rigorous than almost everyone else's.

"No," one of the girls that stood around us replied. "Good luck though."

James made a small groan of distress.

I asked, "So does the bookstore order at least one book for everyone that's enrolled in a class? And will your professor give you an extension if you can't get a book for a class?" I'd noticed some of the shelves looked bare the closer we got to the entryway.

Resounding laughter from all around was the only response I received.

"So what are you supposed to do to make sure that you get your books?" James said so shrilly over the laughter, I turned to make sure she hadn't been replaced by a teakettle.

A smattering of responses cut through the din all of which equated to, "Buy your books at the first possible moment, hope it isn't on back order, or wait for it to come back in stock. And when it's back in stock, run the whole gauntlet again while praying the bookstore gods decide to bestow their grace upon you. Or drop the class."

Odie started biting her lip, a telltale sign she was worried, and it was no wonder—getting books should not have been this hard.

When the clerk that was monitoring how many students were in the store finally waved us in, we wiggled our way across the threshold.

In the home economics section, there were two, count them *two,* copies of *Introduction to Modern Textiles* left lying in a broken carton when I reached it. I grabbed mine happily and then almost dropped it again when I saw the pink sticker on the spine.

Thirty-five dollars?

That couldn't be right. Maybe they misplaced the decimal and the book was three dollars and fifty cents.

I glanced to my right and saw Odie pluck a book from a shelf and then stare at the price, equally confused. She looked over at me, and mouthed, "fifty-six dollars?"

I held my book tighter; there was a girl in a pink peplum ruffled dress that was eyeing it like it was gold bullion. And for the price they expected us to pay for these damned books they may as well have been actual gold. Knowledge was priceless, but this was a bit ridiculous.

A half hour and *$116* later, I'd obtained four of my books and found out the rest were on back order. I needed a nap and a summer vacation.

Odie trailed into the lobby a few minutes later, and James came out nearly twenty minutes later holding only a used copy of *War and Peace.*

"Jamesy, I can't believe they only had one of your books."

Her attention snapped to Odie and me like she'd just realized we were there. She smiled, looking rattled. "I know. Unbelievable, right?"

Odie stared at her sympathetically. "I didn't get my bio lab book. The lady said it's back ordered till next week. I guess I'll just have to . . . I don't know. Hopefully, my lab partner got one and I can just use hers. Did they say when your books will be in?"

"I . . . uhh, forgot to check," James said distractedly. "I'll come back when it's less crowded to see when they'll be available."

"What are you going to do until then, Jamesy?" she prodded gently.

"Oh, I'll figure it out. I just . . . I had no *idea* about all this—" She waved her hands around, signaling all we'd just endured. She frowned and looked even more disconcerted. "No one mentioned textbooks were so expensive. I don't know, I just . . . no one told me about this part." She sounded more distressed by the second.

"It's a racket!" Odie declared.

I'd gleaned a few things about James in the time we'd spent together. She didn't talk about her parents, but she mentioned that she came from "modest means"—her words. She also told me that she was the first person in her family to go to college, something I told her she should be immensely proud of even though she'd said it like it was something to be ashamed of. I also knew that when I'd gone to get my English 101 book for the whopping price of $45.82—the most insulting part had been the eighty-two cents—I'd noticed a stack of books for the 202 course sitting right there. It was entirely possible that James's professors had assigned some books that weren't part of the standard curriculum, but I suspected James only got one book not because there weren't any there, but because she couldn't *afford* them. And that made my heart clench. I wanted to usher her back into the bookstore, force her to pick out all her books, and put them on my account. But I also knew there was nothing James would like less than my help right now. She'd see it as pity and she'd see it as charity. This was nothing like the gift she gave me in private; this would happen in front of a whole host of folks. And if she was too embarrassed to tell us outright, then she'd be humiliated if I knew and made a big fuss about paying her way. I made a mental note to come up with a plan to try to get her books, even if I had to just anonymously buy them one at a time and leave them in her dorm room.

James led the way out of the Spence and as soon as her back was to us Odie shot me a look that said, "What are we gonna do?" and I knew she'd figured it out too.

I tapped my temple and raised my eyebrows so she'd know I was thinking of a plan and she nodded.

The work seemed to never stop, and toward the end of the week I was definitely feeling a bit like a guppy that was learning to swim, but I was managing. The remainder of the week was gauntlet free—well, not totally gauntlet free. The emotional one was still there.

When I got home from my last class on Thursday, a note was on my door—*Call Dolly.*

I'd just checked in three days ago. Dolly was being ridiculous. *One step forward, one hundred steps back with her.*

I ignored the note and started my studying, which went slowly because thoughts of my scheduled meeting with Trevor tomorrow kept invading my mind. Both Odie and James offered to walk me to the library but I told them I'd be fine. I would have to face Trevor once a week, every week, for the rest of the semester. I might as well rip the Band-Aid off.

Besides, in the very public library where everyone was required to remain quiet and calm, nothing too bad could happen. Plus, I had my plan. My plan that was rock solid. So rock solid I decided to start executing it that very moment. I pulled out a slip of paper and began jotting down my course updates. I was prepared. I would be fine.

I am prepared, I'll be fine. I am prepared . . .

I was not prepared.

CHAPTER FIFTEEN

Daisy

I woke up Friday with a boulder of dread in the pit of my stomach. The feeling grew every hour I got closer to having to meet Trevor. I found myself regretting my bravery, wishing instead that I'd been a coward and accepted my friends' offer to come with me.

I have a plan . . . Yeah.

I'd stopped telling myself that I was prepared, because not even my inner cheerleader was buying that lie anymore.

I headed to my room after my last class ended at noon, and tried to study but when I read the line, *"Textiles as they are today wouldn't be possible without the advent of the cotton gin"* as *"Trevors today wouldn't be possible without the Trevor of cotton gin,"* I realized the effort was futile. I closed my book and took a nap.

When my alarm went off at three thirty I saw that someone had slid a note under my door while I'd been asleep. I was tempted to throw it directly in the trash, thinking the *Call Dolly* messages had escalated to the next level of absurdity, but just before I tossed it I noticed my name written in pretty script across the folded square.

Unfolding it, I took in the words *"Meet me at Harris instead of the Library, same time."*

I reread the note, sure I must have it wrong. Surely not even Trevor was that cruel.

But isn't he? a voice responded.

Look at the way he chose to tell you he had a girlfriend.

And then there was the timing of the note's delivery. I didn't have time to refuse to change the location even if I wanted to. And I sure as hell wanted to.

And just like that, the pitcher of no feelings cracked. Feelings were seeping through the sieve.

He wasn't just content to humiliate me. No. I thought as I left my dorm and navigated down the drive in front, marching thunderously because I was *feeling* thunderous.

Like I could strike and kill at any moment.

He wanted to *keep* humiliating me.

Making me walk through this crowd, forcing me relive that moment is an asshole move.

Trevor Boone is an asshole.

I kept my head low as I snaked through the beginnings of what would morph into the block party all the while fighting to keep my temper under control. It was a futile effort. By the time the Harris building and Trevor propped against the archway at the top of the stairs were in my sights, all the feelings I'd spent the week containing were so very near the surface.

If I weren't so mad I may have noticed how he looked tired, like the week had worn him down to a nub. I may have cared how his eyes looked earnest, imploring, and a little sad. I did take note, even in my anger, that he still looked incredibly handsome, a fact that only served as kindling to my fire.

He saw me approaching and stood up straight, speaking while I was still on the sidewalk, "I thought we might meet here. There are less people, and besides, this building reminds me of you."

"I hate this building, because it reminds me of you too," I spat.

He rocked back on his heels like I'd slapped him as he looked down at me from the top of the stairs like he was king of the goddamned campus, and I'd just had it.

"You made me walk over here, the *same* as last week so I could be reminded—" I heard my voice crack on the last word and was ashamed that I'd shown him any of my hurt because there was nothing he deserved less. He didn't get to see me hurt. He didn't get to know that I care. *Cared.* Trevor deserved nothing. Less than nothing.

"Daisy, no! It wasn't like that. I didn't think about—"

"Of course you didn't. You're great at not thinking about how things make me feel, aren't you?"

I closed my eyes and sucked in a deep breath, already ready to have this over with.

When I opened them, my movements were efficient. I slid my hand into my purse and tossed him the slip of paper.

"That's an update on all my coursework and when I anticipate having the assignments done. I'll see you next week."

"Daisy, wait! Please!" He sounded so wounded that my steps stopped abruptly. My mind protested, *keep walking, Daisy.*

My feet however, did not get the signal.

I felt him draw closer, close enough that the hairs on the back of my neck stood. Close enough that his shadow eclipsed mine.

And then common sense hit me like a ton of bricks. I took a deep breath and stepped away.

He treated you like dirt and he has a girlfriend. A girlfriend that he's still treating like dirt. Trevor Boone is an asshole. He has no business standing close to me.

"Daisy, don't go. Please. I am going crazy. *This is killing me.* Stay. Talk to me or don't talk and just listen to me. Let me explain. Please, I've never felt like this. I—"

"Felt like what? Guilty?" I snapped.

"Yes. No. I mean, I *do* feel guilty but not for the reason you think," he said. I saw in my periphery his head drop into his hands.

"I miss you," he blurted. He sounded so desperate, so sincere.

And it was like a boot to my gut. I was angry at him for saying those words. Angrier still at myself for wanting to believe them when I knew they were lies. And I was angriest of all that it didn't matter if it was the truth or a lie. He had a girlfriend.

He didn't get to miss me.

He didn't get to unload his guilt on me.

He didn't get to ask me to talk, to give him my words when he hadn't even given me an apology.

He doesn't get anything.

The fury I felt made me turn, face him head on, and say the only words large enough to suffice in the moment. Ugly words, words of anger and pain, words that I couldn't take back once they were out.

"I hate you."

Not waiting to see his response, I turned and marched off and I vowed to myself those would be the last words I'd ever say to Trevor Boone.

He wanted my words? He would never get them.

When I arrived back at my dorm the ever-present yellow sticker was affixed to it. I didn't even glance at it. I crumpled the words *Call Dolly* and tossed them in the trash.

Trevor

I didn't remember walking home but I must've because I was sitting at my kitchen table—physically. Mentally, I was still at the moment Daisy said those three little words. They'd felt like a physical kick to the face. My stomach twisted, I'd felt a wave of nausea, I'd started sweating, and my heart tried to jump out of my chest and follow Daisy.

Three little words.

So absolute. So final. So devastating.

Definitely not the three little words I'd been wanting to hear. I'd have loved to have heard "I miss you."

I'd have settled for "Let's talk, Trevor."

My first mistake, of course, had been changing the location. Well, my first mistake had been dragging Daisy into my mess, but aside from that I hadn't considered that Daisy would see the parallel between when we were supposed to meet at Harris for our date last week and meeting to talk this week.

Mistake after mistake.

She'd been right. My only thought was finding a place where we could speak privately.

All week I'd hoped and prayed that time would have given her the opportunity to cool off before we spoke. When I realized the library was too public for the conversation I wanted to have, I'd changed the location to the music building for the same reason I'd chosen it as the starting point for our first date.

It reminded me of Daisy.

I'd just wanted to . . . not plead my case, but explain as best I could what happened last week. I couldn't tell her everything. And even if I could've told her everything it might not have made a differ-ence, but I wanted to tell her as much of the truth as I could. I owed her that much.

I wanted to apologize to her. Not for getting to know her, as selfish as it might have been; I wouldn't ever regret getting to know Daisy.

But I was sorrier than she'd ever know that I hurt her.

Stupid, Trevor. You should've led with that.

Maybe then she wouldn't have said . . . Her words snaked through my mind and my stomach lurched as the sick feeling began to rise again. I couldn't turn the memory off—Daisy looking at me with that same accusatory expression as she had last week, her eyes flat and hard. Daisy saying that she hated me.

She hates me. She hates me.

I had to figure out a way to make this right. This couldn't be the end of it—couldn't be the end of us.

We'd only just started. We'd barely begun to be a we.

I realized the folly of my plan to wait until graduation to pursue her properly.

She won't speak to you in a few months. She won't want to know you in a few months. Daisy is the sun and everyone is drawn to the sun. Everyone needs light. Do you really think she'll still be single at the end of the year?

Dread filled me. I shouldn't have left Daisy to cool down this week. She didn't cool down; she'd heated up, and now she was an inferno.

My regret multiplied.

In retrospect it all seemed so clear. Perhaps I could've waited until the end of the year to try to get to know her, but I'd been so caught up. I felt like Daisy had swept me off my feet with her generous spirit, her quick wit, and her easy smiles.

But none of that mattered now. Because she *hated* me.

She hates me.

I couldn't move past that moment. I couldn't go back and undo what was already done, and I couldn't see a way past this. I also couldn't let go of the hope that one day Daisy might not hate me.

I was a mess of conflicting emotions and it left me paralyzed.

I'm not sure how long I sat at the kitchen table before Jules came home, but when I snapped back into the moment he was standing in front of me clapping his hands just inches from my face.

"Thank God! For a second I thought I was going to have to call our damned parents and you know neither of us wants to deal with that," Jules joked.

When I didn't respond to his joke he turned from the sink and said, "What the hell is wrong with you?"

"Daisy hates me," I blurted.

Logically, I knew Julian was the wrong person to talk to about this. I was allegedly dating his cousin for Pete's sake. This was desperately unfair to him. But I was desperate. I had to get this sick feeling of helplessness out of me some way because I was so close to walking back to campus and telling Daisy the whole truth and nothing but the truth. And then begging for her forgiveness every which way.

I couldn't tell Jules the truth either but maybe I could share my . . .

Heartbreak?

Is that what this is?

Did Daisy break my heart? Could you have your heart broken if you weren't in love?

I wasn't in love.

But I saw now that I had been falling.

Julian looked at me like I'd grown another head and then said calmly, "Well, yeah, of course she does. You lead her on and then you dropped her as soon as your girlfriend returned to town."

He turned back toward the sink, twisting the knife. "If I were her, I'd hate your ass too. Hell, I only know about it and I'm two minutes away from hating you myself."

He grabbed his apple slices and sauntered toward his room.

Then he stopped and turned back around, and walked back to the table with what sounded like laborious steps. I heard the chair scape against the ceramic floor and he said, "Okay. I'm here. Talk."

I dropped my head in my hands because I didn't know where to begin.

After a second Jules joked, "Trevor, we both know I'm not known for my patience, but I really am trying here."

I nodded but otherwise said nothing.

"Look—I know we don't typically even talk about this type of stuff." I looked over at him expecting a grimace of distaste, but his expression wasn't that at all.

Jules looked confused and concerned. "I have to ask—do you love my cousin?"

"Of course I do," I answered automatically.

"Then I have to say I'm baffled. I don't know what's gotten into you, Trev, but something is clearly wrong. You're *not* an asshole. You are not indecisive. And you certainly aren't a womanizer. So what is this really all about?"

I didn't respond. I couldn't.

Julian raised his eyebrow, took his glasses off, and rubbed his eyes at my continued silence. When he spoke again he sounded surprisingly wistful, "I was always grateful that Elodie chose you. That you chose each other. I knew you were both good people. I knew that you'd both been through way too much. I knew you would be gentle with each other's hearts."

I cleared my throat but remained silent.

"But lately . . . Do you love *Daisy*, Trevor?" His gaze was piercing.

"No," I said quietly.

Please, Julian, don't ask me if I was falling in love with her.

Julian exhaled impatiently. "So this is just about guilt then?"

"Yes, I feel guilty. I took things too far with Daisy and I never should have done that. She didn't deserve that."

Julian looked chagrined. "I understand guilt better than you know. If that is true, then pull yourself together. I know this might be new to you because you don't normally mess up this awfully. You don't normally mess up at *all*—but this is the world we regular humans inhabit all the time. Sometimes you mess up *badly.* You say or do something horrific and you're *not* forgiven. You did a bad thing to Daisy. That is your bag to deal with. And it is not everyone else's job to feel bad for you because you feel guilty."

I knew all of that, but I couldn't give him any more context, so I just agreed. "Thanks, Jules. You're absolutely right. I'll work on getting myself . . . I'll work on it."

He nodded, grabbed his plate of apples, and headed back toward his room.

Stopping halfway, he called over his shoulder, "Trev?"

"Yeah?"

"You know . . . you know if you don't want to be with El, then I wouldn't have an issue with that, right? Same for her—I just want both of you to be happy."

"I know that, Jules."

Then he added, with a bit of flint in his voice, "Good, then I'll just say this plainly. Something about this whole thing still doesn't sit right with me, but I can't figure out what it is. You and Elodie are always so secretive about your relationship. You claim you're in love with her—"

I hadn't said I was in love with her; I'd said I loved her, but I held my tongue.

"But you still asked Daisy out. Elodie claims she loves you too, and yet she was all too happy to just move past what happened like it was nothing. And you might not have gone on an actual date with Daisy, but it was definitely not nothing. None of this makes any sense."

Julian was so damned smart it was amazing we'd been able to keep the ruse up for this long. I made a note to redouble my effort to convince Elodie to just tell him.

"I have to wonder why something that on the surface seems so easy has to be so hard."

He stood staring at me, one hand on his hip like a parent lecturing a wayward child. "Trevor, if you want to be with Daisy and Daisy, by some strange miracle, still wants to be with you, then apologize to Elodie and leave my cousin alone. If you want to be with Elodie, then be with Elodie! And stop moping around acting like you're doing her some favor by denying yourself Daisy. But Trevor—if you don't know *who* you want to be with, then be with your damned self. This *isn't* hard."

He turned his back and strode to his room.

I'd never take away Elodie's autonomy. God knew she had enough to deal with on her own, but this?

Julian was wrong. This was hard.

And it was *lonely.*

I hoped I would be able to convince her to let go of the notion that telling him would somehow result in calamity but I knew well how much guilt hooked a person.

I reminded myself to stay patient with her. She'd only ever told one other person, and then tragedy had ensued.

I got up from the from the table and hid away in my room. I found my graphite pencils and my pad and let myself get lost in the rote movements. When I'd first come to live with the Marshalls, drawing was the only thing that would soothe the ache of missing home. I'd draw my parents' store. I'd draw way the trees looked in the fall as the leaves abandoned them one by one. I'd draw little slices of Green Valley all the time. At the time, I'd thought it was just me testing my memory on how clearly it could remember, but as I got older I realized that maybe I was drawing things so I wouldn't forget them. For the first time in a long, long time, I thought of Green Valley and I felt even more melancholy. Could a place still be home if you hadn't lived there for nine years?

I sighed and let the thought go. I let the sound of the pencils scraping and scratching into paper and carving their marks, soothe me and lull me into a trance. It felt fitting somehow; I'd had marks carved into me this week.

Julian poked his head in to check on me at some point. I heard the note of surprise in his voice. "Drawing? You haven't done that in an age." I nodded—or at least, I thought I did—but I couldn't respond. It was the first bit of peace I'd felt all week and I was desperate to hold on to it. I heard the door close as he left me to my solitude.

I drew until the sides of my hand were stained grey and black, until my hands cramped, and even then I kept tweaking, opening the irises a bit, filling out the lashes.

I exhaled a resigned breath when I realized where my mind had taken me. Those were Daisy's eyes. *Just her eyes.* Vivid, beautiful, crinkled at the edges and full of joy. Her eyes the way they looked when she'd laughed with me. I stared at them for a long time, and I wondered if she'd ever look at me that way again.

CHAPTER SIXTEEN

Daisy

A lmost a month into the semester I felt like I was finally beginning to get my legs under me. The weeks had been filled with small victories. I'd attended every weekly check in with Trevor and hadn't said a blessed word to him. Our routine was as follows: we met in the library, I handed him my paper, he read it, and would give me a curt nod if he didn't have any questions. He would watch me leave.

Initially he'd tried making conversation, questioning me about whether or not any of my professors were giving me a hard time or asking if I had any questions about an upcoming project, but I'd been prepared. I'd calmly pull a small notebook out and written my responses. He'd raised his eyebrows and smiled like he couldn't help himself, then he'd read the answers and given me back my notebook.

I did not notice his gorgeous smile. Okay I did—I wasn't blind—but I didn't moon over it, and that felt like a victory.

And last week, I'd updated my weekly report with a line at the very top that said, *"All answers to questions will be responded to in writing within 72 hours and may be picked up from the office of Jubilee Hall."*

He'd raised his eyebrows and smirked but just shook his head. After he'd read over my update he'd nodded and I'd left.

I'd also run into Elodie Mayhew, literally.

I'd been coming out of the shower and bumped into her as she was walking to the next stall. Part of my mind wondered what she was doing here. I'd guessed she was visiting a friend; there were a handful of upperclassmen who lived in Jubilee, like our Resident's Assistants and some like Odie's roommate Janice, who had filled out her housing application late.

After I'd gasped from the shock of the impact and then gasped again from the recognition, I said what I'd been wanting to say to her. "I'm so sorry!" Because I was sorry. I wasn't sorry I'd kissed Trevor. I had no idea Elodie was his girlfriend when that happened. But I was sorry that I played any part in her getting hurt. And even though she wouldn't know that's what was behind my sorry, I wanted to give it to her anyway.

I had no idea if Elodie knew what happened, but Jules had seen Trevor and me kiss, and if he were any kind of cousin he would have told her about it.

Then again, if he were any kind of cousin he wouldn't still be hanging out with Trevor, yet I'd spotted them around campus, still thick as thieves. Either way, I wasn't going to tell her if she didn't already know what happened. I suspected she wouldn't take too kindly to a total stranger telling her two of the people she was close to had betrayed her. Especially if the person who was telling her also played a role in the story.

No, I was going to keep my mouth shut.

She'd grabbed her towel a little tighter, flashed a quick and sort of sad-looking smile, and said, "No, no it's my fault. This one's all on me." Then she sidestepped me and darted into the shower.

In addition to surviving the Elodie awkwardness and the Trevor meetings, I'd also gotten word that the last of my books that were back ordered were in stock.

Speaking of books, I still needed to figure out how we were going to help James. We were getting too far into the semester for her to still be without books. At my last count she had exactly three books. She'd been able to get a copy of the English 202 text from someone, and a copy of the *AP Stylebook* whose origins were unknown. I'd snuck a look at a couple of her syllabi and part of the issue was that English majors had a lot of supplemental reading. There were at least three books for each class. I had to give it to her though—the girl was resourceful. She had become the xerox queen. I didn't know where she was getting the copies but I suspected James had charmed some poor boy in her class into copying the first five chapters of each book for her.

I was ruminating on this and trying to study for my first round of exams that were slated for the following week when I heard a knock at my door. Odie, who was past waiting for responses from me, pranced in cheerily, singing, "Happy Friday! Wanna go with me on a mission?"

The clock read 4:58. Odie should've been in class.

She followed my line of sight and sang, "Cancelled!" And made jazz hands. "The professor didn't show up. Isn't the fifteen-minute rule glorious?"

I laughed and shook my head. "That is not a real thing."

She shrugged. "Well she didn't show. And I didn't feel like waiting around to dissect sheep brains or cow liver or baby geese wing membranes or whatever sadism she had planned for today."

"*Baby Geese* wing membranes?" I laughed. Odie hated her biology lab class with a passion.

"You know what I mean! Anyway, are you tied to your life of mathematics and fabrics or can you get away? I haven't seen you all week."

I stood, stretched, and grabbed my shoes and a light jacket since the weather was starting to change.

"Where are we headed?"

"Post office and then Sonny's to get a few things."

I grabbed the key to my P.O. box which I hadn't checked in a while. There was probably a check from my father waiting for me. Before I'd left home he'd told me that he would send me twenty dollars a month for my living expenses and that I needed to manage my money appropriately or I'd have to wait until the next month.

I'd brought some cash with me from Green Valley, but my funds were getting low.

When we opened Odie's P.O. box, she opened it eagerly and shouted "JACKPOT!" when she spotted two cards.

She did a little dance that made me crack a smile and then she ripped them open right there on the spot.

She grabbed a twenty from one card, squealed in delight, blew a kiss at the bill and then stuffed it in her pocket. Then she flipped the other card open, grabbed the five inside, hugged it to her chest, and read the card twice.

My P.O. box was empty.

"Who were the cards from?" I asked curiously as we headed toward Sonny's Convenience Store.

"My mom and pop sent me the card with five bucks," Odie replied her voice radiant. "They also sent me a note saying, 'Don't spend it all in one place.'"

We both laughed.

"And who was the big money from?"

"Oh that, that was from this sweet old lady at my church back home. She's absolutely loaded and has no grandkids. She loves spoiling all the kids from my church."

We arrived at Sonny's a few minutes later and I helped Odie as she picked out a few goodies for her room. Odie wasn't a big snacker. As a matter of fact, she wasn't a big eater, period, from what I'd noticed. Over the last month she'd become noticeably thinner, but she didn't look unhealthy at all. And when I'd asked her about her lack of appetite she'd just smiled and said she was a finicky eater and the food in the cafeteria didn't taste the same as home. I'd heard a few others ask about her slimmed-down figure and she'd dismissed them too saying she was "watching her figure" or "trying to lose her baby fat." The thing was—there was nothing wrong with how Odie already looked. She was heavier than both James and me but she was just curvier. Both James and I had told her that and she'd smiled in a way that meant, "I don't care what you say."

I wandered the aisles aimlessly since I was the closest I'd ever been to flat broke in my life until I ended up staring at a bag of flour. If I could have afforded it, I would've picked up the ingredients for some chocolate chip cookies. The ones I'd made in the skillet hadn't been half bad.

Odie snuck up behind me. Her "Boo!" caused me to jump a mile.

"What you dreaming of, Daisy?"

"Cookies," I said, dreamily. If my father sent me money next week I'd come back to the store and get the ingredients. I'd hoped to be doing a little more cooking in my Intro to Culinary Arts course, but the first four weeks had been heavy on food safety and light on cooking.

I spent that evening in Odie's room. Her roommate was rarely around but we made it a point to keep to Odie's side of the room anyway.

James eventually danced in holding a fish sandwich from Ed's Fish House and I jumped up and down as she held it high in the air above my head.

"Share, James! Share! Don't make me tickle you," I threatened.

Ed's Fish House sold the best fish sandwiches in all of Nashville.

"Why didn't you tell me you were going to Ed's!" I demanded.

"First of all, I didn't know myself. My study buddy, Calvin, asked me to go after class."

I raised one brow skeptically, at the use of the use of the term "study buddy." Calvin was a sophomore who was in James's Creative Writing class and English 202 class. I'd seen him around James a few times, and bless his poor bound-to-be-broken heart, he was half in love with her. I was not sure if James was unaware of his feelings or really good at pretending, but it was also clear that James saw him as a friend.

Only a friend.

James finally relented and handed me the sandwich.

"You didn't eat there?" I asked around a mouthful of warm white bread, sweet and tangy barbecue sauce, and white fish seasoned and fried to perfection.

She laughed. "I did, as a matter of fact . . . but I mentioned to him that you loved this sandwich so he sent one to you. Calvin said any friend of mine was a friend of his."

I tossed my arms around her midsection.

"Thank you, James!! And Calvin," I added belatedly. But really James because who was I kidding? He hadn't gotten this sandwich for me; he'd done it to impress James.

She gave me a look. "Well I didn't do anything. But I'll pass your sentiment on to Calvin when I see him again."

"And when will you be seeing him again?" Odie asked, raising an eyebrow at James.

"On Tuesday in class," James said lightly.

"Oh, don't give me that! You can't tell me that boy hasn't asked you out."

James shrugged. "Calvin is my study buddy. I'm not going out with him."

"Does he know that?" Odie asked.

"I don't know, Odie, but if he ever asks me on a date I will tell him!" James snapped.

"Unngghh." Odie growled in the back of her throat.

"James!"

"What?"

"It's not right to take advantage of someone's niceness just because you can! You're going to break that boy's heart. If you're not interested, don't lead him on. You saw what just happened to poor Dai—"

Her words died before she finished.

Humiliation I'd considered long dead flared and then simmered.

"I'm sorry, Daisy! I—I shouldn't have said that."

I shrugged. "It's fine. I was led on, and it did hurt. Folks shouldn't do it. But I don't think that's what James is doing."

Odie made that strangled sound again. "She shouldn't accept things from him or . . ."

"Odie, James isn't responsible for her looks. Neither are you, neither am I. And we certainly can't control how other people *react* to those looks. To my knowledge, James hasn't given that boy any reason to think she's interested in him."

James nodded her head in agreement.

But I wasn't letting her off the hook that easy.

Then I turned to my devastatingly gorgeous friend. "Odie has a point, you know. He does like you. And because he likes you, you should make it perfectly clear that he has no chance with you. That is —if you haven't already done that. And if you're spending time with him just because you want to get free stuff out of it, then you need to quit that too."

She shook her head. "I'm not, but I see what you mean. Calvin is nice, but he's my study buddy, full-stop. He knows we're just friends."

Odie changed the subject and the mood lightened as she caught James up on our afternoon excursion. I made them both laugh by doing a dramatic reenactment of Odie seeing all that money fall out of the cards.

"Hey, I was broke. I really needed that cash."

"I hear you. I'm running low on cash myself." I laughed.

James shook her head defiantly. "Neither of you will know broke until you walk a mile in my shoes. At least you came to school with money—I came here with lint in my pockets."

She smiled and then looked away like she'd said too much.

"What would you buy if money was no object?" Odie asked from her spot on the bed as we lay on the rug.

"Easy," said James. "A Canon F-1 and all the film to go with it."

I knew James was interested photography. She'd mentioned once that she had been in the photography club in high school and that they'd lent them cameras to use. She sounded like she missed it a lot.

"James, if you love photography so much why aren't you majoring in it?" Odie asked before I could get the words out.

James laughed. "Because I need to be employed—*stably* employed—when I graduate. There's always gonna be newspapers, so journalism is a better bet."

Odie nodded as if that rationale makes sense.

"But couldn't you take photographs for the paper?" I countered.

James shrugged noncommittally. "Yes, I suppose I could. But that's not the type of photography I love. I don't want to snap people when they've just been pulled from their burning house or whatever tragedy has befallen them that day. Besides, I really do like writing too—it's not a hardship."

I wanted to argue with James that tragedies were not the only types of photographs printed in the papers, but I didn't because I realized that was beside the point. I bit my tongue. I had no right to encourage James to act recklessly when it came to financial preparation for her future. Even if I felt like she was giving up on her dream.

Odie piped up, "I'd hire a person to help me get as thin as you and James." Before either of us could interject she added, "And I'd buy *yarn.*"

She said the word yarn with such deep longing I wondered if I was missing out by not knowing how to knit. "I hardly ever get new yarn at home, so I take apart old projects and reuse it."

"That's so resourceful," James said diplomatically.

James was right. It was resourceful, but it too made me sad.

The distance between how my friends and I were raised—no, not how we were raised, how we were provided for—and how that had shaped our dreams for the future felt acute.

Because the first thing that came to my mind when Odie asked me what I'd buy if money was no object was the ten-acre lot off Route 40 that would be the perfect spot for my eatery. My friends wanted cameras and yarn. I wanted a business.

The moment I'd been dreading came, "What about you, Daize?"

By divine intervention, I was struck with an idea. An idea so brilliant I blurted it as soon as it popped into my mind. "James, I think I know how to help you get your books!"

James looked to Odie, bewildered.

"What?"

"You can't afford them, right? That's why you haven't gotten your books yet?"

James bristled and I realized I was handling this wrong. Odie shot me a wide-eyed "What the hell are you doing?" look and I rushed to finish.

"Please don't be ashamed—like you told me: this isn't charity, we're friends."

James fidgeted with her hands and then nodded once curtly.

"I think we should have a bake sale!"

As soon as the words were out of my mouth, I realized it was a colossally dumb plan.

Odie stared at me.

James stared at me.

It was like someone had made that whoopee cushion, balloon deflating sound in the silence and that someone was me.

I felt compelled to explain the direction in which my brain had been headed. "I'm sorry! I just have had a hankering for some cookies. Then I remembered the night I *did* make cookies and how folks were stopping me for days after Diana and Ruth told them how good they were. And y'all kept asking me to make them. I thought I could just make a bunch of cookies since I have access to the home ec building . . . but I see that this . . . is a dumb plan." Even if I could figure out how to move the cookies back and forth it would bring too much attention to my dorm room and I'd get caught.

Odie was squinting her eyes and scrunching her nose at the same time. "No. It's not a dumb plan, but it is one that needs a bit of ironing."

To my surprise, James appeared to have her thinking cap on too.

"How much you think we can sell those cookies for, Daisy?"

"I-I don't know. Maybe three for a dime, or quarter. But we can't . . ." I looked at my friends confused. This was a patently bad plan.

"Jamesy, how much do those books of yours cost all totaled?"

James dropped her head in her hands. "One hundred forty-eight dollars and seventy cents."

Odie whistled. "That's a helluva lot of cookies."

James laughed. "Yeah, but I think . . ." She squinted back at Odie. "That we might be able to pull it off."

"Y'all can't be serious! I just told you it isn't possible."

"What if we used a password?" Odie suggested.

"What do you mean?" This from James.

"Folks could only buy cookies if they knew the password."

"It still wouldn't work. You heard how much money we need to raise. It would just be too many folks coming in and out—password or not. Besides, selling something out of your dorm room seems like the best way to get caught."

"Okay well, how should be do it, Daisy?" James looked at me expectantly and so did Odie.

"What? We shouldn't do it! I told you all it was a bad plan. There is no fixing it."

"Fine then, I guess Jamesy here will just fail all her classes," Odie said with sass.

"Hey!" James and I yelled in unison.

I bit my lip and began talking through the plan, absurd as it was. "If we could figure out a way to let folks know to come to one of the three of us when we're out and about on campus . . . then maybe it would work. But that would mean we would have to carry cookies all the time and that would be a pain."

My friends and I went back and forth discussing various aspects of my idea but we couldn't get past the impractical nature of having to carry a bunch of cookies along with all our books and personal items.

It was James that finally solved the problem.

"Let outs! All we have to do is show up to a few parties as they're ending and sell the cookies there. It will be late, most things will be closed, and everyone will have been drinking and will be hungry . . . and then *BAM!* We show up like the cookie fairies."

I ignored the way her words made my heart skip a beat as I remembered Trevor telling me that I looked like a fairy with my sunshades on.

I blinked away the memory and refocused. "Okay, that part is solid, but we still have one big problem. We're broke. Even Odie with her sixty bucks doesn't have enough money to buy all the flour and eggs and butter and chocolate chips that we'd need to get started."

"You don't have that stuff in the home ec building? Don't y'all cook in there?"

"Yes, but not to this scale. In order to get as much of each item as we'd need, we'd need access to like, an industrial kitchen . . ."

James and I turned to stare at Odie, obviously having the same thought.

"What? Why are you looking at me like that?" Odie demanded.

James looked at her imploringly. "Odie. We need access to an industrial kitchen. This plan depends on us getting access to the things in that kitchen. My *education* depends on it. I've been getting by but having books would make things a lot easier."

"Okay, I got that but—"

"Who do we know who has access to the university kitchen, Odessa?"

Odie looked between the two of us and I could see the moment comprehension hit. She closed her eyes, dropped her head in her hands, nodded once, and whispered, "*Dammit.*"

Saturday morning we headed to breakfast and Odie repeated the same litany she'd been echoing all that night. "James, you owe me. You owe me so big for doing this. I don't even think you know how big you owe me. Anything. Anytime. Anywhere. James, I'm serious."

"Okay, Okay." James laughed. "I said yes!" Then she added, "I mean, if you want, I can ask Lucy to ask her brother."

Odie glared at her. "You leave Lucy out of our cookie capers. It's bad enough that I'm going to have to keep this from her."

I realized immediately that Odie was right. Asking Lucy's little brother to steal from the university kitchen *probably* wouldn't go over well.

I bit my lip again.

We probably shouldn't go through with this.

Even though the plan had been mine, I'd been trying to talk us out of it since it had first come out of my mouth, but James and Odie were committed to it.

The last time I'd suggested we drop the plan James looked at me and said, "I know I should've said something earlier but I didn't because, I don't know . . . I was too embarrassed and too proud and didn't want to burden you all with my problems. But Daisy, I really need these books. And this plan can help me get them."

After that I'd dropped it.

It wasn't until we were leaving breakfast that Odie made her move. Charlie was bussing a table as we approached. When she said his name, he dropped a hard plastic cup he'd been holding. It slammed into the floor and broke into two pieces with an ear-splitting crack.

Charlie didn't even glance toward the cup. "Is Lucy okay?"

"What? I think so," Odie said shrilly. "Why? What's happened?"

Charlie shook his head and said, "You're talking to me is what happened. It caught me by surprise is all and I thought . . ."

"No. Lucy is fine," Odie said firmly. Then she took a deep breath and said, "Listen, can you meet me outside for a few minutes? I have something I need—we need—to ask you."

Charlie looked confused for a second then . . . his expression morphed into one that was so hopeful that my stomach bottomed out. *We should back out of this plan. Immediately. He likely thinks this conversation is going in a far different direction than it's headed.*

Charlie excitedly agreed and asked us to wait outside for him, promising that he'd join in a few minutes.

When he came jogging out of the building, I teased him to break some of the tension I was feeling. "I can't believe Mrs. Dot let you go on break."

He smiled wanly. "She doesn't work most weekends. Sometimes on Saturdays, but never on Sunday's because she goes to church. Mr. Jimmy is usually off too. On the weekends, Miss Julia runs the kitchen." He said it in the same wistful admiring tone a five-year-old boy would use as he spoke about his love for his kindergarten teacher.

"Listen, Charlie," Odie started, never one for beating around the bush. "I need a favor from you." She gestured to James and me. "*We* need a favor from you. We need you to get us some butter, milk, flour, eggs, and cinnamon from the kitchen."

He stared at us. And stared at us . . . Then Charlie Love laughed and said, "Okay, why did you really call me out here?"

Odie looked pointedly at James, shrugged and said, "Well, I tried." Then she threw her hands up and began walking away.

"Wait!" Charlie called, sounding desperate, even though James and I hadn't moved a muscle.

I stepped in and quickly explained the predicament and our solution, leaving James out of it. I summed it up by saying, "In short we need to earn one hundred-fifty dollars."

When I was finished I asked him, "Will you help us?"

He looked blown away.

Then he surprised me by saying, "I'm not saying I'll help you, but if I do, why not just use the university's kitchen instead of moving all this stuff back and forth?"

"Is that an option? I figured you didn't have a key to the building and that there was likely very little time when the kitchen wasn't occupied. I'd guess you probably don't get out until nine thirty or ten on nights the kitchen closes at eight and Mrs. Dot and crew are probably back at four a.m. to start cooking."

I saw him about to object so I added, "Plus the home economics building is completely unoccupied over the weekend and that part of campus isn't as heavily trafficked. Whereas this"—I pointed to all the people passing nearby—"almost always looks like this. Someone would see us even if you could sneak us in."

He agreed with me reluctantly.

"I'm not saying I'm in, but . . . if I do this, what's in it for me?"

My eyes bugged out. "Charlie man! I just said that we're broke!"

He shook his head. "I don't want money."

"Odie," he called, and she looked up at the sky like she was begging the Lord to come and save her.

When no crack of lightning came from above, Odessa looked at Charlie and exhaled a long suffering, "Yes, Charles."

"If I do this, then you have to make a deal with me."

She looked warier than I'd ever seen her.

"Not them, Odie, you. This is between me and you. And if I get involved in all this it'll be because of you." He was looking at her with the intensity of seven suns and Odie was fighting back with every ounce of her being.

Charlie was also not one to mince words. There must have been something in the water down in Charleston.

What the hell happened between these two?

"What do you want?"

"I want you to forgive me."

"No."

"Odie, please . . . this is *killing* me."

"No. Next."

A prickle of unease coursed through me as I realized I'd seen this situation play out before . . . only with me and Trevor. Trevor had used those exact same words. *This is killing me.*

I looked at Charlie who, up until that very moment, I'd always felt a modicum of sympathy for. The question reframed itself in my mind.

What the hell did he do to her?

Because those puppy dog eyes Charlie gave her were suddenly very clearly filled with guilt.

"Fine." Charlie huffed. Then he said so softly I almost didn't hear him, "Then I want you to start really eating."

Odie reared back and her hand flew up as if she was going to slap him, but James caught her arm midair.

She looked at James, blinked and swallowed before saying, "Thank you, James."

James nodded, stepped back, and let her hand go.

Her words were venom, heat, and little more than a hiss when she addressed him again. "*You* don't get to talk to me about that. You don't *ever* get to mention that to me."

She turned her back to him, looked to me and James, and opened her palms placatingly.

"I can't do this anymore. I'm sorry. I just can't."

As Odie walked away, James whirled on Charlie, her eyes full of recrimination. "What the hell did you do to my friend, Charles Love?"

He hung his head and then looked up, guilt and shame written all over his handsome face. "I think . . . I broke her. And I have no idea how to fix it."

In the end, Charlie refused to tell us what he'd done to Odie but he agreed to help us. The only assurance we were able to give him when it came to Odie was that we would try to get her to say hello or acknowledge him, and we assured him that we did see her eat.

"She's picky for sure, but she eats," James said. It felt very strange to be asked to ensure that another adult ate food. James and I were baffled by the whole thing but it seemed to set Charlie's mind at ease.

As Charlie walked back in the building I had the distinct feeling we were setting him up to become a bird flying at its own reflection.

So I called to him, "Charlie, why is it so important to you? Getting Odie to speak to you—why is it so important?"

It was never gonna happen between the two of them; he had to know that. He turned to face me, walking backward with hands in his pockets. "Because I love her. And when you love someone you never stop fighting for them. Odessa Mae Boyd taught me that."

Trevor

Dr. Gwinn closed the door behind her and sat on the edge of her desk. I already knew why I'd been summoned and that this was going to be mildly painful, so I was ready to get it over with.

"I had an interesting faculty meeting this morning. Can you guess why it was interesting, Trevor?"

I could but I wouldn't, so I just stared at her. Dr. Gwinn was not the type to blink first, so of course I ended up looking down at my hands.

"Your name came up five different times. Your professors are all saying that you've gone from their star pupil to someone they hardly recognize. Even here with me, you are withdrawn. What on earth is going on? I've seen seniors become unfocused, but this is so unlike you."

Oh, I'd been focused all right. The seven sketchbooks in my room filled with butterflies, daisies, and *Daisy* could attest to just how focused I'd been, but I'd not been paying attention to school.

As if she pulled the thoughts from my mind Dr. Gwinn said, "Is it Daisy?"

"What?" I responded, wide-eyed and flabbergasted because as far as I was aware, she didn't know anything had happened between Daisy and me. I prayed daily that she'd never find out.

"Is Daisy taking too much of your time? I've gotten your reports and I see that she's done well on her first exams. I'm wondering if you're spending so much time helping her that you're sacrificing your grades for hers?"

She had no idea. I wanted to both laugh and cry at her question.

Imagine Daisy letting me help her. Imagine Daisy letting me anywhere near her.

Daisy had been ruthlessly efficient over the last few weeks; she always gave a very detailed report on her grades, she was always on time, and she was totally silent.

She hadn't given me a word or a lingering glance.

And that was fine. I deserved her silence.

"No, Daisy isn't taking up too much of my time."

It was lie because she occupied an ungodly amount of my head-space, but it was also the truth because she gave me less than ten minutes of her time a week. I smiled and shook my head at how stubborn she was. Part of me was proud of her for sticking to her guns. If I was the person she believed me to be, I'd want her to stay far away from me too.

The other part of me wanted to shake her senseless.

Regardless, it was clearly time for me to put Daisy out of my mind. She was out of reach for now. Maybe even forever.

No, not forever.

But definitely for now.

This week had been a wake-up call. Seeing professor after professor concernedly hand me back my papers with C's or D's or worse.

I couldn't afford to continue on like this. Midterms were in three short weeks, and if I performed the same way I had on these first exams then everything I'd worked the last three years for would be erased.

I could still swing an A in most of my classes, but I was going to have to bust my ass to do it. More importantly, I'd opened up the door for someone else—probably Gracie; she was right behind me the last time I'd checked—to finish number one in our class.

It wasn't just Daisy that had been weighing on me, although she'd been the biggest part for certain. Everything was taking its toll on me. Keeping this secret of Elodie's from Jules and the friction in our relationship that it'd created. Seeing Gracie hurt every time El was out and about pretending to be in love with me. It was all too much. I knew I hadn't been myself; I'd been reclusive and withdrawn. I hadn't even attended any of our frat functions.

I didn't go to anything except classes and occasionally to the cafeteria to grab a bite . . . and that was fine with me. I didn't have to pretend when I was alone.

"I've just been unfocused, but these test scores sent the message loud and clear. I won't let it happen again." I squirmed because Dr. Gwinn was looking at me like she was trying to peel back my skullcap and look directly into my brain.

"Trevor—"

"Yes, Dr. Gwinn?"

"Are you sure this mentorship isn't too much for you? It's the only thing that's changed and I can't help but lean toward eliminating it as an extra time suck for you."

I didn't hesitate. "Dr. Gwinn, Daisy is the most efficient person

I've ever met. It's a pleasure"—the word burned my tongue—"to mentor her. You trusted me to mentor her, please trust me to see it through."

Panic had my hand shaking so I discreetly shoved it in my pocket. The idea of not even seeing Daisy once a week, even if it was to just glare at me and hand me a piece of paper, had me on edge.

"Fine. But on Monday mornings I want a status report on *you* added to your status report on her."

She looked back down at the papers on her desk and I stood, understanding that I was dismissed.

I was going to get my act together. I was going to get my grades together.

And for the time being I was going to put Daisy out of my mind. Timing was everything. I'd overplayed my hand, and now . . . now was not our time. I hoped and I prayed that I would and could have a chance with her in the future but for now, it was cemented in my head that she was firmly out of reach.

When I arrived home Julian was sitting in my bedroom. I glanced around to make sure I'd put away my drawing materials before my come-to-Jesus meeting with Dr. Gwinn. Relief flooded me when I saw that I'd been smart enough to hide my Daisy obsession. The last thing my relationship with Julian needed was for him to have found notebooks filled with my longing for Daisy.

"You and Elodie both. Neither of y'all know how to knock and wait for me to say you can come in."

Jules smiled but it looked uncharacteristically melancholy. "I missed my best friend and thought maybe you'd hidden him in here."

The comment stung because it was true.

I'd been holding Julian at arm's length, through no fault of his own. It seemed it was everyone's day to have their come-to-Jesus meeting with me.

"Jules, I—"

He held up his hand. "I just wanted to ask you to reconsider coming to the party tonight, I think . . ." He paused and looked around my room. "I think getting out of this room would be good for you."

I agreed instantly, "You're right, and I'm in."

He looked surprised. The first genuine smile I'd seen on his face in a long time flashed.

"You'll come?"

I nodded. "Of course I will. It's our party, after all. Give me some time to grab a bite and get ready." It wasn't my frat's first party of the year, but it would be the first one where I'd be in attendance.

He smiled hugely. "Of course. Take all the time you need."

The last thing I felt like doing was going to this party. But after tonight I'd have very little time for socializing. I would need to hunker down and focus on my studies. And besides, Julian was right —I needed to pull myself out of my funk and move on with enjoying some of my senior year.

Daisy

"I am not wearing that, James. Where did you even get this? We're supposed to be making money, not spending it!"

James waved me off. "It was donated."

"Donated? James, who had these shirts just lying around?"

"Who said anything about them lying around? If someone wants to support enterprising young ladies then who am I to keep them from making shirts for us? Besides they really aren't that bad, they're promoting the product!" Her words were a bit too innocent, and by the glint in her eye she knew it.

We'd fleshed out the final version of the plan and put James on marketing and promotion for the cookies. It made sense as James knew about all the best parties and she had the gift of gab, but now . .

. to say I was having second thoughts was an understatement. Matching outfits had not been a part of the deal.

"Enterprising young ladies," Odie said drily. "And what product precisely did this kind and generous sponsor think we were selling, Jamesy?"

James rolled her eyes.

"Listen, I am a creative! I have vision! These shirts will help us sell these damned cookies faster which means we get to stop selling cookies faster. Now put your shirts on! Daisy, please let your hair down, guys like it better that way. Both of you find a pair of your best black hot pants or you can wear the ones I supplied, and let's get a move on! The Roll with Black and Gold skate party ends at two a.m., it's already one thirty, and I don't have time to argue with you."

For what it was worth, I was too tired to argue with James.

But not so tired that I was going to wear the hot pants she'd supplied; they may as well have been panties. I would wear my own hot pants, thank you very much.

I was grumbling because I was tired—I'd spent the last six hours mixing batter and baking cookies. And I had only had a five-minute shower and two minutes to sit before James had barged into my room with her wardrobe demands.

I grabbed the shirt and started to dress.

Things had gone blessedly smoothly. Charlie had met Odie and James by the dumpsters behind Spence, and he'd delivered goods in the two empty duffle bags Odie had "mistakenly" left earlier that day in the cafeteria. I'd confirmed the coast was clear in the home economics building around five forty-five, after which we'd gone to work.

And that was how we ended up in the parking lot of the skate rink holding baskets of still-warm cookies wrapped with bows. The three of us all wore matching outfits: knee-high boots, hot pants, fishnets, and black T-shirts with the words *Wanna Eat My Cookie?* emblazoned across the bosom.

The picture of a bitten cookie added a nice effect.

Odie had volunteered to pick Lucy up from the party so we rode there in Lucy's vehicle.

My hair fell around my shoulders and I was grateful for the little warmth it provided. As it was, James and I huddled in the back seat, shivering from the chill in the October air, in our too few clothes.

The doors to the roller rink opened and people began to stream out.

James, Odie, and I locked our pageant smiles into place and stepped out of the car.

The first sale was almost immediate. Two guys walked up to James—surprise, surprise—and bought three bags of cookies. From the smell coming off the guys, there was a high probability that they had a case of the munchies.

Two girls approached me to buy one bag each. "Nice shirt." One giggled as her friend smiled and quipped, "I should get it for you to wear even though you're not selling any cookies."

I began to relax. Maybe I'd overreacted a bit. People saw the joke of the shirt and, even better, they were hungry and snapping up the cookies. I hadn't even been out there five minutes when my basket started running low and I had to head back to the car to refill it.

The parking lot was full now, the noise around us rising to a cacophony.

People lingered, chatting and making plans for the after party or deciding which party to hit next. Couples paired up and slunk off for what I could only imagine would be steamy nights.

I couldn't let my mind dwell on that, not when I had no steamy night prospects, and more importantly, not when I had people clamoring for cookies. Thank God for small, home-baked miracles.

All around us folks were opening wrappers and passing cookies to their friends who'd then come over to buy a packet for themselves. Some folks were even coming back to stand in line, yes there was a *line,* in front of Odie and one forming in front of me. I doled out the little packets, took the dollar bills and made change as fast as I could, and before long I was so caught up with customers that I didn't hear the commotion until was too late to prevent it.

Suddenly, there were two guys fighting right in front of James. She stepped back and looked up at me, her expression morphing quickly from surprised to bemused.

Then a familiar voice rang out over the clamor. "What in the ever-loving hell is going on here?" I recognized Julian's bombastic twang instantly.

Lovely.

Julian moved through the crowd easily. They parted to get out of his way, some fleeing from the ruckus the two fighting idiots created. He didn't hesitate before jumping into the fray and pulling the two boys, who wore the same fraternity colors as Julian, apart.

"I dare either of you to take the first swing at me!"

They both backed up. I'd never heard Julian's voice thunder the way it was booming. Even in the dead of night, his coloring had turned pink. He was livid.

"You are fighting at one of *our* parties?" He made no attempt to hide how incensed he was.

Odie had come over from where she was standing and we both silently pressed closer to James.

My steps faltered when I saw Trevor exit the rink and move hurriedly to Julian's flank.

He locked eyes with me, and for a second his appeared to flare. I couldn't tell if it was from the shock of seeing me or if it was from the shock of seeing me wearing this outfit.

I held my breath. I'd known this was Trevor's fraternity; I just hadn't allowed myself to dwell on that fact. I wouldn't look away and I wouldn't be ashamed. I had nothing to be ashamed of. My feet started working again and I caught up to Odie and James.

The big guy on Julian's left said, "I saw her first and Mike comes in and tries to snake me—"

"No, I saw her first! And besides, she's not interested in you," the guy who I could only assume was Mike responded.

Julian spoke over them. "*I* saw her first and if I see either of you two idiots near her again, you'll have to deal with me. Get out of here, go back to the house. Trev and I will be there to deal with you when we're done here."

I saw the guys slink away, seeming smaller after the stupid exchange. James, on the other hand, crackled with anger. Her eyes were slits and she'd shoved her basket into Odie's hands and stepped into Julian's face, finger wagging. "What the hell was that, Julian? You don't just get to come up here and claim me."

"Is that what I did? I just prevented two idiots from fighting over you! I just prevented two sloppy fools from possibly hurting you or any number of people around you. And James—if I were to claim you, would absolutely know it."

James did an admirable job of not responding to the last part. Instead I saw her chin jut out indignantly. "You just lost me two paying customers."

Julian took his time looking her up and down and then leveled her with his honey brown eyes and said lazily, "Those two can't afford what you're selling."

James eyes met him head-on. Without her mask in place, I could see that there were emotions, deep ones that simmered just under the surface, when it came to Julian. I couldn't tell if they were positive or negative emotions but what was evident were the sparks firing between them.

With the mischievous look of a schoolboy pulling his crush's pigtails, Julian reached into the basket Odie still held, grabbed a bag of cookies, opened the packet, and took a bite.

She snatched her basket back from Odie indignantly and hissed, "You don't get to just take my cookies, Julian P. Marshall."

He stepped into her space fully and with James's height, they were chest to chest, almost eye to eye.

I heard Odie suck in a breath as she reached for my hand. I could see why—the tension and heat coming off the two of them was almost palpable. It felt like the energy in the air right before the storm.

Julian leaned in near James's ear and said so low I almost missed it, "You're absolutely right. I'm not going to take your cookies, gorgeous, you're going to *give* them to me."

He stepped back and looked at me and Odie. "How much for all the cookies?"

Odie didn't answer him. Instead, she whispered by my side so softly only I could hear her, "My word, he can have all the cookies."

I could see what she meant. Julian's handsomeness was borderline lethal when he focused all of it on you.

James hissed, "Daisy's cookies are delectable delights, and we would never sell any to the likes of you!"

Lightning fast, Trevor and I made eye contact—remembering my confession that my doughnuts would melt in his mouth.

Then I saw his eyes widen as he read my shirt, and I had no doubt when I saw his nostrils flare and his fists ball that he was wondering if the same thing were true of my cookies.

I looked away.

Odie had regained her wits, and stepped in front of James who had clearly lost the ability for rational thought. "One twenty!"

Jules reached into his back pocket, pulled out his wallet, and handed Odie a stack of twenties. She quickly tallied them.

"You gave me one forty." She extended the extra bill back in his direction.

He shook his head. "Keep the extra twenty if it means you'll stay *away* from our parties from here on out. There's something about the three of you that makes men lose their goddamned minds and I'll be damned if I need that kryptonite around my idiot frat brothers . . . or me," he added quietly.

"We're not agreeing to—"

"Deal!" I said. Disregarding Julian's insults, we were not responsible for his idiot frat brothers' behavior. Or his.

I pulled James, who still seemed verklempt, back toward Lucy's car.

I felt Trevor's eyes on me as I walked briskly away. Just as I was almost out of his range, he reached into my basket and grabbed a packet of cookies.

I did not turn around, even though I felt the weight of his gaze as I forced James to get in the car.

In the safety of Lucy's car, I could still feel those magnetic eyes of his calling me. Finally, I turned and looked out of the window. He was still watching me and as he held my eyes, he licked his lip, raised my cookie to his mouth, and took a bite.

I shuddered then broke eye contact, feeling disappointed in myself.

He has a girlfriend, Daisy. Get a grip.

Lucy climbed in the vehicle a few seconds later and brought me back to reality swiftly.

"Why the hell are you three always into something? And why on earth does my car smell like chocolate chip cookies?"

CHAPTER SEVENTEEN

Trevor

I t was nearly four in the morning and I was weary to the bone, turned on, and unable to get the taste of Daisy's delicious cookie out of my mouth.

There had to be more than flour and eggs in the batter. It seemed Daisy was destined to bewitch all she touched; food was no exception. It was the best cookie I'd ever tasted, so much so that I wanted to savor it.

That's not all you want to savor.

We're in Julian's car headed home finally, after having dealt with our knuckleheaded frat brothers. I downshifted, stopping at the light. Jules had been drinking, which meant I was driving. Julian wasn't drunk, thank goodness. Liquor made him chatty and silly, and I was too tired to deal with either.

I hadn't been able to get Daisy out of my mind.

Daisy in that outfit, wearing that shirt . . . Daisy with those long legs on full display, with that hair wild and . . . sexed up.

Yes, Daisy had that just-rolled-out-of-bed thing going on with her hair and it was . . . I shifted uncomfortably in my seat.

Daisy haunted and taunted me.

And I hated what thoughts of her did to me. I hated the way she hijacked my thoughts. Except . . .

I also loved it. Because no one had ever captured my attention so completely. The way she'd looked at me defiantly, letting me know she was uncowed by my presence. In addition to being gorgeous, she was strong . . . and stubborn.

"You've got the light," Jules said tiredly.

I accelerated and then glanced over at my friend who was unusually quiet. Julian didn't just look tired, he looked out of sorts and I figured I knew why.

"So, James?" I said. I was going for light but it came out sounding incredulous.

James and Julian would've made a lot of sense. She might be the only girl I'd ever seen that could handle that combination of ego and charm without being overshadowed by it. And by Julian's reaction tonight, he was all too aware of it. So I was puzzled on why he would elect to insult her instead of turning on the charm the first time he'd seen her.

And it would have seemed to me that if you liked Daisy, you should have made sure you were completely free to pursue her before you started to woo her. I told my inner monologue to stop being judge and jury and to shut up.

He dropped his head low, bracketing the sides of his face with his hands. I could imagine why.

Julian had just shown his whole hand to James. If she hadn't known that he liked her before, she sure as hell knew it now.

To top it off, he wasn't really given to public displays of any kind. Tonight was completely out of character for him.

Then again lov—*I wouldn't think that word.*

Attraction made you do strange things.

Julian was still silent but had shifted slightly and was slumped against the window looking totally dejected.

"Since when did she leave her mark on you?" I prompted.

He laughed without any mirth whatsoever. "That's a very accurate way to put it. Since the first time I saw her. I thought James was the most beautiful girl I've ever seen since day one. And I've wanted her since then. I've seen her this entire semester, she's in my—"

"Wait, back up, the day you insulted her?"

"No," he said firmly. "That was a few days later. I'd already spotted her before then. I saw her the morning of freshman move-in. She saw me too, but she pretended she didn't. She has a way of making a person feel invisible if she wants to."

I did vaguely remember Jules mentioning something about a pretty girl that morning but I'd had my own pretty girl on my mind.

"And that was no small part of my anger with you the day I saw you with her and Daisy, if you want to know the truth."

"I didn't make you insult her, Julian! You could've chosen another way to get me alone, you know."

"I know that." His voice was quiet, introspective. "She makes me trip over my tongue like you wouldn't believe."

This confession from him was a shock and judging by the grimace on his face, it cost him to admit it. Jules was a born orator. There was a reason he was the one that wanted to go into law, the reason that he was the one at the top of the ticket. Julian was persuasive. He didn't get tongue-tied.

"It wasn't logical, but it was easier to blame you for what I said than to take responsibility for it myself." He paused and sighed heavily.

"The other part of it was self-sabotage. I know that I can't have James. I always knew that I couldn't have her, even if she were interested in me. So it would be better to remove any temptation of her ever liking me. It's better that she hates me, I couldn't—"

Jules was blind.

"That girl does not hate you." I laughed because it was patently obvious to anyone that was watching tonight that Jules and James wanted to maul one another.

"I have news for you, Trevor, she absolutely does. I've seen her, what? Twice a week this entire semester, and she makes that hatred abundantly clear."

I glanced at my friend, registering the bleak expression on his face while switching lanes to turn into our apartment complex.

Then I really heard what he said. "What do you mean you know you can't have her? If she likes you and you like her—"

He shook his head. "First off, she doesn't like me. But second, what you said about my family was true. My mother and father are very old-school. You and I know that. I'm expected to date a certain type of girl. I'm supposed to *marry* a certain type of woman. Trev, I may not agree with it but . . ."

He shrugged helplessly.

What type of craziness?

I couldn't even find words.

"Trevor, I am not like you. I've never had an illusion that I would marry for love. I will marry Romona or whoever and maybe one day we will grow to love one another, maybe we won't. It doesn't really matter; it is what it is. My ex's family is the same way. Her parents went to school with mine. You know, all of their friends are kind of like that. That's why we broke up. We both realized we were wasting our free years. She and I always felt more like friends than like lovers anyway. We both wanted to experience . . . I don't know, something more. Passion, maybe."

I didn't say anything. I didn't need to. Most people would think that Jules was choosing money over love, but the money was only part of it. I knew Julian was faced with a terrible choice. May and Marcus Marshall would never accept a girl they believed to be beneath him.

Never.

And they would actively work to make sure her life and his by extension was a living hell. The only thing worse than watching someone you love be tormented was watching someone you loved be tormented by someone else that you also loved.

There was no way he could have both.

Because having a relationship based on love would mean defying his parents. And I knew deep down Julian still wanted their approval.

Who wouldn't want that?

I felt an uncomfortable pang at that thought. A swift tide of sadness rose within me from nowhere.

Having the approval of my parents, wanting it . . . was a feeling I could only remember. I wracked my brain trying to recall the last time I'd sought to sacrifice something, anything, to make my parents proud. I couldn't even recall the last time I'd spoken to them voluntarily.

I redirected my thoughts from that unpleasantness to the issue at hand. Just because James and Julian wouldn't be skipping down the aisle didn't mean that they couldn't enjoy one another's company for the time being.

James likely wasn't interested in marrying Julian anyway.

"Well, if you are so worried about wasting your youth, isn't that all the more reason for you to run full speed after James? You two have chemistry for sure."

"No. That's not chemistry, and it's not passion. It's *madness.* It doesn't know reason. It's never seen logic. It's volatile. And it makes me stupid. There is nothing, *nothing,* I need more than to stay as far away from James as possible.

"I mean, you saw what I just did back then. I just spent one hundred and forty dollars on cookies and I don't even like sweets! If that's not proof enough that I lose my mind around James, then I don't know what is."

"Technically you only spent one twenty on the cookies, and to be fair, Daisy's cookies are really good," I added, feeling an unnecessary desire to defend Daisy's baking.

He sat up straight as if jolted. "I didn't take the damned cookies!"

I couldn't help the laugh that escaped me.

Then Julian was laughing at himself and he rolled his eyes and said, "I was jealous and I was stupid. And I deserved to be overcharged. All in all, one hundred and forty bucks is a steal if it means that I never have to watch a bunch of men ogling James in a midriff and barely-there shorts."

I laughed. "Just be glad they didn't ask for four hundred."

He winced. "I probably would've paid a thousand and it still would've been a steal. A thousand dollars is cheaper than lawyers and bail, and I was so jealous"—he tapped his head against the window lightly—"I was liable to do something stupid enough to need lawyers and bail."

"Thanks, by the way," he said changing the topic so quickly that I didn't follow.

"For?"

"Having my back. I know things haven't been easy between us and I know Daisy was there. And I didn't know if you would just avoid the whole situation. I was, uhh . . . relieved to have you beside me."

He had the decency to sound ashamed and I knew it wasn't about fighting. Julian could've taken the two of them without me if it had come to that. This was about loyalty.

I swallowed the distaste in my mouth.

Julian had never trusted easily. I hated that he had a valid reason to question my loyalties now. I followed his reasoning. If I had been unfaithful in my promises to Elodie, who's to say I wouldn't do the same to him?

"Always, cousin. Always," I replied simply.

He rubbed his forehead tiredly as we pulled into a parking space then inquired absently, "Hey, I've been trying to get up with my cousin for a few days, but every evening I've swung by her dorm she's not been there."

Unsurprising. Elodie spent a few nights a week in her girlfriend's room.

"Uhh, I haven't spoken with her but she's probably with Gracie. I have her dorm number if you need it."

"She's a RA in Jubilee this year, right? I'll call her."

Jules bade me goodnight at the door and headed to his room. I headed to mine and pulled from my pocket the last two cookies still wrapped in their paper bag.

I'd only intended to take a bite, my curiosity having crested to an unbearable degree, but once I'd bitten into it as Daisy had driven away I hadn't been able to help myself from devouring the entire thing.

The still-warm cookie had been perfect—just a little soft and chewy but not mushy, sweet and buttery with a hint of salt to boost the savory taste. I let out a little groan just thinking about it.

I placed the packet reverently on my nightstand. I'd treat myself to a little piece each night, hold on to a bit of Daisy for as long as I could.

When I closed my eyes and gave myself over to sleep still lying atop my covers, I dreamed an impossible dream. One that was filled with Daisy's laughter, and us building a life together that was sweet, replete, and full of cookies.

The next morning when I awoke Jules and El were already sitting at the small dining table in our kitchen. Someone had made eggs, bacon, and orange juice. I had no idea who that someone could've been, because neither Elodie nor Julian could cook.

I wandered in, gave Elodie a hug and then stumbled to the cabinet to grab a plate because the food not only smelled edible, it smelled delicious.

"Who cooked? Did you hire a chef?" I joked to Jules.

"Prepared with my own two hands."

I looked at him like he was speaking French. "Jules, when did you learn to cook?"

I loaded up on bacon and added some scrambled eggs to my plate.

"It's really good, too." El smiled around a mouthful of crispy bacon.

"You don't know everything about me." Julian's voice carried a smile. "I have my secrets."

El and I caught each other's eye. *Jules doesn't know about secrets.*

Breakfast was great. It was the first time all three of us had been together all semester where the conversation had been easy and languid, just like old times.

Julian talked about grad school applications; he had finished his for Columbia Law School and would be mailing it the coming week. He reminded me to drop my application for their MBA program in the mail. Elodie mentioned that her "best friend" Gracie had spent the week applying for CUNY Law; she'd already been accepted to NYU.

After that Julian had turned the conversation to our plans for break. Elodie informed us that she planned to spend the holiday in New York with her Gracie and her family.

"Trevor and I are contemplating spending time in Green Valley, but I'm sure you already knew that." Julian said lifting his glass to take a sip of water.

Elodie schooled her surprise admirably fast because of course I hadn't gotten around to telling her that. I'd seen her less this semester than I had ever before, and that was my fault.

"Yeah, he told me when we spoke yesterday."

Julian raised his eyebrows at me questioningly. "I thought you told me in the car last night you hadn't talked to Elodie this week."

"Oh well, maybe it was last week," Elodie said quickly with a shrug.

"So if we go, you'll be coming with us to Green Valley, right? I'm sure Gracie's parents would understand how important it is for you to be there for Trevor given that this will be the first time he's gone home to spend time with his folks in years. Matter of fact, I'm sure my car could fit both you and Gracie if she wanted to tag along."

"Uhh . . ." El looked to me for help and I opened up my mouth to smooth things over, but before I could speak Julian held up his hand.

"Don't—just stop."

I closed my mouth.

He looked at us, accusation in his eyes. "Y'all never spend time together unless you have to. Y'all never touch unless it's in public. You couldn't care less about one another's whereabouts. You spend all summer apart and don't talk." Julian ticked off each point of our fake relationship on his fingers.

Then he looked up, eyes clear and calm and full of simmering fury. "The amount of lies y'all are asking me to swallow is too much for even me to bear. If you're not going to tell me the truth, then at least stop with the lies. I can't take it anymore."

He shoved off from the table and went to his room.

Elodie and I looked at each other for only a second before moving at the same time to go after him.

We needed to fix this mess.

Elodie went to sit on the bed next to him and said, "Julian, I'm—"

Jules looked at her and I saw the fatigue written clear as day on his face when he stopped her. "El, there's no one I love more than you."

He nodded in my direction and said, "That goes for you too, Trevor. I love you both more than anyone in the world. You two are my closest friends, my closest family."

He closed his eyes and shook his head.

"We're so close that I already know what you're about to say. I already know what both of you are about to do. Don't apologize to me unless you're ready to stop lying to me. And don't waste your time trying to convince me that I'm crazy because I've already caught you in a lie, and I know for a fact that I'm not. I may have been blind, maybe even willfully so, but I am not stupid. So stop treating me like an idiot."

I sat down in the chair because, finally, this was going to end. There was no way forward that didn't involve lying to him and I didn't have it in me to lie to Jules anymore.

Not now that I knew the secrets were poisoning him too.

"Trev, you got nothing to say?" he asked me wearily.

"I've got a lot to say but most of it isn't my place, Julian."

Elodie was growing paler by the second, I could see her leg bouncing under her long flowing dress.

"El, you've got nothing to say?" he asked.

She opened her mouth, closed it, and then repeated the motion twice more. Elodie bit her nails, then finally shook her head no.

Julian exhaled. "All right, I guess we're done here. You two can stay and try to get your story straight. *I'll* leave."

Julian exited and a second later I heard the apartment door slam.

Elodie wiped tears from the corners of her eyes.

I was gentle in my approach because one wrong word would have her fleeing.

"El, Jules is not your father. There is no one I know with more zeal for life. There is no one I know who—"

"Don't you think I know that!" she screamed, making me sit back in the seat. Elodie rarely raised her voice, least of all to me. For the first time, I heard the frustration and exhaustion in it.

She continued, red faced and glassy eyed. "You think that I didn't wanted to tell him? You think I haven't practice in my head a hundred —a thousand times—just looking at my cousin and saying, "Ju-Ju, Trevor and I are just friends. We've always been nothing but friends. He's a good and kind and noble guy, but I will never love him because I cannot love him. I am in love with Gracie Freeman and she loves me."

"Then say it," I implored. "It *won't* matter to him."

She flinched and shook her head.

She blinked away a tear and looked at me, all fire and grit. "You know I can't afford to take that chance. You know what happened when I told my father. Julian is my *only* family. Do you think I would risk him in that way—"

"Look at what this is doing to him. To us, to you! Gracie said when you guys graduate and move to New York you planned to live together and not worry about what other people thought. How are you going to do that, Elodie, when you can't even be honest with Julian?"

She twisted her hands. "Gracie is *naive*. Her folks are wonderful, so Gracie thinks if we just live our lives and fight hard enough then everyone will eventually just . . . come around. And had I been raised by her folks, then maybe I'd feel that way too. But I told my father and he said it was fine and then he took his own life. So forgive me for thinking that people don't just come around because in my experience people abso-fucking-lutley do *not* just come around to the idea of two women being in love with one another."

I knew her parents' death was the source of all her fears with Julian. That she'd told her father, and he'd promised it didn't matter that he loved her anyway, then *he'd* told her mother who had *not* responded that way.

And then days later her father had driven his car off a cliff with her mother in it. Neither of them survived the wreck.

Just this past summer I'd found out that her father's company had been deeply insolvent, and that was the most likely reason he'd killed himself. I'd shared this news with El, but she'd spent the last five years telling herself she was responsible for her parents' death. Convincing her otherwise was nearly impossible.

"We need to tell him, Elodie. This? What we're doing? It can't work anymore. He's already figured most of it out."

"We just have to try harder. Maybe if I stay here a few nights . . ."

"Stay here and what? Pretend to have sex with my pretend girl-friend? So Gracie has to feel yet again like she's second place? So she has to call me and get assurances that I really do see you as nothing but a sister. This is destructive—how can you not see that? Elodie, it is not your fault your parents died."

She was quiet when she responded. "You know, Trevor, we've been doing this for the last few years and you've never had a problem with it until now. I can't help but think that this is more about you wanting to be free to be with Daisy than it is about it being good for Julian or me and Gracie."

I sighed. "You're right, I'd love to be free to be with Daisy. Daisy made me feel for the first time like maybe I could have the same thing you have with Gracie. Someone that cares for me, that sees me, that understands me, that . . ." I couldn't say love because that would sting a little too much. "Someone that is just for me. I want to belong to her. I want her to belong to me. I know that sounds selfish, maybe even barbaric, but that's how I feel when I look at her."

"I had no idea you felt so strongly about her."

"Neither did I until it was too late. But that doesn't matter. What should matter to you is that knowing all that now, I'll continue to hold up my end of this charade knowing full-well it's probably obliterating my chances with Daisy."

Not that I deserved Daisy to begin with.

"And that should tell you that I *am* willing to do what is right, even if it is to my personal detriment."

She looked back at me, eyebrows bunched in confusion. Before she could argue I finished, "But I don't think what we're doing is right, not anymore. And that has nothing to do with Daisy. I haven't once mentioned telling her. At this point it wouldn't matter if she knew or not. This is wrong because you're letting your fear dictate everything. You've already decided the worst possible outcome is the only outcome and that's just not true. You're afraid Julian won't be there for you, that if you tell him, you'll lose him. But not telling him is pushing him away. I understand that you're scared. Maybe I don't understand the exact situation you're in, but God knows I understand rejection."

After all, the object of my affection hasn't spoken to me in five weeks, but who's counting?

"Julian deserves a chance, Elodie. Trust him. Give him the chance to show you who he is and what he's made of. Give him the chance to be there—"

I stopped with a jolt as I heard a noise in the living room. A few seconds later the bedroom door opened.

I made eye contact with Jules and saw that his glasses were off and his eyes were red.

He walked over to Elodie and crouched until he was face-to-face with her. He took her hand and waited for her eyes to find his. Then he said simply, "Elodie Mayhew, I love you and I don't care who you love."

Her eyes bounced back and forth between his as he squeezed her hand.

Jules rocked back on his haunches with a smile. Eyebrows raised, he prompted, "Now, is there something you want to tell me?"

Elodie's sobs broke through the room.

The cousins clung to one another. Julian shushed Elodie's cries and apologies, and rocked her like a child.

And I rose from chair, and left the two to talk.

A few hours later Jules found me in my room studying even though my hand twitched every few minutes, tempted to ditch the books and grab my pencils and charcoals.

He took a seat on my bed and got right to the point. "I have half a mind to beat the shit outta you for keeping this from me," he half-joked.

I smirked. Jules and I were evenly matched; he could *try* to kick my ass.

I opened my mouth and he held up his hands.

"I know why you did it. Thank you, by the way, for going to bat for me. Also, thank you for looking out for my cousin when she wouldn't let me." He shook his head in disbelief.

"She's like family to me too," I responded simply.

"So when are you going to tell Daisy?"

I looked at him, eyebrows raised. "I'm not."

Jules confusion was palpable. "Why? Everything you said about that girl in there . . ."

I stared at him. "Julian, did you not hear how hard it was for me to get your cousin to tell *you*?"

I *still* wasn't sure if Elodie would've told him in the end if Julian hadn't overheard us.

"What on earth makes you think she'll be comfortable with me telling a total stranger her secret?" I used the words Elodie had used when I'd proposed the idea to her a few weeks ago for effect.

Julian shrugged and opened his mouth but I cut him off. "This is still her secret, Jules. Please tell me you get that. Just because you know doesn't mean you have the right to tell anyone. I wanted to tell you every single day since I found out, but it wasn't my information to give away."

"I get that." His tone was understanding but his eyes gleamed in a way that made me fearful. "But I also know Elodie's happiness and comfort is not more important than yours. You and Daisy are clearly crazy about each other."

I brought my hand down in a swiping motion. "No. In case you forgot, that ship has sailed. Daisy hates my guts."

Jules squinted, examining the situation. "You're right, of course. Daisy has a skewed version of you. And I didn't really like that version of you either. Trevor, if you meant what you said about how you feel about her, then that's not something you wait on, and it's not something you whiff on."

Frustration bleeds into my words. "What are my options Jules?"

268
268

"Apologize to her. Tell her that you were wrong. That you and Elodie are over and you want to start over."

"I tried to apologize. I messed it up. And it ended up with her telling me she hated me. Besides, I've agreed to keep up this farce with El through the end of the year so—"

"You don't have to, actually. I talked to my cousin and she agrees. She's tired of it, you're tired of it. And I've convinced her to move off campus where folks are less nosey. I think there's a place downstairs that's open. Maybe she'll want to be somewhere else, but either way, she and Gracie will have more privacy."

I was glad to have that settled but unsure of how that helped me with Daisy. "Julian, nothing but the truth is going to explain my behavior to Daisy, and even that might not be enough. I publicly humiliated her. I hurt her feelings. Even if I was able to somehow get her to forget all that and give me a second chance . . .

"All of that is beside the point. I don't want to have a relationship with Daisy if it can't be an honest one. She doesn't deserve a relationship based on a lie, and neither do I. I don't want secrets between us, not even other people's."

"I get it. What if there were a way to guarantee Daisy wouldn't talk?"

I shrugged. "I don't need assurances where she's concerned. She wouldn't tell anyone. But didn't you just hear me say—"

"But El does need assurances," mused Julian. "What if there were assurances we could offer to El? Do you think that would help?"

I shrugged noncommittally, not sure where he was going with it, but ready to have this conversation done. "I supposed it might."

"Good," he spoke quietly as he left my room.

I'm not sure what Julian thought he could offer Elodie but I knew it wasn't going to be enough. He would find that out when he spoke to her, and rather than hang my hopes on something that was never going to happen, I pushed it from my mind and got back to work.

CHAPTER EIGHTEEN

Daisy

My room looked like a cookie factory had exploded in it, and there was nothing to be done for it. There was contraband under my bed, under the other bed, and the closet was full of it.

The first weekend we'd made four hundred and twenty-five dollars selling cookies. Odie had donated fifty and James had come up with the rest of the money on her own, thereby allowing her to buy her books.

That should've been the end of our time as cookie pushers.

However, people wouldn't stop talking about the cookies and asking about the cookies; figuratively speaking, folks couldn't keep the damned cookies out of their mouths.

And as an added bonus, I was now being propositioned by guys *all* the time telling me in detail what they'd like to do to my cookie.

Fun, fun, fun times.

I was content, nay overjoyed, *nay* ecstatic that we'd pulled our dumb plan off and that not one of us had been caught. My friends, however, were addicted to a life of crime.

Odie argued that she was tired of being broke and that this was the perfect way to make a little side cash. She wanted to sell cookies every freaking weekend. I pointed out to her although that had been the original plan it was *never* going to work.

There was too much risk involved. It'd been a miracle that we'd been able to pull it off the first time. Anyone could've come into the home ec building while we'd been in there baking. Someone could've spotted Charlie transporting dry goods into garbage bags.

It worked out because of hubris and luck, and thank you, God, amen.

James agreed that we shouldn't do it *every* weekend but disagreed that we should never do it again.

"We're careful," she argued.

As if careful would stop a wayward janitor from floating through the home economics building at seven p.m. on a Friday night. James thought I was being paranoid and ridiculous as the staff—even the janitorial staff—would most likely be at home enjoying supper at that time.

She was right; I was being paranoid. Because paranoia would save us from stupidity. I couldn't help thinking that we got away with it the first time, so we should quit while we were ahead.

James was the one that broke my resolve in the end.

"Daisy, I don't have money for books for the second semester. And I won't have the money. Eventually we're going to have to do this again. So let's just do it one more time, and we will set aside most of it for books and then if there's anything left after that you and Odie can use it for pocket change."

"I'm in!" Odie said immediately sounding like a jewel thief.

I groaned. "James, if it wasn't for Julian ..."

I didn't know what James and Julian were. Attracted, that's for damn sure, but James acted like we'd witnessed nothing, like nothing had happened.

"If it weren't for Julian basically giving us one hundred dollars we wouldn't have made enough in one weekend the first time. There aren't enough parties and there isn't enough time to make all these cookies."

"Not usually, but . . ." James grinned and I knew I was going to hate whatever came out of her mouth next. "Homecoming is this weekend. There'll be triple, if not quadruple, the number of parties. And there'll be a lot more people in town to sell to. Class is almost certain to be cancelled on Friday so we should have an extra day to prepare all the goodies."

I looked at Odie ,who was wearing a smug little smile, and then to James, who looked just a little too sanguine.

"Y'all planned this ahead of time."

"Come on, Daize, one last cookie caper and then we can quit!"

I closed my eyes and exhaled defeatedly.

"Okay. I'm in."

I knew with certainty as soon as the words left my mouth I was going to live to regret them.

When I told Charlie how much of each item I thought we'd need, he'd braced his hands on his knees and lowered his head, sucking in air. He replied, "I can maybe get you half of that. And definitely only about a third of the chocolate chips you need."

He looked at me meaningfully, because the week after the original cookie caper the cafeteria dessert bar had been curiously void of its normal subpar chocolate chip cookies.

I'd switched the recipes on the spot and redid the calculations for the ingredients. Sugar cookies, snickerdoodles, oatmeal raisin.

"Cream of tartar?" Charlie asked befuddled.

"Dry good." I reassured him.

It had been Odie's idea to meet him every night that week to start stockpiling the dry goods. We'd have to get the perishables all in one big run but we could store the dry goods in my room since I didn't have a roommate—thank you, Daddy.

And that was how my room ended up looking like the storeroom of a cookie factory. I tried to hide everything but there was just no space. James had us hitting a whopping eleven parties; five on Friday and six on Saturday night. We were considering dividing and conquering and maybe drafting Lucy to sell at a few. James had somehow convinced Calvin to let her borrow his car for the weekend and we'd use that as our primary means of transport.

I was lost in thought, thinking of everything that still needed to be done as I walked to the library Wednesday evening. There was literally no space to study in my room anymore. Therefore, I didn't see him until I was halfway down the drive and it was too late to turn tail and run back inside.

Julian.

He was sitting on one of the benches in his navy blue peacoat but stood when I approached.

I hadn't seen Julian since the night of the first cookie caper over two weeks ago. My first instinct was that he was looking for James, so I blurted out, "I haven't seen James this evening. I'm not sure where she is."

It was already dark outside, but not so dark that I couldn't see a faint red undertone creep across his complexion.

Oh my.

Just the mention of James's name made him blush. He rolled those pretty eyes behind his glasses. "I am not looking for James. I'm looking for you."

"You do know you could've just come inside and asked for me, right? There's a person at—"

"I know. And I tried. But you must've done something to piss your dorm mother off because she heard your name and told me, 'I'm not that girl's damned secretary. If she's going to need this many notes passed along, she needs to get her own phone.'"

I groaned. Dolly must've been calling incessantly. I thought it was suspicious the notes had suddenly dried up. I hadn't gotten a *Call Dolly* note since the night after the cookie caper.

"All right. Well, what can I do for you, Mr. Marshall?" I said, wanting to get whatever Julian needed out of the way.

Whatever this was about it couldn't be good. Nothing good ever came from conversations with Trevor or Julian.

The wrong sort.

"Mr. Marshall?" he squinted at me, smiling like I was amusing. "You don't like me, do you?"

No, I do not.

"I don't know you to like you or not like you. But I do have to get to the library so . . ."

"I have something I need to discuss with you, and I promise you want to hear it. But not here." His eyes followed two girls passing by and another two approaching from the sidewalk. All of whom were trying way too hard to look like they weren't listening.

"It's too public here, and this is a private matter. Will you take a drive with me?"

I'm not sure what look I gave him but he burst into laughter and said, "Daisy, you're looking at me like I just told you I assassinated Santa Claus."

I raised my eyebrows meaningfully.

He laughed again.

"We don't even have to leave the parking lot if you don't want. I know I am asking you to do a colossally stupid thing, that is to get in the car with a strange man—"

"At night," I added.

"Yes, but I promise you it'll be worth your time. And I promise I come in peace and mean you no harm."

"Yeah, I appreciate the offer, but seeing as how you've pointed out plenty of *very* valid reasons for me to say no, I'm going to have to decline."

Julian nodded his head and shoved his hands in his peacoat, I got about five paces away before he called just loud enough for me to hear, "Your loss, Daisy Payton."

I whipped my head around, stared at him, and then whipped my head around to see if anyone else heard what he said.

I stalked back to Julian's grinning face and said through gritted teeth, "Where are you parked?"

CHAPTER NINETEEN

Daisy

The alarm in my room went off at six forty-five on Friday morning. It was hard to believe that it had only been a little over twenty-four hours since Julian had told me that everything I thought I knew to be written in stone was, in fact, written in spaghetti sauce. It was a bloody mess.

Julian had been purposely mysterious when it came to revealing how he'd figured out my identity; he'd only mentioned had something to do with my mother's gold watch—the one I wore all the time, and how the watch was rare and expensive. Apparently, it had been part of her prizes from winning the Miss Negro Tennessee pageant some years back. Who knew?

Then he'd pivoted the conversation to the true nature of Elodie and Trevor's "relationship." The information Julian provided hit like a sledgehammer. My heart had beat painfully for the girl, and then my heart had broken for Trevor. I realized how lonely Trevor must've been.

You told him you hated him. You've been an icicle to him.

He should've told me. He couldn't have told you!

He's so noble. He's so damned stubborn.

Julian spoke and the jar of no feelings effectively toppled and shattered.

My emotions were a mess of *Trevor*.

Longing for Trevor, wistful over the wasted time we could've had, anxious for the next time we'd speak, and still angry at Trevor's idiocy. He should've told me. He should've *trusted* me.

Sigh.

I spent the night replaying all of the memories I'd suppressed these last few weeks, relishing in them, letting them smash and grind the wall I'd tried to build around my heart.

I wished . . .

There were a lot of things I wished. I wished that I hadn't gotten hurt. I *wish* I hadn't hurt Trevor, because Julian told me, *boy, oh boy,* had Trevor been hurting.

I couldn't wait to find him and kiss all of his cares away.

Oh, Trevor.

Hope surged more powerfully, lodging itself painfully in my chest and in my throat. The butterflies were back full force, wreaking havoc in my stomach and making it hard to eat or think of anything of except when I'd see him again. When I could apologize to him for saying such a hurtful thing. When I could kiss those lips . . .

The only reason I didn't go to him immediately was because Julian told me that Trevor was likely to be furious with him for telling me and he needed to get to Elodie and reassure her that I wouldn't say a word.

And then I'd been hit with a mountain of self-doubt.

Maybe Trevor didn't *want* to see me anymore. After all, I hadn't spoken to him for weeks.

Julian had laughed in my face when I'd spoken that thought aloud.

"Daisy, I wouldn't be here if that was the case." Then he'd added very softly, "I know you don't like me or trust me, but know this—I will do anything for the people I love, Daisy. Trevor is my best friend and he's the best man I know. You two are good together. I could see that from the beginning, even if I couldn't understand it."

"Tell him I'm sorry," I said.

He shook his head. "You tell him yourself." Jules looked out the windshield and then he'd turned to me and said, "Speaking of things you're going to tell Trevor yourself . . ."

I swallowed hard. I knew what Jules wanted me to do. Maybe I wore my apprehension on my face because the question he asked next, came out gentle and that made it even worse.

"What are you so afraid of, Daisy?"

That he'll care about me being a Payton more than he'll care about me. That they'll see me as a means to an end instead of a person.

I sighed, resignedly. Trevor and I were still so . . . fragile. I was enamored with him. I hoped he felt the same about me, but even the idea that we could be together was new. Telling him about the Mill, right now, would leave me . . . vulnerable. The idea of placing my vulnerability back in Trevor's hands scared me.

"Daisy, you have to tell Trevor who you really are."

"I will. But not right now." I hedged. I just needed time. *We* needed time.

"It has to be right now, Daisy."

"It's not the right time."

"When exactly is going to be the right time to tell him you lied about your identity?"

"I didn't lie about my identity. I only lied about one letter in my last name."

"Daisy, you cannot out bullshit me, I promise you. You lied about your *identity* and you lied about where you're from."

I sat there gnawing on my lip, trying to figure out a way to get Jules to understand. Julian seemed to know where my mind was going, or rather, *not* going, and leveled me with a frank glare. "Look,

Daisy, the other day I tried to get Trevor to come to you and *not* tell you anything about Elodie. I wanted him to let you continue believing the lie about their relationship and just tell you that they'd broken up. I told him he could apologize for the way he'd treated you and that he wanted to start over."

Jules paused searching my face for a second.

"And do you know what he told me?"

I stared at him waiting for him to continue.

He said, "'She's never going to go for anything other than the truth.'"

I smiled at how well Trevor knew me—knows me.

"Then he said he wouldn't want to be with you if he couldn't tell you the truth. Trevor has been living a relationship that was based on a lie wrapped in a secret for a very long time. Don't make him go through that again. Tell him the truth."

My smile dropped, processing the truth of Julian's words.

He was right. If I wanted this time around to be different then I had to trust Trevor and he'd have to trust me. Trusting him meant telling him the truth.

A little tiny selfish voice spoke: *Why should you tell him the truth right now when he was fine with you believing a lie for so long?* I told the voice to hush and then responded to Julian.

"Okay."

"Good. And Daisy, make it soon. Because if you don't, know that I will."

Even though he was threatening me, I couldn't help but love how much Julian wanted to protect Trevor.

As I exited the car, Julian again casually mentioned that he was content to keep my secret from everyone except Trevor, as long as I did the same for Elodie. I let Julian know the threat was not needed and also recommended that he work on not threatening me—or anyone, really—if he wanted folks to like him. He laughed and shook his head like I'd said something funny.

And then I'd spent the next twenty-four hours in agony.

Okay, maybe not agony—but in a state of impatience.

Julian said Trevor would come find me after he'd told him about our conversation, so I'd just have to be patient.

I was being patient. I was waiting so hard.

Any moment Trevor was going to show up at my dorm. *Any moment.* I was positive!

I was not positive.

To make matters worse I wasn't scheduled to see him today. Our mentor session had been cancelled due to Friday classes being cancelled for Homecoming weekend.

But I was considering sneaking away from the bake-a-thon later to see if he'd show up anyway. Maybe that was when he planned to find me. I hoped he hadn't left a note with my dorm mother. Given what Julian said, I'd probably never get it.

Much as I'd liked to have stayed in bed to ride the runaway freight train of Daisy's thoughts and feelings about Trevor, I had to get up. There were cookies to bake, scandalous T-shirts to don, and knee-high boots to rock.

Although . . . I bit my lip as I grabbed my Dopp kit, the idea of seeing Trevor *now* in those knee-high boots and fishnets caused my stomach to swoop and drop. I grinned and stepped into the very quiet hallway. Most of my dormmates were still sleeping, enjoying the rare Friday off from class.

I stopped short.

On the wall in front of my door, there was a yellow sticky note with the familiar refrain written on it.

Call Dolly.

My dorm mother had become clever. She'd placed it where I was sure to see it since I wasn't responding to the ones left on my door. I turned to pull my door shut and—for the love of . . . there was an identical note plastered there.

I walked down the hall to the ladies' room. *Then* I looked at the mirrors over the sinks in horror. Every single sink: one, two, three, four, *five*—*Call Dolly* notes.

I snatched the notes down while I brushed my teeth, wondering who was nuttier—my dorm mother, Mrs. Johnson, or my sister. I decided it was draw but when I walked to the shower and saw *another* note, dread slid through me. If something was really, really wrong Dolly wouldn't have let my dorm mother tell me, Dolly would've wanted to tell me herself.

And maybe my dorm mother had knocked, but I'd been sleeping so hard I hadn't heard. Suddenly I wasn't sure if this was just my sister being over the top or something much, much worse. Therefore, instead of taking my shower I headed back to my room, grabbed a couple of dimes, and headed down the hall to the payphone. I put the dime in, and the phone ate it.

Lovely.

I stuck another dime in and the phone ate that one too.

I sighed and hit the stairs headed toward my dorm mother's office. There was a phone in there I could borrow.

I couldn't turn off the voice in my head that told me something was wrong, wrong, *wrong*.

Not even Dolly was this extreme under normal circumstances. But I held on to a small modicum of hope; if something were truly wrong Dolly wouldn't be calling at all. She would've just shown up.

Please let everything be okay, please let everything be okay, I chanted in my mind.

I peeked into Mrs. Johnson's office ready to face her wrath. After all, all those *Call Dolly* requests were because of me.

But it was empty—just the fuzzy portable black and white TV blaring in the background.

I bit my lip, wondering if this was worth waking Odie up. Her roommate had a phone in their room. Maybe I could borrow hers.

As I stepped back out of the office I glanced toward the lobby and saw . . . Dolly.

My sister was sitting there dressed to the nines. Black YSL dress, black pumps, black cardigan, white pearls. She looked like a diminutive, beautiful grim reaper.

And it was the black coupled with her being here that made my heart race and my palms sweat.

Dolly *never* wore all black, she said it was too depressing.

"Dolly?" I said, approaching her slowly because I wasn't sure if this was a dream or a nightmare.

She looked up from the cup of piping hot tea—Dolly hated coffee —and raised a single eyebrow at me.

"Is everything okay? Is Daddy okay?" I blurted, my voice cracking a little because the idea of something happening to my father was too devastating to even entertain.

BOOM! I turned my head, momentarily distracted by a ruckus directly overhead. It sounded like someone was pounding on the doors before opening and slamming them all at once.

"Is everything *okay*? Now you're worried, Daisy? I wonder what *that's* like. To be worried if someone you love is okay."

I stood there staring at her because even though I knew Dolly wouldn't be glib if something were truly wrong with my father, I needed to hear her say those words and she knew that.

"No, Daisy, nothing is wrong with our father. Well, nothing except wondering if his baby girl has been kidnapped."

"*Kidnapped?*"

BOOM! The floor shook.

"Why on earth would Daddy think I've been kidnapped?"

"What else was he supposed to think, Daisy, when your mail was returned to us as 'recipient not at address'? You won't return any of my calls. And we call the Registrar's Office and they told us no one with the name Daisy Payton is enrolled."

Oh shit. *OH. SHIT!*

"Dolly, I can explain, I—"

"Daisy!" I turned to see a very panicked looking James, still in her head scarf and PJ's running full speed to me.

"I've been looking for you! We gotta go now!" She yanked my hand.

"What? James?"

"DAISY! Surprise room checks just started on the first floor. We gotta go *now*!"

OH. SHIT.

I left Dolly standing in the lobby yelling, "Daisy—Daisy!"

I ran so fast I beat James's long legs up the stairs and practically knocked my door down. I felt bile rising up in my throat as I surveyed the sight in front of me. I was going to be sick. Bags of flour, sugar, cream of tartar, oats, raisins all containing *Property of Fisk University Dining Services* littered almost every surface of my room.

"James, where the fuck are we gonna hide all this stuff? There's no more space!"

James shook her head in bewilderment, Odie joined us a moment later wearing the same panicked look. "Throw it out the window!" she declared. We both ran to the window and looked down.

"That isn't going to work. The bags are going to break and then you'll have a bunch of *destroyed* school property you'll have to worry about. And they're sure as hell going to know it came from one of the windows directly over the spot where it landed." We all turned to see Dolly standing in my doorway.

Shit, shit, shit.

Dolly calmly addressed my friends, "Frick and Frack, this looks like an ungodly amount of trouble. If I were you, I would get out of here right now."

"We're not leaving, Daisy!" James said indignantly. Odie immediately agreed. My sister was still looking around the room in wonder.

"No! She's right, I'll be fine! Y'all need to *leave*." I had a father who could move mountains. They did not.

"Daisy!" James protested, looking at me like I had two heads.

"Please, James and Odessa, trust me. Y'all need to go right now."

My friends looked confused and scared.

"Go!" I urged them and they both started toward the door. As soon were they across the threshold my sister said, "Daisy, what in the world is going on here?"

"I was just about to ask the same thing." My dorm mother and two RA's stepped into the room holding clipboards, looking around wide-eyed and miffed.

I hung my head.

"I too have my share of questions about what's going on here. Daisy Marie Payton. What on earth is all of this?" I closed my eyes, hearing the voice of my father.

When I opened them, I saw him standing in the doorframe, his tall figure blocking almost the entire thing. The look of disappointment on my father's face filled me with a shame hotter than any I'd ever felt. Letting him or my mother down was just about the worst feeling in the world.

Someone coughed from behind my father and he stepped to the side, revealing Billy Jo and Della Boone, business owners who ran the bait and tackle shop in Green Valley. And standing there next to them, staring at me with those gorgeous brown eyes full of confusion, recognition, and betrayal, was Trevor Boone.

Silence reigned as I struggled to come up with any kind of explanation.

And then the final nail in my coffin hammered into place in the rapid-fire, accusatory, and unmistakable clip of James Jones. "Daisy *Payton*? I thought you said your last name was Paxton."

CHAPTER TWENTY

Daisy

My homecoming weekend had officially been turned into been hell-coming weekend.

As my world began to unravel, the Boones, *all* of them, made their leave. Trevor goddamned Boone.

He's from Green Valley.

No, he's wasn't from Green Valley, not really. I knew the Boones had another son older than me, but folks were always real secretive when talking about him.

My friends had left again right after the Boones.

The look on my father's face when I told him I'd changed my last name on purpose and that it wasn't a clerical error, that I'd wanted to be known by some other name . . . was crushing.

I'd expected him to be angry, I'd expected him to even be disappointed. I had not expected him to be hurt.

But hurt he'd been.

Very hurt.

I'd tried to explain that it wasn't about him, that it was about me and not wanting all the attention and expectations that came with being a Payton, but the words hadn't come out right.

I said, "I just needed a break from the Payton name, I wanted—to not be known and examined and scrutinized just because of my last name."

My father was quiet for a very long time and then he said, "Well . . . I've worked hard to build on the things my father gave me, our good name being one of them. I've not been perfect, but every day I've worked to make the Payton name one my family could be proud of. And you've never had a problem with benefitting from that name when it suited you. Now though, you get to college and you don't want to be associated with us?"

"Daddy, it's not that I don't want to be associated . . . I just didn't want to be that Daisy."

My father was trying—he was really grasping at straws trying to follow my logic. But it wasn't his fault, it was mine. I didn't have the words to explain and my mind and emotions were all jumbled up. This was not how the day was supposed to go.

My father's frown deepened then he spoke again, "I know there are people who think we put on airs, that any person that looks like us, that strives for more than just scraps, is uppity. I just never expected to have it thrown in my face by my own child. I can't understand what I've done to make you reject how you were raised, reject everything I stand for."

I objected but couldn't offer any additional explanation for my feelings. My father quietly responded, "If that's the case, then look me in my eye and explain what's really going on here. Tell me that my daughter is not a liar and a thief."

And I couldn't tell him those things because I'd been both. I hadn't meant for . . . This wasn't how it had played out in my mind. When people on TV or in the movies were discovered to have a fake identity it always drew laughs. In reality, people didn't take deception the same way.

And I wanted to explain about the stolen items but there was no good way to do that without James, Odie, and Charlie involved in this mess too. And I wouldn't do that to them.

Therefore, my father still sounded dismayed when he said very, very quietly, "I don't think any of my children has ever wounded me as deeply."

I'd absorbed the blow and unable to do anything else, apologized again.

My father asked Mrs. Johnson what the next steps would be for me. She told him she'd file a formal report with the Housing Department and that they'd most likely report all my violations of the Honor Code and the Code of Student Conduct to the Tribunal Disciplinary Council. The disciplinary council would conduct an investigation and hold a hearing to decide my fate.

I already knew what my father would want to do. He'd want to by-pass the system and go to the directly to the president, where my father could exercise his influence and swoop in to save the day.

"Daddy please don't interfere. I want to face the council without your help" I said quietly, as soon as the door closed and Mrs. Johnson left.

I'd expected my father to argue with me and to insist that I choose the path with the highest probability of a favorable outcome.

He did not.

Instead my father made it perfectly clear swooping in to save the day was the last thing on his mind.

"Daisy, I've always preached to you that actions have consequences. Perhaps it's my fault. Maybe I didn't let you feel the consequences enough growing up, and maybe this is my consequence." He looked tired and I'd felt guilty about that too; my father worked what would be considered two full-time jobs—helping to oversee things at the Mill and his judgeship. He had finally taken a day off and what did I give him for his troubles?

Guilt had me gnawing at my fingernails.

"You've made it abundantly clear that you don't want any of the trappings or privileges of being a Payton. And even if you did, you are *still* electing to refrain from telling the whole truth; Mrs. Johnson and I were not born yesterday. I know that there is no way my one-hundred-pound daughter smuggled a fifty-pound bag of flour up three flights of stairs unassisted, much less did it several times over. Unless you've also been training for the Montreal Summer Olympics and that's another thing you've been keeping from me?"

He raised an eyebrow in a move that I hadn't realized Dolly emulated perfectly until now.

"I'm not entirely sure how, or which, of your friends play into this, but I do know that you didn't steal all this on your own. And I don't for one second buy the story that you needed money for the first time in your life so you figured this was a good way to get it. That doesn't even make any sense. You've never shirked from an honest day's work. I know you would've gotten a regular job, not turned to a life of larceny."

"No, she couldn't have. Daisy can't work a regular job—she doesn't have the time." Dolly looked up from where she'd been quietly standing by the window. "Daisy is double majoring."

I looked at her like she had sprouted horns. And a tail. And claws. Bus, meet your new driver, Dolly Payton.

My father looked at me, eyes wide in surprise and then narrowed in confusion. "I thought we'd discussed majoring in business? It's what you said you wanted."

Because that's what I thought you wanted me to want. And because I did a little too . . . maybe not as much as I'd wanted to major in home economics, but I did like business.

My father sighed mightily when I didn't respond and then said, "Is there anything else you're keeping from me, Daisy? Anything else I need to know?"

I shook my head and took a deep breath, successfully holding back the tears that were threatening, but I didn't cry. I'd done all of this to myself. I'd hurt . . . well, I'd hurt everyone. I shook my head again and said, "No."

He rubbed his hands through his hair, in a move that reminded me of Trevor.

Don't think of Trevor.

"Very well, Daisy. You've made a lot of very poor choices, and you're going to have to suffer some hard consequences because of your actions. Since I know for a fact you didn't make those choices on your own, I wish you'd reconsider." He stopped and changed course. "No, what I wish is that you'd tell the whole truth about what's going on here. Then maybe I could understand, maybe I could help you help yourself, because for the love of God, I don't even recognize my own child right now."

I wanted to tell him everything, but I couldn't because even though he had every right to be angry with me, I knew my father was still my father, and if I told him, he would go directly to the president and tell him everything. And when justice was metered out, I'd be spared and James and Odie and Charlie would all bear the brunt of the punishment.

Therefore, I stood there quietly staring at the floor, unable to meet his gaze.

After a long beat of silence he said, "You've chosen to exercise your right to remain silent. I hope it gets you what you're looking for."

He left after that.

My sister, who was still standing quietly looking out of the window, finally spoke. "I don't understand you. I do love you. But I may never understand you, Daisy. Why are you so eager to give up privileges most people are dying to have?"

I stared at Dolly and felt my frustrations start to rise. Instead of answering her question I lobbed my own back at her, because no one could bring out the worst in me more than my sister. Dolly was *always* perfect and *always* content to flaunt that perfection even at the worst of times.

"Why did you mention the major thing to Daddy! Why didn't you let me tell him myself? And why didn't you tell me he was coming up here? Why didn't you stop him? I thought we were supposed to be sisters!" I spat.

I was raw and aching and there was Dolly in all her perfection, having just ratted me out for no good reason when I was already in trouble. So I yelled at her because what I really wanted to scream was, *Why do you always have to be right? Why do you always have to be perfect? Why can't you leave a little space, just a sliver of space for less than perfect people like me?*

Dolly's posture stayed ramrod straight; she didn't cross her arms defensively or twitch. Dolly had never had an emotional tell, therefore I was shocked when she exploded at me.

"I thought that too! Wouldn't it be nice for me to have a sister? Wouldn't it be nice for me to have someone that calls me once in a while to see how I'm doing? To see if the stress of stepping into a role that was custom-made for Ado was working out well for me? To see if I was exhausted from having to wrangle and keep power every single *goddamned* day because some idiot has the smart dumb idea to try to test me, because I have the audacity to be young, and female, and Black, and in charge, *and unapologetic*! Wouldn't it be nice to have someone to answer my calls? Perhaps then I could've warned you. Perhaps then I could've said two weeks ago, 'Daisy, Daddy is getting really, really worried that we can't get mail to you, and he's thinking about calling some of his hotshot friends at the university to see if they can get the issue fixed.' Perhaps if I had a sister, I could've called her over and over and over again to check on her, to see if she was safe, to *warn* her that her family back home were beginning to lose their minds with worry. Maybe I even would've told her that I'd tried to tell our father that he was totally overreacting. After all, it's not like bad things ever happen to anyone in our family!"

Her voice was getting louder and shriller by the second. And while her body hadn't moved except the heaving of her chest, her eyes were getting wilder and wilder.

I'd pushed Dolly too far.

In all my days I'd never seen her look at me quite so upset and angry. And I'd definitely never heard Dolly lose it; she was absolutely on the razor's edge of doing so. I tried to break in to stop her, to apologize, "Dolly, I—"

"I am *not* finished! You had your say, it's my turn now, Daisy! You never listen to me! Ever! You think you know every single thing there is to know and that I must have cheese curds for brains or something. You value your friends, girls you've known for *three* months over me"—she pointed her palms to her chest—"the sister that's loved you since before you were born."

Tears brimmed in her eyes and I opened my mouth to apologize, but she shut me up with, "Save it, Daisy. Whatever you're about to say to try to rewrite the truth, just don't. No matter what you say to me, I know the real deal. If your friends were here right now, you'd turn and walk out that door, and leave me behind just like you did the first day."

It landed like a blow because there was a kernel of truth to it. I didn't love my friends more than my sister but I'd always seen Dolly as so strong and totally together, I didn't think she needed me.

And I had neglected to consider her feelings.

You neglected them a lot.

She took a deep breath and one of the tears that had been brimming spilled over. I had to look away.

"You want to know why I told Daddy about you being a double major? Because you weren't *ever* going to tell him. You avoid *everything*. You smother your feelings. Maybe not the fun ones, but the big, messy, ugly, feelings we all have? You try to pretend yours don't exist! You don't own up to them at all even when asked about them directly. You think ignoring something will make it all just go away."

293

She glanced around then looked at the ceiling and said bitingly, "And how has that worked out for you?"

Every word hit hard because it was the truth. I had no idea Dolly saw me so well, but it also irrationally made me angry, because what else did she want me to do? *Maybe ignoring it is my way of dealing with it. Perhaps, putting bad feelings in a jar and sealing them off wasn't the best way to deal with them, but it'd helped me face the day. Perhaps Dolly wouldn't be so pushy if she tried sealing her own feelings in a jar once in a while.*

"Dolly, I do deal with my feelings, I just don't deal with things the same way as you," I responded a little defensive.

"You're still lying," she said tiredly.

"And I was going to tell Daddy," I responded, letting her comment go by.

"When, Daisy? You've been in school for three months. When were you planning to tell him? At the end of the semester? At the end of the year? When you graduated from college?"

I remained quiet during her inquisition. I had no answers and she knew it.

"If I hadn't been the one paying for your tuition you probably wouldn't have told me either. But this isn't even about you double majoring. The double major is just indicative of my point. You're double majoring *because* you don't know how to deal. You don't know how to cope with big emotions, Daisy, so instead of telling Daddy the truth, that you wanted to be a home economics major because you couldn't give a flipping flying fish what happens at or to Payton Mills . . ." Her tone was so accusatory even if her words were right. Saying I didn't care about the Mill was like saying I was less of a Payton. Further, I knew how important the Mill was to Dolly. Of all of us, she'd been the only one interested in it since we were children. Ado had wanted to be an architect, and my father had suggested that maybe he could add a design portion to our lumberyard *when* he took over the Mill. Dolly had been listening to their conversation and she'd stonily countered my father's surety with one word: "*If.*"

I winced. "I do care what happens to the Mill. I just . . ."

I trailed off and she crossed her arms over her chest and stared at the ceiling.

"I told Daddy this was a bad idea."

"What?"

"I told Daddy back in July I didn't think you were ready to go away to school, that you needed to stay home in Green Valley and work on your issues."

"*What?*" This felt like a betrayal—that Dolly hadn't believed in me, or thought I was ready to go off to school. *She may have been right.*

She rubbed her forehead like she was getting a headache.

"Dolly, why would you—how could you have . . . what?"

Dolly closed her eyes and when she opened them again she slipped a knife right between my ribs. "Do you know one of the last things Mommy told me before she died? She said—"

"Stop," I said. *I can't deal with this right now.*

"She told me to make sure you would be okay."

"Stop, please, Dolly." *Please, please, please.*

She shook her head and laughed a little and said so softly I wondered if she spoke to me or to herself, "Look at how hugely I've failed with that. How am I supposed to take care of someone when I can't even get them to return my phone calls?"

I will not cry.

"And I get it. You're mad at me. And you're mad at Daddy. We dropped the ball on you." A twinge of something clawed at my gut. *I refuse. I refuse.* I stood there hoping my sister would run out of fuel, that she'd change the topic or leave. Anything to keep from . . . feeling. *I can't.*

But she didn't stop. She kept poking and prodding and tossing her pebbles at the dam that held back all the things I couldn't afford to feel. Nope. Nope. Nope. I'd deal with those feelings later.

"When Ado died, Mommy held us together. But when Mommy died . . . me and Daddy . . . we didn't show up for you. We weren't there for you."

I closed my eyes.

"We didn't even celebrate one of the biggest milestones of your life—graduating from high school."

I flinched, then squeezed my eyes tighter, digging deep, deep, deep, finding my calm. I dressed myself in numbness, warding off the tide of emotions trying to spill over the walls.

I opened my eyes and said calmly, "Dolly, why are we are we talking about this? Mommy had just . . . no one felt like celebrating. It was no big deal."

"Is it ever a big deal to you, Daisy? You stand here preternaturally calm despite facing expulsion and the possibility of *criminal* charges. You've ripped out our father's heart and disowned our family."

"I did not disown my family."

"You've shown me one hundred different ways that you could take or leave our relationship. Even your precious friends, who jumped ship like rats on a sinking boat as soon as things got really, really serious—not that I blame them since you've been lying to them too—are upset with you. Doesn't any of that make you feel . . . anything?"

The blanket of calm rippled but it did not tear. I tried to think of the words my sister wanted me to say, words that would make this right.

Either I took too long, or she never expected me to answer because a second later, she stepped back as if coming out of a daze. Likely noticing that under the sacks of dry goods, all of the things she'd placed to remind me of home were gone. Likely noticing the way I'd erased them. Seeing my room through Dolly's eyes multiplied my shame.

My sister, who was made of iron and who hardly ever cried, blinked away another tear. Then she nodded her head twice and said quietly, "So be it."

She nodded again as if reassuring herself, and she didn't look back as she left.

I didn't know if my sister and father left that day or if they stayed the rest of the weekend. The only person I could even think to ask was Trevor goddamned Boone.

And I couldn't ask him.

What on earth were the odds of Trevor and I being from the same place and only meeting in college? *Of all the gin joints, in all the towns, in all the world.* Or I guess more accurately, of all the dorm rooms, in all the colleges, in all the world, he had to walk into mine. Irony was determined to have its way with me, because I'd finally found a practical application for statistics.

Around midday there was a knock on my door. I opened it to find Charlie Love and Mr. Jimmy standing there with a dolly.

Mr. Jimmy's eyes popped open as he took in the scene of the crime. "Well I'll be *damned*! You had a whole 'nother storeroom in here!"

Charlie was mostly silent but looked at me with pleading eyes. I tried to communicate that I was not going to snitch on him.

They worked diligently loading the items on their hand truck and wheeling them out of my room and returning for more as Mr. Jimmy's comments got more colorful with each trip. "I thought I'd seen it all, but this here takes the cake. Or, I guess it takes the cookie!"

I was glad he could find humor in the situation. I was really, really glad. Honestly, I was ecstatic for him.

Before he wheeled his last load out, he paused, introspective for a moment, then asked, "What in the world possessed you to do something like this?"

I gave a half-hearted shrug, tired of trying to explain myself. He looked back at me. "Well, if it weren't for the room checks you *might* not have gotten caught. I mean how did you did manage to steal all this stuff out of our pantry anyway?" he said it as if it had just occurred to him that the goods had been stolen under his nose. Then he looked at Charlie with unbridled suspicion. "Y'all two know each other?"

Charlie looked down at the floor silent, so I responded, not wanting to tell any more lies. "We've seen one another around."

"Mm hmm, seen each other around? I just bet you have." Then he pointed to Charlie. "If I get wind that you had anything to do with this, you're gonna be cleaning toilets for the next four years, you understand me?"

Charlie swallowed hard and nodded.

"Girl, I can't decide if you're crazy smart or crazy stupid, but either way you're *crazy*."

I sighed as he shook his head and began to push the dolly out of the door until the only sound I could hear was the soft *click, click, click* of the wheels as they moved down the hall.

At four, I headed to the library to see if Trevor would show. I hoped and prayed he'd come so I could offer him an explanation.

I knew what it was like to have doubts and I wanted to set any that he had about me to rights. I wanted to let him know that this wasn't a big deal, that it changed nothing. I wanted to put his mind at ease.

I waited and waited and waited. When it became clear that Trevor wasn't going to show, I told myself the session was already cancelled and that there was no reason to worry. That his absence didn't mean anything. But in the back of my mind, I couldn't shake the worry.

Why should he give you the chance to explain when you didn't give him the same chance? I told that voice to shut up and headed back to my room, realizing I needed to apologize to my friends next.

As soon as I'd heard James's voice I knew what had happened. My friends returned to the scene of the crime because they hadn't wanted me to go down alone.

They didn't know everything, but they knew *enough*. And they were owed an explanation. Therefore as soon as I apologized, I would come clean on the whole story and then let them know that I would not reveal their part in the great cookie caper.

I knocked on Odie's door first with a quick *rap-rap-rap*.

There was no motion from inside, no response at all.

I knocked again, and called to the door, "Odie, this is Daisy. Please let me in."

No response.

The knot in my stomach churned harder with each successive knock, but Odie never came to the door.

I headed to James's room next and she *did* open the door, sliding out and shutting it behind her. Obviously Odie was inside and she didn't want to see me.

My stomach felt queasy and my chest felt hot and tight at the thought of sweet and kind Odie avoiding me.

James stepped into the hallway with her arms crossed and looked down at me with that famous impassive glare.

She stared at me for a beat and then raised her eyebrows as if to say, "What do you want?"

All at once I realized I was so used to James being the one to take over, to initiate conversations, that it felt one hundred times worse to have her be totally silent.

"James—I am so sorry," I blurted. "I wanted to tell you hundreds of times. I wanted to come clean and just . . ."

"But you didn't," she said with a shrug.

"I was *going* to at the end of the semester. I was so afraid it would change the way you saw me."

"The way we saw you? What about the way you saw us? What, were we some poor charity cases? You wanted to know what it would be like to mingle with the common folks instead of your usual caviar eating set?"

"I've never had caviar in my life, James. I didn't grow up . . . that way."

"What way? Rich? Because I grew up dirt fucking poor, Daisy. You can't even imagine." Anger was radiating off her in waves that were almost palpable.

"James, come on, you *know* me. You know how much you and Odie mean to me. You're my *best* friends."

She flinched when I said "best friends" and then she responded quietly, "Daisy, we can't be your best friends. We don't even know who you are."

She looked patient and calm, like she was explaining something obvious to a child. If Dolly hadn't already sliced my heart out earlier it would've been stabbed in that moment.

"You made me think you were like me. That you could understand. I couldn't even afford books and you were probably just laughing at me. Did you call your rich friends and tell them you'd come up with a crazy plan to help the poor girl get books? Was this all a game to you, Daisy? Because it is my real fucking life. It is Odie's real fucking life!"

"Call my rich friends? I don't even have any rich friends, James! I didn't even want to go through with the plan. You and Odie wanted to go through with it and I'm the one taking the rap for it!" I felt a hot pang of panic shoot through me because this apology was going all wrong.

James eyes flared and she said, "So what now? Do you want me and Odie to apologize to *you*, Daisy? Are we supposed to grovel at the feet of the spoiled little rich girl who's been lying to us this entire time? Should we be grateful that you're going to take this slap on the wrist that they surely would've expelled us commoners for?"

My heart was racing and my hands couldn't stop shaking. James was icing me out and I could not get through to her.

"James, please! I can make this up to you. I can . . . just tell me how to make this right. I will do whatever it takes."

She looked at me for a long time and then her face changed from angry and withdrawn to a little sad.

She exhaled deeply and shook her head. "Daisy, our entire friendship was built on lies."

She turned the doorknob and took a step back and I sensed my window of opportunity closing.

"It wasn't! I was *really* being myself when I was with you and Odie. All I lied about was *one* letter of my last name."

"And where you're from."

Dammit! "Yes, that too."

"And what your parents do for a living." I technically hadn't lied about that but now was not the time to bring that up.

"I—"

"And who your family is. And how much *money* y'all have." She said the word money like a curse.

I looked her dead in the eyes so she could see just how sincere I was. "James, I am so, so sorry. Please. Just tell me how to make this up to you."

She smiled sadly and said, "You *can't* make this up to me. I've learned the hard way that nothing undoes a wrong. And nothing stops people from doing it again, no matter how many promises they make. I do not forgive people and you are no exception, Daisy Marie Payton."

She closed the door in my face.

I returned and only left my room for the cafeteria as soon as it opened on Saturday morning. I grabbed a muffin and ate it on the way back to my dorm. I didn't have much of an appetite for the rest of the day, so I spent it hiding in my dorm room, sleeping in a cocoon of numbness. Occasionally I would wake and go to Odie's door and knock, but she never answered.

CHAPTER TWENTY-ONE

Daisy

The consequences—the scholastic ones, that is—began rolling in swiftly.

On Sunday I got word via letter that I was being kicked out of my dorm. I had a week to vacate the premises. Another irony of ironies it was signed Director of Residential Affairs, Bessie Mitchell.

On Monday, a note was hand delivered to me in my macroeconomics class, instructing me to visit Dean Gwinn immediately after the end of class.

When I arrived at her office, I was caught off-guard.

Trevor sat in the corner at a small table. He didn't look up when I entered.

Dean Gwinn was impersonal with none of the hints of humor I witnessed before. She didn't overtly mention what I'd done, the only indicator that she knew was the way she drew out the Y in my last name when calling me Ms. Payton.

She explained that until a verdict was reached in my case, I was still a student and that I was expected to continue all of my coursework. I listened, but every few seconds my eyes drifted to Trevor, willing him to look at me, willing our eyes to connect so I could see if there was still the same magnetic pull as before.

He steadfastly refused to look at me.

I was so distracted with Trevor, I almost missed her saying, "Effective immediately, Trevor Boone is no longer your mentor. You will need to talk to my secretary and schedule a meeting time with me. I expect a full reporting of your grades this Friday."

And then Trevor did look up at me. I saw those amber eyes, beautiful as ever, flat, hard, and full of accusation.

The hope I'd been holding onto that Trevor would want to see me, talk to me, know me, vanished in a split second, and I realized from the expression on his face Trevor didn't want any of those things at all.

That evening, when I arrived back to what was still my room for the next six days, I had two more slips of paper slid under my door. The first one was from University Dining Services:

Pending the results of the investigation, your dining privileges have been revoked.

- Doretha "Mrs. Dot" Bushnell

The second paper was a notice that listed all the rules in the Code of Student Conduct I was accused of violating, along with where I could find a resource on campus to help me navigate the university's judicial system.

The list of citations was even longer than I'd expected.

"Jeopardy of public infestation" was my favorite one. "Egregious theft of school property" was the most serious one. Actually no, "falsification of student identity" was the one that was most likely to get me expelled.

I got to the line that read, *The University reserves the right to refer the student for criminal charges in the case of theft or other illegal acts,* and took a deep calming breath, but I was unable to find my calm.

I had no place to eat, very shortly I'd have no place to live. I might be facing criminal charges. I was almost certainly going to get expelled from school. My father and sister weren't speaking to me, and neither were my friends. Trevor was finished with me.

I lay down on my bed, fighting against the tide of emotions rising in me.

I lay down on my bed feeling numb and worn out, and I welcomed both feelings.

You did this, Daisy. You did this to yourself. You don't get to cry. Worse things have happened to you in your life, Daisy. Crying won't fix it. It's already done, all you can do is accept it.

"There's no use in crying over spilled milk." My mother's words suddenly popped in my head.

My *mother. I wanted* my *mother. I need my mother.*

I miss my mother.

I didn't even realize the tears had started until I felt them on my cheeks. And then I let go and I really, really cried.

I cried because if my mother were here, she would've told me no matter how badly I messed up or failed that things were going to be okay. She would've told me that she loved me. She wouldn't have made excuses for me or taken over and fixed everything, but she would've told me that she'd help me figure out how to make things right. I cried because she was not there and instead of hearing my mother's beautiful voice all I heard was silence.

And then in the midst of a sob, a thick choking spasm of anger rocked me. *Why aren't you here, Mommy? You said you'd always be there for me. You promised you'd fight. You promised nothing would happen to you.*

Because she *had* promised all those things. I'd become paranoid, especially after Ado died, that something would happen to my sister or my parents. My mother had laughed and reassured me that she and my father would be old and getting on my nerves telling me how to raise my own kids one day. My mother would never get to know my children. My brother . . . oh God. Would my brother even know me now? If he were alive, he wouldn't even recognize me.

The racing thoughts wouldn't stop, and the tears wouldn't stop. It felt like the switch I used to control my emotions, to numb everything, had been broken. The dull ache that I'd carried inside me constantly since I'd lost my brother and then my mother bloomed and spread until all I could feel was pain; lung collapsing pain. I couldn't catch my breath with how hard I was crying. Sobs wracked my entire body; the emptiness and loss felt so acute and like their deaths had only happened moments ago.

Things will never be okay again. Things will never be the same again.

I lay there thinking of my family.

I thought of how my father had had his heart broken three times—once when we lost Ado, then when he lost the love of his life last October, and again by how much I'd hurt him today—and I cried some more. I thought about how Dolly had been trying to hold us all together and how she was right—I had been inconsiderate, and I'd hurt her. But she was also wrong; I didn't avoid Dolly because I was angry with her, I avoided Dolly because she reminded me of my mother. I thought about Trevor and how maybe he could have been my first love, but now he was just another thing that I'd messed up. I thought about my friends and how they hated me and how there was nothing I could do change it. All the while I cried. I cried until my chest hurt and my eyes were swollen and still I couldn't stop crying. I cried until my nose was swollen shut and I hiccupped. Every emotion that I'd tried so hard for so long to avoid was coming down to bear on me at once and I couldn't stop crying. After a long while, sleep won over the tears and I drifted into oblivion.

The next morning I awoke with a start, scrambling to get my bearings. I heard three quick knocks at my door again, and scrambled out of bed daring to hope that maybe James or Odie decided they wanted to talk to me.

It was completely dark and my eyes are almost swollen shut so I stumbled on my way to the door and yelped painfully as I stubbed my toe. I snatched the door open and my hope evaporated instantly.

That's what you get for hoping, Daisy.

One of the RA's I recognized from room check stared back at me, likely taking in my disheveled state, my puffy swollen eyes, and the tissues that were littered all over my bed.

She pursed her lips and said matter-of-factly, "You have a visitor downstairs." Before I could ask who, she'd turned and left.

I'd already decided I wasn't going to class today. Instead, after I finished talking to this visitor, I would make my way over to the building listed in the letter as the place for students to get help navigating the judicial process.

When I got to the lobby it only took me a second to spot my visitor. Julian P. Marshall stood against the wall, in his navy blue peacoat and charcoal gray slacks.

His eyes widened in surprise as he took in my disheveled state and then he nodded to himself. When I was standing directly in front of him, he said, "Took you long enough."

It was eight o'clock in the morning and I'd already been disappointed once already. I couldn't allow myself hope that Julian was here on Trevor's behalf, so I spoke plainly. "Well, I'm not accustomed to having visitors at eight a.m. What are you doing here, Julian?"

"You look like you need a friend, Daisy."

A knot welled up in my throat. I'd never in my life needed a friend more. I couldn't speak or I'd cry, and I was already mighty tired of crying so I nodded.

"Then I'm here to be a friend, and hopefully, keep you enrolled."

No longer armed by the thin layer of fog I'd been wearing around my emotions for as long as I could remember, it was totally logical that I would cry in the lobby right in front of Julian.

He reared back in shock, huffed a little laugh, and then draped me in a half-hug and patted my shoulder awkwardly. This was not the uncontrollable torrent of tears from last night. I stopped almost as soon as I started. Julian looked at me, squinted his eyes like he was trying to determine if I were truly done crying, and then said, "All right, little chicken, let's get out of here."

On the walk to Spence, Julian explained to me that the Tribunal Disciplinary Council, or TDC, was made of the Dean of Student Affairs, two faculty members and two students. As student body president he'd been asked to be one of the students that were a part of the council.

"I declined," he said with a smirk. "But I was a junior senator last year and was a member of the TDC then, so if you want it, my guidance is available to you, free of charge."

"Thank you." I exhaled gratefully, stepping into the cramped space as Julian held the door for me.

I took a seat at the desk next to Julian and put my head down on it.

Julian laughed.

I turned toward him, head still on the desk. "What?"

"Nothing—just there are twenty pieces of furniture in this office and you choose the one spot that belongs to Trevor. This is our office and that's his desk. You two can't get together but you can't seem to stay apart, either."

I closed my eyes. It was bad enough being in his space. I didn't want to think about Trevor because I didn't want to cry again; I had stuff to do today. It felt like my emotions were having an autoimmune response, like they were overreacting to every emotional stimulus after having underreacted for so long.

I rose and went to sit in the seat by the windowsill.

He laughed again and shook his head. I didn't ask why because I didn't *want* to know. I couldn't play musical chairs with every single seat in this room. I wasn't at his desk anymore; that was going to have to be good enough.

"Now, do you have the piece of paper that shows which rules you're accused of breaking?"

I fished it out of my purse and handed it to him.

I watched as his eyes bounced back and forth reading line after line.

Julian began to frown. Then he sighed. His frown deepened, then he sighed again.

Then he flipped the page and continued reading, his eyebrows bounced up. "Violation of the fire code? What . . .?"

"Ah. Hot plate," I responded.

He took his glasses off, rubbed his eyes, and sighed.

"Well, you don't do anything by half measures, do you?"

"I'm a Payton, Julian," I deadpanned. "We don't know how to do things by half measures."

He squinted at me some more, but a smile tugged at his lips. "A Payton—you sure? Cause I met a girl a few weeks ago—looked *just* like you too. Said her name was Paxton something or other. Uncanny resemblance."

"Shut up, Julian," I said, cracking a small smile.

He put his glasses on and got back to business.

"I'm not entirely sure who you pissed off . . ."

It was my turn to raise my eyebrows because Julian knew exactly who I'd pissed off.

The slight smile was back at his lips. "Pissed off inside the *administration* but they threw the book at you. I don't even know if I've ever seen anyone get cited for having a hot plate even though we all know we're not supposed to have them."

He continued reading the paper in his hands. "Well, you're definitely going to get expelled from your dorm. There's nothing I can do about that. You've got too many hits against you in that area."

"I know. They already sent the letter. I have to be out by Sunday."

"Where will you go?"

I shrugged.

He rubbed his forehead and muttered, "Okay, lets save that for the end."

"I think . . . you might be able to get out of being expelled. But I need you to tell me the truth about everything that happened with this whole 'eat my cookie' business."

Of course Julian would choose *that* to remember.

I hesitated. James already hated my guts. But telling Julian about her financial situation felt like a betrayal that was a step too far.

"Daisy, I am trying to help, but I can't if I don't know what I'm up against. I trusted you with information that was just about as delicate as could be. You told me that we shouldn't have a friendship based on threats. I'm offering you one based on trust."

"Why are you helping me?"

He stared at his desk for a long time before he answered. "Since we are being *honest* with one another, I am going to tell you *all* my reasons and you will not hold them against me."

I nodded in concession. It seemed Julian couldn't help being a little imperious.

"Because I get wanting to escape pressure. That's why you lied right?"

I nodded, even though his question was rhetorical.

"I guess I can see myself in you in some ways."

I opened my mouth to politely object but he continued before I could. "Not in our personalities. But in our life circumstances; I guess I empathize with you in that way. And you need help." He glanced back down at the sheet of paper on his desk. "You need a lot of help. I'm in a position to help you and so I should. And . . . my best friend wants me to help you and he doesn't know how to ask me, so I'm doing it without his asking. Don't get me wrong, Daisy, you and Trevor—y'all need to work on your communication. And you two have the worst timing of anyone I've ever seen. But despite all that and despite what he says or how he's acting right now, I know he still cares about you. Because if he didn't, he wouldn't be upset at all. So regardless of the fact that he's kinda being an ass right now, I know that there will be a point where he'll come to his senses and in that moment he'll be glad that I'm helping you."

I don't have it in me to hope that Julian was right about Trevor.

"Those are the largest and most altruistic reasons . . . but I'd be lying if I didn't also acknowledge that as an aspiring judge, your father is someone I greatly respect and admire. After everything he's done to open doors for people like me . . . Well, it would be an honor to help anyone in his family."

Julian was actually blushing a little as he hero-worshipped my father. I smiled slightly because he was right; my dad was the best. Julian had been more honest with me than I had any right to ask for. I was not in a position to ask anything of anyone trying to help me.

As if he'd read my thoughts, he cleared his throat and smiled his half smile. "Was that honest enough for you?"

I nodded.

"All right then. Now it's your turn, little chicken. Tell me how you ended up stealing all the cookies from the cookie jar."

I told Julian the whole story about James, the books, and the cookies. I even told him about Charlie getting the stuff for us and us smuggling it out in duffle bags from the service corridor and baking it in the home economics kitchens.

311

When I finished my story, Julian was quiet for a moment and then said in frustration, "James should've asked me for the books. I would've loaned them to her."

I stared back at him blankly.

"Why would James ask you for anything? She doesn't really even know you."

To my knowledge, she'd interacted with Julian only a handful of times and those interactions hadn't all been pleasant.

He shot me a disbelieving look.

"What are you talking about? She sees me twice a week. I'm the TA for her English 202 class. Even when I'm not teaching the class, I'm usually in the class to hand back papers at the start or to collect assignments at the end. There is no way James didn't know I could help her get those books."

He added more quietly as if he was speaking to himself, "She's *so* stubborn. She just didn't want *my* help."

I felt compelled to defend my friend . . . former friend. "Or she didn't think you would give it."

Either way, James knew she had another way to get books for the *second* semester, and she sat on that info in order to get me to agree to sell that second batch of cookies.

I am going to kill James. Just as soon as I get her to speak to me again.

Julian said, "Well, after hearing that story, they only caught you on half the criminal stuff you did."

I hung my head. "Will the university refer me to the police for criminal charges?"

"I don't know. Right now the only criminal charge I see is possession of stolen goods. But they can't prove without a shadow of a doubt *you* stole them. But we're toeing a fine line. I want to help you stay in school without pissing in the face of the administration, because if they feel like you're trying to pull one over on them or that you're not remorseful, then they're absolutely going to refer this to the law. And it won't just be possession of stolen goods. If the cops investigate it'll be trespassing, conspiracy to commit theft, and all of your nobility—"

"Nobility?"

"Daisy—Odie, James, and Charlie are *just* as culpable as you are. All of your asses should be lined up answering for this craziness together. Just because you lied to them about one thing doesn't absolve them of their responsibility over something else. Those two things aren't really related and you're letting your guilt over lying to your friends cause you take responsibility for something that you didn't do by yourself."

"What are you saying? Are you saying I should tell on my fr—" I stopped. "You're saying that I should tell on James and Odie?" Telling on Charlie was out of the question. He had the most to lose and was the least involved.

He exhaled. "Dai—"

I cut him off. "Would you do it? Would you rat on Trevor?"

"No."

I raised my eyebrows meaningfully.

"I wouldn't have to rat on Trevor because no matter how angry he was he'd never let me go down alone for any shit we did *together*. Daisy, if you're hell bent on shouldering the blame alone, then here's what I got—you should preemptively acknowledge what you did was wrong and try to make a case for why you should be allowed to stay."

"And you think this is my best chance?" I bit my thumbnail. Confessing seemed risky.

"I think it's your *only* chance. You can try telling the TDC you're not guilty and try to get out of *everything* you've been accused of. But there will be an investigation. Your friends are going to be questioned —that's inevitable. There were a hundred people at our party that night, and all of them saw the three of you together. Not to mention you were already caught with contraband in your room."

Julian had very valid points, but I was overwhelmed and something in my expression must've given away how close I was to losing it.

He softened his tone. "I'm not saying what y'all did wasn't stupid, but it wasn't *serious*. Even the changing your name thing is weird as hell, but you didn't impersonate another student, you didn't cheat. You still did all your work. You just did it under a different name. In all this foolery, no one got physically harmed, and the university hasn't gotten any bad press from it, so it's a little puzzling to me why they're taking this to the nth degree.

"Actually, it's not puzzling. I think they're trying to make an example out of you *because you're Daisy Payton,* and I hate that. The assumption is probably that you're spoiled and you think the rules don't apply to you. When I said everybody has a hot plate and no one gets cited for it, I meant it. The normal punishment is that it gets confiscated, end of story. But I think if you go in there—humble, sorry and ready to make amends, then you have a chance."

The irony that my last name would be used as a reason to punish me instead of protecting me would have been a little funny if I'd been less terrified.

"The school already reclaimed all the stuff y'all stole for the second batch of cookies, so there doesn't need to be any restitution there. How much money did you even make from selling the first batch?" Julian inquired.

"One hundred and sixty dollars."

Julian's voice was incredulous. "Y'all made almost *two hundred* dollars selling cookies in one night? I have been wasting my time preparing for law school. I should've been banging down the door trying to get into the Girl Scouts!"

I smiled despite myself. "We met a very generous patron who paid us very well to leave a party."

His mouth snapped shut and his blush was back. He rolled his eyes and muttered something that sounded like, "It was cheaper than bail."

314

He cleared his throat, shifted in his seat, and then said, "And how much of that money did you keep?"

I stared at him confused. "I just told you James needed the money for books. Why would I keep the money?"

"Daisy . . ." He made a strangled sound.

Comprehension dawned. "Let me get this straight. You risk getting kicked out of school by taking the fall and you didn't reap *any* of the benefits?"

"It wasn't like that . . ."

He stared at me with his mouth open. Then prompted, "Then what was it like?"

"James . . . needed help." I struggled to clarify because the way Julian framed it was technically true, but not how it happened.

"This is some bullshit. James needs to come forth with that information."

"James isn't even speaking to me. She'll never do it. Also, she would most likely spit in my face if she knew I told you about her financial situation."

"What about Odie?"

"She's not speaking to me either."

Julian rubbed his temple. "Okay. We will figure out this stuff later. In the meantime, you need to think about which one of those three options you want to take, and I need to eat—Actually, are you hungry?"

"I am starving." I hadn't had dinner or breakfast due to my dining privileges being withdrawn.

"Okay then, we need to eat breakfast. And then you need to pack."

He was right. I did need to pack, although I had no clue where I would go.

Julian walked me to his car and this time I didn't hesitate getting in.

As he pulled out of the parking lot and into traffic the thing that'd been on the tip of my tongue all morning long spilled out.

"Julian?"

"Yes?"

"Thank you."

He was quiet for a second. "What, no tears this time?"

"Shut up, Julian." I laughed.

"Daisy?"

"Yes?"

"You're welcome."

Trevor

I decided to skip my third class of the day and head home around four. I needed to get some sleep. I hadn't been sleeping this week.

This semester.

I was past tired. I was past cranky.

I was exhausted and I was *irritated.*

My prodigal parents had shown up, completely unannounced, at o' dark thirty last weekend and had been single-handedly responsible for derailing my senior year homecoming weekend.

Years. Years without a visit.

Then they'd showed up completely unannounced on my doorstep. I'd been in a state of perpetual discombobulation ever since.

My father, upon popping up on my doorstep, calmly explained, "A man gets tired of having to chase his offspring down via telephone. Eventually he figures he should come see him directly."

They'd informed me that we'd be having breakfast with the Paytons and that I needed to get dressed quickly because Mr. Payton was waiting in the car and we needed to go fetch his daughters from campus.

I'd wanted to tell my parents they could leave without me, since they'd been totally fine living their life without me thus far.

The nerve. They showed up like they'd just seen me this past summer. Like we'd spent the past few years together as a family.

I'd wanted to tell my father in particular that he did not get to show up and order me around like . . . well, like he was my father.

But I'd wished to maintain the peace. Julian had been preaching to me about working on my relationship with my parents. "Look on the bright side, at least you know your parents love you."

I wasn't sure about his assessment but I could—given how his parents behaved—see why he'd say that.

So instead of telling my father and mother to leave, I'd gotten dressed and headed out to the car. An eerie sensation of déjà vu hit me as I recognized the face of the older man driving. The unsettling feeling quickly gave way to a knot that bounced between my stomach and my throat.

I had no particular ill will against the Paytons. In fact, I hadn't thought of or heard the name in years. But Mr. Payton had been the one to drive me from Green Valley to Charlotte, so my only real memory of him was of him taking me away from home. By that time, my parents had sold their car in an effort to stave off foreclosure. I didn't remember the drive all that well, but I did remember Mr. Payton had his daughter with him, and she'd been sick. As in, laying-on-me-warm-and-feverish, in-and-out-of-sleep-the-whole-long-car-ride sick. We weren't in the same grade at school, and I vaguely recalled she must've been maybe seven or eight to my eleven.

I also remembered how I'd *felt* during that ride.

Abandoned.

Confused.

We'll come fetch you later. We promise.

Immeasurably sad.

I pushed aside the pang at the memory—at the promise.

At the *broken* promise.

317

I remembered feeling kinship with the girl in the car that day. The type that could only exist between children. The feeling of being totally powerless along with another small human that had been tossed into the same scenario—that could understand with no words how you felt. Because that sick little girl hadn't wanted to be in the back seat of that car any more than I had. We'd held hands and lain on one another and I'd felt a sort of comfort.

My comfort during the ride to school had been successfully tuning out most of the conversation around me. I'd listened for my name and answered whatever question was thrown my way without embellishment.

How were my grades? Great.

What were my plans for after graduation? Still deciding.

Somewhere it had dawned on me that one of the sisters we were about to pick up from the dorms was the girl that was in the car with me that day.

I didn't remember there being two girls in the Payton family. Then again, there was a lot I didn't know or had forgotten about Green Valley families. I'd wondered if I'd crossed paths with the girl from the car. I'd wondered if she'd recognize me, and immediately realized I'd been silly. We'd seen each maybe a handful of times that I could recall in my life, and the last time had been almost a decade ago. Of course she wouldn't.

When we'd arrived, I'd been allowed by the RA to go upstairs since I was escorted by my parents and then . . . in a matter of seconds Daisy Marie *Payton* had detonated my world.

That's how it'd felt. Like a bomb had gone off and the walls and the ceiling and the floor were falling down around me. Comprehension clicked in rapid succession. Seeing Mr. Payton speak to his daughters. Realizing his daughter *was* Daisy. And that meant she'd been the little girl in the car.

And then realizing his daughter *is* Daisy and that meant she'd lied to me.

She'd lied to me a lot.

I'd realized she was from Green Valley and must have known that my parents had given me away.

Oh. God.

Between my parents arriving and Daisy's deception, I hadn't been able to get a grasp on my emotions. I'd felt like I'd had an out-of-body experience, like I'd been observing someone else's life. And that was before I'd even gotten around to comprehending that Daisy's room looked like a baker's pantry.

I'd felt like a damned fool.

Note to self. The next time you and a girl don't want to talk about some topics? Make those the first things you discuss.

Even after my parents and I had left, I hadn't been able to turn my mind off. I wondered if Daisy had known who *I* was the whole time. I'd had no clue about her identity but she'd lied to me about everything else, so maybe this was some sort of sick joke she'd been playing.

On top of all that, things had not gone well with my parents. I'd told them I wasn't feeling well, mostly because I had felt like I was going to be sick. It must've been believable because they'd let me return to my apartment without too much fuss.

But not without consequences.

My mother likely knew that once I returned to my room I was going to disconnect my phone and not open the door for the remainder of the weekend. She'd decided to strike while she had the advantage over me in my out-of-sorts state. And that was how she'd extracted a promise from me that I'd return "home" for the Christmas break.

Walking back to my apartment now, I wondered how I would get out of spending the holidays in Green Valley with my folks.

Because I was absolutely not going. The idea was barely tenable at the start of the semester before everything happened with Daisy. It was completely impossible now that it meant sharing a town with her.

Daisy.

Over the past few days I'd tried not to think about her. If I thought about her, then I'd have to feel the sensation of my heart going crazy *still*, even after she'd lied to me, and that pissed me off. And I'd have to stave off the longing that welled up in my chest, even now.

I almost wanted to laugh, because the timing had *almost* come together after all.

After Julian had told me about his plans to tell Daisy the truth, I *had* decided to seek her out. I'd decided what I felt for her was worth taking a chance on, if she would have me, then I—*we*—should give it a try. I'd wanted to start over and I'd been grateful that the timing had finally, finally worked in our favor.

But now I didn't know.

I'd held El's secret back from Daisy it because it wasn't mine to set free.

I had no idea why she'd held back the truth from me, but I knew it hurt.

I couldn't help but wonder what else she'd lied about.

Did the girl I'd begun to fall for really even exist or was that all a part of her deception too?

One thing was for certain: Daisy and I weren't good for one another.

Between my parents stirring emotions that I thought I was long past and Daisy, I was fraught.

And I was too tired to think straight.

My thoughts couldn't stay linear. They collided with one another, split apart, and fractured like atoms.

I couldn't concentrate for shit.

Therefore, when Dr. Gwinn got ahold of the disciplinary file on Daisy and informed me that she'd be taking over as her mentor I'd had no objections. When she told me she wanted me there when she told Daisy, I didn't say a peep.

When I'd finally steeled myself enough to lay eyes on what was still the prettiest face I'd ever seen and caught Daisy's wide brown eyes staring back at me, my heart had taken flight in my chest. But I'd ignored it.

It was a foolish organ. It had been driving all my poor decisions and it was finally time to let sleeping dogs lie.

I heard voices before I opened my apartment door and figured Elodie and Gracie must be visiting from downstairs. It had been nice having them close by. It had been nicer still not having Gracie glare daggers at me every time El and I were in the same room together.

That part of Julian's idea had been good.

Gracie had been happy to give up her position as a RA and move out of the dorms and into a place with El. Elodie, however, was *not* a naturally hopeful person and had been rightfully furious at Julian for telling Daisy, and hadn't spoken to him in days.

I didn't blame her. But I also hadn't waded in; my mind was already full of my own problems. Not to mention, I was steeped in regret over another obligation I'd foolishly agreed to.

If El was at the apartment that meant she'd forgiven Julian and that was something to be glad of—my life was better when the people I loved were getting along.

I stepped into my apartment and sitting in technicolor at my drab kitchen table was Daisy Payton. I blinked, sure I was hallucinating, and then she laughed and goosebumps that I did not want appeared on my skin. And *then* I realized who she smiled at.

My best friend sat at the table doubled over in laughter. I heard Daisy's voice, all sweet southern syrup with a bit of spice, finish some previous joke or story with, "And *that* was the last time *anyone* in my family ever tried to make pecan pie!"

Jules and Daisy were smiling at each other like they were the best of friends. My mind, rife with exhaustion, frustration and jealousy, went haywire.

Before I could catch my words they were out of my mouth. "What in the hell is going on here?"

Daisy jumped at my voice and I didn't blame her. I hadn't meant for it to boom like thunder, but then again, I also didn't expect my Daisy and my best friend to be laughing it up together.

Jules looked up from where he was sitting and said all casually, "Hey, Trevor. Daisy and I are having sandwiches. Would you like one?"

All this cooking Julian was doing lately—what was he trying to do? Get into Le Cordon Bleu?

"Since when do you cook, Julian?" I boomed again.

"I didn't." He took a big bite of his sandwich, gesturing at Daisy with his free hand. "Daisy here is a panini-making wizard."

Daisy made sandwiches for Jules. Daisy and Jules were eating sandwiches together. Daisy hadn't even made a sandwich for me.

Oh, hell no.

"Since when do you cook sandwiches for Julian?" It sounded like an accusation. It *was* an accusation. Daisy and I had eaten sandwiches together the first time, the only time we'd had something resembling a date.

This felt like a mockery of that moment and all of the resentment I was feeling rose to the surface.

If I were more rested or less discombobulated, maybe I would've listened to the voice in my head that said I had no right to ask Daisy any questions, but I wasn't either of those things. I was fraught, tense, and suddenly angry, so I unwisely ignored it.

Daisy, who'd moved to the sink and was washing dishes in *my* sink, the dishes she and Jules used for *their* sandwiches answered without even looking at me, "Since I was hungry and he offered me food. What's it to you?"

I couldn't answer that question. It would expose me too much.

So I spoke to cut her in the way she'd cut me. "I just didn't think you were the type of girl to just give *anyone* your sandwich."

She whipped around from the sink and assaulted me with eyes narrowed into slits and fiery as hell. My heart kicked up and I was glad my hands were in my pockets because they'd be shaking from the amount of adrenaline hitting my system. I could practically see her biting her tongue. And I was even hotter because I was angry and turned on, and angrier that I still reacted this way to her. After a moment she bit her bottom lip hard, then licked it in a mesmerizing little move and said, "Sometimes a sandwich is just a sandwich, Trevor."

Then she looked at Jules, and said, "Julian, thanks for the food and the company. I'm going to head back downstairs to Gracie and El."

My eyebrows were on the ceiling with how hard they jumped. Since when did Daisy hang out with El and Gracie?

Then Daisy walked over to Jules' chair, leaned over, and *hugged* him.

I was wrong before. That was the moment my eyebrows hit the roof.

When he was finished *embracing* her, he leaned away and said, "I'll come by and check on you later, little chicken."

Little chicken? I think St. Peter just saw my eyebrows.

"Little chicken? You have a *nickname* for Daisy?" My voice was as high as I'd ever heard it.

Jules looked sheepish. "Yeah, I guess I do."

"You let Julian give you a nickname?" The blood was whooshing in my ears and my heart was pounding so hard I knew my blood pressure had shot up so fast I had to be in danger of having a stroke.

Did anything between us mean anything to Daisy? Had it ever? Of course not, Trevor, you're the type of person that it's easy to move on from.

"Trevor." She called my name like she was exasperated. "Yes, Julian calls me a nickname. Julian showed up, and Julian is helping me, so at this point he could call me Rudolph the Red-Nosed Reindeer and I wouldn't give a damn."

"More like Pinocchio the liar."

Her head whipped back like I'd slapped her.

She walked to me slowly, staring me down. Those hypnotic eyes pierced me, as if they could will me into submission with their weight alone.

I stared right back, ignoring the pull to obey because I'd left sanity behind.

Daisy was literally driving me crazy.

She lied to me.

She deceived me.

She hurt me.

And now she was sitting here, laughing with my best friend like none of that ever happened.

Like we never mattered?

She's spent all semester making me feel badly about lying, all while doing the exact same thing? Then she came into my kitchen and made sandwiches for Jules? He got to have her company and I didn't?

No. No. And no again.

Daisy didn't get to be the offended party today. I would not apologize. She needed to apologize.

She needed to grovel for a change.

But it was clear from the sparks I saw in her eyes, from the heat radiating off her when she got close, that she had no intention of apologizing.

"You really want to have this conversation with me? You of all people? Well, I guess we're both liars, Trevor. Is that what you want to hear? And you lied to me about something much bigger—"

"I was myself with you!" I pounded my chest for emphasis. "I was honest with you about who I was—"

"Oh yes, Trevor, how could I ever forget? You were so very, very honest with me. I knew all about your fake relationship with your fake girlfriend, and I willingly made a damn fool of myself by agreeing to go out with you. How silly of me to have brought it up," she deadpanned.

Then she looked up at me and she *smirked.*

It was the unrepentant little smile that broke me.

This girl had broken my brain because it should not have been possible to want to kiss her, strip her, pin her against a wall, and make love to her until we were both sated and exhausted and also to *never* see her again.

I was so upside down that fury and lust were coursing through me and I didn't know which of them I wanted to win.

I didn't even know this person I'd become—who got into shouting matches with women, who lost sleep, and who ached and pined for women.

Not women, just her.

Suddenly, my fire went out and I was bone-weary and tender-hearted. I would not cry in front of this girl, but my eyes pricked and I blinked the tears back before she could see them.

I took a deep breath.

"Daisy, I was wrong to have not told you about Elodie. I've spent almost the entire semester trying to tell you I knew I was wrong. I've been trying to apologize. And when you made it clear that you didn't want to speak to me, I spent all of my time respecting that *because* I was wrong."

I looked up to see that Jules had made his way from the kitchen to his bedroom and I loved him for giving us privacy.

I continued, "But in all of my wrongs—being with you felt right. It felt like something real and honest, and new and fragile and vulnerable and . . . perfect. And now I don't know if—"

The person I was falling for. I am absolutely not giving her that.

"I don't know if any of that was real because I have no clue who you are. What you did was worse," I finished, shaking my head.

"I was *myself,*" she countered. "Whether I have an X or Y in my last name, my favorite color is still the same! My favorite book is still the same. My dreams are the same! I showed you parts of myself that no one gets to see. And it *was not* worse, Trevor, it only *feels* worse because *you're* the one who got lied to this time."

"You didn't even apologize."

"You didn't give me the chance! You wouldn't even look at me in Dr. Gwinn's office. I felt like you'd given up on me without even giving me a shot to explain."

"That sounds mighty familiar. How does your medicine taste, Daisy?"

She closed her mouth, which had already been preparing her rebuttal, before I'd even finished speaking and dropped her head in her hands. When she looked back at me, she may as well have cut my heart out, dropped it on floor, and stomped on it.

She was crying.

I'd never seen her cry before and it was a special type of torture. My fingers twitched and ached with the need to reach for her as fat tears rolled down her cheeks.

Daisy was right. We'd both been wrong. There was no *worse*. I'd hurt her, she'd hurt me. I didn't know now if it were possible for us to be together without barbs between us, but I didn't want to fight with her.

Before I could voice my thoughts, she spoke, "I can't do this with you. I had an apology all planned out. I was going to explain everything and beg you to forgive me. I was going to . . ." She sighed. "But what's the point?"

Every other word out her mouth broke as her chest heaved up and down, but she was the one breaking me.

My will strained under the force that it took to hear her cry and not fold her into my arms and kiss all her tears away.

Her voice trembled. "We're going in circles, Trevor. This isn't good for either of us. I *am* sorry I lied to you but it doesn't even matter. So here's what we'll do—I'll stay away from you, you'll stay away from me, and we'll call ourselves even."

I couldn't bring myself to speak for a moment because she was right; we were going in circles and this couldn't continue.

"Fine, we go our own ways." I closed my eyes knowing what I was going to say next would truly sound the death knell for Daisy and me.

"But you should know you'll have to see me again. I'm one of the student representatives on the TDC and I know for a fact that you're guilty."

I didn't think it was possible to feel worse than I already did, but when I opened my eyes the look Daisy gave me—no anger, no guilting me, just endless hurt—stole my breath away. The only noise in the room was the sound of her tears and the soft click of the door as she left.

When I turned around Julian was standing there, looking accusatory.

"I am not going to clean your clock for what you basically accused me of earlier. But I am telling you right now, get your head out of your ass when it comes to this girl."

I was so tired of Julian meddling in my life and thinking he was always right.

I was tired, period.

"Why did you bring her here, Jules?"

"Because I didn't think you'd be home and because she had nowhere else to go. She's being kicked out of her dorm."

"Of course she is! You weren't there, you didn't see what I saw. She *should* be put out of her dorm, Julian. Daisy deserves what's happening to her!" I turned toward my room. I didn't want to talk about Daisy anymore.

"Not all of it, she doesn't. And you know that. And you're going to feel like a jackass when you finally come around."

I didn't respond.

"I'm advising her."

Of course he was. Jules had never learned that sticking his nose in other people's business led to bad outcomes.

I turned slowly and exhaled all my frustration. "Of course you are."

"Did you even give her the chance to explain, Trevor? She has a good reason for why she—"

"*Everybody* feels like they have a good reason to do the shit they do, Julian, or they wouldn't do it! You know what your problem is? You and Daisy both think that the reason for your actions are all that matter!

"Doesn't matter who gets hurt or what you have to do, as long as it's for a 'good reason.' But life does *not* work that way. If you do a bad thing for a good reason, *you still did a bad thing*. Telling Elodie's secret without her permission was a bad thing. Lying to people about who you are is a bad thing. Stealing is a bad thing. I am so tired of you trying to excuse her bad behavior—just because she had a 'good reason' to do it. And I'm tired of you trying to excuse your own."

I stalked to my room and tried to sleep but rest evaded me. I tossed and turned, a phantom ache running down my arms like they were missing something or someone, and I was haunted by the sound of Daisy's cries.

CHAPTER TWENTY-TWO

Daisy

In the two seconds it took me to get downstairs to the apartment I now shared with Elodie and Gracie, I still hadn't managed to get my tears under control. The apartment was mercifully empty and I made my way to my room quickly before I lost my nerve.

I was listening to my feelings, I was owning my feelings, and I was feeling like I needed to get the hell out of here. I picked up the phone in my room, and dialed the same number I'd been punching since I first learned to dial. She picked up on the fourth ring.

"Dolly?"

"Daisy? What's wrong?"

That made me cry harder. Even with all the noise and clamor from the Mill in the background, my sister could still tell something was wrong with one word. *Oh Dolly, I've been so unfair to you.*

"*Everything.* I miss Mommy. And I miss you. And I want to come home," I said, my voice breaking.

My sister didn't hesitate for even a second. "I'm on my way."

On the drive home I told Dolly everything.

Every. Single. Thing.

And to my sister's eternal credit she responded with Dolly-like poise and un-Dolly like compassion. She smiled knowingly when I told her about Trevor. How he'd made me giddy and breathless. How I'd felt like when we were together, we were the only people that existed in the entire world. She laughed and was especially appreciative when I told her about the fake Fisk-tory facts, given her love for history.

Then she'd almost crashed us into a tree when I'd told her about how I thought Trevor had made a fool of me.

"You just wait till I see the Boones! I'm going to . . . I will . . . That son of a—"

"Wait, there's more!"

I explained the whole Elodie thing and Dolly's eyes went round and wide before shooting me a look. "And this is who you're staying with?" she asked after a minute.

"Yes, they took me in after . . . well, after . . ."

"Are you comfortable with that?" I looked at my sister, and saw that there was no judgement in her face or tone. Dolly was just being Dolly—looking out for me, making sure that I was okay. She would've asked me that question no matter who I'd ended up staying with.

"I'm fine." Then I amended, "I'm fine with it for now. I don't care that they're two girls in love, but I may hate their habits as roommates though. Either way, I'll ride it out for the rest of the semester. I'm just glad they're letting me stay."

"That was mighty kind of them," she agreed. "So, you and Trevor?"

I sighed mightily. "Trevor and I are finished with each other."

Dolly nodded, her face impassive, but I heard a short soft snicker.

I turned to look at her, puzzled.

"What?"

"Nothing. Nothing."

Snicker, Snicker.

"Dolly. Are you . . . are you laughing?"

"No," she said as a grin finally punctured her façade. "I would"— *snicker*—"never laugh at you."

"I can't believe this! You are laughing at me."

She huffed a little, bringing her amusement back under control and then in a voice closer to her normal soft soprano said, "I am not laughing *at* you, but the idea of you and that boy being finished is laughable. Y'all are just getting started."

"Dolly, did you not just hear everything I told you?"

"I heard it all. You had a really bad week and a really bad fight with your boyfriend."

I blinked rapid-fire and stared at her in disbelief. Surely my sister, who was not known for her jokes, must've miraculously located her funny bone and was pulling my leg.

She continued to drive straight faced as ever.

"He's not my boyfriend."

"Daisy, I *have* been listening and it seems to me like this is a good, decent guy who was working with a terrible hand. He was damned if he told you and damned if hadn't. Even if he thought you were the most trustworthy person in the world he couldn't have gone blabbing a very sensitive secret because it wasn't his secret to tell. And that lets me know, dear sister, that you can trust him with your secrets."

I leaned my head back against the headrest. I'd never thought about it quite that way before. Dolly was right. Trevor was loyal to a fault.

Not loyal to you though.

I shook my head. "It doesn't matter. He thinks I'm a liar."

"Because you lied to him," she said softly.

"I know."

"Daisy, let me ask you a question. If you could erase the mistakes you both made what would you want?"

Trevor. A yearning so deep and intense rose in my chest, I felt it in my heart and in my bones. I'd want charming, sweet, clever, stubborn, infuriating Trevor.

"I—"

"*Gosh.*" She glanced over at me and then back to the road. "You don't even have to say anything. I can see it all over your lovesick little face."

Lovesick? I was not lovesick! This was not what love felt like. This feeling of anxiousness, of neediness, of desire, and hope, and fear . . . this couldn't be love.

At least I hoped it wasn't.

Dolly proceeded to burst my bubble.

"The way you describe your relationship with Trevor, the push and pull? All the angst and joy, the feeling of being the only two people in the world? Losing track of time when you're with that person? Thinking about them constantly?" She laughed. "If y'all aren't already falling in love, y'all are thirty seconds from it. And you don't just give up on folks you love."

She glanced over at me again. "You *can't.* Something in the way we're made won't let us."

She gave a half-shrug. "That's how I know this is nowhere near finished."

I wouldn't allow myself to hope that there could be something for me and Trevor in the future, even though I wanted so badly for Dolly to be right. Dolly understood logic, therefore logically speaking she had to see that Trevor and I weren't good for each other.

"Dolly, maybe that would be so if we could just erase the past, but that's not reality—"

"I disagree. It's reality all the time."

"But he—"

"He lied. You lied. Now what? You've been swinging back and forth between brooding and mooning for the last two and a half hours. You've. Got. It. Bad. And he clearly still cares for you because he's getting into shouting matches with you. If a man doesn't care about you, he doesn't spare two words in your direction, let alone all the energy it takes to get angry. He's shouting at you when he'd very clearly rather be making you scream. And y'all have been carrying on like this all semester? He's probably so frustrated he's near out of his mind."

"Dolly! You're the one who warned me to stay away from him the first place!"

"Of course I warned you away, Daisy, you were just getting to school and I could see the way he was looking at you—"

My head whipped toward my sister.

"How was he looking at me?"

She smiled like she knew a secret. "Like he could not *wait* for your big sister to leave. Like he wanted to get you alone to 'touch and agree'—and I do not mean he wanted to be your prayer partner."

"Dolly!" I spluttered. Though the idea of Trevor looking at me like he . . . he *wanted* gave me butterflies. I resigned myself to the idea that perhaps Trevor would always give me butterflies.

Dolly ignored my affronted tone. "We had this talk, Daisy. Mommy covered the birds and the bees, and I covered the teeth and the tongue." Her smile was barely there but her tone was as cheeky as ever.

My sister—my prim, buttoned-up sister—was unfailingly proper and rigidly circumspect, but she was not, much to my eternal surprise, a prude.

I'd blushed when James mentioned the birds and the bees because my mother had, in fact, had that very painful talk with me when I'd turned fifteen. And as soon as she'd left my sister slipped into my room, closed the door, and began to drop some enlightening facts my mother omitted.

"No sister of mine is going out into the world unprepared. Mommy just gave you the basics. I'm going to give you notes on the advanced study, including the DIY version."

So yes, I'd blushed, because Dolly was as detailed and thorough with explaining the "advanced study" as she was with everything else. Not that I'd had anyone to practice advanced study with. Not that I'd had anyone to practice *basic* study with.

That was all beside the point. "Dolly, I'm not talking about any of Trevor's *looks* with you."

She raised her eyebrows as if to say, *suit yourself.*

"It doesn't matter that we're attracted to each other. We have terrible communication."

"Then fix it, Daisy. You're acting like your life is happening to someone else. Like you don't have any control over this situation. From what you've told me Trevor's pride is wounded—"

"His pride?"

"Yes, Daisy, his pride. He trusted you with pieces of himself and he feels like you didn't do the same thing. Before you say anything—I *know* that there are things he didn't trust you with. I got that part, okay? But saying 'oh well, we both messed up so let's go our own ways' isn't your *only* option. You could try meeting him with a little grace. You could try forgiving *and* forgetting."

"Nobody ever really forgets anything. That's just a lie we tell ourselves." I quote my own sister, affecting her voice.

She smiled at my impersonation. "Fine. You could try forgiving and *deciding* to leave your mistakes in the past and stop throwing them in each other's faces. Or you can continue to not be with the person who, imperfections aside, sounds like a good person that makes you happy."

"Even if I wanted to do that, I couldn't right now. Trevor's part of the group that will investigate me. I wouldn't—"

"Back up. Investigating you?"

I brought Dolly up to speed. When I finished, she said, "So let me get this straight. They'll be a hearing to determine if you get to stay in school. The boy you just fought with, the one that is most likely head over heels with you, is one of the people responsible for deciding your fate, and his best friend is helping you to try and get out of this mess?"

Except for the head over heels part she had it right. "Yes."

"Daisy, yours might be the first relationship to ever die because Cupid just gave up and decided to shoot himself in the face with an arrow."

I smiled despite myself and griped, "It's not a relationship."

"And what type of kangaroo court is this? There are so many conflicts of interest, Daddy would have all of this dropped in a second"—she snapped her fingers—"if he—"

If he were involved. If he was speaking to me. If he hadn't disowned me.

She pulled into our driveway and navigated into the garage on the side of the house.

It was dark and late, near midnight, so we were silent as we climbed the veranda stairs and entered the house.

By some unspoken agreement, we both made our way to the second-floor den and closed the door behind us. My father was most likely already upstairs asleep.

Dolly glanced at the clock, rubbing her eyes tiredly.

She made her way to my mother's favorite chair and tossed my mom's afghan to me. I clutched it tightly and collapsed on the sofa, exhausted.

"Sniff it."

I closed my eyes and inhaled deeply.

It still smelled very, very faintly of my mother's perfume and even more faintly of my mother.

And that felt comforting, like a little of her was in the room with us.

"I don't usually touch it. I don't even usually sit in this chair." Her soprano was a bit too high. "But when I need . . . When it feels unbearable, I come here and I just . . . try to feel her, you know?"

I nodded and I felt my eyes prick, I but managed not to cry.

Dolly and I lounged in silence for a long time.

What would my mother think of what had happened between me and Dolly? How I'd pushed her away and shut her out?

She'd hate it.

I stared at my sister through the dim moonlight in the room. Her eyes were closed but she still fidgeted every few seconds.

"I'm so sorry, Dolly. I'm so, so, so, so sorry. Everything you said about me in my dorm room was true."

She opened her eyes and blinked tiredly, then yawned and half lifted her hand to make a flicking motion. "Daisy, it's all right."

"It's *not*. It's not all right. I haven't been a great sister to you. I haven't . . . You remind me of Mommy so much. And it hurts. It hurt to be reminded all the time. I was terrible to you and I'm sorry."

"I'm not like Mommy, *you're* just like her. Sweet to everybody," she mumbled ,closing her eyes.

"Dolly, please what can I do to make this up to you? I need you to forgive me," I whispered.

She said on a soft exhale, "Okay. You're forgiven."

She sounded like she was only a few minutes from dropping off to sleep.

I didn't deserve my sister. And I also didn't understand my sister.

Her forgiveness didn't feel real. It felt too easy, like I hadn't earned it and since I was trying to be honest and own my feelings, I asked, "Dolly, how can you just forgive me, just like that?"

I'd been expecting to have to beg, to plead. Dolly was not known for her magnanimity. She was president, CEO, and lead talent recruiter for Grudge Holders, Inc.

"Grace," she said around a yawn.

"Grace?"

She struggled to open her eyes and then she sighed and opened them a little more fully. "The way I see it, I can continue being angry with my sister. Not speaking to her and wind up with the type of relationship that I do *not* want." She looked me in my eyes and I could see the sincerity of her words. "Or, I can believe my sister is sorry and forgive her. Grace."

"Grace," I repeated.

"Paul . . . taught me that . . ." she said, her eyes closing again.

Paul?! Who in the world was Paul?

"Reverend . . . Smith . . . taught . . . me . . . lot . . . grace." A few seconds later Dolly's eyes were closed and her breathing even.

Interesting.

Dolly Pearl Payton was holding out on me. I stared at my sister's now-sleeping form knowing I was going to interrogate the hell out of her in the morning. Two years ago a new minister had been installed as pastor of our church. He was young and, in the words of James, he was *fine. He was also single.* Church got a lot livelier after that. I remembered him coming by the house a lot to pray with my mom when she'd been sick and to sit with us after she passed. He'd performed her eulogy.

Very, very interesting.

I recalled Dolly's eagerness to get back for Sunday service when she'd dropped me off at school and wondered if Reverend Smith, or as Dolly called him, *Paul,* was the driver behind that determination.

Oh yes, I would be launching the Spanish Inquisition the moment she opened her eyes.

I lay down on the sofa, wanting to stay near Dolly for the night. When we were younger, on special occasions like the Fourth of July or Labor Day—never Memorial Day; *that* was never a fun occasion— my parents would let us make an indoor camp in the den and have a slumber party. I snuggled under the warmth of the blanket, surrounded by faint echoes of my mother, feeling lighter and closer to my sister than I had in a long time.

Dolly's chair was empty when I awoke the next morning and the room was filled with light, which meant it was already mid-morning. I must've slept wrong because there was a crick in my neck. I stood up and stretched, trying to realign my neck when motion from other side of the room caused me to jump lose my balance and fall back into the sofa with an *OOMPH*!

My father stood in the doorway, looking confused.

"Daisy?"

"Yes?" I gasped, still trying to catch my breath from the fright. My father must've been working from his home office downstairs. Dolly had finally moved into his office at Payton Mills this past summer, but he still had an office in the municipal building and worked there most days.

I saw his eyes look up as if he was trying to recall something and then he blinked in confusion.

"What are you doing here? Did the school . . .? Were you asked to leave?"

"No. I just needed to come home. I was . . ."

On the verge of a mental breakdown.

"Homesick. And so I called Dolly and she came to get me."

"You just decided to take a vacation from school in the middle of the week?"

He sounded even more confused.

"No, I . . ."

I trailed off as realization dawned that technically what my father said was true. I had decided to leave school in the middle of the week for what was a vacation. I looked down at the floor, a deep ingrained reflex at making my parents ashamed. I was tired of being the girl that let her father down.

After a moment of my silence I heard my father say in frustration, "Daisy, I wish you would talk to me."

My response slipped out before I could catch it.

"I wish I *could* talk to you."

My eyes snapped up to meet his in surprise and before I could take the words back, before I could apologize for my sass, he whistled lowly. "All right, well now we seem to be getting somewhere."

My father sat in the chair Dolly had occupied in the night before.

"Now that's a pretty big statement. Before we get to what you *aren't* telling me, maybe we should back up and talk about why you feel like you *can't* tell me."

I closed my eyes and tried to will the panic coursing through me to recede. "I'm sorry. I didn't mean it. I shouldn't have said that. I'm sorry."

My father shook his head at me implacably. "Oh no. While I'd love nothing more than to believe that my youngest daughter feels like she can come to me to discuss anything, I'm more inclined to believe what you said the first time is what you meant."

"I don't know how to explain it so you'll understand."

"Don't worry about my understanding, Daisy. Just tell me what's on your mind. I'm here to listen even if I don't understand."

"You don't know what this feels like. I've failed everyone, including *you*. And I was having a hard time dealing with that. So I asked Dolly to come and get me."

He frowned. "Why on earth do you think I wouldn't understand *that* feeling?"

"Because you've never failed at anything."

My father began chuckling before I'd even finished my sentence.

"This is all your fault, Kendra," he spoke to the ceiling. "You should not have left me alone with these crazy, stubborn girls. And you should not have coddled them so much while you were here."

He looked at me and answered the question in my eyes.

"Yes, I still talk to your mother. It makes the day a little easier to face if it feels like I'm bringing her along through it."

My heart sank at the idea of my father missing my mother so much that he talked to her throughout his day.

"And I want you to know if she was here she would have blamed me and said I'm the one that coddled you all. Then she would have laughed harder than I did at your statement, Daisy, because no one could tell you better how imperfect I am. I fail *all* the time."

He shook his head in disbelief, but was still grinning.

I found this hard to believe. My father was pretty much perfect in my eyes.

"When your mother and I were still newlyweds, I was balancing my burgeoning law career, working at the Mill, and my young family. I was failing miserably until your mother told me she would leave me if I didn't get my act together."

I reared back in surprise and he laughed.

"I was so caught up in my own ambition that I was letting my family down. Even when I was home, I was so overworked that I was neglecting y'all half the time. But it didn't have to be that way—I didn't *have* to do everything. I eventually hired a general manager and then, as we grew, an entire executive team to help me manage.

"But hiring help hadn't even felt like a choice until your mother pointed out how I was hurting our family. My father did it all when he was starting the Mill so in trying to emulate him, I did it all too. But his point was *never* for me to do things his way. He was just trying to show me the ropes. And so now I have to wonder what things I've unintentionally made you think needed to be done my way when I was just trying to show you the ropes."

He leveled me with his gaze again.

It was time for me to explain myself.

"I don't want to work at Payton Mills." The words burned. I don't know why I started there, maybe because my father just told me a story about how he'd worked two careers to keep his father happy and I absolutely did not want to do that.

My father's face morphed into one of confusion. "Okay . . .?"

"I know that's what's expected of me. I know that in order to be a perfect Payton I'm supposed to work at the Mill and if I want to do something *else* then I can do that *too*, like you did with being a judge. But I don't want to do that. I just want to be free to follow my dreams."

"Daisy, first of all, there's no such thing as a perfect Payton. Second of all, I don't work at the Mill because I have to, I work there because I *want* to. I love it! I love the noise and the movement. I worked two careers because I was fortunate enough to have that many opportunities. But of course that doesn't have to be your reality. Why would you think that?"

"Because Ado told me he wanted to be an architect and you—you always told him he could do that and do the Mill. And now Dolly works there and Dolly is an engineer—she could've gotten a job anywhere in the world."

"You have a very good memory."

He paused for a long time, seemingly trying to figure out what to say.

"If your sister were here, she'd tell you that she feels the exact same way as you. That I always pushed Ado toward the Mill. And I just don't know. When you're a parent you see things differently than your children a lot of the time. But that was never my intention. I just figured that expanding our family brand to include services of how you could use the wood we supplied would be an added bonus. Dolly says she had to fight me to get her place at Payton Mills and she's right. I actually wanted her to go elsewhere. It was never my intention that all my children would work at the Mill. I wanted you to find your own paths."

"What?"

He looked at me, surprised. "Why wouldn't I want that for you?"

"But what about all that stuff about being leaders, assuming our place in the world, and setting ourselves apart from the people we lead?"

"Daisy, all of that is still true. *Whatever* your pursuits I expect you to pursue them with excellence and I expect you to lead. I did not raise you to have low expectations of yourself. I did not raise you to dream small. I did not raise you to be a follower of anything except your own ambition and heart. Raising you that way was done with intention and I make no apologies for it." He continued, "So what do you want to do? Since you don't want to work at the Mill?"

I told my father about the ideas I'd been tossing around and he listened, asking questions, making suggestions, and nodding in approval in some places.

Once I started talking to him, I couldn't stop. I'd missed our daddy-daughter conversations and I'd missed his insights. "Daisy's Doughnut House is a mouthful," he said over the eggs, sausage, and cheese grits I'd prepared for breakfast. "Maybe you should just change it to Daisy's Nut House. Honestly, nothing would be more fitting." His eyes twinkled with humor as he laughed at his joke.

Around lunchtime, I finally worked up the courage to ask for his forgiveness. His response surprised me. "I overreacted a bit. I'm not saying that I wasn't disappointed in you for lying or that I didn't feel rejected in the moment. And goodness knows I have never been more furious with you than I was when I found out you'd been involved in any type of thievery. But a few days after we got back, Dolly came by my office to tell me that she absolutely understood why I was upset but also that I didn't get what it was like to grow up as a Payton after Payton Mills had become *Payton Mills*.

"Dolly told me, 'Daddy, I was *fine*. I adapted, developed retractable barbs to keep myself safe.' I asked her if that was what changing your name was, you developing a barb to keep yourself safe? And she told me, '*No*. I'm trying to tell you I stood in front of Daisy with mine so she never had to develop barbs. She didn't know how to keep herself safe.'"

He frowned as if thinking on something deeply troubling. "And so I'd like to say I'm sor—"

"Don't apologize, Daddy, please!" I rushed to assure him. "It'll just make me feel worse. He opened his hands in a beseeching manner, a motion that reminded me of the way Trevor moved his hands when he explained something and my heart gave a lurch.

"If I'm forgiven for overreacting then you're forgiven for your dishonesty. Deal?"

"Deal," I said immediately.

My father and I talked all day and it was wonderful. During lunch, we chatted as I pulled together a quick meal of tossed salad, tomato soup, and fresh baked bread, marveling at the sparse contents of the refrigerator.

He looked at me somberly. "We eat simply around here these days."

I laughed and nodded. Dolly *could* bake because "baking was science" in her words. But cooking? Well for starters, Dolly hated cooking on the fly. She'd lament, "A dash of this, a pinch of that. *How much is a pinch?*"

Her food wasn't bad, exactly. It was more like . . . it was terrible.

What was worse, her food *looked* delicious. Probably because she was a perfectionist, but it tasted like Dolly made it. Her saving grace was that she *could* follow a recipe. I decided to take time while I was home to go through some of my father and sister's favorite dishes and transcribe them into recipes, that way Dolly could maybe feed herself and our father every now and again.

By evening, we'd made a run to the store, restocked the pantry, and my father stood sentry in the kitchen over the oven waiting for the pot roast with onions, potatoes, and carrots to be finished. The butterbeans with dumplings and cabbage with peppers and carrots was already done.

While he waited for the roast to finish, I finally got around to telling my father about the great cookie caper with the caveat that I would not include the names of anyone involved and that he would not call any of his friends to solicit help.

After a moment of hesitation, he agreed.

I shared most of the story but conveniently forget to mention the hot pants and cookie T-shirts, but he got the gist.

"Daisy, I get that your heart was in the right place but . . . ."

"I know. I shouldn't have done it. I'm sorry."

He waved his hand to dismiss my apology and I moved on to Julian helping me and my three paths forward.

My father seemed impressed. "Tell Julian to call me and we can talk strategy! Better yet, I think I still have May's number. I'll call and—"

I groaned. "Stay out of it, Daddy."

"You didn't ban me from talking to *your* friends, you only said I couldn't discuss it with mine."

"Daddy!"

He shrugged, unrepentant. "Be more careful with the deals you cut."

"Who's cutting who?" Dolly's voice carried from the hallway. She walked into the kitchen and greeted us both with hugs.

"Your sister doesn't want me talking to her student-lawyer friend but too bad, because that wasn't part of our deal."

Dolly laughed and meandered to the sink to wash her hands and then took a seat at the table, throwing a compliment my way.

"It smells divine in here, Daisy."

"It does indeed," my father agreed.

As my family sat around our dinner table talking about our lives, filling one another in on town gossip, retelling old stories, and joking like old times, something sharp and painful that I'd been carrying inside me began to mend—just a bit. I still found myself glancing toward my mother's chair or expecting to hear her voice fill the lulls in the conversation, but with my family and in my home, I felt a little more whole.

CHAPTER TWENTY-THREE

Trevor

It had taken less than twenty-four hours for me to come to my senses after my fight with Daisy.

I was an idiot. I needed to apologize. I still didn't know if it was possible for Daisy and me to be together but it didn't matter. I was tired of letting my emotions turn me into the worst version of myself. My feet were on autopilot as I navigated the short flight of stairs down to El and Gracie's place.

El and Gracie's *and Daisy's* place.

Gracie opened the door after a few knocks.

She stepped aside to let me in and then returned to the living room, sprawled on the sofa, and gestured for me to have a seat.

Their apartment was the same size as ours but far better appointed.

"El's not home. She had a meeting." Gracie didn't look up from the book she had open in her lap.

I was clearly interrupting her study time.

"I'm actually looking for Daisy."

"Daisy left." She turned the page.

What did she mean, Daisy left?

"Daisy left and went where?"

"Home, her note said." Gracie didn't look up from her book.

My stomach sank.

It had to be just for a few days, right? Jules would've told me if Daisy left school permanently. Wouldn't he?

Gracie turned another page in silence. I got the feeling she was being intentionally oblique.

"Do you have any idea when she'll be back?"

"Yep. But I'm not sure I should tell you." Gracie's Manhattan accent punctuated her frank tone.

"That's fair," I responded.

I didn't like it, but it was fair. I stood to leave. Gracie closed the book and looked up at me. "You know, you offend me, Trevor."

I rocked back on my heels. That surprised me.

Gracie and I had always had a good relationship in spite of my pretend relationship with El. She served as a senior senator in our student government cabinet. We worked well together.

At least I'd *thought* we worked well together.

"Well, Gracie, it seems I owe you an apology too. Though I can't say I know precisely what I've done."

I knew I wouldn't have to prompt her to tell me more. Gracie was on her way to law school for a reason. She could lay out a case like nobody's business.

Speaking of case, I would need to head to the Student Affairs' office today to tell them that I wouldn't be working on Daisy's case.

"I'm offended by people that abuse their power. You, sir, abused your power."

That snagged my attention.

"*Abused* my power?"

"Birdies have been talking to me. Knowing what I know about

346

you and Daisy, it seems ludicrous that you'd agree to one of the students serving on the TDC for her case. I can only assume—"

"I'm not going through with it. I haven't touched the case. And I'm swinging by today to tell them I'm stepping down from it. There are any number of people—you for example—that are more qualified, with less entanglement."

"I would *never*. She's my roommate—that would be a conflict of interest." She stressed the words as if to make a point.

"Agreed."

"Forgive me if I'm overstepping my boundaries here. Actually, I am most definitely overstepping my boundaries, but given that I've spent the last few months watching my girlfriend tread through endless guilt over how your fake romance was preventing you from being with your one true love—"

This was news to me. I'd never intended for Elodie to feel guilty. One more thing to feel bad about, to try to set right.

"I feel like I'm owed the opportunity to speak."

I sat and braced myself for my dressing-down. I was surprised when her tone turned gentle. "Why are you sabotaging your chances with Daisy?"

It felt like a sock to my gut. The truth I'd been hiding from was made all the more painful by the softness of Gracie's tone.

She's too good for me. She will eventually leave me. Everyone does.

I pushed aside those thoughts. I hadn't wanted to acknowledge them. I *knew* they were irrational. But that didn't make it any easier to shake them.

"I'm not pushing her away."

"I never said that you were. I said you were sabotaging your chances with her, but I think your subconscious just told me what's really going on here."

Gracie was the child of two shrinks; she was big on the subconscious. She was also correct.

I frowned down at my hands. There was no way I could earn Daisy's forgiveness after all we'd endured. After the way that I'd hurt her.

It was the earnestness of her expression and that loosened my tongue.

"I don't know what I can do to get her to forgive me."

"You could try apologizing," she prompted softly.

"That's what I came here to do. But after I apologize I don't know what to do—how to *earn* her forgiveness. I don't know how to prove that I'm worthy."

She cocked her head at me, examining me in a way that made my tongue clam up. Gracie looked at me like I'd unintentionally revealed a secret and it made me self-conscious.

After a moment of us both being silent she cleared her throat and said, "I'm sorry, I just—I forget sometimes how badly you all had it in that house. And child abuse—"

Child abuse was serious and I needed to set her straight. "I wasn't abused growing up, Gracie. Nothing happened to me in the Marshall's house."

"Sure." Her tone was unconvinced.

"I mean it. I was mostly just left alone."

"You were ignored," she countered.

"I was . . ." *Ignored.*

But I didn't like the way she said it, as if it was something to be pitied instead of it being a gift. In that house, being ignored was basically something to be celebrated.

Before I could counter she shook her head and closed her eyes, then opened them and looked at me beseechingly. "Trevor, I need you to listen to me and really try to *hear* me. I know this goes against everything you've been taught, but there is *nothing* you can do to *earn* Daisy's forgiveness."

I know that. It's too late. Bleakness unfurled in the pit of my stomach.

"That's not how forgiveness works." My attention snapped to hers.

"Forgiveness is *given*. It's not earned. It *can't* be. If a person wants to forgive you, they will. And if they don't want to forgive you, then they won't. And no amount of hoops you jump through is going to change that.

"*Atonement* is different. When you hurt someone, you can and absolutely should atone for what you did. You should seek them out and try to determine what you can do to ease or erase that hurt—but even in doing that, they don't have to forgive you. It's not owed to you because it can't be earned. And sometimes even if a person does nothing to atone they'll be forgiven anyway. Do you understand what I'm saying?"

I thought I did, but it was a difficult concept to accept. In my experience, everything had to be earned.

"So you're saying I should stop trying to get Daisy to forgive me?"

She laughed. "Daisy is a sweetheart. She's probably already forgiven you. What I'm saying is *fight*."

I laughed humorlessly. All Daisy and I seemed to do was fight.

"Stop fighting with her, and start fighting *for* her. And stop fighting *yourself*. You care about her. So care for her. No caveats. No requirements."

"What if Daisy doesn't want me as her champion?"

"Then she'll let you know. But right now Daisy probably doesn't even know that's an option."

"What if—"

"Trevor, you used Elodie as an excuse to keep from pursuing this girl. Then you used the fact that you'd messed up as an excuse, then you used her secrets as an excuse, and now you're using whatever happened between you guys yesterday to make Daisy leave here in a tear as an excuse. No more excuses. Either you want her or you don't."

Gracie's words sounded so wistful they made my heart clench. "The only thing blocking the path for you and Daisy is you and Daisy. You can have your happy ending. Why won't you take it?"

Gracie and I had talked a bit more after that. She'd told me that Elodie was in Knoxville meeting with a caterer that had flown in at May's request to do a food tasting for the engagement party.

I'd asked Gracie how she felt about the whole thing. Her response had been practical if not melancholy. "I accepted a long time ago that El and I might not have a happy ending . . ." Then her melancholy fell away and all that was left was grit. "But I still fight."

Long after I'd left her words reverberated through my mind. *You can have your happy ending. Why won't you take it?*

I began to formulate a plan. I would apologize to Daisy and then . . .I needed an ally. I needed more resources. I needed to show her how I felt. I needed to find her *friends*.

Daisy

Dolly deposited me back at school on Sunday night, with sage parting words. "Try not to get expelled over the next three weeks."

I shot back, "Try not to fall in love with Reverend *Paul* Smith over the next three weeks."

It was worth it to see her head almost spin thee hundred and sixty degrees on its axis.

I'd taken mercy on my sister and decided not to question her about why our Reverend was the last thing on her mind before she drifted off to sleep at night. I had, however, kept a careful watch over them both during this morning's Sunday service. And they'd been so dang circumspect.

My suspicions weren't confirmed until after service ended and we got near the door to leave. I snuck a peak back at the Reverend's face as he watched my sister leave, his expression one I was all too familiar with. *Yearning* clear as day flashed across his face for less than a second as my sister stepped out the door. Then a parishioner was in front of him and his smile was back.

I'd let my father and sister know that I was going to stick it out at school for Thanksgiving because I needed to study and all that commuting back and forth would just take away from study time. My father relented after a few protestations when I pointed out I was already behind on my classwork due to my impromptu vacation and I'd be home the week after Thanksgiving as soon as I finished my finals. I promised to cook a big meal for them with all the trimmings then.

The next morning, I opened my apartment door and was greeted by ruckus on the stairs over my head.

"Take me to her right now! Or I will—"

"Ow! Calm down! I will go get her and then you can see she's fine! No one has hurt Daisy, least of all me!"

"Why do you need to go get her? Why can't you just tell me where she is or take me to her!"

A very harassed-sounding Trevor and a very worried-sounding Odie were having a very loud conversation in our stairwell.

I wasn't sure about the whole "least of all me" part, but I was sure that his loyalty to his friends was evergreen and that he would not show Odie where Gracie and El lived. I was tempted to be evil and leave Trevor to fend for himself against Odie's demands . . .

Grace, Daisy. Grace.

I called her name and headed up the stairs instead.

"Daisy!"

As I came into view, Odie bounded down the steps and launched herself at me. I looked up to see Trevor wince as we hit the wall and the air was knocked out of me.

Odie jumped up and grabbed me from the floor before I could get my bearings straight. She clung to me and hugged me so tightly I could hardly breathe.

"Daisy, I was so worried about you! Where have you been? I couldn't find you and I was looking everywhere. I kept hearing that you'd gotten kicked out of the dorm and I came to our room and sure 'nuff it was empty. And folks were saying that they hadn't seen you in your classes and that you'd dropped out!"

"I'm fine, Odie." I patted her reassuringly, while I gasped for more breath.

Odie was still near hysterical.

"And then *he* found me, and offered to bring me to you. But I didn't know if I could trust—"

"Found you? What do you mean he found you?"

Trevor cleared his throat and I looked up where he stood above us on the stairs. He squeezed his hand on the back of his neck. "I, uh . . . waited outside her class."

"Why?" I couldn't help the suspicion in my voice. Why would Trevor help Odie find me? Why would Trevor help me, *period?*

We weren't even supposed to be speaking to one another. He was trying to get me expelled from school.

Maybe he'd been waiting for Odie so he could interview her and this was just part of a trap to get us both together so he could kill two birds with one stone.

"Because she's your friend and she was looking for you."

That was . . . nice?

"Thank you?" I said, unsure of what to make of his kindness.

Trevor shifted uncomfortably on his feet and then said, "I've done my part. I'll be on my way now."

He brushed against me as he passed on the stairs and just that brief, soft contact was enough to send my heart rate up a notch. I reminded myself to be cool, and to keep cool. Just because Trevor had done a nice-ish thing didn't mean a thing.

I stalled in the stairwell because I wanted to give Trevor a head start. I didn't want to have to see him just ahead, just out of reach, the entire walk to campus.

"Daisy, I'm so, so sorry," Odie called my attention back to her.

I raised my eyebrows in surprise. "You're sorry? What are you sorry for? I thought you hated me? *I'm* sorry. I didn't mean for my lie to get that big and I never meant to hurt you. I promise you I didn't . . . I just wanted the chance to be seen as something other than my family's name."

"Oh, I know that." She pulled me into another hug. "I'm not mad anymore and I *never* hated you. I just needed time to sort through my feelings before we talked. You didn't even want to do that second batch of cookies and if we hadn't have talked you into it, none of this would be happening to you."

"It's okay, Odie."

Odie was still my friend. Thank God.

She slid her arms through mine, and with arms linked we headed out into the cold late November air.

Odie questioned me about my troubles as we walked. I brought her up to speed on the options I faced—how Julian was helping me and how Trevor was . . . not.

"That's odd. Trevor had the perfect opportunity to ask me questions about what happened today, but he didn't. Well, he did ask me questions, but not about that."

Before I could interrogate her further, she pivoted.

"It doesn't matter, I'm going to confess. It's not right that you should get in trouble alone."

We argued. And argued. And she was finally persuaded when I told her, "More people getting in trouble for this won't make it better for me."

Odie relented, but her expression was like a raccoon trying to figure its way into someone's trashcan: determined. I had a feeling she was placating me and that the subject was going to come up again.

I caught her up on what happened with my father and my sister after she left and how I'd been home to try to set things right.

When we arrived to campus, we split up but made plans to meet up later in the week to study. She gave me another hug in parting.

Before she was too far out of range, I called to her. "Odie?"

"Yeah?"

"James?"

She shook her head sadly. "Daisy, sometimes the hurt is just too big."

I nodded.

James doesn't forgive me. James doesn't forgive.

CHAPTER TWENTY-FOUR

Daisy

I was holed up in my room studying when something weird and wonderful happened.

There was a knock at the door. I opened without checking, figuring Elodie had left her keys. In the short time we'd been roommates I'd already learned she was remarkably bad about remembering her keys.

When Elodie wasn't around, Gracie had calmly explained to me that Elodie had grown up having doors opened by someone else so keys were hard for her.

The person on the other side of the door was not Elodie.

It was Trevor.

I stood frozen like a deer for a few seconds before I was able to come to my senses. "Gracie and Elodie aren't home."

Trevor's dimple showed as he smiled. "I know. They're up in my apartment. Can I come in and set this down? It's a little hot."

I took stock of him, and realized belatedly that he held a casserole dish in his hands.

I opened the door wide so he could come in and watched as he sat the dish down on the counter, taking extra care to leave the tatty potholder beneath it.

"I made you baked beans."

That was . . . *weird?*

Trevor looked unmistakably shy and also a little . . . proud.

He fidgeted. "I've never cooked them before, but I did have help with the recipe."

This was definitely weird.

"Trevor, why are you making me beans?"

"Before we get to that, I have something I want—something I *need* to say."

"Okay." I looked at him, confused. Trevor was confusing me. One minute he was agreeing we should stay far away from one another and telling me he was going to help usher me into expulsion's welcome arms and the next he was bringing Odie to me and making me beans.

"I'm sorry. I'm so sorry. If I could go back and undo the hurt, erase the humiliation you experienced because of my poor choices, I would. I would in a heartbeat. I know that you'll probably never forgive me."

"I already forgave you. I forgave you weeks ago. I forgave you the minute I found out the truth about the situation."

His mouth fell open, and seemed so shocked that I took my opportunity to apologize too. "I'm sorry, too. I understand why you wouldn't want to know me. I did mislead you about who I am, and for that I'm sorry."

"I want to know you."

It was my turn to be shocked.

"You do?"

"Of course I do."

"So I'm forgiven?"

"If there's anything to forgive, it's already been forgiven. And

Daisy, how could I not want to know you?" His eyes swept over my face in a way that made me feel cherished.

My heartbeat went staccato. I hadn't ever expected to see that look from him again.

"I have no right to ask anything of you, Daisy. I know that. But I won't lie. I do want things from you. And you don't have to answer now. In fact, it's probably better if you don't, seeing as we both need to hunker down so that we're not on Dr. Gwinn's *list*."

Trevor's eyes looked at me, blazing and fierce. "But I want you to know that if you want me, I'm here. Agreeing to go our own separate ways and never speak again was the furthest thing from what I really wanted. I just want to be a part of your world. However I can, whatever you need—a friend, a mentor, *whatever* you want."

I wanted Trevor. I did. But he was right; now wasn't the time. I was up to my eyeballs in work.

Dr. Gwinn was right; double majoring was a disaster.

I needed time, and Trevor was giving me—giving us—time. It was both the right and the smart decision. Last time we'd rushed headlong into a relationship and made a mess of it.

We needed time. Therefore, I started slowly.

"I think starting as friends would be good."

"Starting?" he repeated and raised his eyebrows playfully. Trevor was being playful.

Sigh and swoon.

"Starting as friends sounds perfect."

I couldn't help my grin.

"Daisy, may I hug you?"

My arms extended instantly. We both took a step and pulled one another into an embrace.

I'd forgotten how strong Trevor's arms were, how good they felt. How good he smelled, like spice and a scent all his own.

We stood like that for an age, my arms wrapped around his waist and his around my shoulders.

My face pressed against his chest. I listened to the sound of his strong heart and allowed myself to enjoy the moment for a long while before I pulled away.

I leaned back and looked up at his eyes that were now lighter, happier than before.

"So, *friend,* beans?" I raised my eyebrows.

"Oh! Yes, the beans. Like I said, I had a little help with the recipe but I made them myself."

"Okay, but Trevor, why on earth did you make me baked beans?"

"Odie said you loved them. Said you were mad for 'em and ate them all the time."

I began to laugh. I laughed so hard, I doubled over. And then I laughed some more. "The candy!"

"What?" Trevor's eyebrows jumped in confusion.

"The candy, Trevor! I love Boston Baked Beans the *candy.*"

He groaned. "Oh no."

I chuckled and walked into the kitchen and grabbed two plates.

"Let's eat some beans!"

"We really don't have to," he groaned again.

I ignored his protest, opened up the casserole dish and scooped a healthy portion of beans onto each plate.

I tasted the dish as Trevor looked on nervously, fork poised. Brown sugar, sautéed onions and peppers, and a hint of salt rolled over my taste buds.

It was delicious and it was familiar.

"Trevor, this tastes just like my dad's baked beans."

If I'd thought he looked bashful before, he was almost flushed with embarrassment now.

"Is this my dad's recipe?"

He nodded.

"How did you get my father's recipe?"

"I, uh, I called him."

"You *called* my father?" I looked at Trevor like he'd grown an extra limb.

He pushed the beans around on his plate.

"I did."

"Why?"

"Odie mentioned that you loved baked beans. I wanted to make sure I made them the way you liked." He shrugged. "I figured your family would know how you liked them. I tried to call your sister, but your father ended up picking up the phone. We chatted for a minute and then I asked him about the beans."

"Oh boy! He was delighted, wasn't he?"

Trevor's grin appeared. "I've never heard anyone talk that long about baked beans."

My father could grill like a champion. But to my knowledge he knew how to make three dishes: boiled eggs, boiled water, and baked beans. And he had opinions about all of them.

"You did good."

He responded with an enormous smile.

"You know what would've been perfect with these beans?"

"Hmm?" he said around a mouthful.

"A Tennessee barbecue sandwich."

Trevor rolled his eyes, but his big grin didn't drop.

We sat for a while longer, eating beans and enjoying the tentative new peace until Elodie and Gracie came downstairs and Trevor departed to study.

The next three weeks passed in a blur.

The second week after I'd returned everyone went into finals mode, and studying became a near-constant thing. I spent most of my time hidden away in my room or at the library. Julian and I found out that my hearing wouldn't be until early next semester and we'd agreed to suspend any discussions around it until after finals were over.

"We can talk about it over the break," he said pragmatically. "But

if I don't start hitting these books I'm going to be on academic probation. Dean Gwinn's class is kicking my ass and finals are *seventy
percent* of your grade."

I was very sure we *would* chat over the break. I'd jokingly
recounted my father's request to speak to Julian and, much to my
horror, Julian had been thrilled at the idea. He'd badgered and badgered
me until I relented and gave him the number to my father's office.

The idea to invite Odie to come home with me over the break
came to me during one of our late-night study sessions as she laughed
at a story about my sister and declared that she'd love to meet Dolly.

Odie looked surprised, then got a gleam in her eye and replied,
"You know—I think that would be a swell idea. I can't wait."

A week later, finals were done, I was exhausted, and I was ready
to get my break started. I felt pretty good about all my finals, even
stupid statistics.

My dream roommates, Gracie and Elodie—tidy and mostly quiet
—had already left to spend the break at Gracie's parent's house in
New York for the holidays.

I was zipping the last of my things into my bag when the phone
rang. Hoping it was Dolly calling from a payphone to tell me she was
a few minutes away, I raced to the phone and picked up.

It was Dolly. "Daisy!" *BANG!* "Listen, I can't talk long. There's
an issue at work and I can't get—" *BANG!* "away. One of the kilns
—" *BANG! BANG!* "—trouble!"

"Okay, is Daddy coming to get me?"

"No. He was going to—" *BANG! BANG! BANG!* "—and he said
he would bring you."

"What, Dolly? I can't hear you?" Every other word was drowned
out.

"I said *Julian* will bring you home. He's headed to Green Valley
today."

I sat on my bed, leg bouncing, as Dolly disconnected. There was only one reason that Julian could be going to Green Valley: *Trevor* was going home.

That meant I'd be in the car with Trevor for three hours.

I was plagued with doubt. Trevor and I'd had a nice moment but that didn't mean that it would last. Three hours was too long to be in a car with him. What if he'd changed his mind and no longer wanted to be friends?

I began formulating a plan to catch the Greyhound home, and had gotten as far as plotting how I'd get to the bus station when there was a knock at my door.

I opened it and unsurprisingly saw Julian.

"You ready to go?"

I stalled, looking for an excuse. "I can't ride with you."

He crossed his arms over his chest and leaned against the doorway as if bored. "And why not? I'm an impeccable driver."

Odie! Sweet, blessed Odie had come to save me from my impending misery.

"Odie! She was supposed to ride home with me. Sorry! I can't abandon her. I'll just take the bus with her tomorrow."

He scratched his chin thoughtfully. "Yeah, your father might've mentioned something about that, and that's why I went to her dorm to pick her up first. She's already downstairs in the car."

"I—"

"You are terrified because you're smart and you've already deduced that my best friend is also downstairs in the car. Daisy, I am tired. Finals kicked my rear end this year, probably because I was distracted a large part of this semester." He threw a pointed look at me.

"Hey! I had nothing—"

"I have a month's vacation that starts right *now*. I have been promised breathtaking mountain views and home-cooked meals." He placed his hands over his tummy and his heart.

"You should've told me you were hungry. I would've cooked for you."

He raised one eyebrow. "Considering that you making me a mere sandwich caused so much unrest in my house, I shudder to think what preparing a full meal would have caused."

He spotted my bag, walked in and grabbed it, and threw it over his shoulder. "Come on, little chicken, be brave! Face the big bad wolf. I assure you his growl is worse than his bite."

I didn't know about that. I'd felt his bark and his bite and they'd both hurt. But I was out of options. Julian was already exiting my apartment, therefore I flipped off the light, locked the door, and turned and followed.

Trevor

When Julian told me he needed to pick something up before we left town, I thought he meant he needed to get a bottle of wine or maybe some flowers for my mother, some trifle of hospitality to give to my parents as a token of appreciation.

I should have known better.

I'd been totally confused when we'd pulled into the driveway of Jubilee Hall. Confusion quickly morphed into annoyance the moment I saw Daisy's friends emerge from the building. I shot Jules a glare and he gave me back a smile and said, "It would seem I'm the Green Valley taxi this year."

"I see." I didn't care if Daisy's friends, or Daisy for that matter, rode with us. In fact, I was looking forward to it. However, my annoyance stemmed with Jules being sneaky since he deliberately withheld the information from me.

He hastily loaded the girls' bags into the car. Then Odie and a very confused James had climbed in.

"Julian is giving us a ride to the bus station?" James asked.

I put down the book I'd been holding on my lap. This ought to be good.

Odie was quiet for a moment. "Well, in a way. Just wait, Jamesy. It'll all be good." James frowned but then noticed me watching and eerily cleared her face of all expression.

"One more stop before we get rolling," Julian said, more to the girls than to me. I already knew how this was going to play out. My saving grace was that it seemed I was not alone in being blindsided by this mess.

The moment I saw her emerging from the building wearing her fitted green coat and boots, I knew I was in trouble. I'd been working on trying to keep my feelings toward Daisy nothing but friendly.

It's what she'd said she wanted. It was likely what we needed. But she was a vision, like water gifted to a thirsty man. I couldn't look away. She was walking slowly like she was being dragged to the guillotine and not to a car with her two best friends and her . . . me. I took her in, noticing the intense frown of worry on her face, how troubled she looked, and I was struck with the innate wrongness of the scene. I hated frowns on her face,;they should never be allowed purchase there. I hated that Julian was touching her things, and that he was the one to usher her to the car. I was out of the car and at Julian's side relieving him of her bag in seconds. I got a glimpse of his too-pleased expression and ignored it.

I opened the rear car door for her and she looked up at me, surprise on beautiful face. "Thank you," she said softly. When she brushed against me while sliding into the car, my heart danced in my chest and the familiar white-hot flame of lust shot down my spine. I realized three weeks was not enough time to get over Daisy Payton. Three lifetimes wouldn't be enough.

I felt a little shaken at the revelation and because of that I *almost* missed the lightning quick voice of James Jones screeching, "Odessa Mae Boyd, what on earth is going on here?"

I quickly deposited Daisy's bag and climbed into the front passenger seat. The girls had arranged themselves so Odie sat in the middle, James sat directly behind me, and Daisy sat directly behind Julian.

Julian took off. He pulled onto the road that would lead us to I-40 while Odie fidgeted with her purse strap.

I was glad Daisy sat catty-corner to me. I could see her facial expressions clearly if I glanced in the rearview mirror. Even better, the mirror was angled toward Julian so she probably couldn't see me admiring her. I couldn't bring myself to feel ashamed of the pleasure I felt at the possibility of being able to covertly watch Daisy Payton for the next three hours.

"Well, we *are* taking the bus to my folk's house. But Daisy here . . ." She waved her hand at Daisy who stared impassively out the window. "Well, she extended an invitation for us to join her in Green Valley for a bit . . . ."

Daisy's expression told me she had no clue James had been part of this invitation.

"And I figured since it's been such a trying semester it might be nice for all of us to have a little R&R in the mountains."

I hoped Odie knew she wasn't going to a ski resort. Green Valley wasn't that.

"Incredible. I can't believe you lied to me too, Odie."

"I *didn't* lie to you. We are taking the bus."

James crossed her arms, clearly not placated. "I guess I shouldn't be surprised. They say you become who you hang around."

"Don't start," Odie warned.

"No, let her start." Daisy turned from the window, and leaned over Odie to face James. "James, you haven't spoken to me in over a month. I am very well aware that you're under the impression that I'm a compulsive liar, but just in case there's any part of you in there that's capable of believing any word that comes out of my mouth—"

"There isn't," James said flatly.

"Hey, hey now! Don't be nasty to Daisy," Jules reprimanded, and it grated on my nerves that he was the one jumping in to defend her.

"Shut up, Julian! Don't tell me what to do."

"Don't tell Julian to shut up, this is his car." This from me, because James was being disrespectful even though she'd been put in a tough spot.

"Don't tell James what to do, Trevor," retorted Daisy, of course, because why the hell not?

Maturity and sanity had all gone out the window. We began talking over one another trying to make our point, until Odessa cut in, more loudly than I thought possible.

"*Everybody* shut the hell up! I'm sick of you all. If you can't be pleasant then at least be silent."

We rode down the road in silence for a second. Just as Jules reached for the knob to turn the radio up, I heard Daisy's voice.

"James, I just want you to know I had *nothing* to do with this. This wasn't some elaborate scheme that I hatched with Odie in order to get you trapped in Green Valley or have you at my mercy so you'd have to forgive me. I *already know* you're not going to forgive me." Daisy shrugged and shook her head at the ceiling. She looked so sad that I wanted to be free from my seatbelt so I could pull her into a hug. But I was being ridiculous. Daisy and I were barely speaking. I needed to move slowly. I'd just gotten out of the same boat as James.

"I'm done trying to apologize to you. I'm done badgering you, hoping you'll speak to me. That said, I'm perfectly fine with you staying at my house. You are welcome there for as long as you'd like. I won't bother you but my father and sister are a delight, and Green Valley is stunning. However, I understand why it might not be appealing to you. I'd never want to be stuck somewhere that I didn't wish to be, particularly with someone I hated. So if the idea of spending time with me and my family in our house is so untenable, I will borrow my sister's car and drive you Merryville to the bus station in the morning."

Daisy leaned back against her seat and stared forward. I turned my head and caught her eye and gave her a sympathetic look. She answered with the barest hint of a smile.

Jules took the continued silence as a sign to turn the radio up and the song "You are Everything" by the Stylistics caught my ear.

Even if the song wasn't by one of Daisy's favorite artists, and even if she hadn't been sitting in the back seat so very, very close to me, the song would've reminded me of her anyway.

My eyes watched her in the mirror while listening to the band sing of not being able to forget the face or memories of being with a girl. I wished Daisy and I could—not start over, because I didn't want to erase what we had in the beginning—but maybe start again.

I sighed. I didn't want to hope or want or push for too much, too soon with Daisy. She wanted me to be her friend so I would be her friend.

I shifted my mind and concentrated on the other thing I'd been avoiding. How in the world was I going to spend almost a month with my parents?

I glanced over at Julian who—despite our very rocky semester— was here by my side like always, and I felt grateful for him. Julian was my brother. We never pulled our punches and we fought like mad sometimes, but we were always there when the other needed it.

Julian turned down the music and cleared his throat.

"James?"

"We are not in class and I don't have to speak to you, Julian."

I saw the quick hit of hurt before he reached for the knob again and I spoke up for him automatically. "Hey James, I know you hate everyone in this car at the moment, but this ride will go a lot faster if we're not constantly laying into each other."

She sighed mightily and said, "Fine. Yes, Julian?"

Julian cut a grateful glance at me, and then quickly looked away, "I, uhh . . . was doing some cleaning in preparation for graduation and noticed I still had a bunch of my old books. Most of them haven't been changed out in the English Department curriculum. I was wondering if you would like to take any of them off my hands? It would do me a favor clearing up some of the clutter."

Julian was lying. I didn't know why he was lying but he was absolutely fibbing. Jules was a goddamned book miser. He didn't loan books, and he didn't give them away *ever*. He hoarded them. I knew he could feel me staring at him because his red undertones began to peek through as he drove.

After a long moment James replied, "Sure, I'll take those off your hands . . . Thanks."

Julian said nothing. He just turned up the radio.

It began to snow shortly thereafter and the rest of the ride was quiet with the exception of the sound of the wipers. Odie and James eventually fell asleep and Daisy stared quietly out of the window while Jules nodded along to the radio. When we got our first view of Green Valley laid out like a painting of sleepy, peaceful hills the sun was just about to sink behind the mountains and the valley looked glorious.

Jules slowed the car. Odie and James, now awake, both gasped. And me? I didn't know how I felt. There was some drumbeat inside me that said *this is home, this is home, home, home.*

But how could it be when I hadn't been here in so long? But I remembered these views. I remembered seeing it just like this, laid out like a postcard as I'd ridden in the car with my father on our way up to his favorite fishing hole. Green Valley, even—or maybe especially—under a thin layer of snow and piping chimneys, was simply beatific. I took a deep breath and steeled myself as we began descending the switchbacks down the mountain.

CHAPTER TWENTY-FIVE

Daisy

I helped Julian navigate to my house from the back seat of the car. Trevor's parents would meet us at my house and would lead Trevor and Jules back to the Boone's home.

My home was set a little way back from the main road and mostly surrounded by trees. As we turned off onto the driveway, I watched the fir trees with their soft boughs bent, weighted with a bit of snow. I'd always loved the way the tall trees looked after a dusting. After a minute of driving, I heard Julian cough and then say, "Daisy, not that I don't trust you but . . . where the hell are we? Why am I driving through the woods?"

"Ye of little faith, Julian. Keep driving. The house will appear shortly." Julian wasn't wrong; for all intents and purposes, we did live in the woods.

"For safety," my mother and father always said. My mother was from Brownsville, and when we'd gotten older, she'd told us a little about how Elbert Williams had been murdered and how Thomas

Davis had to abandon his business and was run out of town for trying to stand up for his rights.

"Not everyone is happy about your father's success," she'd said simply.

Julian rounded the last corner and my house came into view. Two cars were parked along the curve of the driveway; one belonged to the Boones but I didn't recognize the other. I saw Julian's eyes bouncing back and forth as he took in the scene. Our house was not grand but it was stately. But what made our home special was the trees that surrounded it on all sides, forming a cover and a shield. There was walking trail that led to Ado's grove behind the house, but you couldn't see from the front. From the front our house appeared to be surrounded by a wall of trees.

It felt amazing to get out and stretch after such a long time in the car. I titled my head, letting the light snowfall hit my face. When I looked back, Trevor was staring at me. Our eyes snapped together like magnets and my heart began beating double time. The way he stared at me and his looks against this background of snow?

They scared me.

He looked just like he belonged here with us, with my family, with me. His stare heated and I felt warm despite the chilly weather. The sound of the door slamming broke his concentration and I reluctantly looked away to see Dolly on the front porch with my father and the Boones trailing behind her.

I did a little dance—the Daisy dance, she called it. It was the way I'd greeted my sister when I was excited to see her for as long as I could remember. And then we were off—running and jumping at each other.

I took extra care to introduce Julian to Dolly since he'd done her a favor in delivering me home.

"Dolly, this is the one and only Julian P. Marshall."

"So you're the one who my father can't stop talking about?"

My sister laughed.

I saw Trevor's head snap in Dolly's direction at that comment.

I cut her off. "Julian, this is my sister Dolly Payton."

"Dolly, like Parton?" he joked.

Oh no.

The laughter died in my sister's throat immediately and she leveled him with a look that made Julian step back.

"No, Dolly like *Payton*."

Julian's eyes were wide and somber as he replied, "Noted."

Bags were brought inside and we were ushered inside to the living room. Reverend Paul Smith, the owner of the unfamiliar vehicle, sat quietly by the fireplace and gave me a friendly smile before standing to give greetings and hugs to our entire cadre.

"Dinner will be served shortly, so go on and freshen up," Dolly announced. I slipped into my role as co-host and directed Julian and Mrs. Boone to the bathrooms on the lower level. Then I ushered James and Odie to the guest bedrooms on the second level.

When I returned, Trevor was holding my bag.

"The boys are carrying your things up! Saves an old man his back." My father declared this dramatically from the sofa, where he appeared to be wading into conversation with the Reverend and Mr. Boone.

"You are not old, Daddy." I rolled my eyes. I looked at Trevor, realized my mistake, and simply waved my hand for him to follow me. I was all too aware of him trudging closely after me, step by step as we took the back stairwell up to the third level. We walked down the long hallway until we got to the back of the house.

"How many rooms are in this house?" I turned to see Trevor looking around.

"Um, there are seven bedrooms. I don't know how many total rooms are in the house. I've never counted. There are two rooms at the back of the main level that aren't in use. They're only ever used when the house is really full, but that hasn't happened in a while. My brother's bedroom is downstairs along with two other guest rooms.

My mother and father's room is on this level along with Dolly's, and my bedroom is up here. But you knew that because we're up here." I was rambling because I was nervous. And I had no idea why I was nervous; it wasn't like anything would happen with Trevor in my bedroom.

I stepped into my room and made way for Trevor to follow. My room wasn't overly small or large; it was cozy, with a white sleigh bed in the center and a large window facing the rear of our property on the far wall. He entered the room and as he walked past the bed he quietly joked, "That is a huge bed, fit for a fairy princess. I'm sure the adjustment to the dorm's twin beds must've been hard for you."

I laughed softly. I didn't know why we were both being quiet; something about the moment seemed tenuous.

"Yes, the dorm beds were an adjustment, but I'm sure you went through the same thing. I'm certain the beds at casa Marshall are huge as well."

He walked over to my window and looked out. The light had faded but you could still make out the backyard surrounded by the shadow of the mountains in the distance.

"I bet this is a million-dollar view when the sun is shining," he said almost awestruck.

"You're right. It's spectacular."

"The beds at casa Marshall are big, but I didn't grow up there really. Jules and I spent most of our time in boarding school. And the beds there are dorm sized. It wasn't hard for me."

He turned from the window, sat my bag down, and began looking around my room. I stood silent, feeling oddly like I was under inspection as he ghosted from my dresser to my side table, looking at the knickknacks and whatnots that make up my life. He picked up a formal family portrait from when I was about five or six. His smile was automatic. "You were a cute kid." His amusement made me grin. Then he squinted and pointed to Ado. "Your brother, right? He looks just like your father."

I nodded.

"Does he live here or somewhere else?"

I raised my eyebrows in surprise. I'd assumed Trevor's parents would've kept him in the know. Part of me wanted to say, "Somewhere else," but I'd learned my lesson. No more lying, please and thank you. I took a deep breath. "He died in Vietnam a few years after that picture was taken. Just after my ninth birthday."

Trevor immediately, carefully, replaced the picture. The reverence with how he handled it made my heart squeeze. He turned and inspected me again, like he was looking for bumps and bruises. I turned from his gaze, afraid he would see too much, and said the thing that pressed on my mind. "Why didn't you know that? Why didn't your parents tell you?"

I peered at him from under my lashes. He slid both hands in his pockets and gave a shrug I thought was supposed to be lighthearted but somehow looked anything but. "My parents and I don't talk much."

"This must be strange for you."

"Very."

"Why did you decide to come back after all this time?"

He stared out the window for a moment into the darkness before he turned and looked at me. "I could say that it's because I promised my mother and I try to keep my word when I give it."

Trevor was nothing if not a man of his word, to his detriment even.

"But that's not really it. My parents . . . I don't know. I guess I'm here to find out if we can even have a relationship. Things right now are so broken between us, I don't know if they can be fixed. But I feel like I owe it to myself to try."

I reached over and rubbed his arm. The move was meant to reassure him but it sent a zing through me and I heard Trevor's voice catch.

"They told me they would come back for me and they never did."

He tried to mask the pain in his voice with a smile but I heard it none-theless and it speared me.

"I guess I want to find out why. What was wrong with me that made them—"

I couldn't let Trevor go down that path. I cut him off the only way I knew how: I slipped my arms around his waist and pulled him in for a hug. His body was rigid and tense so I held on tighter and squeezed. After a moment, he relaxed and his arm came around me and held me back. He tucked me under his cheek and I held him until his racing heart slowed.

"You are perfect," I whispered.

"You of all people know that's not true. You know just how imperfect I am."

"You're perfect to me."

I felt him shake his head in disagreement and I had a dawning realization. I wondered if maybe a small part of Trevor thought he didn't deserve the same devotion he showed to everyone else.

"Trevor, you are perfect even though your actions may not always be perfect. But your soul?" I leaned back and stared into his eyes. They probed mine with an intensity I'd never seen before. "Your soul is beautiful."

He flinched and I knew I was right. And it made me sad. I couldn't fix Trevor's perception of himself and I wouldn't try; that was something he was going to have to work on himself. But I could be there to hold his hand while he attempted it. We all had things we needed to sort out. God knew I could attest to that.

His throat worked on a swallow and then he said, "*You* are perfect, but I suspect you already know that."

I laughed. "How about this? Maybe neither of us is perfect." He opened his mouth to object so I added, "But maybe we're perfect for each other."

His smile was immediate and, when he gazed at me, I didn't break the connection. I held his gaze, letting him see how I felt, letting him see the way he lit me up inside.

"May I kiss you?" he whispered.

I shook my head.

Before the hurt could appear, before he could disentangle himself from me, I leaned in, pressed up on my toes, and I kissed him.

It only took Trevor a second to react.

He gasped in shock, then groaned and pressed his lips to mine, hard. Then he coaxed my mouth open wider and slid his tongue against mine.

It was *delicious.* And then it was over.

He broke away with a chuckle.

"I meant on your hand or your cheek or your forehead," he said, still catching his breath. He smiled broadly, squinted at me, and said, "Daisy Payton, I am scandalized. Making out with a boy in your daddy's house. If I didn't know any better, I'd think you were trying to get me shot."

"Har-har." I rolled my eyes, still trying to cool down from the scorching hot kiss.

He tugged my hand. "Come on. We'd better get back downstairs before your father comes up here with his shotgun. I wouldn't want him thinking I was doing something untoward with his daughter."

"Yes, heaven forbid we should do something untoward when we're alone in a bedroom." I shocked myself by saying it.

Trevor groaned. "Daisy . . ."

"Trevor . . ." I said, my voice husky even to my own ears. I turned and fled the room as he trailed after me, and I could feel his eyes on my backside the whole way down the stairs.

As soon as I hit the first floor something struck me as odd. Dolly had said dinner would be ready in a few minutes but I hadn't *smelled* dinner when we came in. Panic had me hustling toward the kitchen.

I paused when I saw the dishes: string beans, rice and gravy, crusty cinnamon-browned candied yams, bubbling macaroni and cheese pulled straight from the oven, fried chicken, and barbecue spareribs. They all glistened delectably on the counter as Mrs. Boone picked up a dish to carry to the table.

My heart sank quickly; none of these were the recipes I transcribed for Dolly.

"Dolly," I hissed, not wanting Mrs. Boone to overhear as she moved dish after dish to the table, where folks were already starting to assemble.

"These are not the recipes I left you."

She waved me off. "Oh Daisy, thank you for those. They were just what I needed to get my confidence up in the kitchen. But I was so tired of eating the same thing, you know? When I cooked today I just decided to make something new. Turns out a pinch of this and a dash of that wasn't so hard."

Waves of panic shot through me. "Dolly, did you *taste* the food while you were cooking?"

She looked at me mystified and a little curious. "Taste it while it's cooking? Why on earth would I do that? Why would I taste food that wasn't done yet?"

God. Please. I don't ask for a lot, but if it is at all possible please, please, please let my sister's abominable cooking skills have produced something edible. Amen.

There was no time to fix it if it was indeed bad, so instead I hustled to help them get the rest of the dishes on the table.

When we were all seated my father looked to Reverend Smith.

"Reverend, we're honored you could drop in for supper this evening. If you would be so kind as to bless the food, I'd be grateful."

Reverend Smith blessed both the food and the hands that prepared it *twice*, and he took time to add at the end that he was grateful he got to share in what he understood to be Trevor's first meal home in a long time. Mrs. Boone beamed, Mr. Boone looked at his son misty-eyed, and Trevor looked . . . uncomfortable.

The sounds of silverware clinking against dishes broke the tension as the entrees and sides began making their rounds.

"This food looks mighty good, Dolly," Mr. Boone said, licking his lips.

My sister beamed with pride. I was in constant contact with the Lord, hoping he'd received my prayer and worked the miracle that was almost certainly needed.

When everyone's plates were absolutely loaded with food—well, everyone's plate but mine, because I knew better—our company dug in.

Knowing my sister's track record, I didn't start with the meat. Meat could go wrong in so many ways. Instead, I tasted a small mouthful of rice. Just as I started to chew the undeniably grainy and hard texture of the rice, Julian, who had made the rookie mistake of starting with the meat, took a big bite of his chicken wing. I watched as his face went from excited anticipation to absolute disgust. He picked up his napkin and discreetly spat the meat out. He set the remainder of it down and I noted the pinkish-red uncooked meat near the bone.

Oh Lord, Dolly undercooked the chicken.

I swallowed my gravelly rice and took a small bite of macaroni and cheese. I was unsurprised that it tasted like mustard. I didn't know why it tasted like mustard considering no one in their right mind would put mustard in macaroni and cheese, but I was not *surprised*.

Reverend Smith took a bite of the spareribs. He began to chew. He chewed and chewed and chewed and chewed.

Dolly had overcooked the ribs.

I took a small bite of yams and registered that they at least were edible. Dolly hadn't added any sugar, nutmeg, or butter, but she did at least remember to put cinnamon on top.

It was at that moment that I heard my sister's voice softly at my side. "That doesn't taste right." I watched as she frantically moved her fork from item to item, *finally* tasting her wares.

"No . . . No. That's not it . . ." she muttered over and over again.

I looked around the table and saw folks pushing their food around with polite disinterest, or taking tiny mouthfuls of the least offensive goods on their plate. Conversation trickled to a halt all at once under the weight of the elephant in the room.

Suddenly my sister pushed her chair back from the table and snatched Reverend Smith's fork from his hand just as he was about to eat a mouthful of macaroni. She began grabbing plates and forks in a frenzy. She plucked a dinner roll from Trevor's hand before he could take a bite, then she grabbed the punch from Mr. Boone's hand and marched into the kitchen with the dishes teetering in her arms. We all jumped at the sound of the crash. She marched back in with a trash can and began moving around the table, violently scraping plates into the garbage.

"There was a little technical . . ." She grabbed the entire pan of mac and cheese and flipped it into the trash. "Difficulty with dinner."

She grabbed the chicken and it landed with a *dra-drump* into the garbage, making Odie jump.

"I will provide you with an alternative form—"

"Dolly!" my father called her name. She froze and looked up. Dolly was a little frenzied and a lot frazzled. Her bun had come undone with the force of scraping and shaking food into the trash. Her eyes were wide and panicked and so very un-Dolly like.

I stood and jumped in to support my sister, "I invite you all to join us in the parlor for a song and drinks while we make arrangements for a replacement meal."

I shot Dolly a panicked look, and started motioning for our very confused guests to follow me.

"Dolly, if you'll go upstairs and get your violin to entertain our guests I'd be ever so grateful."

My sister blinked out of her haze, and then moved. "Yes, my violin. Of course."

Everyone looked a bit wide-eyed and shell-shocked as they followed me. I asked my father to make a round of drinks for everyone and he slid right into the role of bartender. When Dolly came back downstairs and began playing beautiful, painful notes, I slipped away to the kitchen and took stock of what I had to work with. Dolly had at least gone grocery shopping. I broke out the griddle and the skillets and got to work. Thirty-five minutes later, an upside-down dinner was ready: bacon, sausage, eggs, French toast with cinnamon, vanilla, and a nutmeg sugar glaze on top, and pancakes with maple syrup and whipped butter.

I didn't have to call anyone; people just started to drift in, chatting and holding glasses as they smelled the aroma.

As we sat back down to eat my sister squeezed my hand.

"Daisy, you're a lifesaver."

I squeezed her hand back. "So are you."

After dinner we moved into the living room and my father served more cordials. Julian and my father got into conversation about an upcoming legal case where my father quizzed him about his knowledge of state law. Julian beamed and preened when responded right and earned my father's praise. James was a bit withdrawn until Dolly showed her the legions of fashion magazines she owned and then James began to happily sift through them. Odie was quizzing the Boones about their Bait and Tackle store.

At one point I noticed my sister and Reverend Paul had both disappeared from the crowd. I set off to find Dolly . . . and I did. The conversation I overheard was so heartbreaking, I had to tuck it away for another day. Dolly would have hated it if she knew I'd overheard them.

When I got back to the living room the party was breaking up. James had already retired upstairs and Mr. and Mrs. Boone were grabbing their coats. I groaned when I heard Julian say, "Yes, sir! I'd love a visit to your offices, sir! I absolutely would."

My father patted him on his shoulder and then trailed down the hall after the Boones, to open the door for them. Julian stood there smiling broader than I'd ever seen, and I, being the epitome of maturity and poise began making kissing noises behind his back. He shot a look at me but fought to wipe the grin off his face.

"I think they're in love," Trevor said jokingly.

Julian eyed both of us with a cocked head, then turned on his heel and mumbled something that sounded a lot like, "I was just about to say the same thing."

The next morning I rose early, headed downstairs, and knocked on James's door.

Her groggy voice called, "Yes."

"May I come in?"

"Yes." I entered and James sat up, disheveled.

"I think I drank too much last night," she groaned, eliciting a smile from me.

"Can't go from a having learner's permit to being a NASCAR driver, James."

She laughed. "Amen to that."

"I'm just coming by to see if you'd like me to take you to Merryville today. I know it's Saturday, but I'd like to get a move on so my sister's car is not tied up too long. She sometimes goes to work on Saturdays."

James was quiet for a long time. She seemed to be wading through a lot of different emotions and I gave her the space to do that.

"Your sister is amazing, Daisy. I've never met anyone with more knowledge about the fashion industry. You can both dress but Dolly follows designers and trends in a way that I've never seen. And she's so smart and so *nice*. She offered me four different handbags last night. She kept saying she needs to keep her closet under control."

That sounded about right. Anyone that I loved, she automatically loved too. "Dolly is the best," I said simply.

"And your father . . . God, it's like they bottled southern charm!"

I laughed. I'd never quite heard him described that way but it was accurate.

"He obviously loves you both so much. Even Julian, who is probably the smartest person I've ever met, is in awe of him."

I laughed again, surprised. I'd never heard James say a kind word about Julian, but her assessment was correct. Julian was definitely a little awestruck by my dad. "You're right, my father is amazing."

She gestured around. "And this place! These trees and the peace . . . and the elegant beauty. I wish I had a camera. It makes me want to shoot all day!"

"The views are breathtaking. I love Green Valley. I couldn't imagine living anywhere else."

She shook her head. "I thought it would be something different. I thought . . ."

"You thought?"

"I thought—I had this idea in my head that I see now wasn't reality. I thought that you'd grown up in a mansion, with butlers and maids—"

"I'm sorry to disappoint you but we don't even have a pool."

She shook her head in what I assumed was disbelief. "Your family seems so normal."

I looked at her out the side of my eye. "Yeah. I mean, *mostly.* My sister's a little scary sometimes and my father is not to be trifled with when he's working but otherwise . . ." I shrugged.

"Daisy, I grew up—" She shook her head and swallowed heard. "Let's just say the poor people around us thought we were poor. Rich people to me were something mythical. And *evil.* How can some people have so much and there still be people that lived the way my family did?"

"When I found out that you were rich, and I thought about the fact that Odie and I bought you clothes when we were barely getting by, I couldn't . . . it just reinforced how I thought rich people behaved. That they want everything for themselves and nothing for the rest of us."

"James, I did feel bad about that and if you recall, I was crying. Those tears weren't just because I was happy, they were also because I felt guilty about you all spending money on me. *However* I also didn't feel bad about it, because I felt like for the first time in my life someone just considered me."

She gestured around. "What are you talking about? Folks consider you all the time. This entire house screams *I consider my offspring.*"

I bit back my laugh. "I wasn't counting my family. Family has to consider you."

She looked at me flatly. "I'm here to testify that they absolutely do not."

I stared at her, unsure of how to respond to that. It was clear that we were raised worlds apart. I didn't know if it was even possible for James to see my point of view.

"This is harder than I thought it would be." She groaned. "I thought you were some spoiled rich girl who deemed it a noble cause to bestow your presence upon the masses."

"Nothing could be further from the truth."

"I know that *now*, Daisy. I've seen you with your family. I saw how you helped your sister yesterday—that was really sweet, by the way."

I shrugged. "It was nothing."

She sighed. "I can't understand why you would deny these people, why anyone that grew up in this house with this life wouldn't want to shout it from the rooftops."

I closed my eyes and tried to think of how to explain this to James so she'd understand.

"James, you're really beautiful. You know that, right? Like, I'm not saying that Odie and I aren't attractive, but you belong on the cover of magazines."

She shrugged. "I am not my face."

"Exactly. And I wanted to feel like I was not my name. You're beautiful and you didn't do anything to *deserve* your beauty. It just is. My family is well off and I didn't do anything to *deserve* this life. People see your beauty and it makes lots of them act foolishly. They give you things you don't deserve or sometimes try to punish you like Julian did when he insulted you. Or they only see you as an object to be used to get something from. People do the same thing with me about money, or whatever influence they believe I have. And for me it was exhausting. I was tired of having to question the motives of everyone. I was tired of feeling like I had to watch my back. I was tired of being judged by something that had very little to do with the real me. So I ask you, James, if you could do something, *anything* to make people disregard your face, and see you—the real you, would you do it?"

"No," she answered harshly.

Well that backfired spectacularly.

"Daisy, those of us who grew up without power, those of us who grew up without *safety* would never dream of giving it up once we got it. It wouldn't even be a consideration. Not even temporarily. So even if I could somehow blind others to my looks, I *wouldn't*. Being beautiful is powerful. Even if I didn't earn it, I have it so I'm going to use it. Like you said, people won't hesitate to try to use my beauty against me, so I won't hesitate to use it to my advantage."

I stared back at James, wondering what happened to her growing up to make her see the world so binary.

Either way, she was never going to see my point. Before I could ask what time she wanted to leave for Maryville, she said, "But I do get why you wouldn't *trust* people. *That* I understand."

I looked at my friend, well my maybe-friend, and my heart

383

cracked for her. It was clear James had been through some heavy experiences.

"I'm not good at forgiving people, Daisy."

I laughed. "I am aware of that, James."

She looked at me and grimaced. "You get on my nerves because you make me want to forgive you."

New comprehension dawned. *James may not know how to forgive me.* I felt like the whole concept of *grace* would be lost on James but the real-world application might not be.

"My sister once told me that forgiving people is choosing the relationship you want over the relationship you have." I paraphrased Dolly's words. "She said you have to believe the person has changed and decide to give them a chance. That you can't forget the past, but that the decision to move forward from it is yours. I propose we move forward from the past, James."

She seemed genuinely engaged in thought before responding, "I think that's a proposal I can live with. I like your sister very much. She's practical."

"Don't I know it!" I laughed.

Then I laughed again as she launched herself back onto the covers. I was happy to hear some of the James lightness return to her voice when she said, "You guys are going to have to drag me back to Fisk. This is the best bed I've ever slept in!"

"I'm going back to bed," I declared, shaking my head.

"Wake me up for breakfast!" James shouted.

James Jones really was something else.

I climbed back up the stairs, tumbled into bed, and fell into a fitful sleep.

Dolly woke me around ten telling me that she was on her way to work and that she'd followed the *recipes* and made oatmeal, eggs, and bacon for everyone. She'd given me a kiss and informed me that my friends were already downstairs eating and that she'd be home around dinnertime.

I marveled a little at how pulled-together Dolly seemed. If I had endured the conversation she'd had last night, I would've been a rattled wreck. I sometimes thought poise under pressure was my sister's superpower.

We ended up making base camp in my room. James lounged on my floor snuggled under blankets and surrounded by a stack of *National Geographic* magazines I gifted her. She was going through each shot, writing notes about the aperture and type of camera, the frame rate, exposure, and other things she'd tried to explain to me to no avail.

Odie, ever the mama bear sniffed, "You're welcome, Jamesy." When she saw that James and I were back on speaking terms.

James threw a pillow a her in response.

Throughout the day we took turns catching one another up on our lives over the past few weeks. Odie revealed that Maurice had asked her out on a date.

My eyes bugged out. "And how did his roommate Charlie take that news?"

Odie shrugged. "I have no idea. But when we come back from break he's taking me to see Mahogany."

Then James revealed that she's had a secret admirer *all semester long* and that she thought she might be falling in love with this stranger. "He leaves me notes, beautiful sonnets, sometimes witty non sequiturs . . . always in the same spot, always on the same day outside my English 202 class."

Odie and I stared at her, awestruck and dumbfounded. Odie said the thing I couldn't. "Is there anything else you've been keeping from us? You gave damn Daisy such a hard time and you've been living an episode of *Spy vs. Spy!*"

James shook her head but I responded, "Speaking of English majors . . . There *is* something else James kept from us, Odie." I effected an instructional tone, "Did you, by any chance, know that

Julian P. Marshall, otherwise known as Jules the gorgeous, was James's TA for English 202 this semester?"

James looked at me and the only way to describe her face was *caught*.

Caught, caught, caught.

"Now why on earth do you think this interesting tidbit never came up?"

Odie stood and placed her thumb theatrically on her chin. "Hmm. I'm not sure, Daisy. Could it be because he's dull and unattractive?"

I pretended to think on it. "Hmm . . . Odie, I think you may be right. It's definitely not because he's smoking hot and very into James."

Whoever said brown girls couldn't blush had never seen James Jones in that moment.

"Shut it, both of you!" she said, rolling over on her back and closing her eyes.

"Jamesy," Odie teased. "Is somebody hot for their TA?"

James growled—actually growled—in response.

"He came to every single class looking like . . ." She sighed and bit her lip. "Looking like Julian."

"You're clearly attracted to him. He's clearly attracted to you. What's the problem here?" Odie says.

"I get why she would hold back."

They both whipped their heads to me.

"I do. Julian is . . . complicated."

James looked at me with what was one-hundred-percent unfiltered jealousy. "I heard you and Julian have been spending a lot of time together. Just how *complicated* have things gotten between the two of you?"

I wanted to laugh in her face. So I did, because she had to know . . . me and Julian? *Absolutely not.*

I laughed so hard at James—cool James, losing her grasp on her tightly-held mask—that I tipped over on my bed.

I wiped tears from my eyes to see Odie shaking with laughter as James barely attempted to disguise her interest.

"James, for the record, no. Just *no*. There are no complications in my relationship with Julian except that his best friend is Trevor. Julian is exactly your brand of crazy, James. Not mine."

"He is not my brand of whatever."

"Oh, he is. He most certainly is. You two both go all the way. I mean *all* the way."

Odie piped up. "Yeah, James, you two seem like the type to get into a fight, break all the dishes in the house, and then have sex on the kitchen countertops."

I burst into laughter because Odie was exactly right.

James snatched a magazine from the floor to hide her face and mumbled, "We're not that bad."

"*We*."

James groaned.

"What's this 'we'? Have you been seeing Jules this semester, Jamesy?" Odie questioned.

"No. I just meant . . . being around him this semester . . . he's not that bad."

I looked at Odie, grinned, and mimicked the narrator from the classic Christmas movie, "*Well, in Whoville they say—that the Grinch's small heart grew three sizes that day.*"

Odie laughed so hard tears streamed down her cheeks. James threw her magazine at me and we both devolved into a riot of laughter.

That night after dinner we went ice-skating. Dolly drove us and the only discernible change in her demeanor happened when she spotted a car that looked like Reverend Smith's in the parking lot and tried to put our car into park twice.

When we cut through the trees to get to the outdoor rink, my friends oohed and ahhed in surprise. The Green Valley skating rink was only around once a year, just before the Christmas holiday in a clearing surrounded by a circle of trees. There were loudspeakers around the rink and a concession stand that abutted the woods that sold hot chocolate, candy, funnel cakes, and other snacks.

Unsurprisingly the ice rink was a favorite date spot for teens. We were lacing up our skates on a bench when I saw Reverend Paul in the distance talking to some teenagers I didn't recognize.

I shot a glance over at Dolly and she said softly, "That's right, the church's youth ministry is here tonight skating. I'd better . . . go speak . . ."

Dolly was off the bench and gliding across the ice seconds later. Superpower.

I heard a voice laugh. "I didn't know chickens could skate."

"I didn't know pretty prep-school boys could skate either." I shot back without even looking up.

Julian and Trevor stood behind our bench, engaged in conversation with . . . little Charlie Boone. *His brother.*

Yikes. I hadn't made the connection until right that moment. I dully realized that Charlie wasn't at dinner the other night. I wondered if his parents had intentionally left him home to give them a chance to reconnect with Trevor first. I wondered if it was hard for Trevor to be back in Green Valley with the brother that was born after him, the one that his parents kept. I did the math and I figured Charlie was maybe a freshman in high school this year. I turned and walked a few paces to my friends and offered my hands. Odie had been on skates before so she could at least stay upright. James, on the other hand, had already fallen twice just attempting to stand and was now firmly planted on the bench biting her nails and bouncing her leg. She rejected my hand while Odie latched onto it for balance.

"James, come on. It won't be as fun without you," I coaxed.

"You girls go ahead! I'll be fine watching."

"You're not the type to sit on the sidelines and watch other people have fun."

This from Julian.

I looked at Odie, eyebrows raised.

Jules walked around the bench, squatted down on his haunches, and offered James his hand.

Her knee bounced faster.

She gave a little shake of her head. "I'll fall."

"I won't let you."

Julian was all smoldering intensity, and I was surprised James didn't melt into a puddle from the heat that was radiating between them.

"James, I'm not asking you to trust me. I know that you can't do that. I'm asking you to hold my hand. Because if you're holding my hand and you go down, you'll pull me down with you. And I have no plans to go down, so that means my only choice is to keep you up."

She hesitated for a second and then slipped her hand in his. The grin on Julian's face was electric.

I took Odie around a few times before she declared she was ready for a break. I ushered her back to the railing and let her go just in the nick of time.

"Daiiisssy! Ahhhh!" A high-pitched, shrill little voice called my name. I smiled and turned because I *knew* that excited scream.

"Daisy! Daisy! Save me!" A pint-sized cloud of blond and chestnut curls cut directly across the ice causing skaters to dodge and some to nearly fall.

Bethany Oliver was flying full speed ahead toward me with arms wide open, pink knitted page-boy hat askew, and mouth screaming at full volume.

"Daisy! Save me!!"

I laughed. Children were the best. I'd babysat for the Olivers more than a few times over the years. Clever and funny, Bethany was rambunctious with an imagination in overdrive.

The six-year-old crashed into my legs, causing me to have to shuffle my feet to keep my balance and clinging to me in the way only small children could. I had a working theory that there were teeny tiny octopus-like suction cups deep in the fingertips of small children. It was the only explanation for why it took the strength of ten adults to detangle one determined child from the legs of their parents.

I saw Bethany's father, Congressman Oliver, skating over to join us the proper way instead of cutting across like his maniac daughter. She saw her father coming and maneuvered behind my legs.

Ah yes, the advanced behind-the-leg cling. There was no way I was getting out of this without eating the ice.

"Save me! Save me, Daisy!"

"What am I saving you from this time? Pirates?"

"No!"

"Monsters?"

"No! Everyone knows monsters aren't real!"

I laughed. Children changed so fast. The last time I'd babysat for her before I went to school I'd had to check beneath her bed five times for monsters just to be sure-sure-sure-sure-*sure*.

"Okay, I give up. What am I saving you from?"

"Bedtime," her father answered. "Bethany, it is time to go. And no amount of screaming or hollering is going to get you out of it, young lady."

"I *can't* go. Daisy just got here. We haven't even had time to catch up." She peeked from behind my legs.

Her father released an exasperated sigh and I winked at him. I gave Bethany my hand and pulled her around to hoist her around my waist as I skated off the ice.

"Where you been?" She squinted at me like I've been up to something suspect.

This kid.

"I've been away at college. You know, the school they send big kids to where you sleep away and learn a lot and make new friends."

"They leave you at school overnight?" She sounded scared.

"Yes, but all the kids are there, and we have our own rooms and our own beds and everything. It's a lot of fun."

She squinted her hazel eyes and tilted her head like she was deliberating if I was the victim of child abuse; she clearly wasn't sold on the whole sleeping at school idea.

"Enough about my school. Let's talk about you."

I jostled her on my hip, readjusting her weight as I waited for her father to pull their car around to us where I planned to deposit her, skates and all.

Hey, her father could deal with that part . . . as I resorted to the oldest child-wrangling technique in the book: blackmail.

"I believe it would be a good idea this time of year in particular to do everything within your power to stay on the *nice* list." I looked at her meaningfully and her little eyes widened.

I could practically see the cogs in her head turning as she worked to find a loophole or exemption for bedtime that would allow her to stay on the nice list, so I preempted it.

"I have it on good authority that listening to one's father and mother about bedtime are the very basics for nice list consideration."

She bit her lip.

"Furthermore, you might want to get into the practice of going to bed at a decent hour about now, Bethany. I'd hate for your house to get skipped when you-know-who drops off all the gifts for you-know-what because you were still awake. Going to bed now will make it easier when you have to fall asleep on Christmas Eve."

She considered it for a second and then surprised me. "Your points are valid," her little voice replied.

Caught completely off guard, I cracked up.

"My points are valid? Well, Bethany," I adopted a haughty tone. "I'm so glad you find no holes in my logic."

She grinned, the full, tiny-teeth grin that I loved.

"What in the world am I going to do with you?"

Her father pulled up, hopped out, rounded the car, and opened the car door in one swift motion. I plopped her in, buckled her up, and closed the door.

Her dad gave me a very grateful, if not a little weary, "Thank you. My wife is under the weather and I'm flying solo."

"Good luck." I laughed.

Just as I made my way back into the rink area I heard his voice. "You're good at that."

Trevor stood off in the shadow of a tree.

I walked over to him. "Good at what?"

"Saving the day."

Trevor

Daisy looked so surprised that I would pay her a compliment and that stung.

I realized I had my work cut out for me but I was up to the task. I would shower her with compliments daily. I would erase the expectation of anything other than kindness coming from me.

But first I had to get out this friendship lane that I was technically still driving in. Yes, Daisy had kissed me. *She enthusiastically kissed you, in her bedroom.* But that didn't matter; no matter how many hints or signs she dropped, it wouldn't be enough. I wanted to make things official between us. The last time I'd left room for ambiguity, we'd had secrets, vagueness, hurt, and deception.

I wanted no part of that moving forward.

This time I wanted something new, something better. Something that would last.

If Daisy needed time, she could take all she needed as long as I got to be near her. I'd be as patient as Jacob waiting for Rachel. And I'd use the time we were both in Green Valley to get to know everything about her.

I loved Daisy. Maybe even since before things fell apart; I didn't know. It was probably too soon to tell her so I would keep it to myself until the time was right.

If I'd had any lingering doubts that the girl I'd started to fall for was the real Daisy, seeing her here in Green Valley would've been a balm to those worries. The way she'd risen to help her sister. Seeing how much satisfaction she seemed to get out of playing hostess and bringing folks together. Seeing the gentle way she calmed down a wound-up child and helped her parent.

Daisy was sweetness incarnate, and I loved her. The realization settled into every part of me as I'd watched her, hair flying, broadly smiling, gently helping her friend around the rink.

"It occurred to me that we made a new deal. But we haven't yet shook on it." My smile was wry because I knew that Daisy would know where I'm going with this.

"Our deal to be friends?"

"Yes, and friends shake hands. If I recall though, you and I have a special handshake."

She smiled and her eyes flared with understanding.

Her voice was a little shaky when she said, "Sounds reasonable. We should definitely shake on it."

I extended my hand to hers and waited just a beat as she took off her glove and gently slide her warm hand against mine.

Something that had been gnashing and aching and sharp soothed in me the moment our palms touched.

I splayed my fingers and slid them in between hers. We both flexed our fingers at the same time, and just like that, she held my hand.

I loved the feel of Daisy's hands. Her soft to my rough; her small to my large. If it was all I ever had of her, it would be enough. I led her back to the ice and saw that Julian and James were still going round. James no longer looked pensive and tense; she was talking and laughing while Jules skated backwards, pulling her along.

Daisy and I still had a lot to learn about one another and I wanted that education to start now.

"Tell me something about you I don't know," I quizzed.

She scrunched her nose and deadpanned, "I hate grapes."

My eyebrow jumped in delighted surprise at her truly disgruntled tone.

"Well, now I guess I won't ever take you to a vineyard. I'd hate for those grapes to have to suffer your wrath." I couldn't help the smile in my voice and I didn't want to.

Daisy's holding my hand again. I thought we'd never get back here.

And I certainly never thought I'd be ice-skating under the moonlight, hand and hand with Daisy.

Life was totally unpredictable, especially with Daisy in it.

"Har-har, Steinbeck," She said, playfully rolled her eyes before wrinkling her nose again. "I don't like the *texture*. The sliminess on the inside plus . . ."

"Plus?"

"Dolly told me they were eyeballs one Halloween and I've never been able to get that visual out of my head."

"Dolly sounds like she gave you a run for your money growing up."

"You have no idea."

"Trevor?"

"Yes," I answered loving the sound of my name on Daisy's lips.

"I'm not mad, you know. I know how strongly you feel about keeping your word. Julian told me that was why you felt you had to serve on the TDC as part of your position. I understand why you agreed to be on the council."

Jules, bless him, was covering for me. I was obligated to serve, but I was not obligated to serve on her case.

"Daisy?"

"Yes."

"I stepped down off the case."

"You did?"

"Weeks ago, yes. I can't believe I forgot to tell you."

"Why?"

"Because I didn't want to work on anything that would hurt you. I was—I *am* tired of hurting you. I just couldn't."

Daisy stopped skating so abruptly that I almost ran into her. I pulled her to the edge under the shadow of a massive snow-dusted fir.

"Are you ok—"

I didn't get to finish my thought. She snaked her hand around my neck, pulled me lower, and kissed me again.

I kissed her back, loving the way her mouth opened the moment our lips touched. Loving the way she pressed into me, as if she couldn't get close enough.

We kissed under the stars and it was perfect. My blood raced and I was wound tight as a drum but it was worth it. I slowed down the kiss, reminding myself to be careful. There were families around. There was even a preacher around.

Daisy slyly licked my lip then bit it. "Why am I always the one kissing you?"

I had trouble responding because I was still trying to gather my thoughts. I wondered if she had any idea—any clue whatsoever—what she did to me.

I took her hand and spun her around so that her back was to my front. Daisy would feel what she did to me, but at least it wouldn't be on full display for every man, woman, and child at the rink.

I maneuvered us from the shadows just in time to see Julian skating *very* close with James, her entire body leaning back against his frame with his arm wrapped round her waist. James's eyes were closed and he was smiling and whispering in her ear.

I shook my head. Only Jules could pull off the impossible with that girl. He was charming as hell when he wanted to be.

We skated all night, Daisy and I and then together with her

friends. Eventually, we all got funnel cakes and Daisy and I argued good-naturedly, like old times. I couldn't stop smiling and neither could she.

"It's too messy."

"It's powdered sugar. Of course it's messy," she replied rolling her eyes.

I resisted the urge to tug her hair. "That's why you have to get it with chocolate sauce instead. Everybody knows that's the only way to eat a funnel cake."

"Everybody knows you have a habit of doing sacrilegious things with food! You're a sicko. What kind person ruins the crispy, fried, doughy bliss that is funnel cakes by adding chocolate sauce instead of powdered sugar! You—"

I didn't know if it was the word bliss, the fact that Daisy always got my blood moving when she sparred with me, or the fact that there was a delectable piece of powdered sugar right at the corner of her mouth, but I leaned down and licked the sugar away with a kiss.

It did not compare to the sweetness of her mouth or the perfection of having her in my arms again.

When it was time to leave, we escorted the girls back to their car. I asked after Daisy's plans for the remainder of the week, wanting to give her space to be with her friends but also desperately wanting to spend every waking moment with her.

We agreed to go Christmas shopping later that week and I left on cloud nine.

CHAPTER TWENTY-SIX

Trevor

C loud nine did not last. The following evening, after returning from Big Bun's Burgers with Julian, my father and mother cornered me in my room.

It was eerie, at least to me, that my room was exactly as I'd left it. Down to the pieces of Bazooka gum that I'd left on my desk and the Hank Aaron baseball card I'd gotten a few days before. The room was dotted with pictures of me that I didn't even remember. Me at about aged six in a little league uniform that read *Green Valley Grizzlies.*

Me and my mother and father posed for a professional portrait when I'd been about four.

Another picture, smaller, of me standing over a baby bugging peering inside at Charlie.

Even my clothes were still in my closet. The room felt like a shrine.

My mother sat at the desk chair and my father stood in front of the door as if he were barring it.

I sat up on the bed and put down the copy of *How to Win Friends and Influence People* that I'd been reading. The book had been an impromptu gift from Dr. Gwinn at the end of the semester. She knew the semester had been a difficult one though she hadn't known the exact reason for it, and she'd inscribed words of motivation behind the jacket. "Seven down, and I'm so proud. One to go. Remember rule number two."

Rule number two was you were either working toward your goal or against it; there was no middle ground. Rule number one was, of course, to be early is to be on time, or as Daisy called it during one of our conversations this week, "time magic."

I smiled thinking of her, then dropped my smile as I remembered my parents were in my room and they wanted . . . something.

"Hey Mom and Dad, what's up?" The terms were stilted from disuse, and my mother began to fidget with the tea towel she held in her hands.

"We wanted to talk to you, Trevor. You've been home almost a week now and we haven't seen you much."

I bit back the urge to snap with something ugly like, "You haven't seen much of me for the last nine years, so what's the difference?"

My parents were right; I hadn't been around. I'd made it my business to get out and explore, and Jules was game to go, too. I think he'd fallen in love with Green Valley the moment he saw it covered in snow and looking like the idyllic countryside of some renaissance painting.

So we'd stayed busy. Sometimes we let Charlie tag along, other times we didn't.

Charlie. The most surprising thing was that I bore no ill will toward my younger brother. He had been a baby and was just as much a victim of circumstance as I was. We'd been deprived of one another's company. He was so eager to get to know me, he was effusive —*too* effusive. He reminded me of a bounding Labrador or a nippy poodle.

I smiled at the thought and could almost hear Gracie saying,

"That's because you grew up in a repressive environment. Look at you, El, and Jules."

Charlie got along great with Jules too, and our decision to let him come along or to leave him behind was based on one thing: a deeply ingrained brotherly instinct to torture my younger brother in a good-natured way.

"You're right, I haven't been around much." There. That was both accurate and not snarky.

My parents stared at me.

I stared at my parents.

I took a deep breath and closed my eyes. And then I prayed for patience because I realized my parents were never going to address the elephant in the room. And I was never, ever going to be able to move forward unless I asked the questions I needed to ask.

I exhaled the calming breath and decided the present was as good a time as any. "Why was it so important for you that I come home?"

"You're my son. Why wouldn't it be important to me for you to come home?" This from my mother, who had twisted the tea towel into a knot.

"I don't know. Maybe because it never has been before." I replied, my voice rising just a little.

"That's not true. We always wanted you home," my father said.

Then my father came and sat next to me on the bed. He sighed mightily. "Trevor, I know this isn't a fancy place like you're used to, and I know that maybe we're a bit too plain spoken. But we're never going to be able to make this work if you can't come down a little off your high horse. We thought when you decided to come home—"

"*What?*" I was incensed. "Come down off my high horse? I have every right to have a high horse. I have all the horses. You all *gave me away*. You sent me to live with people that barely cared if I lived or died. You have no right to imply I'm a snob because of the people you chose to send me to live with!"

My father and mother sat in stunned silence for a moment. And then my mother got up and she hugged me.

My chest heaved and I felt suffocated by her touch. It was too much; too soft, too caring. She placed her palms on the side of my face and tilted my head to meet her eyes.

"I'm sorry." She wept.

I flinched.

"Trevor, I'm sorry. I'm sorry. I'm *so* sorry."

She repeated the words over and over again until something in me broke. Hearing the tenderness and remorse in my mother's voice sliced me open.

I began to cry and she pulled me in to her, holding me tightly. She rocked me, patted me on the back and whispered, "It's okay, son, let it out," until my tears slowed. I hadn't realized it but something inside me needed to hear those words. I needed to hear my parents apologize. My tears didn't last long, but they were hot and cathartic.

Then my father apologized.

"I had no idea you felt that way, son. We had no idea." He kept repeating solemnly.

And then he told me a story.

"In '62 me and Adolpho decided we were going to support the Movement. We were both too high profile to organize church meetings and the like, but we had financial means and knew we could help out in that way. It was all very hush-hush. We didn't want to draw attention to ourselves. We were local business owners and we had enough to deal with facing the jealously that came with *that*.

"We were funneling money to Brownsville, to Birmingham, to Memphis, wherever they needed it to do the work. Then the person we were using to move the money *died*, and we had to figure out another way to get the money to where it needed to go. We couldn't wire it from anywhere in Green Valley so we tried sending it out of Maryville. We never did prove it, but Adolpho and I believe that's where all the trouble started. Somehow or another, folks got wind of what we were doing and decided they should send us a message to stop."

I sat on my bed engrossed in his words. I had no clue my parents had been a part of any Civil Rights causes.

"So that's when business started to trickle and dry up. They boycotted my shop and Adolpho had to deal with a mutiny at the Mill. The difference though, was that too many folks needed Payton Mills for their livelihood so the Paytons weren't hurt nearly as bad as we were. Us though? They nearly put us under."

"The boycott went on for over three years," my mother said.

"There years? Humph. Some folks still won't shop there," my father countered.

"And we were desperate. We tried to get a loan from the bank and they called in our debts instead." He shook his head in disgust.

That, I remembered. My father coming home looking so defeated after being denied at the bank. My mother and father discussing it in hushed tones, thinking I had no clue what was going on.

My father blinked hard twice, like he was fighting tears. "That was the lowest point in my life. To not be able to provide for y'all. One day, if you're lucky, you'll have a family of your own and it'll be the honor of your life to work to give them everything they need.

"I don't think you remember how bad it was but there were nights when there was no food in the house. It was winter and I couldn't pay for oil to be delivered to the house. I was afraid you were going to catch your death."

"And you . . ." He looked at me and I was floored by the sincerity in his eyes, in his tone. "You deserved everything. Every good thing. Still do. I knew we had to get you out of here."

I felt a lump in my throat and struggled to swallow as I let this information sink in.

My father cleared his throat a few times, unable to speak. My mother squeezed my hand and began speaking. "I called my cousin Marcus. He'd been able to help us in the past. He'd even been an investor when we'd first started the business. He put me in touch with May and she and I spoke about having you finish the school year and spending the summer with them," my mother said.

"She wasn't supposed to *steal* you, Trevor. They were family."

"Steal me?"

"We sent you there so you'd be spared the worst of our blight. Admittedly, we didn't come and get you at the end of the summer. We were still in dire straits. But I was in constant communication with May and she insisted that you never wanted to come to the phone, that you had adjusted so well, and that you never even mentioned our names."

I felt my blood pressure rise and my stomach churn. Of course I hadn't mentioned their names. May told me there was no use whining about people who didn't want me enough to keep me and who weren't coming back to get me.

"But a year went by and that next summer I couldn't take it anymore. I told your father, poor or not, we needed to go get you. I hadn't spoken to my baby. I didn't know if you were all right. I needed to see you." She gingerly touched my face. "And so we did."

"What?!"

"Borrowed a car and drove all night to Charlotte."

Something in the back of my mind whispered, *They kept their word. They came for you.*

"No one was there."

I knew immediately what had happened. "Julian and I split summers between sleepaway camps and the Marshall's house in Hamptons." I whispered more to myself than to my parents.

"No one that worked at the house would tell us where you were, who you were with, if you were okay, when you'd be back. Nothing."

"We went to the cops," my father said with a disgusted head shake. "They told us if we'd dropped our baby off a year ago, then why were we worried just now. And then they implied that we were making it up for attention, because 'you know how our people like to carry on for attention.'" The disgust in his voice was palpable.

"Nobody would help us," my mother repeated sadly.

"Adolpho was finally able to hunt down May and Marshall. He was important enough for them to answer his calls," my father added.

"And that was how we found you, two and half years later. We were still struggling financially, but things were starting to look up. We told May that we would be coming to get you and she told me flat out, 'Children aren't handbags. You can't just give them away and pick them up when it's convenient. He's settled here and happy here.' And then it was Julian, Julian, Julian. How unfair it was to Julian to lose his playmate. How you and Julian were like brothers. How you and Julian kept one another entertained. I told her I didn't care, I wanted my son back!"

Seeing that my mother had become emotional, my father cut in. "And then . . . Marshall called me and said that if we tried to take you they'd deploy an arsenal of lawyers and would keep us in court until you were eighteen. We were just getting back on our feet and we couldn't have afforded to fight them even if we'd tried. We had no reason to think that the law or anyone else would help us out.

"I tried to reason with them so many times." He shook his head.

Then my mother said quietly, "May called me one day and told me she'd let me talk to you. And you got on the phone . . ."

Horror twisted my gut because I knew before she spoke what she was going to say.

"And you told me that you wanted to stay. You didn't want to come home and that you were having the time of your life."

I felt sick.

Three years had gone by and I'd thought my parents didn't want me. They hadn't come for me. So yes, I'd lied to them on the phone. I'd wanted them to think I didn't need them and that I was happy.

"I lied. I wanted to come home every day." I was cried out, yet tears still threatened to fall. I was so drained. I thought of how my parents had been consistently trying to contact me these last three years upon finding out I was going to Fisk University.

I'd ignored their letters and their calls. I'd made it worse.

I couldn't process how or why May or Marcus would fight to keep me when they never really wanted me. I suspected that May just hadn't wanted my parents to have me; maybe she enjoyed pitting Jules and me against one another. I had no clue. What I did have was anger. Boiling and bright for that woman and her husband. I would have to work though it because they were Julian's parents, but I couldn't help but feel disdain at the thought of them.

My father sighed wearily. "It never got easier not having you around. In fact, it hurt a lot. But we were able to console ourselves with thinking that you were thriving. Your mother . . ."

My parents shared a furtive look. My mother looked away and my father swallowed hard before continuing, "You should know your mother was never on board with sending you away."

"BJ, there's no reason to go down this road again—" My mother shook her head but my father cut her off.

"No, Dell, he should know. They say mothers know best, right? And your mother . . ." He sighed again as if releasing a weight. "She had her doubts from the outset. Said something about May rubbed her the wrong way when they spoke. Tried to convince me that maybe you'd be better off here."

My mother squeezed my hand but otherwise remained silent. I couldn't even begin to wonder how that conflict had played out between the two of them. It was clear after all this time that it was still touchy. My father finished with, "I know you probably don't agree with the decision to send you away in the first place, but you should know it was me that pushed for it. So if you're going to lay blame anywhere, it belongs with me."

My mother spoke and shook her head. "Stop that. We've had enough of that, haven't we? Where have blame and shame gotten us? Nowhere. Same with anger. This is our chance. Our second chance, one I wasn't always sure we'd get. Trevor, I might not have one hundred percent agreed with your father but I understood where he was coming from. He thought it would be temporary, he thought the time away would give you access to a better world." My mother's defense of my father's decision, one that had clearly hurt, touched me. She was the type to always look for the good in a situation. I realized faintly that Daisy had that same trait, and maybe I'd been destined to love her because of that.

My father's voice cut through. "Not a day has passed that I haven't missed you. And not a day has passed when I haven't been filled with regret for creating the hole your absence left in this family."

I hugged my father. Then I stood and scooped my mother up into a hug. That made her laugh, which was a magical sound. Almost as magical as Daisy's laugh.

After a long time of us just standing there hugging my father spoke again. "So . . ." My father drew out the word in a clear attempt to change the subject, making my mother and me laugh again in the process. "What are your plans for tonight? I was thinking we could have a little father-son time. We have a game to finish."

My mouth dropped in disbelief. Before I'd left, my father had been teaching me to play chess.

I trailed behind him to the family room and sure enough the board was set up precisely as it had been. Next to it was another board with pieces lined up. My father motioned to it. "I tried to teach Charlie but he's rubbish. He's got too much energy to focus and be deliberate."

I felt a little—okay, a lot—choked up at the thought that my father would be so dedicated to the idea that we'd finish our game one day that he'd purchased another board to play with my brother.

My father stood looking at me as I stared at the pieces, almost afraid to touch them.

And I realized he waited for my answer. "Father-son time sounds perfect, Pop."

We spent the entire night playing games. When Charlie came home from school we played a game of Monopoly that sent Jules to jail and my mother to skid row while my father and I split the middling properties and my brother bought Park Place and Boardwalk.

That night around nine the phone rang and I dashed to the kitchen and picked up before anyone could grab the call.

"Trevor?" Daisy's sweet voice came through on my line. From somewhere in the house I heard Jules shout, "UNO! OUT!" followed by my little brother's, "Cheater!"

"Daisy," I responded, unable to keep the grin off my face. Daisy and I hadn't been able to see one another every day since we'd been in Green Valley but she'd call me or I'd call her daily. We chatted for a minute, and she told me of the small pieces of her day that I'd missed. The jokes Odie made, the heads James turned. Julian was in for a world of trouble with that one. And then I told her all about my own day. It was miracle because of the smallness of the thing. I didn't want or need anything for Christmas; it was a gift to share in her day and to have her want to share in mine.

―――――

Over the next few days and weeks my parents and I had lots of conversations. We began to mend our relationship and I began to regrow roots in Green Valley.

Through it all, Daisy had been my joy.

After I told her all about my conversation with my parents, she made it her mission to be my "official Green Valley homecoming guide." Her words. For me, she became a memory-jogger and historian. She was the thread sewing me back into Green Valley society, one stitch at a time.

Instead of introducing me to the locals the same way she did for the rest of our friends, she'd say something like, "You know Trevor, the Boone's oldest boy? Would you believe he and I both ended up at the best HBCU in the world? Must be something in the Green Valley water! I persuaded him to drop into Green Valley for the holidays."

The other person would look at me blankly at first. After recognizing my name, they'd offer me a hearty handshake, and *then* they'd ask after my parents or my brother. Or they'd ask about my grades and tell me what a good student my father had been. The number of times I'd been told that they hadn't seen me since I was "knee high to a grasshopper" was astounding.

And during each conversation, Daisy would take the time to discreetly explain who they were and how their family history intersected or totally diverged from mine.

That's Eugene Lee, who your Grandaddy Toby couldn't stand. Said he cheated in cards and you couldn't trust him. Those are the Donners. They own a local lodge in town, and rumor has it they're thinking of adding a bakery.

There was genuine southern charm—the kind Daisy showed when we sat in her kitchen and she insisted we have just one more of her delicious lemon and nutmeg glazed doughnuts—and there was southern charm as performance art. Daisy had mastered them both.

She planned trips for all of us to the local haunts. When we'd gone to the Green Valley Christmas Market we'd eaten pretzels, corndogs, popcorn, and drank ale until we'd just about burst.

Just a few days ago we'd all gone shopping downtown. Daisy and Dolly pointed out which store was best for which type of gift while all of us dipped in and out of stores, discretely purchasing presents or trinkets.

We all became especially enamored with Scratches Records and Cassettes. It'd been there that I'd found my Christmas gift to Daisy. I'd taken a deep breath at the price but it was a *signed* copy. I'd forked over the cash and then made an excuse so that Julian and I could leave before Daisy could see it. He'd been more than happy to leave, only pausing to stop once at Shutters. I waited outside. I had no idea what Julian would want in a camera store.

All in all, my time in Green Valley had been restorative. I still had a way to go but my path forward with both my folks and Daisy was mostly clear.

Julian, on the other hand, had been wracked with guilt. His working theory was that his parents, his mother especially, intentionally kept me apart from my parents because she wanted me as a playmate for him.

I had no idea if that theory held water and I didn't care. I needed to work through my anger at my own pace, but for now, in this moment, May and Marcus couldn't have any of more of my headspace. They'd already taken too much time from my life.

Speaking of time, I didn't want to waste any more of what I had with Daisy. Tonight, her family was hosting their annual Christmas Eve cocktail party and we were all going. I would find time to tell Daisy that she had my heart. I would beg for hers.

James and Odie would head to South Carolina to spend the rest of break with Odie's folks early tomorrow. Interestingly enough, Julian had offered to chauffeur them. I don't know if Jules felt terrible and wanted to let me spend time with my family or if he wanted to spend more time with James. I suspected it was a little of both, although Julian denied there was anything going on between him and James. "We're just friends. That's all we are and that's all we'll ever be."

In my opinion, he doth protest too much, but it was none of my business. Either way I'd tried to make it clear to him that there was no need to shoulder any of the blame for his parents and that I was in no hurry to be rid of him.

Jules peeked his head in my room just as I was slipping into my jacket. He whistled as he theatrically brushed off my shoulders. "Whoo-whee! You clean up nice!"

I laughed at his antics. We were both decked out in formal attire; I was in a navy blue herringbone suit with brown leather pockets and elbow patches. Julian's tux was black with a notched lapel—Italian and bespoke, as always.

We headed out around eight fifteen. My little brother, looking adorable in his tuxedo, trailed after us trying to adjust his cufflinks.

"Hey guys, wait up! Trev—can you show me how?" I spun on my heels, quickly fastened his cuffs, and then patted him on his head.

"Charlie, there is no way in H-E-double-hockey sticks Jules and I are letting you ride with us. Go wait for Mom and Pop."

He bounced on the balls of his feet. "But, but . . ."

Jules and I laughed as we walked out the door.

"Man, little brothers are great. I may have to borrow him sometime," Jules quipped.

"You can take 'em, just make sure you bring 'em back."

Jules eyes widened and I realized what I'd said. "Julian, I'm sorry."

"Got it."

I would have to be extra careful. Jules had a habit of getting addicted to guilt.

When we arrived the party was already in full swing. The house had been decorated with garland sweeping the front porch. There were red bows on the railing and candles shone in each of the windows.

Entering the house, I found myself grateful to Daisy again as I was able to greet everyone by name, ask about their work at the Mill or at the Piggly Wiggly, or inquire after their family.

I was there for about ten minutes before I began to get antsy.

I landed against the bar and watched with a schadenfreude-like fascination as Julian spotted James descend the stairs, wearing red from head to toe.

I sidled up to my best friend who had turned red as a Christmas ornament. "I don't know who's redder."

"Shut up, Trevor." Julian was looking everywhere but at the stunner. But James had other plans. She sauntered right up to him and twirled. "Julian, do you like my gown?"

He threw me a pleading look, his hands fisted at his sides.

I shrugged, nodded a hello to James—who grinned like she knew exactly what she was doing—and walked away, on the hunt for Daisy.

Julian started playing with that fire. I hoped he wouldn't get burned.

I found Dolly and Odie, both wearing black and gold, milling about in the room where Dolly played the violin for us my first night home. I couldn't help but quip, "Nice colors." Dolly laughed.

I asked after Daisy, but neither of them had seen her in a while.

"You might try near the ugly Christmas tree," suggested Dolly.

"There are like, twenty Christmas trees in this house. Which one is the ugly one?"

Dolly narrowed her eyes. "Trevor, are you calling my house poorly decorated?"

Realizing I'd stepped in it, I quickly clarified. "No! Of course not. I'm saying *none* of these trees look ugly."

"Oh well, the ugly one *is* ugly. It has tinsel and garland and every single homemade ornament we created as children. We put it up in the family room." I'd just left their family room and I hadn't seen a tree that looked like that. Or Daisy.

"The upstairs family room," she clarified.

She motioned for me to come closer so I leaned my head down. "No one is allowed past the second level. But my sister is crazy about you. You will go and spend some quality *alone* time with my sister, and Trevor? If you even think about hurting my sister again or disrespecting my father's house tonight, I will personally hunt you down and make you a one-nut-Chuck. Are we clear?"

"Crystal!" I said, stepping back. Daisy was right. Dolly was a little scary sometimes.

I followed Dolly's instructions and took the back stairs until I spotted Daisy in a darkened room off a long hallway.

Daisy stood in profile staring out the back window. Backlit by the glow of the Christmas tree, I didn't think I'd ever seen her look more beautiful.

She wore a long, deep blue gown with pleats at the bottom and a satiny looking fabric wrapping her bosom. Her curls were free and fell around her shoulders, caught back by a gold headband that looked like it was made of laurel leaves. The effect made her look like a queen or a goddess. If God made words for how beautiful she looked I didn't know them. I stood there speechless, watching her until I saw a coy smile pull at her lips and she said, "How long are you going to watch me?"

I laughed. "How long have you known I was here?"

"A while," she answered.

"And here I thought I was being sneaky."

"You can't be sneaky around me."

I walked to her, allowing the fullness of my joy to overtake me. "Yeah? Why's that? You use your fairy powers to put a tracker on me, Daisy?"

She smiled ruefully. Then her smile dropped and she looked at me with those mahogany eyes. "I can always feel you when you're near."

That did it.

I leaned down to capture her lips.

I smiled at her responsiveness, at the way her breath caught.

I skimmed all that soft, warm bare skin, from her shoulder blades down to the dip of her waist on display for me and suddenly I was so hard it hurt.

Daisy trailed her hand down my shirt, reached down, and pressed her hand against my bulge and suddenly I was the one gasping.

"Wait, wait, wait." I stumbled back, rock-hard and off-kilter from Daisy's exploring fingers.

She looked up at me wide-eyed and curious. "Did I do it wrong?"

Definitely not.

I shook my head but didn't say anything and then walked to the window to try regain some of my sanity.

Daisy was at my back a second later, her hands running along my shoulder blades, her melodic voice husky in my ear. "What's wrong, Trevor?" She nipped my ear and I shuddered.

Daisy was making me mindless and I could not afford to lose my mind. *Or any other body part.* Dolly's words rang through my ears.

"What's wrong is I want you so badly I can hardly think straight so I'm trying to catch my breath but the gorgeous, insanely sexy love of my life keeps touching me and it's driving me out of my mind."

"What did you say?"

I turned to see her shocked expression and then ran my words back again.

Oh God. I stepped away from her and hung my head.

"Trevor, what did you just say?"

I took a deep breath and looked up. My eyes moved over Daisy and she didn't look upset or angry the way I'd expected; her eyes were lit with excitement.

Interesting. Maybe this wasn't so bad after all. I said it and she was still here.

I tested my theory. I took a half step back and Daisy took a half step forward coming into my space. I tried to hide my smile.

"Uhh, I'm not sure. What did I just say?"

I stepped back again. She stepped forward and warned, "*Trevor!*"

"Are you talking about the part where I called you gorgeous?" I took a step back.

Daisy took two forward. "*No.*"

"The part where I called you insanely sexy?"

I took a half step back and my back hit the wall.

She looked at me from underneath those coal black lashes. "Maybe."

I laughed. Then I looked down at Daisy with every ounce of tenderness I could muster. "Or maybe you mean the part where I called you the love of my life."

Her smile was brighter than all the twinkling lights of the tree. Brighter than the stars that shone in the sky.

But I was the one who lit up when she looked at me and whispered, "I love you, too."

EPILOGUE

May 3rd, 1976

Trevor

When James and Odie had asked me during Christmas break to help in crafting their confession letters, I'd immediately agreed. On one condition: they had to tell Daisy.

That was the rule. There would be no more secrets between Daisy and me ever again. Therefore, on Christmas morning before they hit the road, the girls had told Daisy and she'd been livid with both them and with me. It was too late though; the confession letters had already been mailed.

We'd had our first fight that morning. The best thing about fighting as a couple with Daisy?

Making up.

Once we returned to school in mid-January, the three of them had stood before the disciplinary council. I'd been allowed to watch the closed-door proceedings as moral support. I suspected that her father, who hadn't been able to make it, pulled some strings to allow me in there.

Dr. Gwinn had served as a character witness for Daisy, much to her surprise, but not mine. When Dr. Gwinn was in your corner she was really in your corner, and you couldn't help but love Daisy.

Well, *most* people couldn't help but love Daisy.

Therefore, when the Dean of Student Affairs announced that all three would be *expelled*, my heart plummeted.

And then something strange happened.

Mrs. Dot stood slowly, and strolled—in the way that only old ladies could—up to the lectern at the front of the room. She began speaking without permission or preamble.

"Nawl, we not goin' put chil'ren outta school for tryin' to get some books. They gonna earn off what they stole from my pantry."

The Dean of Student Affairs objected. "Mrs. Bushnell, I appreciate your concern for our students but these three violated the code—"

"Don't talk back to me, Leonard. I know what they did. Was you the one tryin' to make the cookies when there were no chocolate chips? Thinkin' you were goin' senile in your old years and worried you couldn't do the orderin' no more? Was that you or me, Leonard?"

The man looked like a chastened little boy. Obviously put out, Mrs. Dot added, "I fed you when you was here. And you're not goin' to listen to me? Do I need to remind you of all the things I caught you doin' when you was here, Len? We got that rule about changin' cups for a reason. Now they stole from me and they gonna come earn it back from me. I got one that I s'pect was involved with all this and he is earnin' it back as we speak. Would it be fair to let the ones confessed go, and keep the one that kept his mouth shut?"

Dr. Gwinn spoke up. "I agree with Mrs. Dot."

The other four members of the council also sided with Mrs. Dot. And the Dean of Student Affairs sighed.

"All three of you are on academic probation for the next *four* semesters. If there are any further infractions you will be expelled. You may continue to be enrolled here, but you will pay the University back what you owe by working gratis for the University Dining Services."

He gaveled out the meeting and Daisy jumped into my arms with joy.

My sweet girl had taken her punishment like a champ. After her first week of work, she'd finished the day talking a mile a minute.

"Trevor, this is actually the best opportunity. Mrs. Dot said that if I continue to do well on tables, she's going to move me up to serving, and if I do well on that, then next semester she'll move me back to the kitchen. And she said that I could come in this Sunday and she'd show me how to make her recipe for smothered chicken fried steak! I could never get the gravy right when I tried it on my own."

Daisy loved the kitchen. Over the last five months, Daisy had talked about work nonstop. That was how I knew she was born to run her own kitchen.

Odie and James? Not so much. James quipped, "I thought I came to college so I wouldn't end up a dish washer." And according to Daisy, Odie was less than thrilled to be working in close proximity to Charlie.

I sat in the cafeteria waiting for Daisy to finish her shift. Odie and James trickled out from the back, their blue shirts untucked and dragging. They tossed me tired goodnights and trudged out the door.

Charlie came out next. He nodded a curt goodbye and was out the door in seconds. From what Daisy had told me, Charlie had a perpetually dejected countenance ever since Odie had started dating his roommate.

I knew Daisy would be coming along any moment. She was usually the last of the student staff to leave.

A few seconds later she exited the doors looking cute in her shapeless royal blue uniform. She walked up to me and snatched her hairnet off, freeing all that hair that I was so enamored with. I watched as it fell to her shoulders. Then she rose on her toes and pressed a quick kiss to my lips. That was all it took for my body to react; I was ready to go.

Thankfully, so was she.

"I'm free! My warden has released me!" she joked cracking a smile. One of the perks of being Mrs. Dot's favorite was that she let me stay after the dining hall had closed. I waited for Daisy every night she worked, and then I walked her home. She joked, but Daisy was now closer to Mrs. Dot than I ever was; she adored the old lady.

The air was warm on our walk and we moved slowly. I wondered if Daisy would like to have a bath tonight. I would draw her one before I went upstairs.

"Has Julian decided what he's going to do for the summer?"

Jules had been accepted into Columbia Law School and would be moving to New York in the fall, but he'd been tying himself in knots over how to spend his summer.

El and Gracie had been trying to convince him to move to New York early to spend time with them. They'd both be enrolled in schools in the city starting in the fall.

I'd also invited him to Green Valley, but he'd seemed reluctant to return. I thought I knew why. Ordinarily his—our—summer would've been spent leaving a trail of hedonism from Charlotte to the Vineyard, with maybe a stint in Europe in between. But now I was happily settled and I wasn't going back to Charlotte. I knew Julian loved his parents and I would never ask him to choose them or me. I knew very well that familial love was not something you could turn off easily. However, his parents were absolutely the type to ask him to choose. I tried to stay out of whatever happened between them and just let him know I'd always be there for him.

"I don't know what Jules is doing. He told me he still hasn't made up his mind."

I tried to push the worry for my friend out of my mind but I couldn't quite manage it. The closer we got to graduation, the more unmoored he seemed. This was the first time in nine years he and I would be apart. The original plan had been for us to both go to Columbia for grad school; he'd get his JD and I'd get my MBA. But New York held no appeal for me, not when my entire world was in Tennessee. I'd turned down Columbia and had been accepted into Vandy for the fall. It kept me closer to Daisy and I could go home on some weekends to visit my folks and to see Charlie in the marching band.

My parents and brother would be up in a few weeks to finally watch me graduate. It felt extra special because they'd been denied so many moments with me.

Jules' parents were coming too. They were throwing a big graduation party for him and allegedly for me. At first, I'd flatly refused to go. I was working through my anger but I didn't feel ready to see them and I didn't want to do or say something in anger that I'd regret. I'd had enough of that for a lifetime.

Then Daisy said, "My love, they have stolen so much joy from you. Don't let them steal celebrating all you have accomplished with your best friend too. We'll just ignore them."

That was Daisy. Always pushing and poking and prodding me to be a little better.

"Have the girls decided which weekend they're coming down to Green Valley?" Daisy's friends had promised to visit her over the summer.

"Odie says the Fourth of July, James says Memorial Day—in other words, no, they haven't picked a date yet." She threw up her hands in an exasperated little motion.

"What are they doing for the summer?"

"James is being vague about her plans, but Odie is going to work at the bus depot in Charleston with her dad."

We entered her apartment and it was dark and quiet. Elodie and Gracie were probably already asleep.

Most nights Daisy passed out shortly after I got her home. Her schedule was crammed since she elected to continue double-majoring and had to work. Dr. Gwinn had been nice enough to give Daisy a reprieve from joining the debate team because of her work-community service, but judging from the way we argued, I would have had to watch my captain's spot if she'd joined the team. I didn't mind sparring with Daisy during the day; it made for hotter and sweeter nights.

Daisy hadn't wanted to take a bath so I waited for her to finish her shower. She was taking a long time and I could feel my eyes getting heavy but I wouldn't leave. I would wait for her, however long she took.

Usually I would lay with her until she fell asleep and then return to my own apartment because I was trying to be a good man for Daisy, but I was *still* a man. I'd just yawned for maybe the third time when the bathroom door swung open.

Daisy stepped in and closed the door.

She wore a robe.

Then she *didn't* wear a robe.

Daisy

I didn't feel shy, not under Trevor's regard. I felt powerful as I met his stunned gaze.

His mouth fell open as he took me in. I felt his eyes like strokes everywhere; he looked at me with such devotion, such love, such smoldering heat that I almost combusted on the spot.

"Daisy?" he questioned. He sounded panicked. He sounded in pain.

Poor love. I can't wait to kiss it and make it better.

I'd been contemplating seducing my man for the better part of the month.

I loved him. I wanted him desperately.

But the clothes kept getting in the way.

Every time we started to progress in the right direction, Trevor would stop my hands from wandering too far on his body. Or he'd stop me from removing too many clothes on my body.

So I'd decided to get rid of the clothes.

I walked over to him and he reached for me instinctively, then hesitated, hands hovering above me.

This would require a bit more persuasion.

I slid between his legs and let my hands begin to stroke the waves of his hair in a soothing motion.

Trevor was frozen still as a statue.

I licked his lips and Trevor went ramrod straight.

I captured his face between my hands and looked deep into his eyes.

I held my face just inches from his, close enough so that he could see the sincerity and passion in my own.

"Trevor Boone, I *love* you. I *want* you. Will you let me have you tonight?"

He groaned my name and then he took my lips. His tongue plunged deep; this kiss was hot and languid and undoubtedly different. It was the smoldering base note we would build our song around.

I groaned and deepened the kiss, and within seconds I was breathless and fumbling to unbutton his shirt.

"You're so gorgeous," he growled, as he batted my hand away from his shirt. I growled back in frustration but then it quickly turned to a moan as Trevor lowered his head and captured one of my aching nipples in his mouth. Searing heat coursed through me, and I shuddered as he reached over and pinched the other.

He laved my breasts with attention; first one, then the other. I cried out with the shock and pleasure of it.

I felt his lips tug into a smile. Then he stopped, pulled me onto my bed, and lowed himself over me.

"What am I going to do with you?" he asked, his hands ghosting over every part of me.

"I have some ideas," I gasped as he kissed a tender spot on my neck. "Trevor, take off your shirt."

I felt him shake his head against my skin.

I pushed his shoulder gently and he immediately retreated and sat on the edge of my bed.

"What's wrong? Why won't you take off your clothes? Don't you want me?"

"You know I do," his voice was hard and frustrated.

"Then what is it?"

"*I'm not ready!*" He exhaled in frustration. "If you had told me that you were ready to take this step then I would've been prepared. I don't have any condoms and—"

I laughed.

He looked at me like I had grown an extra head. I opened my nightstand drawer and pulled out a box of condoms.

Trevor's eyes went wide.

"Now that's settled."

Trevor looked at me with fierce intensity. "You're sure?"

"I've never been more sure of anything in my life."

He returned to my neglected breasts and lavished them with attention. He laid me back on the bed and slid himself between my legs. He moved, sliding down and trailing hot, wet kisses along my stomach. He nipped, then licked the delicate skin on the inside of my hips and I moaned. All the while Trevor whispered soft, hot words of ardent devotion.

You're my everything, as he skimmed the back of my legs with kisses.

I love you. You're mine. You taste so good, I want more. I closed my eyes and gave myself over to the deliciousness of Trevor's words and touch.

My eyes flew open as I felt him quickly part me and then his mouth was on me, languidly licking between my folds. I couldn't think because Trevor sucked on a *spot*.

My body reacted violently, going from hot to inferno, liquid heat flooding where he licked and I clenched down hard. "Mmm, you like that," his rumbly voice washed over me.

I loved that.

I gasped his name.

And he smiled up at me wickedly. "I love hearing you say my name like that."

Before I could react he dipped his head back between my legs, licking, sucking, and worrying that spot that drove me wild.

I became an unintelligible mess of moans and grunts.

Then he surprised me by slipping one finger inside me. He slid and curled it, coaxing me. The extra sensation was almost too much to bear. I felt my stomach coiling, stretching to reach something and I let out a loud moan. He murmured lowly, "That's it, love. Let go for me," against my wet slit. The friction of his sucking and the motion of his finger made the sensation that much more intense.

It made it *unbearable*.

My insides clenched as he drove me higher and higher until there were white sparks at the edge of my vision and something inside me spasmed hard before releasing with a rush.

I collapsed back on the bed and Trevor was there pulling me into his arms, kissing me deeply, slowly, hotly.

After a long moment, I began to come back to earth. Our kisses morphed from white hot to soft and sweet. I noted with some frustration that he was still fully clothed and made a noise of distress.

He pulled back, pushed my hair from my face but held me still. His eyes searched mine cautiously. "That's a noise I haven't heard before. What was that noise for?"

I smiled, temporarily thrown off by his declaration. "You don't know all my noises."

He smiled at me smugly. "I know a lot more of them than I did before."

I looked away bashfully, and he kissed my neck.

Then he began to rain kisses on me.

"Daisy, there is nothing"—kiss—"to be shy about"—kiss—"when you're making love"—kiss—"to the"—kiss—"one you love."

His words melted me and I relaxed into him with a sigh and I felt his erection prodding my navel angrily.

"Oh! You're still . . ." I moved my hand down to his waistband, but he stilled me.

He kissed me until I was languid and senseless and then he kissed me some more.

"Tonight is not my night."

"But . . . I want . . ."

"Daisy, I have everything I need. Tonight was more than I could have ever dreamed."

He was assaulting me with his sweet words and with his care.

"I enjoyed what we just did."

His smile could have lit the whole campus, maybe the whole city.

"But what about—"

His hands roamed all over my body like they couldn't stop. Like he needed to be touching me, pinching my nipple, biting the curve between my shoulder and my neck, winding me up, distracting me.

"Trevor, you are making it very difficult to have this conversation."

"Good!" he said simply.

"Trevor!"

He took a deep breath. "Daisy, you wanted to have me tonight, and I will give myself to you. I will do whatever I can to make you feel amazing. But that doesn't mean that *I* get to have *you* tonight. Tonight is just for you. There will be a night." His eyes roamed over my body hotly. "Hopefully, there'll be lots of nights that will be just for us."

His palm slid over my belly and down to my hips. It made me tremble.

"But tonight is just for you, love."

His expression stole all my breath. His eyes were full of devotion, of promise, and of love.

The End

ACKNOWLEDGEMENTS & AUTHOR'S NOTE

Mommie, you lent yearbooks, personal photos, sat for interviews, and were so selfless with your time. I absolutely could not have written this without you. I love you. Aunties, your closeness and sartorial choices were the inspiration for Daisy and her friends; I'm forever indebted to you! Thank you Uncle for the Fisk-tory lesson. Cousin Collective—you all are the best confidantes I could ever dream of. Family, I appreciate you letting me disappear for long stretches of time to write this, and for still being there when I returned to you. Rah you let me vent and cry and never gave up on me. Love you. To the ladies who brunch, you saved my sanity when I needed a writing break. All my gratitude to Smartypants Romance, especially Penny, for her selflessness with her characters, and to Fiona and Brooke for having the patience of Job and spirit of the beatitudes. Lastly, thank you to my editors Michelle and Rebecca, and to my beta readers Heather and Nicole for your invaluable insight.

A note about Fisk University:

When I was presented with a chance to write Daisy and Trevor's story, I knew it would occur on the campus of an HBCU. The Payton and Boone families have such deep Tennessee roots it seemed natural that they would have a relationship with the oldest HBCU in the state. Despite the research I conducted to ensure historical accuracy, there may be errors present; it may help the reader to think of this version of Fisk as I do, as a fictional version of the real university meant as an homage.

That being said, there are areas where I elected to diverge from reality to serve the purpose of the story. For example, Daisy would've needed approval from more than just Dean Gwinn in order to double major, and the judicial process is a little more complex than stated in the story. It's my fervent hope that these minor transgressions can be forgiven by any readers, especially any Fiskites that read this story.

ABOUT THE AUTHOR

Chelsie Edwards' mother declared her a smarty-pants at 4 years old; now she gets to be one professionally. She manages project timelines by day and book timelines by night. She resides in the suburbs of Washington, D.C. and has no dogs, fish, or birds, but her neighbors cat "Buddy" keeps her company by sunbathing on her porch.

Find Chelsie online:
Facebook: https://www.facebook.com/chelsieedwardswrites/
Goodreads: https://www.goodreads.com/author/show/19916501.Chelsie_Edwards
Twitter: https://twitter.com/ChelsieEWrites
Instagram: https://www.instagram.com/stillchelsie/

Find Smartypants Romance online:
Website: www.smartypantsromance.com
Facebook: www.facebook.com/smartypantsromance/
Goodreads: www.goodreads.com/smartypantsromance
Twitter: @smartypantsrom
Instagram: @smartypantsromance

ALSO BY SMARTYPANTS ROMANCE

<u>Green Valley Chronicles</u>

<u>The Donner Bakery Series</u>

Baking Me Crazy by Karla Sorensen (#1)

Stud Muffin by Jiffy Kate (#2)

No Whisk, No Reward by Ellie Kay (#3)

Beef Cake by Jiffy Kate (#4)

Batter of Wits by Karla Sorensen (#5)

<u>The Green Valley Library Series</u>

Love in Due Time by L.B. Dunbar (#1)

Crime and Periodicals by Nora Everly (#2)

Prose Before Bros by Cathy Yardley (#3)

Shelf Awareness by Katie Ashley (#4)

Carpentry and Cocktails by Nora Everly (#5)

Love in Deed by L.B. Dunbar (#6)

<u>Scorned Women's Society Series</u>

My Bare Lady by Piper Sheldon (#1)

The Treble with Men by Piper Sheldon (#2)

<u>Park Ranger Series</u>

Happy Trail by Daisy Prescott (#1)

Stranger Ranger by Daisy Prescott (#2)

<u>The Leffersbee Series</u>

Been There Done That by Hope Ellis (#1)

The Higher Learning Series

Upsy Daisy by Chelsie Edwards (#1)

Seduction in the City

Cipher Security Series

Code of Conduct by April White (#1)

Code of Honor by April White (#2)

Cipher Office Series

Weight Expectations by M.E. Carter (#1)

Sticking to the Script by Stella Weaver (#2)

Cutie and the Beast by M.E. Carter (#3)

CPSIA information can be obtained
at www.ICGtesting.com
Printed in the USA
LVHW041953061120
670968LV00004B/682